Nightshade and Fire

Todd Woofenden

Signal Light Books
Bowdoinham, Maine

Nightshade and Fire

Copyright © 2019 Signal Light Books

Print Edition
ISBN: 978-1-7342473-0-5

Cover Design by Braden Todd Curtis

CONTENTS

Draw nightshade blades on the fire floor.
No oil, no wick, no tinderbox or match.
Follow the sun in darkness
To see nightshade's fire.

1. The Drop

Late sun lit the treetops as if fire had touched them, but the road was dark. Tagan dodged, narrowly avoiding a collision with an old woman.

"Apologies!" he called over his shoulder as the startled woman reeled back and upended her basket, scattering apples in the road. He didn't stop. He held tightly to a paper-wrapped parcel and willed himself to run faster.

The woman froze as two men in gray gis flew after the boy, crushing apples underfoot and cursing. No apology was issued, and the woman didn't ask for one. She watched them disappear around the bend, and only after waiting to be certain no more were coming did she stoop to collect the apples that were still good.

A door opened, and a shopkeeper hurried over with a lantern. "The master's grandson. He's got fire in him, that boy. Have you seen him on the mats? But it might be more trouble than he can manage, this time."

"Don't you go telling Saor Tieg or the Talla that I saw a kill team chasing the boy," the woman hissed. "I never saw nothing."

"Let's get off the street."

Tagan's muscles burned as he ran uphill. At nineteen he was wiry and light, and he could run. At the House Kamine fighting school, his speed and raw fighting ability had put him at the top of his class. He could win a sparring match against any of the other young men. But it didn't make him a match for the gray-gi assassins. He pumped hard, trying to go just a little faster.

At a fork in the path, the gray-gis split up, one taking the left fork and the other the right. They could navigate in the dark as well as the boy could, and they knew this trail. It ran up to the cliffs and looped back onto itself. The boy had nowhere to go.

Tagan charged to the peak and stopped. His eyes widened and his jaw dropped as the gray-gis closed in. He backed up onto a stone outcrop, approaching the drop to the ocean. "What do you want?" he demanded. The last rays of the setting sun behind him cast the faces of the gray-gis in deep red, a warning of the blood about to be spilled.

"You don't know?" one of the men said in a slow drawl. "Or do you mean you're unsure which particular misdeed has caught up with you?" He grinned menacingly.

"Who sent you? What's this about?"

"You're wondering, was it cheating at the tables? Humiliating fighters twice your age in front of the others? Or the knife-throwing contests. Or possibly that business with the trade route? So many things to choose from."

"You know about the trade route?" Tagan's eyebrows went up.

1

"The smugglers still don't know what happened to their shipment. But the Turning are less easy to fool."

"Turning? What would the Turning want with me?"

"They call you the *Talla's tinderbox*. You make sparks all up and down the shores. The card games at the fire pit pavilion, for instance. That was a fine, clever job. They know you cheated, but still haven't worked out how."

"That was two years ago."

"The Turning are annoyed by your little cheats and swindles, boy, and have often wished to slap your hand. But there are certain things even the son of Talla Undine can't get away with. One of them is to put your hands on the young lovely."

"Put my hands ... What are you talking about?" Tagan slipped the parcel into his belt and held his palms up.

"You saw the nightshade flower on her forehead. You knew who she was. Did you think the clan would allow it, you and the Turning chieftain's daughter? The Turning protects its bloodline. Foolish boy."

"Abbie? You're talking about Abigail?" He backed up until his heels found the edge of the drop. "Abigail introduced herself, and we talked. That's all. I would never have presumed!"

"Foolish boy," the gray-gi repeated. "To presume is what you do, young tinderbox. And this time you sparked a fire. But never mind." He waved a hand, dismissing the matter. "Come easy, and we'll take you unharmed. You can tell your story to the Turning chieftain yourself."

The man's hand slid to his blade, and Tagan stiffened. Gray-gis didn't take their targets alive. He readied his feet, and with a final glance as the gray-gi rushed forward to attack, Tagan sprang backward. The blade flashed as he dropped over the edge. He cried out, and his wail was cut off abruptly as he plunged into ice-cold water.

The gray-gi stood at the edge of the cliff, and his companion stepped up next to him. At first they saw nothing. The last of the sun's rays danced on the ripples of high tide. Then they spotted it, a plume of darker red in the water, which rose and dissipated as the waves lapped against the stone. A single nod from his companion acknowledged the kill. The mark was down; his blood was mixing with the sea. Nonetheless they stayed and watched, scanning the surface. Their grim smiles widened as shark fins appeared, and the relative calm of the water turned to a roiling fury. The long shapes in the water fought and tore, and then finished and moved away from the cliff face.

2. Drive

It wasn't just the spiral of black diamonds tattooed on the woman's face that caused the boy behind the counter to flinch. It was the blades sheathed at her waist, and her all-black outfit. This was not a woman on her way to a costume party dressed as an assassin. She looked like the real thing.

Her dark eyes pinned him, and he realized he was staring. "Find everything?" he said, trying to keep his voice from cracking. He couldn't help notice she was buying the same outfit she had on: black jeans, a black tee shirt, and black underwear. Even black socks and a pair of black sneakers. He tried not to look at her as he scanned the underwear. She might take it to be suggestive, and skewer him with her blades.

She nodded, waving an impatient hand as the boy stopped working to gawk.

"Sorry." He jerked his head down and stuffed the items into a bag.

Camilla counted out the cash and dropped it on the counter. "There's a motorcycle dealership near here, right? Where is it?"

The boy felt a shiver up his spine. That voice! If he were directing one of those comic book movies with a killer fighter woman, that would be the voice, soft and demanding. "Yuh – yeah," he stuttered. "Um, turn right at the light. It's like a few miles down. Probably closed, though."

"All right." She took the bag, and the boy stared at her backside as she pushed through the doors.

"Holy shit," he muttered.

Camilla kept to an artificially slow pace, ambling across the lot. She set the bag on the passenger seat of the car, and pulled out. She knew how spot a tail, and recognized the pattern: The man in the khaki pants hovering at the far corner of the building was a scout. No doubt his car was just out of sight. He had tracked her, and would stick with her until the kill team arrived. She had to convince him that she wasn't running, or he'd come at her, himself.

"Damn it," she quietly cursed. This had happened once before, when she was a kid. Twelve-year-old Camilla had run to Canada with her grandfather. She had been forced to change into an oversized tee shirt and shorts from a tourist shop, because someone had planted a tracking device in her clothes. Eighteen-year-old Camilla was supposed to know better. She should have checked more carefully. But it was too late for that now, and the best solution was the same as it had been back then: ditch the clothes.

Camilla sighed and closed her eyes, holding back the hollow feeling. Horace! They had shot her grandfather, the bastards. She had wanted so much to believe in her grandfather's plan. But what could she have done, anyway? She was just a kid. ...

Twelve-year-old Camilla stood at the edge of the driveway, looking up at their new house. The tidiness of the place was foreign to her: the wide plane of the walk curving up to the stairs, not a single brick out of alignment; the neatly edged, paved driveway and the three-car garage; and the perfect cut of the grass. And the house was even more foreign: three stories, newly painted white trim against pale gray, a thick slate roof, copper gutters— and all of this for her and her grandfather, and the couple he'd enlisted to live with them?

Robbie stood next to her and patted her on the shoulder. "What do you think, honey?" he said, playing his new part as her father.

"You sure this is the right place?" Camilla said, drawing a pleasant laugh from the man.

"You get your own room. Come on inside, and let's have a look."

Camilla had had her own room in the last place, too, her foster-family's trailer home. Her room had been a laundry room, just big enough to hold an apartment-sized, stacking washer and dryer set, had her foster parents had enough money for that kind of thing. Instead it held a mat and a sleeping bag for the foster kid, and plastic drawers to serve as her bureau.

"But you can see everywhere," she said, as they climbed to the porch. Aside from a few token trees, the yard was mown grass and flower beds, all wide open. She could see a row of other stately homes on each side of the road, stretching down the street. "We're supposed to hide out here?"

Her grandfather, a gray-haired man about to celebrate his seventieth birthday, stepped up behind her and leaned in. "Remember where you are," Horace whispered, and Camilla stopped talking without further prompting. The front porch was not the place to discuss their plans. Someone could be listening.

"Want something to eat, Calista, honey?" said a blonde woman pushing past them with a bag of groceries. "We can have sandwiches. Have to do real shopping later."

"Sure, mom," Camilla said, no more used to her new name than she was used to calling this woman *mom*.

Later that night, Horace came in and sat on her bed. Camilla was idly fingering the fabric of her new silk pajamas. She wasn't used to them yet, but she had given Grace high points for the selection, and for her other new clothes. Grace was the first one who seemed to realize that although she was tiny, Camilla wasn't a little kid. There were no duckies and bunnies on her pajamas, and her new slippers weren't alligators or bears.

"You're nervous," Horace said, putting an arm around her shoulders.

4

"Yeah, duh. We're supposed to be safe here? They're gonna come after us—after you. We're not even hiding."

"That's the strategy. They won't be looking for a family of four living in Boston. They're hunting an old man on the run with a little girl."

"You took their money. They're gonna want it back."

"We've been over this." Her grandfather's mood darkened. "I hold them responsible for my son's death."

"Yeah, my dad." Camilla looked away. "My dad the assassin."

"He chose that road, honey. And Walter Turcotte hired him, and got him killed. So yes, I took the man's money. Turcotte needed to be stopped."

"Right. Some guy is running a big, powerful company, and they kill people who get in their way, and *you* have to stop them? That not the reason. It's because you blame yourself, isn't it? For my dad. For not teaching him right, or whatever."

"Well now, that's not ..."

"Or was it revenge? He took something from you, so you took something from him."

Horace sighed. "Camilla, dear ..."

"I thought I was *Calista*," the girl spat.

"Yes, yes. Good lord, child, I have to hold up my end of this little charade, too, don't I. So, Calista, dear, listen to me. This business between me and the man I blame for my son's death, that's mine to own. And this house, and our new family—this is my solution."

"Why didn't you just shoot him?" Camilla blurted. She jumped from the bed and turned her back, and stared out the window. "Then we wouldn't have to hide. He's just gonna come find us."

"You leave that to Robbie and Grace and me. You'll see. Even if he gets back on his feet, Walter Turcotte will never think to look right under his nose, here in Boston. He'll be hunting for me in Singapore, or Belize, or on the coast of Norway."

"Right. You left trails. Robbie told me."

Horace didn't see the eye-roll, but he could feel it. "Robbie left trails, dear. And he's good at it. Trust him. He's your father, now. He'll keep you safe, he and Grace." ...

And for six years, he did just that. And then something happened, and Turcotte's men found them and killed Robbie and her grandfather. If not for the fact that Grace had recognized the danger and had run early, the woman she had called mom for six years would be lying in a pool of blood next to them.

"The only reason I'm not dead, too," Camilla muttered, stepping on the gas, "is that I was upstairs."

She had counted at least four shooters, that night, too many to take on alone. It had left her with two choices: run or die. And Horace had taught her that foolish heroics were just that, foolish. *You won't honor my memory by pointlessly sacrificing yourself, Camilla*, he had often told her, when they were talking strategy. *Protect yourself. It's important to me.*

"So why didn't *you* protect yourself? I told you this would happen. I told you."

Back at the motel she pushed into her room and shoved the door closed with her foot. She flipped on the lamp by the bed and turned on the TV, and then turned on the shower. But instead of stepping under hot water, she quickly stripped and pulled on the new clothes. She checked her knives and the sheaths. There was no way a tracker could have been placed on the blades, and the sheaths were simple leather with no place to hide a tracker. But she checked them anyway. Satisfied, she fastened the belt, and dropped to the floor.

She crawled out of the bathroom and across the room to the locked door connecting her room to the next. Moments later she had the lock open, and was in the empty adjoining room working the lock to the next room after that. Soon she was sliding through a bathroom window two doors down. Horace had taught her to plan ahead, especially when staying in a new place. She had cased the motel earlier, and designed the exit strategy before she had rented the room.

It was a good plan. No one would expect her to emerge down the hall, and even if they had someone watching the back, she wouldn't be seen behind the stockade fence enclosing the propane tanks near the bathroom window. Yet the moment her feet hit the dirt, she felt it, a presence just past the corner of the stockade fence enclosure.

Her blades came out, and she ran wide, so that as the man turned the corner and fired, she was next to him instead of in front. She slashed his wrist, and drove her other blade into his gut. But the scout's instincts weren't bad. In spite of the blade in his side, he pushed toward her instead of pulling away from the strike. Still Camilla had the advantage. The gun fell from his hand, and she pegged it with her foot, sending it thumping against the vinyl siding. She ducked a strike, and as she pulled her blade free, she sank the other into chest, finding just the right spot between his ribs.

The man in khaki struggled, and sank to the ground. Camilla retrieved his gun and fired a single shot into his head. This was another thing Horace had drilled into her: Your opponent isn't down until you're certain he's down. Those TV moments where the bad guy rises after being soundly defeated to launch yet another attack were ninety-nine percent Hollywood, but no one was ever subjected to a last-moment turnaround in a fight by being too careful.

"You didn't do that yourself, though, did you?" she bitterly accused, as she ran to the back of the lot.

She jumped the fence and ran for the two-lane, tossing the gun into a wet ditch and stopping only briefly, to wipe down her blades and clean the blood spatter. Not bad. She wouldn't have to change her clothes again.

Being dressed in black and armed with knives ruled out one class of driver, but attracted another. None of the family cars stopped for her. Instead they pretended not to see her, and sped up to get past the dangerous character on the side of the road with her thumb out. But the first oversized pickup truck to come along pulled right over, engine roaring.

"Hop in, babe," the burly man at the wheel said, without asking where she was going.

She hopped in. "Could you drop me at the motorcycle dealership?" She didn't need to ask if he knew where it was. The Harley sticker half covering the rear window told her that he did.

"How 'bout we stop off for a drink on the way? You ain't in a hurry, are you? You a Harley girl? Nice."

Camilla grinned. "I'm more of a fastest-bike-on-the-lot girl." She ignored the pick-up line. This man looked to be around forty. But he wasn't being creepy, hitting on an eighteen-year-old. Horace had taught her the craft of looking older or younger than she was. Right now she looked to be around thirty.

"What, like Ducatis and shit? You race?" He pulled back onto the road fast, spinning the tires to show that he appreciated speed as well.

"They have a Ducati? That would be perfect."

The man laughed. "At Ken's? Nah. Ken don't sell no fancy-ass racing bikes. Nobody around here's got that kind of scratch. And he's gonna be closed. You hungry? There's a place across town. We could have a bite. They got Jimmy on the guitar tonight. Just one guy, but he can play."

"Thanks, but I'm meeting someone."

The dealership was a typical small-town place, two repair bays and a showroom with grimy windows mostly covered with posters, and a parking lot that needed to be repaved. But these little places were usually run by enthusiasts. Maybe she would find something.

"Want me to stick around? Don't look like nobody's here."

"No, he'll be here in a minute. And I'll be fine." Camilla patted the handles of the blades at her waist. "Thanks for the ride."

"Mm," the man grinned. "Mind if I stay and watch? If you're planning to use them things."

Camilla turned and smiled back at him, and winked. "Then I'd have to kill you too, wouldn't I?"

"Right," the man laughed. "But if it don't work out, the diner's a half mile down. I'll save you a seat." He winked back, and Camilla watched him peel across the lot and jump the curb.

The driver was right. There were no brand-new racing bikes. The showroom displayed a few Harleys and lots of chrome parts on dusty peg board. She waited for the truck to disappear, and slipped around back. In the first repair bay was just the right thing. It wasn't new, but the blue and silver Yamaha YZF-R1 would do nicely. She jimmied the lock on the rear door to the repair bay, clicked on the lights, and ran over. A light started blinking, but she didn't see any cameras, and there wasn't an annoying klaxon sounding. Someone at a security company was getting a message, though, and soon the cops would be coming.

Conveniently, the key was on the workbench next to the bike. She grabbed a helmet someone had left on the workbench. It was big on her, but would have to do. She punched the button to raise the door, and mounted the motorcycle. Out of habit, she patted her waist—her blades were there—and snapped the leather straps over the hilts. Then she wound the throttle and rocketed down the road.

Camilla made it to the interstate, and was doing ninety when she saw a black Beamer in her rearview, weaving around a slow car in the fast lane and putting on the speed. Damn it! A kill team! She raced ahead. But she didn't know about the second car. A mile or two up, a black car came the other direction, pulling into a median crossover. The car stopped in the median, and two men got out. One pulled out a revolver, and the other set a rifle on a short tripod on the hood of the car.

Pushing the bike to 110, Camilla raced up the highway trying to lose her tail. Then at a curve she had to slow to maneuver around slowing cars. Something was happening on the bridge up ahead. An accident? Everyone was slowing down. When she discovered what it was, it was too late. Just as she spotted the black car and the sniper rifle, the gun fired, and a round struck the engine. Camilla swerved and crashed into the cement barrier along the side of the bridge. She flew over the handlebars and over the edge, and plunged into cold water.

As she struggled for air, things seemed to change. Instead of sinking in a sunlit river, she was in a dark, water-filled cavern—and someone else was there.

Was it happening again? She had thought all of that was over, with her grandfather's death.

It's important to me. ... Her grandfather's words came back to her, and stuck. Was this Horace, struggling in the water alongside her? How could it be? Horace was dead. Was it Una? ...

"We're not like other people," her grandfather had told a much younger Camilla, seemingly forever ago. "You understand?"

"My friend thinks I'm nuts," the young girl holding his hand said, as they strolled down a Boston street looking for a place to have lunch.

"You told your friend." His voice tightened. "What did you tell her?"

"Just about seeing Una. You know, before I came to live with you. I had to tell someone."

"And what did she think?"

"I said it was clairvoyance. Like a sixth sense. And maybe I was seeing Una 'cause she was in just as much trouble as I was."

Horace smiled. "That was certainly true. But I suppose your friend didn't believe you."

"Of course not. Someone tells you they see this amazing fighter girl from some other time and place—and not in a book, or something, but you're actually looking at her, for real? That's nuts."

"I suppose most people would think so."

"You would, if you didn't see her, too."

"Did you tell anyone else? Robbie, or Grace?"

"You said don't tell them anything. About *that*, anyway. About seeing stuff. It would spoil everything. Nuh-uh. I'm never telling them. But I'm gonna be a fighter like Una when I grow up."

"Honey," Horace gave her hand a squeeze of solidarity, "you already are a fighter like she is—or like she will be. Or ... you know what I mean."

"Yeah."

"You know, there's a saying, in Una's time. It's their version of living to fight another day. They say, *Live on and join in the hunt tomorrow.* That's what I want you to do, Camilla. You're my granddaughter. Live on. Join in the hunt, and one day have some children to carry on after us." ...

As she hit the bottom of the river, haunted by his words, it seemed like such a burden, to *live on* and to bear Horace a great-grandchild.

But I have to! she silently demanded of herself. She ripped the helmet off and fought her way up, and drew in a panicked breath as she surfaced.

Now what? Men would be coming. They were probably on the bridge by now. She had mere seconds. She looked around and began climbing the cribwork under the bridge, heading for the massive I beams just under the road bed. Cars rumbled overhead as she scrambled up and pressed herself into a gap above one of the beams.

Then it happened again: Her vision blurred, and she was in a water-filled cavern. She could breathe, but someone else was fighting for air. Who was it? Her link to Una had been broken the moment the bullet went into Horace's brain. She had felt it, the connection severed. Had she somehow reconnected?

"Relax. There's air. Just breathe," she muttered, although she knew she wouldn't be heard. Una had never heard her. Horace could speak to Una, but that wasn't a skill Camilla possessed.

Then she sensed words: "Abbie, is that you? Are you coming to me in my thoughts?"

"Wait. You can hear me?" Camilla said. "Who are you? You're not Una."

3. The Caves

The tide was higher than he had expected. As he struggled to hold his face in the pocket of air at the top of the cavity, Tagan silently scolded himself for the lack of planning. The science of sea tides was captured in charts. There were men who spent their lives keeping track of that kind of thing. He could have checked.

He drew in air, and spluttered and coughed as water came with it. Not enough air! His heart raced, and he uselessly swept his hands across the stone as if there might be a door. Panic swept in.

Then a thought came to him, words forming in his head. "Relax. There's air. Just breathe." It was strange, almost as if someone were talking to him. Was it panic? Was he hearing things?

But somehow there was an element of command to it. In spite of the panic, he tipped his head up and breathed, and the panic subsided. Whatever it was, the voice in his head was right. He swam along the edge of the chamber until he found a spot where the ceiling was higher. Scraping with his feet, he found a ledge that he could grip, and pushed himself up to rest. He sighed. Plenty of air.

"Abbie, is that you talking to me? Are you coming to me in my thoughts?" he said to the wet, dark cavern.

Clear as can be, words formed in his head. "Wait. You can hear me? Who are you? You're not Una."

"Una. My mother's old name from the time she trained under a Gatto master in the north." Tagan wiped the sea water from his eyes and blinked in the blackness. "I must be in shock. Half-drowned in a cave, and I'm recalling my mother's old name from her stories about the cat-fighter clan."

"Your mother. Una's your mother? That's weird."

"Next I'll be fancying that her old muse is talking to me. *What shall I do now, Horace?* she would say to the stars. Even twenty years since the voice stopped speaking to her, she looks upward. *What shall I do, Horace? What would Camilla do?*"

"Horace is dead." The voice in his head grew cold. "But it was two days ago, not twenty years. And I would execute my plan. And, damn it, you can *hear* me? I'm talking to you, and you can *hear* it? Una could never hear me."

"Words are coming to me. I'm delirious, thinking of home and my mother." Tagan closed his eyes hard, and tried to push it away. "It brings back thoughts of my mother's old Gatto name."

"She changed her name to Undine when she left the Gatto. But listen, you do have a plan, don't you?" the voice chided. "Was it to get stuck in an underwater cave? Although, I'm a fine one to talk, hiding under this damned bridge."

"A plan. Yes, I do. Yes, that's right." Tagan drew in a deep breath, then another, then a third, drawing in as much air as possible. Then he dove, and the words in his head ceased.

The opening was almost ten feet down, and he had to hold his breath long enough to fight his way along the passage. He pumped through, concentrating on moving forward and not hitting the rocks above and below. Five feet. Ten feet. Fifteen … He rocketed up and drew in a big breath.

His heart pounding, he swam toward a dimly lit ledge. Why was there light? He pulled himself up and rolled onto the stone slab, and lay on his back with his arms out like a crucifix.

"You're bleeding," said a young voice.

Tagan jumped up with a startled cry, and bumped his head on the overhanging stone. "Damn it! Rebecca? What are you doing here?" He looked over at a little dark-haired girl lounging on the stone slab, dressed in black pants and a white shirt much too big for her.

"Tagan, you're bleeding," the little girl repeated. She held up an oil lamp.

"It's a cut. The gray-gi nicked my arm. And pike me, what are you wearing?"

"My clothes got wet," the girl shrugged. "I found these."

With a loud exhale, Tagan turned and sat, stooping in the cramped space. He rubbed the new bump on his head. "Becca, you found them because I put them there. Those were for me to change into."

"Oh. They're yours? I'll take them off." The girl fingered a button, and looked at him with faux-innocent doe-eyes.

"No you won't." Tagan waved a finger. "Don't even start with that. Did you bring food? I'm starving."

The girl clicked her tongue. "Of course. What do you think I came down here for? You're always hungry. I'll get fat from eating because of you." She picked up a paper-wrapped parcel. "Now get your wet things off," she said in a matronly voice, holding it away from him. "You'll catch a cold and die."

"Becca, stop it. First, it won't work. You're not the first girl to flirt with me. And second, you're *ten*, damn it. You need to forget all that. All of that is over. You're supposed to be saying boys are gross."

She shrugged. "Boys *are* gross. But you're not a boy, and you're definitely not gross."

"Give me the food."

She handed it over. "Killjoy. Here I am, bringing food to a dead man. Shouldn't you be grateful? You could at least give me a kiss."

"Anyone else," Tagan muttered, "and I'd tell your mother." He unwrapped the package and pulled out a sandwich of thick molasses bread filled with smoked fish and crumbled cheese. "Oh, wow," he said.

"Oh wow is right," the girl sniffed. "And I don't have a mother, so that's mean."

Tagan sighed. She was right. It was mean. He couldn't blame her for her behavior. And she was making progress. But she didn't always make it easy to be nice. "I'm sorry, Becca."

"And if I did have a mother, you'd tell her I demanded a kiss?" Rebecca laughed. "I'm ten. You'd look like an ass."

"Which is why wouldn't tell her."

"That, and because even though you're chasing after that Turning girl—which is amazingly stupid, you know—secretly you're deeply in love with me. I know you are. I can feel it. It's why I'm still here."

He tore the sandwich in half. "Share," he said. "And shut up. That's not why you're here."

Rebecca grinned and scooted up close, and took the half-sandwich. "Your plan worked." She leaned against him, then pulled away and grimaced at the wet spot on the white shirt. "Ick. You're soaked."

"Someone took my dry clothes." He rolled his eyes. "But yes, it worked. The package of pig innards was a nice touch, if I say so myself. I could almost hear the sharks thrashing out there. The gray-gi assassins have got to think I'm dead."

"Everyone will think you're dead. That Turning girl might hurl herself off a cliff." She sighed dramatically, and swept an arm across her forehead.

"Damn it, Becca. She won't kill herself."

"Whoa!" Rebecca shivered, and shook her shoulders. "Is that panic I'm feeling? I was kidding. Abbie won't hurl herself off a cliff, stupid. At least, maybe she won't. But what about your mother and your grandfather? Don't we have to tell them?"

Tagan grabbed Rebecca's arm. "You're to tell no one. Understand? And there's no *we* in this. You'll go to the funeral and cry. You hear me?"

"There's *we* in everything." She shook herself free and moved away. "And you'll let your own mother think you're dead?"

"Who do you think showed me this place? We were up on that ledge one time, and she told me that if she ever had to disappear, she'd jump off the cliff at that spot and swim to the caves."

"Your mother told you that? Wow. She's as devious as you." Rebecca grinned.

"I come to it naturally, all right? Just don't worry about my mother. She'll figure it out. Abbie will too, somehow. She has to." He offered a strained smile.

Rebecca shivered again. "Fine," she said. "Relax. You're gonna kill me with that."

Tagan wolfed down the half-sandwich, and rose and headed for the entrance to a dark passage. The girl rose also, and hurried behind him.

"Listen to me, Rebecca," he said, turning and taking her by the shoulders.

"Oh, this is serious," the girl said in a mock-stern voice. "You're calling me Rebecca."

"Listen to me. I'm going. You're staying. Count to a hundred, before you even think of going up. I have to disappear, and you have to go home and cry because your friend is dead."

"Fine. I'll bawl my eyes out. I'll turn the waterworks up to high, all right?" the girl said.

Tagan swept her into his arms. "I do love you, Becca. And I want to see you grow up and fall in love with someone, and have kids."

"Whoa, hey. Who said anything about kids?" The girl pushed back. "I just said a kiss! And yuck, Tagan. Now I'm all wet."

He took hold of her shoulders again, and kissed her on the forehead. "A kiss. All right? I promise I'll come back as soon as I can. I'm sorry. I don't have a choice. Count to a hundred." He vanished into the passage, leaving the girl staring after him.

Tagan emerged from the caverns in nondescript Tallach garb, black pants tucked into his boots, a white shirt, and a black vest, carrying the small bag he'd left inside the entrance. It was a good thing that he'd thought to stash some clothes inside the entrance, or he'd be soaking wet. He pulled his cap down and stepped into the night with the bag over his shoulder.

This part he had practiced. Up on the cliffs there had been enough light to see. But under cover of the trees it was almost completely black. He didn't head for the main road, but instead climbed up the rise to the high path along the ridge. His grandfather would assign people to scout the roads, but they would have searched the ridge trail already.

It took him a long time to reach the trail, feeling his way like a blind man. But he kept moving, ever upward, feeling for rocks and roots and picking his way past them. Would Dimon be there? They hadn't planned for it to happen so soon. He had told his friend that gray-gi assassins might come, but he had figured it would be weeks from now.

"He'll be there," he reassured himself. Of course he would. Tagan tripped on a root and almost fell, and exhaled loudly. "He had better be there."

At the ridge, he stopped just off the trail. The crescent moon was enough to show the gray thread of the path winding upward. Cupping his hands over his mouth, he made the call of a coyote, and within moments heard answering cries from the forest. He called again; then he stepped into the path.

"Join in the hunt," Tagan said, reciting the password almost in a whisper— and heard a low sigh.

"Tagan! Damn it, you're here." A young man stepped onto the trail, his short, light hair glimmering in the dull moonlight.

"They came early. What could I do?"

His friend laughed and wrapped his arms around him. "Fire and daggers, you're alive!"

"That was the plan. Come on. Let's get going." Tagan started down the trail. "Did you bring my pack?"

"I couldn't get yours." The light-haired man held up his palms as his friend spun on him. "I couldn't! The whole town is out, Tagan. Everyone. Every soldier, every man who can hold a blade. Your grandfather has half of them hunting for gray-gis, and the other half making sure the gray-gis don't get to him or your mother."

"But surely my mother knows it was a ruse." Tagan folded his arms and stood blocking the trail.

"Your mother *invented* the ruse. Raptors, she's good. Even I thought you were dead. Nobody—including Saor Tieg—would suspect she's putting on a show. She wrecked her room, Tagan. Broke everything in it. She's inconsolable."

Tagan tipped his head. "How would you know that?"

The young man's shoulders drooped. "Because I thought they got you, too, and I went to see her. The guards told me nobody was allowed in, but I insisted. So they knocked on her door, pushed me in, and shut the door behind me. They're frightened as hell of your mother, you know. And it looked as if a hoard of bandits had ransacked the place. Your mother was standing by the window—the *open* window—ranting about her lost boy. And she turns and looks at me. And calm as can be, she lowers her voice and says, *What in hell are you doing here, Dimon? Are you letting him leave on his own?* I was so shocked that I stood there like a statue until she stepped over, patted me on the butt, and shoved me out the door."

"All right," Tagan grinned, "that I can believe." He turned and continued down the path.

"But I don't think your grandfather knows," Dimon said, running along after him. "And I couldn't get anywhere near your rooms. I couldn't, Tagan. Trust me. I tried."

"The money was in my pack," Tagan said. "And I only have one extra set of clothes."

"I know," Dimon sighed. "Damn it, I know. At least I have food."

They reached the road, and they ran.

As he was nodding off, warm by the campfire, Tagan's mind wandered back to those frightening moments under water in the caves.

The voice came back to him. "Can you hear me? Tell me you can hear me."

Tagan sat up and looked at his friend, but Dimon was curled up asleep. No one had said anything, and yet, just as in the cave, someone was speaking to him somehow. Words were forming in his mind.

"I'm not under water now. What is this? Why does it seem that someone is speaking to me?"

"Your name is Tagan. The girl called you that. She's adorable. Tagan. Is that after *Tieg*, your grandfather's name?"

Tagan's mouth fell open. "Do I have an inner voice of my own, like mother's old voice? Did it pass to me somehow? I never believed her. Is this her revenge, to pass it on to me?" He looked up at the sky. "Yes, muse, I'm Tagan of Deadrise Bay. My mother is Talla Undine, and my grandfather is Saor Tieg. But shouldn't you know this already? You're in my head."

"Oh, this is excellent! Your mother never heard me. Not a damned word. I don't think she would even know about me, if not for my grandfather. And now that he's gone, I can't even see her."

"Is someone toying with me?" Tagan looked around, as if a prankster might pop out of the forest to continue the conversation with him. "Or is it delirium? I've hit my head, perhaps. Who or what are you?"

"You said it yourself. Camilla. That's me."

"Camilla." Tagan lay back down. "*The silent one.* But that's impossible. Mother told me the last time Horace spoke to her was before I was born. I'm nineteen. The voice stopped almost twenty years ago."

"It's shifted," the words in his head told him. "Horace told me that might happen. Your mother was a child, and then things shifted and she was older. Now it's shifted again."

"Delirium, for sure," Tagan said, and pressed his eyes closed. "I need sleep."

4. The Stone Walk

"She refuses to speak you, Allton. Are you certain this was the right thing to do?" Eyes downcast, her fingers nervously drumming against the handle of a basket, a woman of around forty stood in the doorway.

At a wooden table, the severe chieftain of the Turning clan turned his head slowly. His black hair was graying around the temples, but the early sign of age seemed to make him appear even more powerful and threatening. The conviction behind the clan's existence, that the world would suffer a mass annihilation, and the chosen people would step in to remake it in proper order, had yet to manifest itself. Most in the south would say that things were getting better, and that the prospect of an apocalypse was fading. But the Turning clan kept its faith, and kept its people cloistered from the rest of the world. For generations they had religiously protected the purity of their bloodlines. Allton had no intention of allowing things to lapse on his watch.

He turned gray eyes to the woman at the door, one of the few people who were allowed liberties in their manner of addressing him. "Am I certain *what* was the right thing to do, Hester?" he said, in a low, menacing tone. "Perhaps you mean sending you to reason with my daughter?"

There were some who saw the need for change. Allton himself was considered almost radical by the older Turning men. When the scepter passed to him, he immediately made plans to open legitimate trade routes instead of trading only through smuggling operations. The old men complained of the dangers of fraternizing with the outside, but Allton brushed away their concerns. Only trusted men would be sent on trade missions, he said, and they would travel armed. There would be no fraternizing.

And what had it gotten him? His own daughter had confirmed the wisdom of the elders and underscored his folly.

"*Our* daughter." The woman clenched her teeth and pressed on. "And I mean the boy, Allton. I don't question your intent. Abigail needs to learn her place. But the grandson of Saor Tieg? Mightn't there have been a lesser means of dealing with the problem? That old man controls the Western Shores. He runs the trade for every merchant line on the entire coast. Aren't you trying to forge an agreement with the Tallachs?"

"Trade is a separate concern," the man scowled. "Some things are sacred. I'll not see my daughter engaging in a dalliance with that lowlife, firestorm son of the Talla. I don't care who his grandfather is."

"Firestorm? I thought he was a tinderbox," Hester said, but quickly shifted to a less sarcastic tone. "Talla Undine is very powerful, dear. Perhaps respected and feared even more than the old man."

"This line of Tallach animals," Allton pounded a fist on the table, "I'll not have them tainting my blood. Abigail will learn to obey. What did she see in that boy, anyway? Are there no young men in our own camp? The captain's boy, for instance. He seems to fancy her. He'll be a general one day."

Hester offered only a strained smile in response. Did a nineteen-year-old girl's infatuation with a boy require a deep explanation? As she turned to leave, her smile changed to a sob. One might have asked her the same question at nineteen. She had fallen for a boy in line to ascend to the rule of the Turning clan. Was her own mistake any worse than her daughter's?

And why did her husband have to make his point so viciously? Why not just let it go? He had said it himself: There were plenty of boys in the Turning. Surely the Tallach boy would have been forgotten. But instead, Allton had brought his daughter to the table and told her that because of her misdeeds at Deadrise Bay, he'd been forced to put a contract on the boy.

"The gray-gis will solve this problem you've created. Now, go," he had barked at the girl "You'll be going on no more trips!"

Abigail had stood frozen, staring, then rushed out of the room. The report from the gray-gis had been delivered soon after: The contract was completed. Abigail stayed in her room, and refused to speak to her father even when ordered to do so. The smiling, agreeable daughter was gone, and in her place the Turning saw the face of despondency.

His wife's demeanor also turned sour. Hester had never been to the Western Shores, and had never met Saor Tieg's grandson. But she knew what Abigail saw in the boy: a taste of freedom and excitement, something she herself had once longed for.

"A better question," Hester muttered when safely out of earshot, "is what did I see in *you*, Allton."

She realized that it had been a mistake to encourage her daughter to learn more about the world outside the Turning. Look what it had led to! Had she discouraged her husband from allowing Abigail to go on the trade mission, Allton would have said no, and none of this would have happened. But at the time it had seemed harmless enough. Abigail had been so excited at the idea of visiting Deadrise Bay. ...

As if offering her a birthday gift, Abigail's father made a rare a concession. Maybe it was the wine he'd had with dinner, Abigail thought. He'd had a bit more than usual. Or maybe it was the timing. They had just made a step toward a lucrative trade deal with the Tallachs. He was in a good mood.

"All right, all right," he'd said. "Damn it, Abigail, go!" he laughed. "I can't stand to hear about it anymore."

The girl had turned her gray eyes to him and blinked. "I can go? To Deadrise Bay?" She sounded confused.

"Your maids will attend, of course. Anne and Evelyn are not to leave

18

your side. The captain will find private accommodations, and you'll stay in your room after the evening meal. Is that understood?"

"I can really go? To the Western Shores?" She flicked her dark bangs from her face and stifled a giggle.

Her father turned and scowled. "See what happens if you ask a third time. Now leave me to my wine, child. Go find your tutor."

Abigail clamped her mouth shut and left.

For weeks she had been pestering him to let her ride along with the trade team. Deadrise Bay! She'd never been. She'd never been anywhere. But she'd heard stories of the Western Shores: sweeping cliffs with the ocean pounding below; terraces of food tents offering everything one could imagine, from the daily catch to spiced meats, and exotic liquors from overseas—everything!

Her mother had tried to temper her idea of the splendor of the place. "It's not all sunshine and roses, dear. Deadrise Bay is a working port. I imagine it can get rough. There are the sailors and merchants ..." She stopped talking when she realized she was dangling further potential pleasures before her young daughter, rather than imparting a useful warning.

Abigail barely slept the night before the journey. She rose filled with energy and distraction. Her tutor, a dark-skinned man of twenty-five in a brown gi, waited outside her room. He put up a hand to stop her from rushing past.

"What did you say you would accomplish yesterday?" he said, and stood silently.

The girl rolled her eyes. "Do we have to do this today, Arran? I'm going to Deadrise Bay! I don't want to do the three questions. Can't we skip it for just one day?"

But the man stood his ground. "What did you say you would accomplish yesterday?" he repeated.

"Fine. I said I would improve the form of my upstroke in making letters." She folded her arms and looked past him.

"What did you accomplish yesterday?" the man said.

"I didn't work on my letters at all, all right? Arran, *I'm going to Deadrise Bay!*"

"And what will you accomplish today?"

"Anything you want. Just let me pass."

The young man furrowed his brows, but stepped aside.

The only thing to dampen her excitement was the riding arrangement. "Why can't I ride my mare?" she complained. "I can ride as well as the soldiers."

"You'll ride in the wagon," her father said, with a measure of finality that caused the girl's shoulders to droop.

She grumbled, mimicking her father as she stormed out. *"It's unbecoming for the daughter of the Turning chieftain to be seen riding a horse like a commoner*. Ha. What he means is, someone might see me and maybe even *talk* to me. Wouldn't that be horrible."

But she packed a trunk, and she and her servants bundled into the wagon. Flanked by guards, the wagon took up the rear of the convoy.

"We're going to Deadrise Bay!" Abigail exclaimed excitedly, as the horses pulled, and they started down the road.

Her father might have amended his order that she and her maids attend the evening meal and then retire directly to their room, had he fully understood what an evening meal was like on the terraces at Deadrise Bay. A meal at Allton's table was precise, executed with military efficiency. Food was served, they ate, and dishes were removed. There was no room for idle conversation. Allton might linger with a glass of wine and interrogate one of his men on a timely topic, but everyone else left promptly.

The atmosphere at Deadrise Bay was startlingly different. The landscape from the inn down to the water was cut into wide, flat terraces with stone steps and walkways joining one to the next, and people sat in open air enjoying the evening. The food vendors near the water served hundreds of sailors. Food and beer were plentiful, and the sailor's voices swept up the terraces.

As one ascended, the rank of the diner ascended likewise. The crowds grew thinner and the food finer, but the mood was equally festive. Just below the inn on the high terrace was Saor Tieg's pergola. Wide strips of bright purple damask moved in the wind. Those below looked up hopefully, eager to catch a glimpse of the important figures seated up there. Maybe they would spot Saor Tieg himself, or his daughter, Talla Undine the fighter. Ship captains might be under the pergola making deals.

The trading company from the Turning had secured the terrace just below, an expensive display of the importance of their mission. Soldiers stood silently while Abigail and her servants sat with Allton's men beneath a colorful canopy, enjoying a fine fish dinner. Abigail, Anne, and Evelyn wore their normal clothes—simple gray dresses buttoned up tight to the chin. Abigail's dress was of a finer material, but someone bumping into them might mistake her for a servant, except for the purple-brown flower tattooed on her forehead—and this tended to be obscured by her uncooperative black bangs.

For the meal on the terrace, Abigail wore a white silk hat, one of the few nonessential things she owned. It wasn't especially fancy. The wide, stiff brim was decorated with a plain silk bow. Her mother had bought it for her from a passing vendor, feeling an impulse to give her daughter something special. And like her mother's words about dangerous sailors, the silk hat had prompted Abigail to dream of exotic encounters with people outside the Turning. Now here she was. She listened to the sounds, a steady background of voices, and peered excitedly at the crowds of sailors near the water.

The men at her table seemed nervous. It struck her that they were no more accustomed to this than she was. Maybe some of them had been on a mission to the Shores, but probably none had been this close to the master's pergola. Occasionally she caught a snippet of conversation from the high terrace, and wondered if the famous Saor Tieg sat up there, and what they were talking about. Were he and his party quietly making fun of the country hicks under the canopy below?

"Are you finished?" Anne said, touching Abigail's arm as she stared at the purple drapery.

"What? Oh," Abigail smiled. "Just thinking. There's still more to the meal, isn't there?"

The servants from the cook tents seemed to keep coming with more and more dishes. A Tallach meal, at least this high up on the terraces, seemed to consist of endless fancy, small courses.

"Shall I ask?" Anne said in a whisper, fearful of appearing not to know the protocol.

Abigail laughed quietly. "Let it keep coming until it stops. But I'll stretch my legs." She leaned in close, and winked. "Do you suppose it's all right to stretch one's legs in Deadrise Bay, or am I about to commit a grave social error?"

The soldiers stiffened as she rose, but they didn't know the customs any better than she did. They moved aside and allowed the chieftain's daughter to step out from the canopy and wander to the iron rail along the walkway. They followed close behind.

She stepped to the edge of the terrace and looked out over the ocean, drawing a long breath of sea air. The view was magnificent. Then as she tipped her head to glance at the pergola, a gust of wind whipped up the walkway and swept her hat from her head. She cried out and reflexively reached for it, but it soared upward and vanished between strips of purple.

"Ow, damn it!" a young voice cursed from beneath the pergola. "Who threw that? Wait, what is this?"

The Turning soldiers hurried to flank the girl as above them the purple damask was pushed roughly aside and a boy the same age as Abigail stormed out, holding the hat accusingly with one hand and clutching the other over his face.

"I'm sorry. The wind." Abigail said, almost inaudibly. She looked up at a young Tallach aristocrat dressed in a white shirt and black silk vest, snug pants down to his shins, and black sandals. She dropped her gaze to the walk.

"Are you trying to blind me?" The boy stepped to the rail, blinking and rubbing at his eyes.

"I'm sorry."

The soldiers pressed closer to the girl. Behind them, others were rising.

"I thought you were here to trade. It's an assassin's mission, then, is it?" He strode down the steps. "You're angry about losing at cards, I suppose. I knew you Turning folk were vindictive, but to try to kill me with a hat?"

There was a lilt to his voice. Was the boy joking? Abigail looked up and stared.

"It's not my fault that your man isn't good at the game table," he continued. Then he caught sight of the cut of the dress, and the wide, dark eyes and open mouth of the startled girl whose hat he was clutching, and he halted. "Oh," he said, blinking and rubbing one eye. His face flushed. "I assumed … This is yours?" He stepped up to the rail that Abigail was still clutching, and held out the hat.

"Yes." Abigail dropped her eyes again and took the hat.

"You're not a staff servant."

"No." She extended a hand and offered a strained smile. "I'm Abbie. And I apologize. I didn't mean to …"

"Tagan." He took her hand, and with a bow and a flourish, planted a kiss on it.

The soldiers stiffened, and one reached out to pull her arm back.

Tagan grinned at the soldier. "Isn't that how one says hello in Turning territory?"

Abigail stared. What was that, a wink? She smiled stupidly at the boy, until the captain broke her gaze by stepping up and extending an arm in front of her. "Good evening, master Tagan," he said stiffly, backing the girl up. "Please accept our apologies for interrupting your meal."

Abigail brushed back her bangs to pull the hat on, and the boy tipped his head. "Whoa," he said, "wait a minute. What's that?" He reached out, but the soldiers swarmed between them and ushered her back beneath the canopy.

Tagan stared, then shook his head and jogged up the stairs. "Nice to meet you, Abbie," he shouted over his shoulder as he vanished behind the tapestry.

"A new friend?" Evelyn whispered. And on Abigail's other side, Anne added, "a good-looking new friend."

"Tagan," Abigail mused. "After Saor Tieg? He must be, mustn't he?

He's the grandson?"

"He's on Saor Tieg's terrace," Anne said. "I suppose you must be right."

At the glowering stare of the captain, the girls stopped talking and returned to picking at the remains of the meal.

Not five minutes later, a servant came down the stairs, bowed to the Turning soldiers, and stepped up bearing a bottle of wine of a significantly better vintage than what they were drinking. "From the master," the man said, "with apologies to the young lady for his grandson's deplorable behavior."

Behind him came women carrying crystal goblets and more bottles. Without waiting for permission, the servant began filling glasses. The captain looked as if he wanted to refuse the gift, but reasoned that one didn't refuse a gift from Saor Tieg, if one wanted negotiations to proceed. He nodded brusquely.

The servant filled glasses for the men first, then came to pour for the maids and Abigail. As he leaned in with Abigail's goblet, he surreptitiously slipped her a note. Abigail palmed it.

Wine, dessert, more wine, more dessert. Clutching the note, Abigail waited and waited for an opportunity to read it. It wasn't until the after-dinner music started that she found her chance. A quartet of musicians beneath the pergola struck up a tune, and all the Turning men under the canopy turned to look. Abigail peered at the slip of paper in her lap.

Walk along the cliff at the late bell?

She blushed in spite of herself. When one of the men looked at her, she coughed and faked having swallowed her wine too quickly.

Getting out of the room proved easier than she had expected. She reflected that the soldiers couldn't really be blamed. Not in their wildest imagination would they envision Allton's daughter defying his order. As a matter of protocol, two men stood outside the door. But they understood their job to be to keep others out, not to keep the girl in. They shared a flask and settled in for a long, uninteresting shift. They would stand there half the night, until another pair of soldiers came to relieve them; and they would continue to do this every night for the duration of the visit.

Abigail knew that she was putting Anne and Evelyn into a tricky position. If she were caught, her servants would be in as much trouble as the soldiers. But they both encouraged her to go.

"Anne's a heavy sleeper," Evelyn said with a wink. "She won't know."

"So is Evelyn," Anne grinned. "She'll sleep through the whole thing."

Abigail quietly opened the window that looked out over the cliffs. She dropped to the grass just as the late bell sounded. At the edge of the terrace was an iron rail to keep unwary guests from stumbling off and crashing to the stone walkway along the cliff. She stopped to look around.

There were sailors down on the wharf heading for their ships, but the walkway was unlit, and the moon was low. It was very dark. As she made her way to the top of the stairs, she felt her heart race. Was this a good idea? Anyone could have written that note. It could be highwaymen looking to kidnap her and demand a ransom. Or men from a slave ship planning to steal her away overseas.

Then she heard the strike of a match.

"I promise I won't shout at you again," said the voice she had heard earlier. As he set the glass chimney on an oil lamp, the boy came into view. "You can come down."

"You're Saor Tieg's grandson," Abigail said, stepping down the stairs slowly.

"I'm more my mother's son than my grandfather's grandson. You'll see what I mean when you get to know me. And you," he said, holding up the lamp. "Show me." He tapped his forehead. Abigail pushed her hair back from her forehead, and he broke into a smile. "I knew it! Nightshade. You're the daughter of the Turning chieftain. What are you doing here?"

Abigail pursed her lips. "I shouldn't be here?"

"Oh, I think here is a fine place for you to be. But I'd have bet Dimon my entire purse against the owner of that hat being Allton's daughter. So I just mean, well, what are you doing here?"

"I thought we were going to walk along the cliff. Isn't that what you proposed?" Abigail sniffed.

"Ha. So it is. Would you care to walk?" Tagan stepped up next to her and offered his arm, and Abigail smiled and took it. "So, Abbie, have you been along the cliff walk before?"

"We just arrived," she said. "I haven't been anywhere."

"Never been here before?" Tagan echoed. "How old are you?" At the girl's scowl, he shrugged. "I know, I'm horribly rude. But I might not have a chance to ask you later. My soldiers won't interfere, but I suspect yours will, if they discover us."

"I'm nineteen."

"Ah! So am I. Do you fight?"

Abigail stopped and pulled her hand back. "Do I *fight*?"

"I'm not challenging you," Tagan said, backing up a step and grinning. "I mean, do you train. I'm hoping to go overseas with the team next year to House Kamine. I mean, the original House Kamine. I train in the satellite pavilion here in Deadrise Bay. We don't have girls. Not usually, anyway. You know about my mother, though, right?"

"Talla Undine. A fourth-tier fighter. Everyone knows of the woman fighter of Deadrise Bay."

"You walk like my mother. Confident. As if you're leading me, and not the other way around. Like a fighter."

"Shall I be the delicate flower?" Abigail batted her eyelids, and dropped her shoulders.

"Raptors, no," Tagan laughed. "Just don't throw any more hats at me. You could've killed me."

"No more hats. I promise." Abigail smiled. "And to answer your question, no, I don't train, although my tutor is the son of a Gatto master. You know of it? The fighting style of the cat."

"An ancient and respectable form of combat. The Gatto have always been a powerful presence. Your tutor is Gatto?"

"If I look confident, it's because of Arran. He teaches me poise. Of course it comes at a price. Every day with his three questions, for instance."

"Three questions?"

"First thing, without even saying hello, it's *What did you say you would achieve yesterday, young miss?* I'm to reflect, you see." Abigail rolled her eyes. "Then, *What did you achieve yesterday?* Did I accomplish what I said I would? And third, *What will you achieve today?* I get that every single day, like a mantra."

"He wants each day to bring you a step forward."

"He wants to annoy me," Abigail snapped. Then she sighed. "Or at least it often seems like it. But yes, I do understand the point. It frustrates me, because what I'm allowed to accomplish is so limited."

"You look to me as if you could accomplish just about anything."

Abigail turned. "Don't you know about the Turning? More than about the nightshade blossom, I mean."

"Only a little."

"We're even more backward than the Gatto, if you can believe that. There are no woman Turning fighters. No soldiers, no scouts—nothing like that. And although my father sits atop the patriarchy, no special status comes down to me on that count. He's stuck with a daughter and not a son."

"For which I thank him," Tagan said with a bow. "I don't think we'd be having this nighttime stroll otherwise."

With a loud exhale, Abigail stopped and folded her arms. "It's maddening. I'm his only child, and yet I'm just a girl."

"Just a girl? Don't let my mother hear you say that."

"In his eyes, I mean. In the eyes of all the Turning. You mentioned fighting. The only reason I know anything about the art of fighting is that I've pressed my tutor. My father would stab him through the heart if he knew I'd walked through a kata or two." She glared. "Why shouldn't I fight?"

"No reason I can think of."

"Not that I want to, but why should it be denied me? Why shouldn't I travel, and attend negotiations, and do any of the hundreds of things I'm not allowed to do? I had to beg for months to be allowed to make this journey to see the coast. And I'm surrounded by soldiers every minute."

"Not every minute," Tagan grinned.

Abigail gave a coy smile. "I can't even try to get a boy's attention by throwing a hat at him, without the soldiers intervening."

"Ha! Well," Tagan said, stepping up close, relieved to see the angry face turn to an inviting one, "there are no meddling soldiers here at the moment."

"No, there aren't, are there? No one to pull me away from that rude Tallach boy, if I were to step even closer." Abigail shifted to close the gap between them, and Tagan smiled, leaned in, and pressed his lips to hers.

No one had seen them. They were certain of it. And yet someone must have, as things abruptly changed. The next morning, Abigail and her servants were taken on tours of the city and then a ride on a schooner. Never once were they left alone. Soldiers flanked them every minute. The noon meal was taken at the inn, but not in the main dining room. Instead they ate in a smaller room to the side, where no mingling with the locals could take place. After the noon meal they were taken on another tour, and just as closely guarded.

Dinner was brought to their room. Then Abigail discovered that the captain had moved her and her servants to a different room. He explained that it was better situated, without saying what was better about it. But it was plain enough. The new room had no window overlooking the terrace. Instead there was a door that led onto a balcony, below which was another balcony. Abigail feigned sleeplessness, and several times stepped outside and peered down, only to receive a nod from a soldier standing watch below.

This routine continued for three days. Never was there any possibility of slipping away, nor any possibility of someone passing a note to Abigail: no notes, no invitations.

"Did they question you?" Abigail demanded of her maids. They swore no one had asked, and they hadn't said a word. "Then how could they know? Someone must have seen us."

The relentless efficiency of the Turning soldiers angered her, and on the fourth day Abigail refused to go on the day's planned trip.

"I don't want to go on another sailing trip down the coast. I don't want to see the islands. I don't want to visit the merchant shops with no one allowed in but me and the soldiers," she insisted. "I've bought enough things already. And my father will take them away, anyway."

This was only partly true. She definitely wanted to visit the merchant shops, and would enjoy buying more things, even knowing they would be confiscated when she returned. But she refused to go as a prisoner of her father's soldiers. When the captain's attempt to reason with her failed, he ordered that they would stay at the inn for the day.

It was at the evening meal that the idea came to her. They sat in the small dining room where she assumed Saor Tieg and his grandson had sat any number of times, and Abigail silently considered her conversation with Tagan. *You know about my mother, right?*

"I want to meet Talla Undine," Abigail demanded, seemingly out of the blue. She set down her glass and stared at the captain. "She's the daughter of the man who runs all of this. And I'm the daughter of Allton. I wish to meet her."

There was a quiet sidebar, but no one could think of a reason to refuse. On the contrary, they thought it might be useful.

"She's a woman of great influence," one soldier said, "and as the master's child notes, the progeny of a leader, as is she. It might offer us an edge in negotiations, to allow them to speak."

"All right," the captain relented. "We'll plan a meeting." Later he knocked on the door of Abigail's room. "It's been arranged, miss," he told her. "You're to meet the Talla in one hour."

Abigail practically slammed the door in his face. She spun to her friends. "Get me the Tallach clothes I bought. I told you I'd get to wear them!"

The girls scurried and fussed, helping her to get ready. Soon she was dressed in a new outfit of a young woman from Ben Atallach, a white silk shirt with mother-of-pearl buttons, a deep blue satin vest, and short, black pants with cuffs tight to her shins just below the knee. Abigail giggled with delight as she pulled on black sandals.

"Your legs are bare," Anne hissed. "Will the captain allow it?"

"I'm meeting Talla Undine," Abigail said with a devious smile. "You just watch." She opened the door and strode into the hall. "I'm prepared to meet the Talla," she announced, "and will honor her by presenting myself dressed in the proper fashion."

The soldiers stared, their eyes fixing on her legs until the captain slapped one of them in the chest with his glove and they snapped their eyes up.

The captain gave her a deep scowl, but made no comment. "Come," he said sourly.

Abigail strode down the hall in her Tallach garb, followed by her servants in their gray dresses, and the soldiers.

Meeting Talla Undine, even with careful planning beforehand, turned out to be entirely different than either the captain or Abigail had expected. They entered the mansion through tall, heavy oak doors flanked by watchmen, and stepped into an opulent foyer. A portrait above an elegant fireplace depicted a young Talla Undine with a redheaded girl behind her, resting an arm on Undine's shoulder. The redhead had a little blue flower on her forehead. Abigail stepped over to look, touching her own forehead.

But Undine herself was not in the foyer. Instead a captain and two soldiers in full dress, complete with polished long blades slung at their waists, stood waiting for them.

The captain of Undine's guard stepped up and bowed. "Talla Undine invites her guests to join us in partaking of a glass while you wait," he said, and with a wave of his arm, servants swept in with trays of small crystal digestif glasses half filled with an amber liquid.

Abigail's captain took a glass, sniffed it, and took a sip.

"Fennel and anise," Undine's captain explained. "The Talla has it made overseas. A recipe from her muse, she says." He dropped his eyes, then straightened. "To many successful trades between the Western Shores and the Turning." He raised his glass; and they all lifted glasses to toast, and drained them. "And now, shall we soldiers retire to the salon while the young lady visits with the Talla?"

There was a moment's hesitation as Abigail's captain realized he and his men wouldn't be attending the meeting. He fixed his eyes on Anne and Evelyn, silently demanding that they not leave Abigail's side.

A Tallach soldier stepped to a stairway and waved a hand. Abigail and her servants followed him up, while the others moved toward a door in the rear. Upstairs the soldier rapped his knuckles on a door.

"Send them in," came a voice from inside.

The soldier opened the door, and closed it behind them. Abigail didn't know exactly what to expect, but the woman who stood looking at them matched the image in her mind. Undine was dark haired, no early gray, with dark eyes and a powerful stance. She was dressed in meticulously stitched finery, and wore a knife belt at her waist with twin Tallach blades. She looked not merely in charge, but ready to defend her position. Abigail's servants halted in their tracks at the spiral of black diamonds inked on the woman's face. None of them, Abigail included, had ever seen a woman with the marking of a fourth-level Tallach warrior.

Undine stepped up, smiled, and took Abigail's nervous hand in hers. "Well, well. You are pretty, aren't you? Look at those gray eyes. He told me about that. I think he said *stunning*. And I believe you are also intelligent, well spoken, shimmering, elegant, and irresistible. He ran out of words after a while. But there's something I want to see. You have a flower inked on your forehead. May I see it? A friend of mine has something similar."

Abigail stared, flustered. "See it?" she echoed stupidly.

"The nightshade blossom."

"Oh." Abigail pushed back her hair.

"Very fine," Undine said. "Very fine, indeed. My friend Tyra will be interested in that. Did you see the portrait in the foyer? Hers is a flax flower, the mark of the daughter of a Tallach sea captain. Yours is the mark of the family line, isn't it?"

Abigail nodded, mutely.

"Do you know its origin? Were your ancestors *in the trade*, as they say?"

"The trade?"

"The killing trade. Were they assassins? You don't take nightshade for a cough. Nightshade is a killer."

"It's a symbol, I think."

Undine laughed. "I'm being overbearing. Horace used to warn me about that. *Be ready to win the fight, but be ready to win the hearts, as well,* he'd say. I'm better at the former. But come. You aren't here to be grilled by Tagan's mother. You two," she pointed at Abigail's servants, "there are some fine chocolates and a pretty good wine in the sitting room. Go on. Pour a glass for me. I'll be with you directly." She nodded her head toward a door. "At a minimum we need to do something about those outfits. Abigail, come with me."

Confused into silence, Abigail followed her along a narrow passage to an interior room. Undine pointed. "Go on. Through that door. If you get into trouble, rap three times and I'll send in the guard." She winked and turned and left.

Through that door. Abigail had expected to spend her time with Talla Undine in subtle conversation, hinting at how she might like to meet the woman's son. But it seemed the Talla was way ahead of her. She breathed in, breathed out, and pulled the door open.

Tagan leaped to his feet, and was about to run forward and wrap his arms around her, but he stopped short, unsure. "Abbie," he said, smiling widely. "You met my mother?" he proposed clumsily.

"Shimmering?" Abigail said, pursing her lips and flashing a pretend scowl. She folded her arms. "Irresistible?"

"Definitely irresistible." He stepped forward and kissed her.

Negotiations were rocky, but proceeded. The connection with Talla Undine seemed to help. The Tallach men paid closer attention when the captain spoke, and offered fewer objections to the arrangements he proposed. And in return, the captain forced a smile and said *yes, of course,* when the Talla repeatedly invited the girl to come back to visit. For the final week of their trip, Abigail spent more time with Saor Tieg's daughter—or so the captain thought—than with her own contingent. This Tallach woman had certainly made an impression, the captain thought. Abigail seemed almost moved to tears when the caravan left Deadrise Bay.

It was only when they were halfway home that it occurred to the captain that he had been played. "Wait," he muttered, reflecting. "The Talla has a reputation for trickiness, doesn't she?"

"She does," said his second.

"And all these visits. Allton's daughter and Saor Tieg's daughter. It had to be that boy." He closed his eyes and fell silent. "We'll not speak of this. Understand? I'll make my report and volunteer for service in the far reaches."

"Yes, captain."

"Hell in a basket," the captain said, slumping. "Allton's daughter, and that brazen Tallach boy."

5. Under the Bridge

The tires on the expansion joints made the booming industrial sound of a gigantic machine. Between the impacts, Camilla could hear footsteps and voices, then more voices. People were stopping to check out the crash. Then she saw the flicker of flashing blue lights reflected in the water below. Soon there were voices right above her, people leaning over the barrier to look.

No time to dwell on the boy in the forest. She had to concentrate on her own situation. It was a warm day, but there was no sun under the roadbed. Stretched out soaking wet on an I beam, she was cold. Worse, water was dripping off her. Would someone see it?

She looked around and spotted a joint in a drain pipe from the roadbed that dripped slowly onto the I beam ahead. It was an early sign of infrastructure decay. In ten years, the pipe would come apart and the beams would start to lose their structural integrity.

Camilla shook her head. This was also no time to be reflecting on the condition of the highway system. She shimmied across the beam and stopped near the slow drip. It would mask the water dripping from her clothes. By now people were scrambling down the embankment to the water. She tried to make herself as small and flat as possible. Wasn't it just her luck that a pack of good Samaritans would be eager to try to save the girl who crashed the motorcycle.

Soon the whole place was buzzing with activity. People were working their way along the side of the river looking for a body, state troopers were waving cars past the crash scene, and radios were barking.

Camilla froze as a pair of officers talked directly overhead.

"That was a nice bike," one man said.

"Stolen," his partner said. "Break-in at the Harley shop over on the strip."

"It's not a Harley."

"Nah. Some hotshot put it down on the town line road a couple weeks ago, and fucked it all up. Harley shop just finished the repairs."

The other officer laughed. "Now they get to do it again. Good business to be in, I guess."

Someone called to them, and the voices moved off.

Camilla sighed, and tried to stop shivering. This could take hours. The good news, she reflected, was that with police on hand, the kill teams would pull back. The bad news was that they wouldn't give up. They would return to perform their own search, the moment the police finished and left.

She waited and waited, listening for the change, the distinctive sound of officers finishing up and leaving the crash site. Finally, it came. There was a little talking, then doors slammed, and cars pulled away sharply.

Those were the cruisers, and that sound meant it was time to go. Cruisers pulling away with conviction marked the end of the incident. Camilla heard others pulling more slowly onto the highway, but she didn't care about them. The gawkers would take their time leaving. They didn't matter. She crawled as fast as she could, looked around, and made her descent.

The next part she had mulled over as she waited: how to get away. The kill teams would be in place already. They had seen her go into the water, and the most obvious thing to do would be to scout the river downstream. Men would be watching the water and the highway. Camilla couldn't see the cars from under the bridge, but she guessed that a black Beamer had passed several times since the crash. At least one of the kill team vehicles would be making a circuit, scouting the roadside for hitchers and looking along the embankment.

Downstream was out, and so was continuing down the highway. She couldn't hitch a ride with police and kill teams on the road. It left only two routes: She could swim upstream. The kill teams would rule that out as impractical, although they might post someone upstream just in case. Or she could go back toward town. They might expect that, and would probably have a few men in the woods. But they would be contractors used to urban settings. They wouldn't have thought to bring trackers with experience in the woods.

She sighed. It wasn't ideal, but it would be easier than trying to swim upstream. She slunk along the bank until she came to a chain link fence that marked the edge of the highway right-of-way, and staying close, worked her way toward town.

As it turned out, there was only one man assigned to the woods on this side, and he was sitting on a rock having a smoke as she approached. Camilla easily skirted him, and then it was all clear. Even so, she grumbled as she pushed her way through the undergrowth. She had escaped the kill teams that had come for Horace and Robbie, and then they had found her in under two days. She thought she'd been especially clever getting away from the motel and taking the motorcycle, like the lead character in one of those dystopia movies, racing off and leaving her pursuers to eat her dust. And then she was flying over the side of a bridge. Nice job, she silently scolded herself. Horace would be proud.

Horace. And Robbie. She stopped and clenched her hands into fists. What had happened? They were supposed to be safe in the house in Boston. Her grandfather had set it up himself. ...

"Your name is Calista now," Horace had told his granddaughter six years ago, as little Camilla sucked soda through a straw.

"Why can't I be Una?" she complained. "Or Undine?"

"Because the goal is to blend in, not to stand out. You're just another new kid. You moved to Boston from Trenton, you're about to enter the eighth grade, and you're worried about making new friends. That kind of thing. Got it?"

"It's so lame," Camilla growled. "*Calista* sucks." The girl made a loud slurp at the bottom of the cup to illustrate. But she understood. She might complain, but beneath the sour demeanor, she got it. Her grandfather's solution was good for her, for him, and for the new people she had met, Robbie and Grace. They were going to be her parents in this charade.

"And none of us—not you, me, or Robbie or Grace—has anything to do with things from the past. Understood? That's all behind you."

Her grandfather didn't need to elaborate. Camilla didn't know all the details, but she understood the general outline. Years ago, when Camilla Rand was a small child, her father had gotten mixed up with very powerful people, who had hired Vergil Rand to assassinate a government advisor. In the end, an agent tracked her father down and shot him. Horace spent years setting up an elaborate scam to take down the men who had hired Vergil. He took their money, and he ran.

Camilla, in the meantime, had lost not only her father, but her mother as well. The woman had run off, leaving Camilla to make her own way. Abandoned, Camilla jumped from one foster family to another, repeatedly getting into trouble. She built her troubles to a climax when she burned down the house of a boy who had been persecuting her. And then she sought refuge with the only person she could think of, her estranged grandfather.

When twelve-year-old Camilla showed up on the porch of Horace's remote cabin in the woods, Horace was forced to run again, this time with the girl in tow. They fled to Canada, and after a narrow escape from Turcotte's men, Horace made a new plan. Camilla needed a normal home, and Horace needed a safe haven. He knew of a couple that needed a safe haven as much as they did. And so he arranged for Camilla to become Calista, the daughter of Robbie and Grace, newly moved to Boston with Grace's elderly father.

And it worked. Calista went to school and found a local karate dojo. She made friends, and earned her belts, and the day she turned eighteen she made a visit to a tattoo parlor.

The tattoo artist tried to talk her out of inking her face. "Hard to get work. Nobody'll hire you. You understand that?"

"Got it," she said.

"But aren't you supposed to do your arms, anyway? You know, like Kung Fu. You carry the brazier with your bare arms, and you get the marks."

"I'm not a Shaolin priest," Camilla said with an eye roll. "And that's an old TV show."

"So Shotokan guys get face tats? I've never seen that."

"It's House Kamine, not Shotokan."

"But you go to a Shotokan dojo. You told me that. What's House Kamine? Never heard of it."

"Because I haven't started my dojo yet. It's gonna be called House Kamine. And House Kamine fighters get this spiral of diamonds. It's a sign of achievement. You gonna do it, or not?"

It was that very day that things turned. Camilla went home expecting the conversation to be dominated by the ink on her face, but all she received was a raised eyebrow from her grandfather, who was standing in the living room doorway as if waiting for someone. Her pretend-mother was lugging a suitcase down the stairs, and almost ran into her in the hall.

"Oh! You're back. I'm so glad," Grace said, and wrapped her arms around her. Their mother-daughter relationship was a ruse, but the hug was genuine. They had grown close over the years. Grace called her *dear*, and Camilla called her *mom*.

"Mom, what's going on?"

Grace winced, white-faced. "I thought I'd missed you. Callie, I love you. You know that, right? But I have to go."

"What do you mean, you have to go? Where are you going?"

"Camping," she said, and smiled sadly. "You and Horace need to pack and get out, too. Look me up when you can." A taxi pulled into the drive, and Grace planted a kiss on her forehead and rushed out the door.

"What's going on? Where's she going?" Camilla turned to her grandfather.

"Robbie will be here soon," Horace said. "We have to make plans. The signs are there. We've been discovered."

She and her grandfather and Robbie stayed up late that night, guns loaded, security cameras on. Neither she nor Horace could get Robbie to tell them what had happened. But Camilla could tell he'd done something. Somehow her pretend-father had blown their cover, and now men were coming for them.

Finally, Horace gave up trying to draw it out of him. "Calista," Horace dropped his eyes, "you should go. Pack light, and move quickly. Get out of the state."

"We should all run," she said. "Robbie, you can go after Grace. You have to, right? You can't just leave her on her own. And you and I can go together." She grasped her grandfather's hand. "Just like before. We can go to Canada."

Horace shook his head. "I'm too old for that. And together we're a bigger target."

"I don't want to split up. I don't care if you're old. We'll account for that."

The argument went on for a long time, until they were exhausted and opted to sleep on it. They would make a plan first thing, and be out of there tomorrow.

With an unmistakable look of guilt, Robbie insisted on taking first watch. He loaded a shotgun and parked himself in front of the monitors. Camilla went upstairs to her attic room, and Horace retreated to his bedroom on the second floor.

The storm that rolled in was a case of bad luck. Rain swept in, and as light streaked across the sky and thunder boomed, the cameras started to go out. Robbie cursed and fiddled with the keyboard, and too late thought to sound the alarm. The front door and back door burst open at the same time, and men streamed in.

Camilla would later reflect that their attackers must have cased the place, as they knew exactly where to go. From the top of the stairs she could hear them move through the kitchen and let loose with automatic rifles. They were shooting through the door and wall to the dining room. That was the space that had been made over into the ops room. But it was just a room in an old house. It wasn't bullet proof. Robbie didn't have a chance to fire a single round. Upstairs, Horace leaped out of bed and raised his gun, and a sniper in a tree caught him in the middle of the forehead.

She heard the shot and then the thump of her grandfather's body hitting the floor.

There was a moment of frozen indecision. But her grandfather had relentlessly admonished her not to do stupid things, and as she stood considering the urge to run downstairs to save him and Robbie, she realized she couldn't. They were already dead. She desperately wanted to run down, anyway. Instead she whipped on her black pants and a black turtleneck, pulled on her gloves, grabbed her go bag, and was up the ladder to the roof hatch in seconds.

It would have been easier to escape on a dry night. Just in the moment it took to raise the hatch, get onto the deck, and close it again, rain pattered down onto the wooden rungs inside. They would see it, and would know someone had gotten out. But there was nothing to be done about it. She pushed the outside hasp down, shoved a bolt through it, and ran along the ridge to the chimney. This was the dangerous part. If a sniper looked her way, she would be dead.

Camilla wrapped a handgrip over a zipline and waited for another flash of lightning, and the instant the flash ceased, she pushed off. The long roll of thunder cloaked the sound of the wheel riding the line, and the man in the tree watching the windows missed the black shape sliding through the air higher up. A few seconds of abject terror later, she held her feet out and stopped herself against a telephone pole by the street, and then she was climbing down and slinking into the night.

Horace was dead. Robbie was dead. The men would discover that a third person had been in the house. They would figure out who she was, and they would come for her and for Grace. But Camilla knew a thing or two about hunting. She would get to Grace before the killers did. She had to. Not only had Grace served as her mother for the past six years, she was the only one left who could help her figure out what this was all about. Camilla needed to find out who was after them, and why.

Slogging through the ditches along the side of the highway, Camilla sighed. Earlier it had all seemed very clear: Find Grace, get the information she needed, and make a plan. Simple. And the crushing sadness of losing her grandfather and Robbie had lent her firm resolve. She would get the bastards. But so far, the bad guys had racked up a lot more points than she had.

There had, however, been one positive outcome of her hours on the I beam. She had worked out where Grace had gone. Their little pretend family had been a web of tricks and subterfuge. The four of them had simultaneously trusted one another implicitly and kept secrets. Grace had been all-in as Calista's mother. She laughed and joked with her teenager, and admonished her to spend more time on her schoolwork and less time lounging around with her friends. But at the mere hint of a threat to Calista, Grace turned into a pit bull. If there was trouble at school, Grace would show up at the office and let loose her wrath. She would then take the girl to her car, and they would drive and drive, talking it out until both of them were ready to go home and go to sleep. In the morning it would seem that a weight had been lifted. Whatever the problem had been, it didn't seem so important anymore.

But for all their hours talking through one problem or another, neither had learned much about the other's past. Grace didn't know Camilla's real name, or that she was in fact Horace's granddaughter. And Camilla knew the woman had been in serious danger, but she didn't know why. This was the deal. The past was sacrosanct; one didn't press. Nonetheless, small things came out. Sometimes her stepmother would tell little stories about her childhood, painting in small pieces of her past. And hiding on that I beam, she centered on one of the little facts she had gleaned.

Where are you going? Camilla had asked. *Camping,* Grace had replied.

Camilla didn't have to hunt for Grace. This was a code word from a story she had once told her. Camilla knew exactly where the woman was going.

6. The Fiddle Game

The road agents crept up just before dawn, and found a lone figure sleeping on the ground by the smoldering remains of a campfire. Nearby was a full pack. They smiled. It could be clothes, food, or valuable goods. Maybe this was a porter, conveniently lost in just the right place for an ambush.

Tagan stepped back from relieving himself in the woods—and halted. The shorter one had a blade out, and was two paces from Dimon, preparing to drop on him and kill him without a fight. The other held back, stepping to the side to cover the road, in case their target should somehow escape the strike and make a run for it.

Slowly, carefully, the road agent crept forward, closing to a single pace. Then two things happened, all at once. Dimon's arm shot out, and he grabbed the road man's ankle and pulled hard. As the man cried out and fell backward, Tagan's blade soared over the man's head and stuck in a tree with a thump, instead of catching the man in the neck. Tagan cursed, and Dimon rose to a crouch, still holding the man's leg. He yanked the leg upward and to the side, flipping the man onto the coals of the campfire.

The larger man was already in motion, but so was Tagan. As the big road agent rushed to the aid of his companion, he received a hard kidney punch from behind, and groaned as he swiveled to face the unexpected threat of a second man. The big man dropped a bag he'd been carrying, and stepped forward.

Dimon had now sprung to his feet and was preparing to take on the smaller one, who had flung himself to the side, screaming and shaking his hands, which he had reflexively pushed into. the coals to protect his face.

"Just these two?" Dimon called out. "I see no others."

"Nor do I. And that one's yours now," Tagan called back. He leveled a kick at the big man, who shimmied backward. "I'd have had him, if you hadn't grabbed his ankle."

Dimon circled. "Don't be so damned quiet, then. I thought you were taking a piss."

"I was. Doesn't mean I'm blind."

As the small one advanced on Dimon, the big man rose. "And you're mine, little shit," he growled, sizing up the boy. Young, wiry, light. One or two shots should take care of him, and then the sorry little bastard would pay for the cheap shot. His fist shot out—and hit nothing.

Dodging the blow, Tagan came up behind the man. He considered repeating the kidney punch. That would bring the man down. But the road agent's sneering retort annoyed him. He glanced at Dimon, decided his friend didn't need any help, and waited for the big man to turn. "What's that you say?" Tagan mocked. "I'm yours? Come get me, then."

The big man wasn't as stupid as Tagan had immediately guessed. He didn't try to rush him. Instead his eyes narrowed, and the man raised his fists and circled.

As if by routine, Dimon drew the smaller man farther away. He ducked and dodged, and put in a few good blows, all the while backing up to separate his own fight from Tagan's. Dimon had trained at House Kamine, too. But it had been down at the docks that he and Tagan had gotten their practical experience in road brawls. One of the rules was not to get tangled up with everyone in the same place at the same time. A couple of one-on-ones was better than a pile of men flailing around in close quarters.

"Two minutes, Dimon!" Tagan called out, as he stepped in and leveled a series of punches at the man. The big man blocked, but Tagan got in several successful strikes, and the man retreated.

"Two minutes until what?" he growled.

Tagan grinned. "Until we're done. Can't spend all morning dancing with you two. If you want to run before the two minutes is up, you'll leave in better shape."

"Smug little bastard, ain't you? I think maybe I only need one minute." The man moved in, and proved that he wasn't altogether unfamiliar with fighting a trained opponent. They engaged, and Tagan blocked several strong punches, and started to pay more attention.

Dimon's opponent was having difficulty. He cursed and swore, moving his fingers between attempts to strike.

"Same deal for you," Dimon said, confident that his man was already spent. "Turn and run. Go find a stream to put those hands into. No shame in it."

In the end, it was a bit under two minutes. Tagan caught the big man in the side of the head, a little harder than he'd intended, and as the man staggered back and stumbled, the smaller one was flying backward as well. He'd hit Dimon in the face—a luck shot, Dimon would later complain—and in return received a vicious kick in the stomach.

The big man rose to his feet and put up his palm. "Let's get the fuck out of here," he growled, stumbling toward the road. His smaller companion followed.

"Get your pack," Tagan said. "I'll carry this one." He scooped up the bag the big man had dropped.

"How much do you have left?" Tagan said, rifling through the bag. The sun was almost up. "Money, I mean. I don't have any. And there's a nice Tallach outfit in the road agent's bag—must have stolen it from a merchant—but there's no money."

They found a downed tree to sit on, safely away from the road, but close enough that they would see if anyone approached.

Dimon rummaged in his pockets and pulled out a handful of coins. "It'll get us a few meals." He pushed back his hair and counted. "A few light meals."

"We'll be broke in two days."

"You said a Tallach outfit. Can we sell it?"

"Do you see any buyers?" Tagan waved an arm.

"You'll come up with something. That, or we'll starve to death."

"Let's get going."

They trudged along the narrow road, picking their way around the muddy wheel ruts. All in all, their exodus had been successful. Apart from being set upon by the road agents, it had gone smoothly. After the fight, it started to rain, but they caught a lucky ride in a wagon. Then they spent hours on foot, and then more hours in the back of another wagon before making camp. And they were already far enough from Deadrise Bay that they didn't need to keep worrying that a sentry might recognize them.

"Do you think they'll buy the story that I'm riding the trade routes to find my father?" Dimon said.

Tagan shrugged. "The timing is suspicious. But you've been talking about it for years, Dimon. Everyone knows you want to find him. Maybe they'll think my death prompted you to get up and do it."

His friend clenched his teeth. "He's out there somewhere, isn't he? Don't you want to find your father? I don't even have a passage token to get into the northlands, and I still plan to find him."

"The token is a reproduction," Tagan said. He pulled a chain around his neck and drew out a cylindrical silver pendant, and fingered the delicate pattern engraved on the surface. "I'm told it's a good reproduction," he added with a snide grimace, "but it's not real. My mother picked it up at a bazaar somewhere, I suppose."

"She told me your father gave it to her. A northerner that she ... well, you know."

Tagan exhaled loudly and rolled his eyes. "The reason I know it's a reproduction is that the story is so ridiculous that I brought it to a silversmith in the old city to have it appraised. He laughed in my face. Told me he'd give me the melt value, seeing as how I'd made such a long journey. It's a fake, Dimon. I wear it because it pleases my mother."

"You think she made up the story about your father giving it to her."

"A secret dalliance with a northern soldier, and she leaves with a token of their night of passion, to wear close to her heart for ever and ever? That's the oldest fairytale in the book, Dimon. Of course she made it up."

"But she's been to the north."

"I know. When she was young. Going overseas, and all that. She's told me the story a million times. And obviously she had an evening with some-one, right? Here I am. But the token is to make me feel better about not having a father. It's supposed to make me feel connected to him somehow. Something for *me* to wear close to *my* heart forever."

Dimon shrugged. "All right, Tagan. Maybe it's not real, but that doesn't mean she didn't get it from a northern soldier. She didn't say a *rich* northern soldier, did she? Maybe the fellow bought it at a bazaar, and gave it to a girl he spent a spectacular night with. Would that be so much less of a story?"

"And maybe I should accept the offer of the melt value. We could get a few good meals out of it."

Dimon stopped and grabbed his arm. "Don't do that!"

Shaking his arm loose, Tagan walked on. "I'm not planning to sell the damned pendant, Dimon. I've no cause to be cruel to my mother. Just stop bothering me about it." He stuffed it back inside his vest. "If I die out here, you can bring it back to her, and she can wear it in remembrance of me. All right?"

"Aren't you cheerful."

Tagan stopped. "I don't mean to diminish your search for your father. I'll do what I can to help. But I'm not looking for my father, all right? I'm looking to stay alive. I need to get the Turning sanction off my back. And the only way I can think to do that is to make my case to the northern lord. No one else holds any sway with the Turning. If my mother wasn't making the whole damned thing up, maybe the Tynan lord will be willing to help. And if not, we'll keep going north."

"Let's keep walking, then," Dimon scowled, and stormed down the road.

A few coins got them a meal from a merchant caravan that had stopped for the night, and an old couple took pity on the young wanderers and let them sleep in their supply wagon. Early in the morning they set out on foot, heading north.

"We'll reach Stockton Line by noon," Dimon said, "if that merchant's account is correct. But we're low on money. What's the plan?"

"The plan? I see. You're expecting me to tell you what to do."

Dimon rolled his eyes. "I bow to the superior mind, Tagan. Command me." He grinned and dodged a punch. "You know I'm no good at coming up with ideas. I'll be your straight man, but don't expect me to think up the con."

"I'm fresh out of ideas at the moment."

"Maybe we can sell something. What do you have in your pack?"

"Aside from the Tallach outfit? Not much," Tagan sighed. He unfastened the closure on his bag. "My lantern and a jar of oil," he said, pulling out a canvas drawstring bag and setting it aside. "That won't even get us lunch. The clothes the road agent had are quite nice. Something I'd wear at home, when I'm ordered to look presentable."

"A nice find, since I couldn't bring your pack," Dimon said.

"Yes, but we can't start selling our clothes. We'll be naked in two days, Dimon, and just as hungry as we are now. Oh, and I've got that old hunter blade that I won at cards that time." Tagan grinned.

"That's a fake, Tagan," Dimon chimed in. "And I mean it's *definitely* a fake."

Tagan slipped a ten-inch, double-edged throwing blade from his pack. Three red stones glinted in the dark handle. "Not a bad reproduction, though. The stones are glass, and the handle's not real ebony. But it's a sharp blade, and it looks good, doesn't it?" He held it up and whipped his arm back and forth, pretending to ward off an attacker. "Not as if you could fool a serious bladesmith, but it's a valuable relic when you're at the pub having a pint. Ha!"

"The fiddle game. You could do the fiddle game."

"The fiddle game?" Tagan put the blade away. "What's the fiddle game?"

Dimon tipped his head. "I don't know. You tell me. Will it get us some money?"

Tagan looked around. "Wait. You didn't say that?" Were words were forming in his head again?

"You've fooled guys in a bar? So do it again," came the words. "Don't you know the fiddle game? It's an oldie."

"Camilla?" Tagan said, out loud. "Are you my muse, now?"

"It's a con. I'll explain."

Dimon flashed a look of concern at his friend. "Tagan, are you all right?"

"I'm fine. Shut up for a minute. I'm thinking." He peered at his friend, who was giving him a look that said perhaps he'd been in the sun too long. "I'm thinking out loud, all right? Quiet for a moment, please."

Dimon raised his palms. "All right, then. Good. I'll leave you to your thinking. Shall we walk while you're doing it?"

"Quiet!" Tagan waved an impatient hand, trying to key in on the words. But he rose and ambled along, following Dimon down the road. As he walked, he offered hushed responses to the words forming in his head, and ignored Dimon's sideways glances. Several times his eyebrows rose, and he smiled and wished he were alone so he could ask questions in a normal voice.

They walked for a long time, Dimon keeping quiet as his friend muttered. Finally Tagan stopped and grinned. "Come on, Dimon," he said at length. "I've got it! I've got a plan. The fiddle game!"

A young, blond Tallach man stepped into a mostly empty tavern, and drew the immediate attention of the proprietor. It was the quiet time of the day. There were a few men lingering at the bar, but most of the regulars had already finished their midday meal and had returned to work. This was the time for cleaning up, sweeping the floor, and getting ready for the evening crowd.

"New in town?" The man said, thumbs hooked into the pockets of his vest. "What can I get you?"

Dimon nodded. "Just came in from the west road. I know I'm late. Anything left by way of a meal? I'm starving."

"I think we can put together a plate. Have a seat. Where've you come from?"

"Sailed in to the south coast," Dimon said. "Got some time off. And last time I was here, I met a girl who lives up in T-town. Thought I'd look her up. That's not far, is it? I'm hoping to get to Steerageway tomorrow."

"Not long by river." The man stepped around the bar and called through a sliding door to the kitchen. "One more plate, Meg." He turned to the young man. "Be right up. Something to drink?"

"Beer."

"Western Shores, eh?" the barkeep said, pulling out a cloth to wipe the bar in front of the young man. "Tallach?"

"Half. My mother. But the Shores are home. I grew up on the Shores."

Dimon kept up the chitchat until his meal came, and then tucked in greedily. He was very hungry, and while he felt guilty that Tagan wasn't getting any of it, he didn't let that stop him.

He polished the plate clean and drained his beer, and then stood and shoved his hand into his pocket. Then he stiffened. "Oh, dear," he said, adopting a serious look. He patted his other pocket, and then crammed his hands into his back pockets. "Damn it," he quietly cursed. "Damn it all."

The proprietor moved up close, and stood directly across the bar from him, and a few men who had been sitting in the rear stood up.

"I've got the money," Dimon protested, holding up a hand. "No need for that." He turned and nodded sheepishly at the rising trio of bouncers. "I've just … it seems I've left my purse in the room."

"You need to pay for that meal, son. We don't give away free plates here." The proprietor folded his arms and nodded, and the men approached.

"I promise, I have the money," Dimon said, now looking worried. "I'm just up at the inn. I'll go fetch my purse, and I'll return straightaway and pay you. On my honor. I won't be but a half hour at most."

The men closed in on him.

"Here, I'll leave my blade as a surety. Will that do? You can hold onto it until I return. It's a good blade. Worth a lot." Dimon frantically unbuckled his leather belt and slipped off the knife sheath and held it up. "See? It's an old northern blade. I was offered five gold pieces for it at a shop on the coast." He set the blade in the sheath on the bar, and raised his palms in an imploring gesture to the bouncers not to throttle him.

"Down at the inn," the proprietor repeated, slipping the dark-handled blade out of the sheath and fingering the red stones in the hilt. He looked at one of the men. "What do you think, Henry? I don't know shit for northern blades."

One of bouncers stepped up, deliberately jostling Dimon. "Let's see it." He took the blade and made a show of holding it up and studying the craftsmanship. "Hunter blade. Looks all right. Nice enough piece of steel, anyway. Don't know about no five gold pieces," he sneered. "But I'll give you the price of that lunch for it, if this Tallach don't come back and pay up."

There was a long moment with Dimon looking worried and the proprietor looking threatening, but finally he gave a single nod. "All right, then. Go on. But you got one hour. Understood? You don't come back, and we come looking for you."

Dimon nodded, held up his hands again in a silent promise that he would keep up his end of the arrangement, and hurried out of the saloon with his head down.

The proprietor took the blade and set it on a narrow shelf above the window to the kitchen, next to a row of liquor bottles.

Half an hour passed, and just as the proprietor was finishing the sweeping, another stranger stepped in. This one was different. He didn't look like a sailor on leave. This young man was dressed in a fine satin outfit, his black vest edged with purple thread. He held his head high, with the air of a young aristocrat. The young man stopped just inside the door and looked around, and then stepped to the bar.

"Pardon, sir," he said, "I've gotten off track. Is the Rose and Star nearby? I was told it's by the stables, but I've walked three blocks."

"The Rose and Star?" The proprietor gave a guarded smile. "I think you might need to sit down and have a drink, young man. The Rose and Star ain't at Stockton Line. That'd be down in Steerageway."

"Oh, damn. This isn't Steerageway?" Tagan exhaled. "I'm afraid those men on the road were having a bit of fun at my expense." He scowled and pulled out a stool and sat. "Aren't I the fool." He turned to the proprietor, and eyed the men at the other side of the room, who were grinning and watching. "Promise you won't say anything. My father mustn't hear. I'd never hear the end of it. Damn it all, they lied to me! And I paid them a sixteenth piece of gold, the highwaymen. Damn it!" He slapped a palm on the bar in frustration.

"Here you go." The proprietor filled a mug with beer and slid it over to him. "Get your spirits back up. You ain't the first to get steered wrong. It's a game with them road gangs. Great sport around here."

Tagan let out a long, exasperated breath, and sipped the beer. He raised the glass. "Thank you. Yes, you're right. I do need this." He pulled several coins from his pocket and clicked them on the counter. "Does this cover it?"

Eyebrows raised, the proprietor nodded and scooped up the money and pocketed it. "It does, young gentleman. Anything else I can get you? Did the rascals on the road feed you at least?"

"Not to the tune of what I paid them," Tagan growled, "but yes. Their little fun didn't involve starving me as well as sending me to the wrong place. They ..." then he stopped, his eyes fixing on the blade on the shelf. "Say, what's that you have there? It looks like a hunter's blade. May I hold it? My father collects antique blades. I'd like to see it."

"That old thing?" the proprietor nodded. "It ain't mine. Fellah came in here with no money. I'm just holding onto it until he comes back to pay. Don't 'spect it's worthy of your father's collection, but sure, you can take a look." He reached up and retrieved it, and handed it to the young aristocrat.

"Mm," Tagan said. "Well, well," he muttered under his breath, sliding the blade out and holding it as if it were a priceless relic. He turned it slowly, and murmured out loud and he ran a finger over the stones. He looked up. "I'll give you ten gold pieces for it."

"You'll ..."

"I know, I know. You could get twelve up over the border. Thirteen, if you find just the right buyer. But you have to know the right people, and it's a long journey. There are costs involved in getting past the border, and so on. Ten is a fair price on this side."

The proprietor stared blankly at him. "You're offering me ten gold pieces for that old thing? Ten full measure gold pieces?"

"Full measure. Yes, of course. It's a fair price. It needs cleaning and oiling. And this sheath is no good. Can't display it like this. It'll need to be replaced with one of the proper style for this weapon. And that's not free, you know. It's a very nice piece, but ten is reasonable."

By this time the bouncers had come over, and were crowding behind Tagan. One of them leaned in to the proprietor. "But it's the boy's," he said.

"Oh, all right. I'll offer eleven," Tagan said, "but not an ounce more."

The proprietor stared. "Now, let's think." He closed his eyes for a moment, and worked to suppress an eager smile. "I suppose the owner might be agreeable to selling. I could try and make it work. Are you staying in town?"

"I hadn't planned to," Tagan grumbled, "but I suppose I'm stuck here for the night."

"All right, then. My man will take you to make arrangements for your lodging. Henry, take my friend here to the Inn down at the water." He emphatically pointed his thumb in the direction opposite the closer inn. "Take him down and show him to the riverside inn. See they tend to him nicely. And when my other young friend returns, I'll see if I can set up the sale."

"Would you do that for me?" Tagan set the blade down. "This would make a fine gift for my father. Shall I return this evening? You have a late meal?"

"You come on by, and we'll set you up with a fine meal, and I'll bet I'll have good news about this old blade." The proprietor scooped up the blade and tucked it safely under the bar, out of sight.

Tagan took another long draft of his beer, then drained the glass and rose. "My thanks to you, sir. But please bear in mind that eleven gold pieces is my top offer."

"Of course." The proprietor smiled, and his bouncer motioned to the door and led Tagan out.

When the other young man returned to the bar, the proprietor was tapping a finger impatiently.

"I'll pay you, as I promised I would," the young Tallach sailor said. "Tell me what I owe. I'll pay it in full."

"Well, now, young fellah," the proprietor said, adopting a guarded smile. "You know, I been thinking about what you said." He pulled the blade from beneath the counter, and set it on the bar. "About this blade. What would you say to selling it? I can't give you no five gold pieces," he laughed, "but it's a fine old throwing blade. I'll give you three for it, and we'll call it even on the meal. How's that?"

The young sailor's eyebrows went down. "Three gold pieces? Sir, I couldn't do that. I'll be back to port in a week, and I'd get five for it. I've a firm offer."

"All right, four then." The proprietor folded his arms in concession. "You could wait until you return, sure. Maybe you'd get five and maybe not. But what's it worth to you then? Wouldn't you like to get something nice for your honey? A sailor wants to show up with something pretty for his young lady, don't he? And four gold pieces, now that'd buy a nice dress, and plenty left over to show her the town."

Dimon sat back and fell silent, as if mulling it over. "You make a good point. I hadn't thought of that. I'd be a sorry sailor to show up empty-handed, wouldn't I?" He looked up. "I could hire a wagon instead of spending the night at the inn and waiting for the morning barge. I'll tell you what. Throw in a plate to go—make it double portions—and we'll call it four. Fair enough?"

The proprietor stifled a smile and leaned down to the sliding window. "A plate to go, Meg!" he called out. "Double!" And then he stacked four gold pieces on the counter and held out his hand. "Deal?"

Dimon nodded solemnly. "Deal," he said. He pushed the blade across the bar, and pocketed the gold.

A few minutes later he was outside turning the corner and ducking down an alley with the wrapped food in one hand, and the gold in the other. Tagan stepped out from the shadows and raised his eyebrows, and Dimon grinned and nodded yes.

"Four gold pieces. And I brought food." He handed over the parcel.

"Nicely done." Tagan slapped him on the shoulder. "And you get extra points for the food, my friend. Now let's get the hell out of here before they catch on." He took the bag of food, and they ran down the road.

"Did your mother teach you that ruse?" Dimon asked, once they were safely away from Stockton Line.

"Not my mother, no," Tagan said, greedily pulling the food from the bag.

"That was brilliant. Four gold pieces for that old replica? It's a hundred times its value. We can get all the way into the north on this."

"It's exactly the kind of thing my mother would do," Tagan grinned, "but this time it was her muse, the one called Camilla."

Dimon tipped his head. "Camilla? Wait. I remember your mother making up an elaborate story about an old man and Camilla."

"Horace. She called the old man Horace," Tagan said. "Horace and Camilla were mother's muses."

"Yes, that's right. Horace taught her the long con. She told me that. It was all his idea." Dimon winked. "But Tagan, I thought Camilla was the *quiet mouse*. Your mother said she never spoke."

"Not the *quiet mouse*. Mother called her *the silent one*. But Dimon, the thing is," Tagan grinned, "she *does* speak to me. And Camilla's a smart one."

Dimon rolled his eyes, and then whacked his friend on the shoulder. "Your grandfather isn't here to lecture you about walking the straight line of a proper Tallach lord, Tagan. Just me, your many-times co-conspirator and friend. There's no need to make up stories."

7. Yellow Silk

"I'm going," Abigail insisted. "Will you help me or not?"

Arran furrowed his brow and sat. "Young miss, your father will pursue. He'll not allow you to travel again to the Western Shores."

"I said, I'm *going*, Arran. He'll pursue only if you won't help."

"I'm a servant of your father."

"You're my tutor. There's no loyalty in that?"

"Your father pays my wages. And if he were to find out …"

"You're Gatto. I thought that came with a sense of honor. Isn't there supposed to be a bond between teacher and student? Isn't that part of your creed?"

Arran sighed. "And you feel that it would be honorable to trick your father and help you secretly to visit Deadrise Bay for the young lord's funeral."

Abigail turned her back on him. "Yes."

The Gatto tutor rose and strode in a wide arc until he faced her, and Abigail spun away again. "I have terms," he said to her back.

"Terms?" She turned back. "That means *yes*."

"There are some things …"

"I agree to your terms. I'll answer six questions a day instead of three, if you want. Anything. Now, let's go."

"The pilgrimage provides a way to clear one's mind," Arran drew his palms out and bowed his head to illustrate the meditative point. He lifted his head and looked into the drilling gray eyes of the Turning master. "Miss Abigail is not Gatto, but the pilgrimage doesn't discriminate. It will be a journey to lose her melancholy."

"Just you and my daughter?" Allton's eyes narrowed. "No soldiers. No guard."

"The pilgrimage is a solitary affair. The young miss will have only herself for company, as I'll be a silent companion. She'll commune with nature, climb the mountain, and return with a new outlook and new respect."

"Hester?" The graying man turned and scowled at his wife.

The woman stepped away from the wall, and ventured closer. "If it will help clear her mind of this, Allton, it would certainly ease mine. And yours, I think."

"Why not send soldiers?" Allton snapped. "She's my daughter. I'm to send her out alone with a young man? When I took you on five years ago, Arran, Abigail was what, fourteen, and you twenty? A young girl and a tutor taking his first student. It was on account of your mother's reputation that I agreed to hire you. But the years seem less separated now. A girl of nineteen and a young man of twenty-five, alone on the road?"

Arran's stony face remained fixed. "Gatto first. Trainer second. Protector of my ward third. Four layers down, a man of twenty-five. Miss Abigail is my pupil and my charge."

"Allton," Hester hissed, "you can't be suggesting …"

"Go, then," Allton barked, waving a hand. "Three weeks, no more. Abigail will stand before me in this room three weeks from today. Understood?"

"Master." Arran bowed and left the room.

Abigail trudged down a hard-baked dirt path heading north, not speaking. The purpose of this journey was to say her final words to a dead boy. She was in no mood to talk.

Even so, she had felt almost a sense of excitement when Arran stepped in with a boy's outfit and told her to put it on and meet him outside. Everything she and her maids had brought back from Deadrise Bay had been taken away, including the Tallach outfits. Even the white hat had been confiscated. And after seeing the Western Shores, the standard gray dress of the Turning seemed like a symbol of subjugation. It had never occurred to her to dress as a boy, but to put on anything besides the drab gray of a Turning woman was in itself a little protest.

But her excitement changed to confusion when she stepped outside to find Arran dressed in his brown Gatto gi, blades at his waist, carrying nothing. He wasn't ready! Where were the supplies? Food, clothes for the road? When he stepped into the road and told her to come, confusion turned to alarm. There was no pack waiting for her, either. No parcels of any kind. There were also no horses or wagons.

"We leave empty handed?" she asked.

"The pilgrimage wants nothing," Arran said.

"And we're going to walk?"

"The pilgrimage wants no horse or wagon."

"But what about meals? Shouldn't we bring food? I don't even have any money."

"The pilgrimage wants no food or money," Arran said.

"But why don't we at least …" Abigail stopped talking. Arran had been her tutor for long enough that she knew how this would go. She could ask a hundred different ways and not get an answer. She drew in a breath, let it out, and looked around. It was a fine day. The sun was up, the air was cool, and the path was dry and clear. What was there to complain about? Leaving was better than staying, even if they weren't prepared.

But her momentary sense of peace with the world evaporated as her mind turned to the purpose of the journey. Tagan had been murdered by gray-gis. Her own father had arranged it. She'd had a brief moment of love and friendship, and now she was alone again, sneaking away to attend the funeral. What then? What could there be afterward but painful remembrance and emptiness?

"One foot before the other," Arran chided.

"What?" Abigail realized she had stopped in the middle of the road. "But I was thinking ..."

"Let us engage in ten leagues of silence as a start to our pilgrimage," Arran interrupted. "Yet to walk is necessary. Come."

Abigail turned and frowned at him, and then picked up on a slight upturn of his mouth. She was about to say something when she realized she was being obtuse. Arran wasn't ignoring her concerns. He had a plan, and he wanted her to shut up until they had gotten away from the compound. She nodded and fell silent, eyes down, and matched his pace.

They walked on silently, hour after hour. Whenever there was a sign of someone on the road, Arran led her into the woods and they hid. He took her on narrow roads that she had never seen before. For hours at a time they encountered no one at all. At midday they stopped next to a stream of clear water, and drank. Arran then took her on a walk through a meadow, and pointed out edible plants. They collected dandelion leaves, lamb's quarters, and purslane.

Back on the road they walked on, silently eating. Abigail felt very hungry, and although it seemed a paltry meal even by Turning standards, the greens tasted good. She said nothing, and trundled along with her tutor.

Several more hours of walking brought them to a range of high, stone-topped foothills. Abigail looked up, wondering what was beyond them. The border was not far. They might even be in the borderlands already. Would they cross? Would she see the northern passes?

Arran nodded, motioning for her to move on. They trudged up a narrow trail, a long, hard climb, and after another hour they reached the tree line and stepped out into blazing sun. They were sweat-soaked and tired. And this, she realized, was just a minor foothill. Much higher hills ahead dwarfed their accomplishment in cresting this one. What had seemed close, now seemed impossibly far.

The trail began to descend again, and halfway down, Arran turned to her. "It's not much farther," he said.

"Aren't we supposed to be silent for ten leagues?" Abigail snapped grouchily, mopping an arm across her brow. "We've got at least three to go."

Arran laughed. "We can continue in silence if you wish, but my sister will wonder at it." He put his fingers to his teeth and called out a sharp whistle. "Your father's men stopped at the peak and turned back. They'll tell Allton that they followed us all the way to the next peak you see there."

He pointed at one of the larger foothills, still quite far away. "That's where I told them we were going. But I believe they'd prefer to make camp in the valley and wait for us to return, rather than follow a Gatto and a girl up and down these hills in the baking sun. Come. We're almost to the meeting point."

Around the next bend Arran halted, and Abigail stopped dead next to him.

"Who goes there?" called a young voice, artificially toned down in an effort to sound menacing. "Who dares venture into the borderlands? Throw down your arms and surrender!" The voice demanded.

Arran grinned, and flopped his arms to his side.

"No, not your arms. Your *arms*, dummy. That's such an old joke." A girl with skin the same rich, dark color as Arran's stepped out from behind a tree. She had long, black hair braided and pinned to her head with a steel rod, and a rigid stance. She held her hands in fists, as if ready for a fight. But her face was young. Abigail guessed she might be thirteen. She wore a brown gi like Arran's, but without blades at her waist.

"Isotta, I'm not giving you the hunter blade," Arran said.

"Why do you get to keep it? The northern lord gave it to mother," the girl whined. "I'm the daughter. Why don't I get it?"

"This is Abigail." Arran ignored her complaint.

Abigail stepped up, and the girl turned her eyes to her. "I'm Isotta," she bowed. "Arran's sister."

Abigail returned the bow. "Abigail. But call me Abbie. I didn't know Arran had a sister."

"He didn't tell you? That figures. You both smell. Arran, stay and watch the path. We're going first. Although I suppose you think *boys* should go first." She rolled her eyes.

Arran's simple nod sent them on, and Isotta grabbed Abigail's wrist and hauled her down the path.

"Come on, Abbie. There's a swimming hole. You can wash. I'll jump in, too."

"But I don't have a costume." Abigail had been taught to swim, although the lessons were more like a military exercise than recreation. Soldiers guarded the trail all the way around the pond at the compound, while covered from wrist to ankle in gray, she got in the water and took her instructions from Arran as he stood on dry ground.

"A costume for what?" the girl said.

"You don't wear a costume?" Abigail immediately felt foolish as the girl stripped out of her clothes and waded in.

"Come on. Arran will call out if anyone comes." She jumped in and hooted enthusiastically at the bracing temperature. "Come on!"

Abigail returned to the trail refreshed and a bit less gloomy. "Your turn," she told Arran.

He nodded and vanished down the trail.

"You do that all the time? Swim with nothing on?"

Isotta laughed. "You Turning. What century are you in? Do you wear special clothes to the outhouse, too?"

Arran finished quickly, and emerged tightening his knife belt. "Come," he said, smiling. "Isotta, the camp is arranged?"

"No, we're going to starve and sleep on the ground," the girl said. She took the lead, and pulled Abigail along. "So you're the Turning chieftain's daughter. What's it like?"

"What's it like? What do you mean?"

"Your father is the *Turning chieftain*," she repeated, with emphasis. "That's like if I were Lord Torin's daughter—which I'm not, by the way. My mother is from the southlands, and my father is one of The Hidden."

"The Hidden …"

"You first. Tell me about what it's like to be the daughter of the Turning chieftain, and I'll tell you about The Hidden. Deal?"

"For starters, we don't swim with nothing on." Abigail offered a thin smile. "I think my father would drop dead if he found out."

"Don't tell him," the girl shrugged. "But I mean, do you have slaves and fancy things? What do you eat?"

"I have servants, not slaves. And there's nothing fancy about the Turning. It's the opposite. The Gatto are fancier."

"No, that's impossible," the girl objected.

Abigail's jaw dropped when she stepped through the trees and discovered what Arran meant by a camp. A canvas pavilion had been set up in a clearing, under which fabric was hung to form two rooms, each with a thatched bed. Outside, a smaller canopy was strung from the trees to cover a low wooden table for dining, and nearby was a stone fire ring with an iron tripod over it. The fire was almost out, but something that smelled good was steaming in an iron pot.

"They'll come back with the horses in the morning," the girl said. "Abbie, are you hungry? I'm starved. I've been waiting for you for hours."

Arran woke them just after dawn by rapping on the center pole with the butt of his short sword. "What did you say you would accomplish yesterday, young miss?"

"I said I'd meet you here and nobody would follow me," came Isotta's voice from behind the curtain.

"Other young miss," Arran said.

"I said I wouldn't cry," said Abigail, sullenly. "And I didn't, and today

I mean to not cry. So you can skip the other two questions."

"Does he do that to you every day?" Isotta asked. "My mother does that to me. *What did you say you would accomplish yesterday*," she said, mimicking an older woman's voice. "*And what did you accomplish? And what will you accomplish today?*"

"Get up," Arran said. "Food. We leave when the horses arrive."

Isotta prepared biscuits with gravy, fried strips of pork, and coffee. Just as they were finishing, someone called from the trail. Arran rose and responded. Two young men rode up on horseback, each towing another horse along with him. They dismounted, bowed to Abigail, and locked wrists with Arran. He stepped to the side for a quiet conference, then walked over to Abigail.

"We ride from here, Miss Abbie. But first you need clothes." He handed her a parcel and nodded at the pavilion.

Abigail emerged in a brown Gatto gi. "Do I get that blade, then?" She turned and winked at Isotta, who scowled.

The two young men left on one horse, leaving the other three for Arran, Abigail, and Isotta.

"Mount up," Arran smiled. "We've a long road."

Abigail discovered that they were well provisioned. They wouldn't be gathering weeds for their meals. The horses carried packs filled with food, clothes, and even some gold.

"How did you come by the gold?" she asked Arran, when they stopped for a meal. "My father certainly didn't offer it."

He shrugged. "We require funds for lodging and food. And you can't attend the young master's funeral dressed in a Gatto gi."

The mood soured. "I'll repay you," Abigail said. "And I'm sorry to make you do this. It's unkind of me."

"I wasn't lying to your father, Miss Abbie. Perhaps I neglected to illuminate the details of the pilgrimage," he offered a thin smile, "but this journey is a pilgrimage. Not as your father envisions, but may it bring you peace."

Deadrise Bay was all black. The colorful tents and canopies were gone. The purple damask of the pergola had been taken down, replaced with black satin, and the windows of the inn were draped in black ribbon. There were sailors down by the water, but none were laughing or singing.

Arran accompanied Abigail to the edge of the terraces, squeezed her arm, and motioned for her to go ahead. "Send a runner to the encampment when you're ready. Stay as long as you want, be it a few hours or a few days."

Abigail tugged her black hat lower on her brow, fixed the veil, and smoothed a hand down the front of her simple, black silk dress. She reflected that the funeral garb of the Tallachs was fancier than a Turning holiday dress. But her outfit was in keeping with what the other women wore. She silently thanked Arran for knowing about such things, and for finding a merchant who could fit her.

Her heart pounded as she approached the groups gathering on the terraces. Would the sentries allow her in? Would she be pushed back and refused? Who was she, after all? She wasn't Tallach. But the pair of sentries flanking the path parted and let her pass. It must be the dress, she thought. They assumed she was someone important.

She didn't know the customs around a Tallach death service, but realized that she didn't care. If she made a mistake, what did it matter? It might as well be her own funeral. She strode steadily up to the terrace just below the pergola, where she had dined the evening she had first met Tagan. It was already packed with people, shoulder-to-shoulder. Every terrace was filled. But she pushed her way in and stood against the rail. This was the same place she had stood the night her hat had been taken by the wind. She felt a tear coming, and fought it back.

Up on the high terrace, people were moving beneath the pergola, and more were lined up outside. Odd, she mused, looking up at the sea of black; she thought she'd seen a flash of yellow. The sun glinting off a surface, maybe? Then she saw it again, a stripe of yellow moving behind the black drapery. She tipped her head in surprise as a little girl stepped out from under the pergola dressed in a fine black dress—with a sash of brilliant yellow silk.

The girl stared at her. Abigail turned to see if she might be looking at someone behind her. She swept off her hat and veil to show her face. Maybe the little girl thought she was someone else. But instead the girl's eyes widened, and she nodded and hurried to the stairs. A pair of sentries immediately moved to let her pass, and the girl walked down.

"Come with me," she said, and took Abigail's hand.

She led her up, and the sentries once again parted and allowed them to pass. The little girl led her right under the pergola. Abigail felt her heart race as she looked over the rows of aristocrats elegantly dressed in black—and caught the eyes of Talla Undine. The Talla nodded silently and closed her eyes, a mournful hello. At the little girl's wave, a servant hurried over with a chair for the newcomer. Abigail sat next to her, at the rear of the group.

Oddly, the girl was winded just from climbing the stairs. She struggled to breathe, in and out. "You're Abbie," the little girl whispered in her ear.

Abigail nodded.

"He's right. You're pretty. Can I see the flower?"

Abigail peered down at the girl. "What?" she whispered distractedly.

"On your forehead. You've got a flower. Tagan told me, but I only caught a glimpse. Can I see it?"

"This isn't the time ..." She looked around again. Would this girl embarrass her at Tagan's service?

"Oh, right." She winked. "After, then." The girl made a locked-lip sign, grinned, and fell silent as a powerful-looking, gray-haired man stood and stepped up onto a platform to speak.

Servants pinned back the black drapes, and everyone on the terraces hushed. Saor Tieg, the elder of Deadrise Bay, paused for a moment, looking around at the crowd. Then he started.

"Nineteen short years ago, my daughter bore me a grandson ..."

The man spoke for a long interval, describing his grandson's educational achievements and his success at House Kamine. His grandson had become an accomplished young man. And now he had been cut down at such a young age. Abigail felt tears form in her eyes, but couldn't help thinking that the man's elegy seemed rather stiff and cold.

Another man stepped up after, the boy's instructor. Abigail listened with rapt attention and then with tears, sometimes with heaving breath, as the dead boy was remembered. The man told stories told of Tagan's childhood and how he had grown into a fine young man. Several times Abigail turned to glare at the fidgety little girl. Couldn't she sit still?

At a pause, Abigail leaned down, rubbing her reddened eyes. "The sash. Yellow?" she whispered vindictively. This girl's lack of respect was an irritation.

"He likes yellow," she whispered back, a bit too loudly. Heads turned to shush her.

"*Liked*, you mean," Abigail added, gloomily.

"Sure, all right," the girl winked again.

Talla Undine was next. Her speech, a mother's retelling of her son's short life, brought Abigail to open, flowing tears. Abigail hadn't heard most of the stories, having only known Tagan for a brief time. His mother spoke at length about what an upstanding, well-intentioned young man her son had been; a lost gem, his life taken prematurely.

As Abigail wept, the little girl wrapped an arm around her shoulder and leaned in. "You're fantastic. Can you teach me?"

"Teach you?" Abigail hissed, pushing the girl away. She wanted this girl to be quiet.

"The crying," the girl whispered. "I completely believe it. And I know, Tagan would punch me if he caught me talking about it. But honestly, you've got it down." Then she halted, and stared at Abigail's look of distress and horror.

"You … what?" Abigail spluttered.

"Wait." The girl put a hand on Abigail's arm. "Oh, no. You don't know?" Rebecca hissed. She noticed a woman giving her a dirty look, and dropped her voice to a soft whisper. "Break into sobs and run up to the Inn. As if you can't take it anymore. I'll follow to console you."

Abigail felt her head start to swim, and realized she had stopped breathing. This little girl wasn't taking the ceremony seriously.

"Do it," the girl insisted, drawing another dirty look. She stopped, thinking, and added, "I have a message for you, from Tagan."

That worked. Abigail stared at her, then wept out loud, which didn't require any artifice. She rose and ran up the stairs. The servants parted, and she dashed across the grass to the entrance of the inn. Attendants in black swept the doors open, and she darted inside.

The little girl stumbled in after her, panting, and grabbed her hand. "Come with me." She wheezed, and led her through the main dining room into a smaller room, richly decorated in black and crystal, opulent places set around the table, ready for the post-funeral meal.

"What is it?" Abigail demanded. "What message? Who are you?" She wiped tears from her eyes.

The girl was bent over, struggling to draw in rasping breaths. She dropped to her knees and lowered her head, and Abigail thought she might collapse.

"Child, are you ill?" Abigail said, shocked from her own reverie.

The girl waved her off, still head-down. "A moment," she said in a choking gasp. Her breathing slowly returned, and the girl raised her head. She drew in air through her nose and blew out long breaths, and finally stood. "I'm Rebecca," she said, still breathing hard. "Tagan's girl. Not his daughter," she insisted, at Abigail's raised eyebrows. "I'm his ward, or sort of a sister." She had to stop and lower her head again and work at her breathing. "Tagan found me, is what I mean to say. Took me from the water. We're joined." She took in another long breath and seemed to settle down. "Tagan's not dead, Abbie. The gray-gis didn't kill him."

Abigail stared wordlessly.

Then the door opened, and a woman in black stepped in and closed the door behind her.

"Talla?" Abigail said weakly, overwrought. Her head spun.

"Tether, get her some water," Undine barked at the little girl. "Quickly. And sit down, Abbie, child." She sighed. "We assumed you knew." The woman stepped over and pulled a chair up close, and took Abigail's hands in her own. "He didn't get word to you?" She clenched her teeth and pressed her eyes shut. "I'll box that boy's ears."

"Tagan, he's ..."

"He faked his death," Rebecca said with a shrug. "There's a cavern below the cliffs with an underwater entrance. He went off the cliff on purpose."

Abigail looked faint, and Undine put her hands on her shoulders to steady her. "Quiet please, tether. A lighter touch is wanted."

"He told me you'd figure it out," Rebecca insisted, ignoring the Talla. "You think he meant like this? 'Cause it seems kind of mean." With a shaking hand, Rebecca set a glass of water on the table.

"Please, tether! Abigail, child, my son was able to slip away from the gray-gis."

As the story came out, Abigail alternately cried and laughed. She put a hand on the girl's shoulder. "I'm so sorry, Rebecca. I thought you were a horrible little creature, talking during the ceremony!" She dabbed at her eyes.

"I am a horrible little creature. You wait. Watch my teeth come out next time I see Tagan."

"No, no, it's all right," Abigail laughed, still wiping her eyes.

"If the young tether doesn't bite him, I will," Talla Undine growled. "*And* box his ears."

Abigail tipped her head. Why did the Talla keep calling the little girl *tether*?

Half a glass of water and a full glass of wine settled Abigail's nerves. "Don't be angry with him, Rebecca. Yes, it's horribly cruel. But now that I know, well, in truth it was a good play. One cruel play to another. You see, my father ..." she halted, and breathed, then closed her eyes. "Talla, my father ordered the killing."

"Allton?" Undine rose to her feet in anger. "It was Allton? The Turning chieftain ordered a hit on my son?"

Abigail buried her face in her hands. "I'm sorry, Talla. This is my fault. If I hadn't come here, and ... and ..."

Undine slowly sat down again, hands clenched into fists, working to hold in her rage. She nodded her head. "And my son is no fool." She spread her hand out and drummed a finger on the table. "He knew your father was behind this, didn't he? And he knew if there were so much as a hint of a charade, those gray-gis would return to finish the job."

"So he let Abbie think he was dead?" Rebecca said, and screwed her face into a scowl. "I still think it's mean. I bet he feels guilty about it. But I can' tell. He's too far away."

Undine patted the girl's shoulder. "Abigail is right, tether. Allton had to believe that the sanction had been carried out. And Tagan had to make sure there was no slip. Perhaps I'll restrain myself from boxing his ears."

"I suppose it says something about me, that I'm not shocked by it," Abigail added. "That he didn't tell me, I mean. But I grew up in the Turning. Everything is danger. Everyone is a threat. My tutor has shown me other ways of understanding the world around me, but that's what I was told by my father. Trust no one but him. Confide everything in him and him alone, so he can protect me. The truth is, I understand why Tagan didn't tell me. It was the wise thing to do." Abigail stopped, and then looked at Undine. "But where is he, then?" she asked. She looked around as if he might be hiding behind the drapes.

Undine shook her head. "Gone. I don't know where. He didn't tell me his plan, either, Abbie. He takes after me far too much. But I'm sure he has a plan."

Abigail nodded mutely, still working through it in her mind. "A plan," she repeated, considering.

"And I'll tell you something else," Undine said. "I watched him with you. Don't think for a minute that he's forgotten about you. Whatever the plan is, be assured, you're part of it."

"You think so?"

"Oh, I can tell you that for a fact," Rebecca interrupted. "He was so worried about you I almost peed my pants. He was terrified."

The Talla scowled and waved the girl off. "We must trust him to work his plan, Abigail, and prepare for the moment when any or all of us might be drawn into it."

"Prepare?" Rebecca asked, drawing another glare.

"Peace, tether. Let me speak to the Turning girl." She turned back to Abigail "It's for us to hold up our end. Play our roles. Mourn his death and return to our lives, as would anyone else suffering a loss. Maintain the routine he'll expect. You'll keep visiting the caves, tether, just as if you were tagging along with my son. I'll keep spending evenings in my chambers with a glass of wine. And Abigail," she turned, "you'll go back to your father, end your mourning, and return to your life in the Turning. And we'll wait and pay attention."

Abigail nodded.

"I have to return to the ceremony. Abigail, sit with the tether. Remain for the meal if you wish, or have her bring you to your tutor, if you'd prefer to be on your way sooner." Undine rose, squeezed Abigail's shoulder in solidarity, and left.

"Tether. What does that mean, Rebecca? Why does the Talla call you *tether*?"

"Because Tagan and I are twined. Since the water."

"I don't understand. The water?"

"When the Gentry turned on me. Last year, in the killspring." …

Warm weather came too early, and stayed. Snow turned to pounding rain, and stripped away the topsoil. In the mountains, rockslides and wash-outs made travel impossible. And in the far reaches, where the Gentry clan still held power, early crops died in the mud. Everyone was hungry, slave and master alike.

The clan leader called for a culling. "One each day. We'll make an offering," he ordered, "until the rain stops and sun shines on the Gentry once more." He cast it as a religious sacrifice, although among his inner guard he was more blunt. "Get rid of those we don't need. Cut down the herd before we all starve."

"The old, then? One each day?" a man asked.

"Not just the old. If the people see us killing off the elders, it could give them cause to reflect. Mix it up. The old, the young, the sick … Set up a lottery. But choose which names are drawn. Rid yourselves of those who task you."

His inner guard nodded in solidarity and set about fixing a lottery. In the first week, seven troublesome Gentry men and women were cast into the water with weights around their ankles. The guards enjoyed watching each of them sink beneath the surface.

Choosing the little girl was a matter of bad luck on her part. Young Rebecca was almost at an age to join the clan leader's harem. Another year or two and his eyes would find her. Already his consorts were beginning to train the girl: how to walk, how to act, what to say, and what not to say. They hid her behind a curtain and ordered her to be silent and watch, and little Rebecca witnessed how pleasuring was done. The women grilled her on it. She had to know these things, so that when it was her time to start, she would please the master. The alternative—well, there was no alterna-tive. The Gentry master didn't retain consorts that he didn't like.

"Practice it," the women ordered. "Walk, talk, act."

But it seemed they weren't clear on the boundaries for practice. When a guard ordered her to fill his cup at the evening meal and the little girl strutted over, nose up and narrow hips moving side to side, he punched her in the stomach, taking her to be mocking his demand. That night she was chosen for the morning cull. She woke to rough hands yanking her from her bed. Her wrists were bound behind her back, her ankles were bound together, and she was silenced with a rough cloth gag.

The cull ceremony proceeded as all the others had: a gathering, the cull strung to a pole and carried like a dressed deer. The clan leader then recited a prayer to the water gods, something he'd written based on a chant he had heard in a Gatto compound. A stone was chosen from the wall surrounding the camp, a symbol of the cull victim's connections. It was affixed to the girl's ankles, and a volunteer was chosen to walk alongside and lug the stone.

The entire camp walked to the lake and crowded together at the overhang, ten feet above the water. This was the sacred culling place, the leader announced. "We give to the water, and we pray for water to return to water, so that the ground may be dry. May the ropes that bind the cull bring her swiftly to join with those who went before her. Stone-bearer, step aside."

The boy carrying the stone handed it to one of the men holding the ends of the pole. Lowering the girl on the pole, the men started to swing, and at a count of three, hurled her over the edge. There was a splash, and people crowded in close to look over the side at the trail of bubbles where the girl had gone down.

No one saw the young man in whites at his morning wash, kneeling on a ledge beneath the overhang and splashing water on his face and arms. When he heard the voices, Tagan froze. He realized several things at once. First, yes indeed he was terribly off course, completely lost. This was not the Gatto post he had been sent to. Second, the captain who had reluctantly agreed to let him play the part of a runner wouldn't make that mistake again, would he? And third, this would be a terrible blow to his efforts to convince his grandfather that he was a responsible young man. Saor Tieg once again would level his lowered eyebrows and nod at the door, sending him away in failure.

Then as he listened to the prayers of the chieftain, he realized what was happening. He had stumbled into a Gentry compound, and they were about to drown someone. Who was it? Had they captured a traveler on the road, or taken someone from a rival camp?

He looked around. He had his blades, but they were up on a higher, dry ledge with his clothes. He turned and saw the figure drop into the water with as splash, and disappear beneath the surface. No time! Tagan slipped silently into the water, drew in a deep breath, and swam down.

A feeling of raw dread filled him as he encountered human shapes— not just one, but many, upright like plants reaching for the sun. He pushed past two, then three, and came to the newest victim, struggling against the bonds. A girl? She seemed small. Was it a child? He tugged down the gag, wrapped a hand behind her neck, and pressed his mouth to hers to push his air into her lungs.

Dark, wide eyes stared at him in panic, and he felt his own heart pounding. He wrapped an arm around her and pulled, but the stone was heavy. He moved her only a little way before he knew he had to surface for air.

Two quick pats on her back, and he pushed for the surface, angling to get as close to the cloaking ledge as possible. It was a struggle to get to the surface, as if the stone were tied around his own ankles. But he had to get more air! He drew in a deep breath, which oddly was also a struggle. He dove, and swam down to give the girl another breath.

Once more he tried to pull her up, but the stone was too heavy, and he made little headway. He fought his way up to the surface. Were the Gentry still there? Sounds from above told him that clan members were moving off. One more breath to be certain. Down to the girl. Then he surfaced again, leaped up to the higher ledge, and pulled a blade from its sheath. He dove, gave the girl her breath, and pulled himself down to slash the rope at her ankles.

As he cut through it, he felt that his own air was expended, but the panic abated. A strange emptiness spread through him. Why was he going to such pains? Did this matter? It would be so much easier to give up. Drift off. The water was fine and comfortable.

But no! He wrapped his arms around the small, limp body and pulled the girl up in spite of the feeling of malaise.

He dragged her onto the stone shelf. "Breathe," he hissed, blowing air into her lungs. She had dark hair, as black as the eyes she had pinned him with at the bottom. "Breathe!" he repeated.

It was a struggle. He felt as if he were dying, himself. But he blew in another breath. He cut her wrists free and pulled her arms to her sides to lie her flat. Straddling her, he pressed his palms to her chest and thrust them down between breaths as he'd been taught.

The little girl spluttered and coughed, and he turned her onto her side to vomit the lake water. Tagan vomited as well, unable to suppress the compulsion. He felt the water choking him, although he hadn't taken any into his lungs or stomach. Yet he choked and gagged as if this little girl had saved him from drowning, and not the other way around. She vomited again, and Tagan fought the urge to copy.

"Be calm. You can breathe," he panted, out of breath.

He looked around warily. If the Gentry were to come down for their own morning wash, they would both end up down there with the others. As the girl lay listlessly, breathing but not moving, he hurriedly pulled on his clothes over his wet whites, strapped on his knife belt, and scooped her up.

"We have to go." He said. He looked around again, and started working his way around the side of the lake, looking for a place to hide. Small arms wrapped around his neck. She said nothing, but the girl pulled herself tight to him, shuddering. Oddly, the sense that swept through him wasn't what he would have expected, the feel-good rush of adrenaline at another's expression of gratitude. Instead what he felt was a release of the terror he'd felt under the water, and a loosening of the tension in his chest. ...

"Tagan breathed for me," Rebecca said to Abigail. "He gave me his breath. Talla Undine calls me tether because I'm tethered to him."

Abigail had listened to the story with rapt attention, almost forgetting about the events that were unfolding in the present. "Tethered," she repeated.

Rebecca nodded. "The sensei at House Kamine calls it *twined*. I can feel what Tagan feels, and sometimes it's the same for him. At least when we're together. Tagan is free of me when he leaves. But when he's gone, I can't breathe."

"It joined you." Abigail looked confused. "His breath in your lungs?"

"The sensei says it will pass in its own time. But it's a year now, and I'm still tethered—not to the bottom of the lake, but to Tagan instead. He still has to breathe for me. Does that make sense?" The girl smiled sadly, looking unsure and guilty.

Abigail nodded slowly. "I don't know, Rebecca. I've not felt such a thing myself. But I'm aware of connections between people. Tagan told me about his mother. Do you know about Talla Undine? About the voices in her head?"

"Her muse. From before Tagan was born. Maybe it's like that." Rebecca stopped talking, breathing hard again.

"The Talla was connected with her muse, and Tagan is connected with you, it seems. Maybe the Talla passed on to him something from herself," Abigail mused. "She's his mother, after all. And maybe there's something in you."

"I have to cut the tether," Rebecca said. "Tagan cut it for me under the water, but it still binds me. I have to cut it. But I don't know how."

"And I have to return home," Abigail said. "I don't want to, but I must."

8. Hunting Grace

Horace had always had a tendency to go on about things, given the opportunity. If Camilla were in danger, he would bark a command. But his preference was to offer a historical explanation of similar improper behavior or bad choices, establishing the context of her foolery within the grand sweep of time. Sometimes his lectures took rambling side trips down literary rabbit holes, as he explained the origins of the little pieces, and the origins of the things the pieces came from.

His talks seemed especially long and convoluted on days when he had to pick her up late from detention. Horace would lecture her on how to blend in and stay out of trouble.

"*Stalky and Company*, for example," he once told her. "Have you read it? It's Kipling. He didn't only write *The Jungle Book*, you know. *Stalky*'s a much better story, if you ask me. A boy about your age gets into all kinds of tricky situations, but he figures out how to get himself out of them. Very clever. I'd have liked to meet Mr. Kipling. I'll get you a copy."

"Fine. So I shouldn't have punched him." Camilla rolled her eyes. "Did Mr. Kipling say that, too?"

"Neither he nor I. Don't miss the point, Camilla. It has nothing to with the ethics of getting into scraps with schoolboys. I suspect Danny will come out of the fracas just fine, and frankly, that's his problem. Let him figure it out. The point is that if you're going to get into mischief, you need to learn to get out of it. Understand?"

"It's detention. I can't skip. I'd end up with two detentions," Camilla growled.

"And you couldn't foresee that outcome? Think, child. Did you even look around first? Did you check your environment?"

"Danny said I look like a skinny boy, so I punched him."

"With the teacher in the room. You were thinking, *This is a good idea.* You couldn't project a moment forward and consider the inevitable outcome? *Detention, here I come.* It's not subtle, Camilla."

"So you think you know what's gonna happen all the time," Camilla snapped. "Even you couldn't have known I'd get detention. I mighta got suspended, or nothing at all might have happened. How could you possibly have known I'd get detention?"

"Oh well, honey, *I Tiresias have foresuffered all,*" Horace told her. "Of course I could see it. That's Eliot, by the way," he explained. "From *The Wasteland*. Tiresias is a reference to Ovid. But *foresuffered*, now that's interesting. Do you know the term hapax legomenon? It means a word that occurs only once in a body of work."

"Great." Camilla rolled her eyes. "Is this somehow about detention?"

"Eliot is saying that like the blind prophet Tiresias, he sees everything. In the context of ... well, never mind. We can discuss that part when you're older. But that word, *foresuffered*. It's the only time Eliot uses it."

"Is this the only time you're gonna tell me this? 'Cause that would be perfect," Camilla grumbled. "This lecture could be a hapax legomenon."

Horace laughed. "Point taken. And extra points for using the term in a sentence and employing literary license at the same time. Nicely done."

She hated to admit it, but a lot of Horace's silly lectures stuck. Pieces of them, anyway. Sometimes the relevant point was lost in the details. The next time Danny Harris teased her in class, she'd punch him again, harder, and she probably wouldn't look around first to see who was watching. But as she contemplated what Grace had said to her, Camilla's mind came around to *hapax legomenon*, and the figurative idea of something occurring only once.

Grace had said she was going camping. But Grace didn't do hikes, or walks in the woods—or camping.

As a young child, Camilla had rarely experienced the wild outdoors. Her father was dead, her mother was gone, and her foster families didn't take the foster kid on camping trips. When at age twelve she re-entered Horace's life, the old man took her on road trips, but her grandfather's idea of roughing it was to stay in a fine French hotel. He didn't do tents and campfires, either.

It wasn't until they moved to Boston that Camilla properly discovered the woods. But it wasn't through Grace. Her new friend Nicola had two older brothers who liked to get together with their friends and drive up to Maine on summer weekends. The deal with their parents was that if they wanted to take the car and go camping, they had to take their little sister with them. It was cloaked in terms of inclusiveness and sibling bonding, but Nicola and her brothers understood the subtext: Their parents wanted the house to themselves.

Nicola insisted on bringing Camilla, and the boys didn't complain. It meant they didn't have to babysit. They could drink beer and have a good time, and Nicola and her friend could amuse themselves. Further, the boys wouldn't admit it, given the age difference, but they were intrigued by the dark-haired, dark-souled girl. Nicola's friend was a kick in the pants. One time one of their friends made the mistake of patting her on the butt as he walked past. To the boy, it was just a bit of playful teasing. He was eighteen, and she was a thirteen-year-old kid. When he was facedown on the ground with the girl pulling his wrists up until he screamed an apology, he learned not to take Nicola's little friend for granted. And the other boys, once the hysterical laughter had stopped, teased him mercilessly for the rest of the weekend. Nobody tried patting Camilla on the butt after that.

On returning home, Camilla would be greeted at the door by Grace, who would ask how the weekend had gone. Camilla would say, *fine*, and that would be the end of the conversation. But one time, as they sat in the park eating ice cream bars, the topic of summer vacations came up. The school year was almost at an end.

Camilla did her best to reassure Grace that there wasn't a need to plan an awkward, contrived trip. "We could just skip that," she said. "It's not like it's a rule that you have to have family vacations."

"You know," Grace said, "there's only one time I remember when my parents and I actually had a good vacation. We went camping up in New Hampshire. Well, sort of. It was funny, really. My dad had talked for weeks about going to the White Mountains, and sleeping in a tent. And he wanted to drive up Mount Washington."

"Drive up?" Camilla asked.

"There's an auto road. Someone at work told him about it. But he didn't plan the trip until the last minute, and couldn't find a campsite. They were all booked, except for places where you had to hike in, and no way was my father going to lug a bunch of camping equipment through the woods. So he tried to get us a room, but the only place he could get was at this cheap motel in Bartlett. Our unit was a dingy little cottage that they rented as a motel room. My parents kept complaining because the TV was old, and the kitchen was old—everything was old. But I thought it was great. I had my own room, and we went hiking, and we drove up to the peak of Mount Washington, and ate at restaurants. It was fun."

That was where the story ended. Grace stopped talking, and Camilla had learned not to ask *what-happened-next*. She knew what had happened next. Grace's parents had both been killed overseas while on a business trip. They had strayed into the wrong part of town, and had been robbed and shot.

But the camping trip story stuck with Camilla. And so, when she asked, *Where are you going?* And Grace said, *Camping*, the image that flashed into Camilla's mind was of a little girl and her parents in the White Mountains. Then as she hid beneath the bridge, wet and shivering, she reflected that Grace had used a single word to tell her exactly where she was going.

"Not bad," Camilla muttered, as she scrambled up from the roadside ditch. "Who would ever guess that you'd run to Bartlett, New Hampshire?"

It was late, and the evening traffic rush was over. Cars zoomed by, but they were spaced out, sometimes a half minute between one and the next. Camilla ducked behind a row of Jersey barriers and watched the approaching cars. No black SUVs. Nobody driving slowly. Not until she saw a single pickup truck driving much too fast did she hop over the barrier and put her thumb out. The driver clomped on the brakes and pulled over.

"Hop in," said a replacement part for the man who had picked her up earlier. He flashed the same smile and patted the seat.

Being short and eighteen made for a wide range of age simulation. Camilla's favorite was to be somewhere in her late twenties. It was an age of maturing strength, ability, and attraction. But it might not be enough of a change from her recent thirty-something. She felt confident that she'd escaped the men tracking her. The man in the pickup had driven her straight through town and through another few towns after it. But the safe bet was to shift to a completely new persona.

And so a sixteen-year-old girl in the white blouse and plaid skirt of a private school stepped up to a ticket window at the bus station. Her face tattoo was covered with makeup, and she had deliberately added too much rouge, emulating the overdone look of a girl trying to look mature.

"I need to get to Bartlett," she said, looking around and grimacing.

The woman at the window gave the girl a bored look. "Bartlett?" she said.

"New Hampshire," Camilla huffed, as if it were obvious.

The woman pushed her glasses up, took her time pulling out a schedule, and ran her finger down the page. "We don't stop in Bartlett, dear. North Conway would be the closest stop." She looked up. "How old are you? Are you traveling on your own?"

"Look, I have to go to Bartlett. My stupid father is there, okay? I have to call him and tell him the time. He said he'll meet me at the bus stop."

"The bus doesn't stop in Bartlett. He could meet you in North Conway."

Camilla let out an exasperated huff and pulled out her phone. She pretended to press a number, and put it to her ear. "There's no stupid bus to Bartlett, dad," she growled, tapping her foot and rolling her eyes at the people behind her in line. "I can get a ticket to North Conway, okay?" She scowled and looked at her feet. "Fine. I'll call back with the time." Shoving the phone back in her pocket, she looked at the ticket clerk. "He says North Conway is okay. When's the next bus?"

"You'll have to switch downtown, honey. I'll write it down for you."

The first part of the bus ride went well. The bus was packed, but she found a seat next to an old woman who smiled at her as she sat. At first Camilla was worried that the woman would be a talker, but she spent the whole ride reading a paperback and knitting. Camilla even slept for part of the trip.

There was a stop in Boston of almost two hours. Camilla pushed outside and strode down the street as if intent to get somewhere. She had no idea what was nearby, but even for a schoolgirl, a determined walk meant less likelihood of being hassled.

Two hours was plenty of time to get supplies. She stepped back into the bus station with fifteen minutes to go, lugging a new duffel bag half filled with clothes and food for the road, and a burner phone. The old woman climbed onto the same bus with her, but didn't recognize her companion from the first leg of the trip. Instead of a schoolgirl, a twenty-something young woman in skinny jeans and a silk blouse stepped past the woman, and picked out a seat next to a big, dark-complexioned man of twenty-five or so, in black chinos and a leather vest. He had full sleeves in black, green, and red tattooed on his arms: vines, leaves, and flowers from wrist to shoulder. Camilla pegged him as Mexican, but wasn't certain. His face showed signs of action, a deep scar over one eye, and a nose that had been broken at least once. But she didn't see any gang symbols. Good enough.

"Okay if I sit here?"

The young man turned and did a double take at the spiral of diamonds on the girl's cheek.

"Whoa. Nice ink," he said.

"Thanks." Camilla smiled.

"Going to the mountains?"

"God, I hope so. That's where this bus is going, right? Otherwise I'm in trouble."

"You alone?" The tattooed man said, then laughed. "Sorry." He held up a palm. "I swear to god, I'm not a sleazy guy trying to hit on you on a bus. Sit down."

Camilla sat. "How about you? Where are you headed?"

"Got a gig in North Conway."

"You're a musician?"

"Bartender. Brick oven place. They call me when someone's out. Vacation, or whatever. Doesn't pay as good as stonework, but slinging rocks is a killer this time of year."

"And bartending isn't?"

"The beer is cold, and you're not out in the sun all day. Beats the hell out of building stone walls when it's ninety out."

"You're a stone mason?"

"Enzo." The man held out a hand.

"Callie," Camilla said, accepting the handshake.

"Stone mason, bartender, and general fuckup. That's me. How about you?"

"Student, orphan, and complete and total fuckup." Camilla grinned. "Pleased to meet you, Enzo."

"You staying in North Conway?"

"Intervale, I think," Camilla lied. "I'm not sure, yet. Visiting a friend. You know the area?"

"I've been working up there off and on forever. Since I was ..." His voice trailed off.

Camilla followed his eyes. Two rows up on the opposite side, a young, bald, very white passenger was giving them the hairy eyeball. Next to him another turned, a clone of the first.

"Skinheads?" Enzo said, looking away. "You'd think you wouldn't have to deal with that up here. It's New England."

"Ignore them," Camilla said, sinking down in her seat. She patted her waist, but wasn't wearing her blades. One didn't hop on a bus openly armed for a knife fight. But in close quarters, with innocent people all around, blades wouldn't be ideal, anyway.

"I just want to get to the apartment, get a hot shower, and sleep a little."

"Amen to that."

The bus pulled out, and soon they were moving through slow traffic toward the highway, and people were settling back to watch movies, sleep, or listen to music. The men in front of them put in their earbuds and seemed to forget about the tattooed devils behind them.

"You know the area around North Conway?" Camilla feigned a tourist's interest in the region. "Know any good places to stay? Cheap places, I mean. I've got some friends who want to come up. Too expensive in town."

They sat back and talked, and Camilla watched the miles pass as she drilled her new tattooed friend for information. She invented a persona on the spot. She was on summer break from the University of Massachusetts in Amherst—a campus she could describe in enough detail to make it work—and was planning a hike in the White Mountains with some friends. "Got any suggestions for good day hikes?"

"Long or short? I mean, you want a walk in the woods, or do you mean a real hike?"

"A real hike. Less talking and more climbing." Camilla grinned.

"Gotcha. Well, I mean, there's tons of places. ..."

In the space of an hour, she had discussed a half dozen hikes that she would never do. But she wove in questions about places for her friends to stay, and came up with a good short list of motels where she might find Grace.

It was getting dark when the bus stopped in front of an old inn in North Conway, but the street and the hotel were brightly lit. Camilla worked her way to the front of the bus and stepped down, Enzo right behind her. The people exiting the bus dispersed, some heading to the inn and others crossing the street or walking down the sidewalk. Camilla hovered with a group of people who seemed to be waiting for rides, and pretended to be looking at a guidebook. She noticed that the skinheads were lingering. Were they after her? It wasn't the modus operandi of Walter Turcotte's operation, but maybe he was switching up his game. Or they might be spotters. Were they calling it in?

Enzo slung his bag over his shoulder, waved goodbye, and walked down an alley next to the inn. "See you around," he said, and Camilla smiled and waved back. Then she ducked down the alley herself, and slid behind a dark set of stairs to watch. Would the skinheads follow? At first they seemed to move off, ambling down the sidewalk. But then they abruptly backtracked and turned into the alley.

"God," Camilla cursed. She hefted her own bag onto her shoulder and silently followed, keeping her distance. She looked for places to conceal herself, should they turn, and scouted ahead for an ideal place to take them on. They'd tracked her to North Conway? How? It seemed impossible.

There were a few store entrances along the first part of the narrow alley, but Enzo passed them, and headed toward one of the buildings in back. Camilla assumed it was apartments. Then partway back, Enzo seemed to sense the movement of the men following. He turned and stopped. He slid his bag off his shoulder and set it on the ground, and raised a single palm.

"Let's not do this, okay?" he said.

"You chose to come up here," one of the men said. "This is what happens." They separated to flank him.

Camilla tipped her head, and then rolled her eyes. She'd been completely wrong. These men weren't spotters sent by Walter Turcotte to trail her. They were punk skinheads preparing to face off against a random person from the bus.

"Look," Enzo said, "You want to come by later, I'll comp you a beer at the hotel, okay? I'm just a guy looking to earn a living."

"You got your green card?" the other man said.

"Where's your little slut friend?" the first one asked. "Girl with her face spoiled? She a wetback too?"

Enzo looked skyward. "Shit. Do we really need to do this?"

"Maybe you can introduce us." One of the skinheads thrust his hips, and the other laughed.

Cracking his knuckles, Enzo closed his eyes and stared at the approaching men. "Okay, fine. Nobody wants you up here. This is not your country."

"It sure as hell is," the other man said, making fists. "It's not *your* country. And we're gonna fix that. Have some fun with you, and then maybe we'll go have some fun with your girlfriend."

"Fuck that," Camilla said, stepping out behind them. "You think I want sloppy seconds? I'm going first." The men spun around to find her in a wide stance, her bag on the ground behind her, unzipped. She patted her palm with a hard rubber truncheon.

There was a round of smug laughter as the men approached.

"Oh, Jesus," Enzo said, striding forward. "Come on, guys. This is not cool. Leave her alone!"

But he didn't get a chance to protect the girl from the bus. One of the men made a move, and Camilla shifted and slammed him in the collarbone with a fast, hard strike. From ten feet away, Enzo saw the hit and heard the crunch. The man howled. The other man rushed in, and Camilla deflected a hit with a sharp inside block, and punched the truncheon straight into his neck. He gasped for air and dropped to his knees, clutching at his throat.

Enzo halted and stared. In two moves, she'd taken them both out.

Camilla looked over. "Time to go now, right?"

"Fucking amen to *that*," he said, grinning. "Shit, Callie."

"I know, I know," Camilla said. "Too hard, right? You're gonna say I didn't have to break the asshole's collarbone, or crush this other guy's trachea. But what a couple of dicks." She pulled out her phone punched in 911. "Hey," she said, "there's a couple of skinhead assholes that need a ride to the hospital. Behind the hotel. ..." She clicked off and pocketed the phone. "Okay? They won't die. Probably."

Enzo laughed. "I didn't mean, *Shit, Callie, why'd you drop those guys like that*. More like, *Shit, Callie, can I have a date?* Jesus."

She linked an arm around his and hurried him down the alley. "You're staying close by?"

"Yeah, right down here."

"I'll take the date under advisement, but a place to crash tonight would be really nice. Just for tonight."

Early in the morning, Camilla pulled on her clothes and smiled at Enzo, half asleep in the bed. Their encounter had all the earmarks of a one-night stand, but neither had a problem with that. He was a single guy trying to make ends meet, and she was a single girl with no basis for a complaint about a guy who didn't have his shit together. She slipped out, expecting that this would be the first and last time she would see Enzo, stone mason and bartender.

Her immediate concern was money. Calista didn't exist in the wider world. Technically she was a high school graduate in Boston. There was a file that listed her parents and home address, and she had credit cards. But having cards was one thing; using them was another. Horace had made the point none too subtly: use the cards locally for routine purchases, but never charge anything if you're on the run. And while her funds were considerable—Horace had amassed quite a fortune, and all of it was hers, now—the money wasn't readily available. She wasn't in Boston, where she could fetch a duffel bag of bills from a safe deposit box, or cash in a tube of gold bullion coins.

She counted what she had, a little over five hundred dollars. Not bad for pocket money, but in a tourist town it wouldn't last long. She thumbed a ride south and rented a silver compact sedan using a fake ID, then headed north again.

As she drove, her mind wandered. It was a beautiful summer morning, which made it hard to concentrate on studying the motels. She found herself thinking about Una's son, and the image of the boy Tagan suddenly came to her.

Tagan! Odd that she had almost forgotten about him. Now here he was again. He appeared to be standing in a stone room.

Form, strength, and skill in combat are the pillars, said an old man in a hooded robe.

Was this a monk? Was Tagan in a monastery? She had time to kill, so she listened in.

A convict who chooses combat faces the Gatto triad: form, strength, and tactical skill, the old man continued.

A convict? Combat? Either his time frame was different from hers, or he'd screwed things up more than she had, since they last talked. Camilla slammed on the brakes, almost running a red light. A man in a pickup truck careening through the intersection leaned on his horn as she stopped well over the line.

Maybe this wasn't the best time to look in on Tagan, after all. She needed to watch the road. She needed to find Grace.

"But what's he doing?" she said out loud.

She resolved to keep half an eye on the road, and half on this other person. As she slowed to look at the motels and then drove on, she saw Tagan get into a fight with another boy. It didn't look like anything to worry about. In fact, it seemed vaguely similar to the fight she'd just been in, except the bad guy seemed to be the one with the truncheon. Yet the boy seemed to be holding his own.

"He can fight," she muttered.

Then she approached a section with a lot of motels, and found her attention drawn back to the present. Chances are, the place Grace had stayed in as a child was gone. That was years ago. But Grace would find a place like it. She'd given Camilla the word: *camping*, and she'd said it in a tone that Camilla knew well. It wasn't just making a casual comment; it was a signal. And she wouldn't sit back and hope Camilla would find her. She'd expect Camilla to figure it out.

The next few places didn't look right. They were too manicured. Too fancy. Camilla slowed as she approached an old, over-painted place, a long, low building with a narrow strip of grass between it and the road, the rest paved for parking. But it didn't look quite right, either. Then at the next place, she caught sight of a black SUV pulled over to the side of the road fifty yards before the motel entrance. She kept her head pointed forward, but looked to the side as she passed. Two men sat in the stopped car. She gripped the wheel tightly. Not a couple of skinheads looking for a fight. That was definitely an advance team! Slowing, she put on her turn signal and pulled into the motel drive.

A few kids were splashing in a small outdoor pool, their parents sitting under sun umbrellas and watching. A few cars were lined up along one side of the drive, but most of the spaces were empty. People didn't drive up north to sit around in a motel. Not most of them, anyway. She pulled into an empty spot and cut the engine. Before she got out, she looked across the street. There were two buildings, one large and one small. The small one was an old cottage. It fit the bill. Was Grace in there?

Then she glanced at the SUV, but she couldn't make out the details from this far away. She imagined one of them aiming a high-powered scope at the cottage. Time to start being careful. She fished in her bag for a baseball cap and pulled it on. Then she pulled out her knife belt, wrapped it in a tee shirt, and stepped out of the car. Instead of heading for the street, she went the other way, crossing the parking area and skirting the side of one of the cottages. In back was a grassy area for the guests, with charcoal grills fixed to steel posts.

Camilla broke into a jog. It would have been a sprint, but people might be watching. A jog meant she was in a hurry, but not in a panic. She stepped around the end of the last building and looked out at the road. The SUV was still there, but the men wouldn't stay for long. The advance teams weren't stupid. They would know that sooner or later a cruiser would stop and ask what they were doing, or a good Samaritan would pull over and ask if they needed help. Sure enough, the engine started, and the SUV pulled onto the road and continued past the motel. Camilla dashed for the street the moment the car was out of sight. She crossed and ran into the woods on the other side.

They would be back soon enough. Was there a second team? She gambled that there wasn't, and crept behind the cottage. She pulled her blades. Then as she turned the corner, she came face to face with a .38 handgun. Camilla froze.

"Don't move. Oh, my god. Calista?" Grace lowered the gun.

"We have to go. Come on." Camilla stuffed her blades back in the sheathes and unceremoniously grabbed Grace's wrist, but then stopped. "Wait. You have guns? Anything else?"

"Calista!" Grace threw her arms around her and gave her a crushing hug. "You got here quickly!"

"Mom, we have to go, right now. You have a bag? Get it. There's an advance team on the road."

They were across the street and driving off in the little silver car in two minutes, Grace behind the wheel and Camilla rooting through Grace's duffel bag.

The guns situation wasn't good, but it would have to do. Grace had brought a .38, plenty of rounds, and a nice little .22 takedown rifle that fit compactly into a soft case with a shoulder strap. The men pursuing them would certainly have more firepower. But even a little pea shooter like the .22 was useful in the right circumstance. A rifle at fifty yards would beat a handgun every time. And she had the .38 if things got close.

She smiled as she pulled out a money clip, fat with bills. Money problem solved. Then she pulled out the boxes of rounds and opened each one, then inspected the rifle case, fishing her fingers into every corner and feeling the seams.

"Pull over. I'll drive," Camilla said.

"Where are we going?" Grace pulled onto the shoulder and stopped, and they raced around the car to switch places.

"Down to the strip." Camilla pulled back onto the road and accelerated. "I'll drop you off. You need to get new clothes, and I need to meet someone. I'll pick you up."

"New clothes?"

"Change in the store. Dump everything you have on. And get a couple of backpacks, and water. And food. Whatever you can find. And bug spray. We might have to run."

"Calista, what's your plan?"

"They've got trackers on you. That team didn't follow you here, and they damned well didn't follow me. They just waited for you to stop."

"Okay, Calista. Maybe you're right."

They made a lucky find of a parking space near the bus stop, and Grace crossed the street and headed at a fast walk to a sports shop. Camilla stopped to deposit Grace's duffel bag, minus the guns and money, in the back of a parked pickup truck. Then she ducked down the alley.

Enzo was still half asleep, but he came to the door. "Hey. Wasn't sure I'd be seeing you again," he said.

"Listen, you know your way around this area, right?"

"Sure. Like I was telling you." He rubbed an arm across his face.

"I need a favor. Can you come with me?"

"Uh, come with you where? My shift starts at two, Callie."

"Fine. Just get dressed, okay? I need your help."

"And I definitely owe you one. But I really gotta be back for my shift. I'm screwed if I'm AWOL on the first day."

"Just come on."

It wasn't until they were all back in the rental car heading down the strip that Camilla realized her error. Grace was introducing herself to Enzo as Callie's mom, keeping up her persona, and Enzo was chitchatting about the north country, and wondering what kind of trouble Callie and her mother were in, and what the plan was, when Camilla stopped short at a red light, this time well before the white line.

"Oh, no. Mom, you threw out your clothes in the store?"

"Yes, as we agreed."

"Shit. What was I thinking? It'll tip them off."

"It'll tip who off?" Enzo asked. "You gonna tell me what's going on?"

She pulled forward at the green light, and glanced at Enzo in the back seat. "Listen, you know this area. If you had someone coming at you—not like those two last night, but armed agents—and all you had was a handgun and a .22 rifle, where would you want to be, to equalize things?"

"Gone," Enzo said. "But, wait a second ..."

"Callie," Grace interrupted, "what's the problem?"

"The trackers. We should have put the damned clothes in the duffel bag. If there's trackers in the bag and also in the clothes you dumped at the store, the signal will split. They'll see it. They'll be on us."

Grace closed her eyes and nodded. "I should have considered that. I'm not on the ball, am I?"

"Not your fault. I told you to ditch the clothes. It was stupid."

"Uh, really, what exactly is going on?" Enzo said.

Camilla glanced in the rearview, and could read his expression easily enough: *I've gotten in a car with a couple of lunatics.* "Enzo, answer the question," she demanded. "Listen, we're the good guys, okay? I thought those guys last night were after me. Turns out they weren't—they were after you—but some bad guys are definitely after me and Grace."

"Callie, just tell me what's going on. I can't get involved in some kind of *thing*. I'll get fired."

"I just need your help getting away. Now, tell me: leveling the playing field. Where would you want to be? They've got bigger guns, but they don't know the landscape. They're most likely from the city. So, you want cover, and you want a chance to get them before they get you. Someplace secluded. You don't want to worry about bystanders getting in the cross-fire. That kind of thing."

"Uh ..."

"Come on, come on! You know this area," Camilla insisted.

"On a mountain, maybe? I mean, there's water, woods, and mountains, right? That's what's up here. If you don't want lots of people around, downtown is no good. Water's no good. You'd be, pardon the expression, a sitting duck. Maybe on a mountain you'd get more chances. But Callie, what the hell is going on?"

Grace nodded. "A trail above the tree line. We get ahead and pick them off. So, which one, Enzo?"

"Um, you want a long hike?" he said, with a strained smile.

"Yeah, definitely," Camilla said. "These guys aren't athletes. They drive around in black SUVs and wait for you. I want them out of their element. Tired, hot, frustrated, pissed off."

"Guys in black SUVs? Shit, Callie."

She turned and looked at him. "They're not Feds. They're private, okay? We're in trouble. We need a plan."

Enzo breathed in. "Long hike and a trail above the tree line. Baldface."

"Okay. Where is it?"

"Turn around. And give me a minute to call in and tell them I missed my bus and won't make my shift. Damn it."

9. Three Rivers

"Crossing the border," Tagan said. "That's the next challenge."

"We can't just cross?" Dimon raised his eyebrows. "We still have plenty of money. Or we could use your safe passage pendant." He grinned.

"You can't just walk over the border, Dimon. Not unless you're Gatto or you have a Gatto porter with you. Not along this stretch. And it's too far to walk around it. And shut up about the pendant."

"The Gatto. I'd heard about that. An agreement with the northern border forts. The Gatto fighters guard the borders in this area now."

"Exactly. They've been granted a large tract of land along the border. Several border forts were decommissioned or reduced to a maintenance staff."

"So we hire a Gatto porter, then. We have the money."

"No." Tagan shook his head. "It doesn't work like that. Tallachs can't just hire a porter. You have to have an arrangement. But I have a plan." Tagan slapped him on the shoulder. "I'll be Gatto." From his pack he pulled a brown gi. "And you'll be my fare."

"You brought a Gatto gi?" Dimon asked. "That's the extra set of clothes you've been carrying around all this time?"

"I thought it might be useful."

"This doesn't seem like such a good idea, Tagan. What if they catch us? What if some real Gatto fighters come along and start asking questions?"

"Trust me. It'll work."

"I think I like the idea of faking it with that old pendant better. Maybe they won't fall for it. But if they catch you pretending to be Gatto, they'll think we're spies."

"Relax," Tagan insisted. "Remember when we were little, and you made fun of me for imitating those Gatto boys who were swindling the sailors?"

"I remember that. You got in as much trouble as they did." ...

As a young boy training at House Kamine, Tagan was eager to learn to fight the Tallach way, but he was also curious about Gatto techniques, or rather, about one technique in particular—throwing knives. He'd seen novice Gatto fighters at the docks playing knife games for money when their master wasn't looking. The young trainees would miss a few times, losing small bets, but would clean up when the stakes were high.

The sailors knew all about Talla Undine, and none would dare play gambling games with the Talla's young son. But disguised as a Gatto he could play, couldn't he? Of course, to get in on the game with any hope of winning, he would need to learn to throw.

He asked the sensei about Gatto fighting, but the man cut him off. *You walk the Tallach road,* he said. So Tagan turned to his mother. She had told him stories about training with the Gatto as a girl, and about her adversary, a girl named Caterione. This Caterione had driven her away from the Gatto, although his mother claimed to have neatly defeated her in a sparring match when they were older.

"Mother," the little boy asked at dinner one night, "tell me about the kata of the Gatto. What are they like? You've done them, haven't you?"

"The Gatto kata? Many of them, Tagan, yes, I have," Undine said. "Why?"

"I see the Gatto teachers with their students, at the docks."

"Ask them about it. You're allowed to talk to them. They might show you a kata or two." Undine shrugged indifferently and took a sip of her wine.

"Couldn't you? You could show me."

This drew a scowl. "Tagan, I promised the sensei I wouldn't interfere with your training. No one wants a Talla meddling with his training regimen."

"I won't do Gatto kata at House Kamine. I just want to see how a Gatto moves—to know a little bit about them." Then he stopped and smiled, as if a great idea had popped into his head. "Wait, I know. You could teach me Gatto knife throwing."

"Tallachs don't throw their weapons, son," his mother said. "Not unless you're surrendering. I could tell you stories about Tallachs who've tried to get clever with their blades."

"But that means you can teach me Gatto knife throwing, and it won't interfere with my training."

Undine looked at him. "I'm getting the sense that this is a trick, dear. What are you trying to pull over on me?"

"Nothing. I swear! Come on. It'll be fun."

Undine relented, and a new mother-son bonding experience was born. They spent pleasant hours laughing and throwing blades at a target, and Tagan learned to throw. He learned other things as well. Cloaked as casual chitchat about the clan whose throwing technique he was practicing, he interrogated his mother. She spun stories about the old times—she couldn't help it—and while he assumed the stories were mostly fabricated, Tagan used the tales to develop his persona, a young Gatto novice who had trained in the north. It was perfect. The Gatto boys wouldn't even be able to challenge his story. None of them were from the north.

The first time he sauntered along the wharf in a Gatto gi, he made a rookie mistake. He was halfway through a game when some sailors coming in on leave warned their fellow sailors off.

"It's a trick. And you, kid, get out of here, if you want to leave in one piece!"

Foolish! He hadn't paid attention to the ship! These men were from a ship the real Gatto novices had already worked. Some fast talking and a hasty retreat got him out of the jam, and he picked a different mark. And it worked. He laughed as he upended a coin purse on a chess table and looked over at Dimon.

"I don't get it," his friend said. "You need the money? What are you swindling sailors for?"

Tagan folded his arms. "Because it's *fun*, Dimon. Don't you see that?"

"No, I really don't." ...

Now the Gatto persona from his boyhood came out again, this time for a more important purpose than taking money from unwary sailors. Tagan moved along the trail at a measured, even pace, with Dimon following. Only one of the blades at the pretend Gatto's waist was a real Gatto blade, complete with an old-style brass hand guard. His mother had lent him one of her old Gatto blades for practice, and Tagan never gave it back. His other blade was a Tallach short blade, but he'd chosen an unmarked one. At a distance, no one would notice.

No one accosted them as they crossed the border. They felt the eyes on them, but nobody stopped them.

"It's working," Tagan said quietly, not looking back at Dimon. "They're letting us pass."

"How many miles to go?" Dimon said, louder. "And what will you prepare for my meal tonight?"

Tagan rolled a small stone under his sandal and flicked it back with his toes, pelting Dimon in the chest.

Dimon laughed, and sauntered along behind. That evening they found a place to camp, and lit a fire. "Tell me something, Tagan," Dimon asked, "why didn't you stop at the border? To take a look, I mean. You didn't point it out, or even look around. Wouldn't a guide do that?"

"Ah. I learned that from mother," Tagan smiled. "It's not that the guides don't know where the line is, or that they don't recognize the change from south to north. The reason a Gatto guide doesn't stop and remark on entering the northlands is that to the Gatto, the trail is the path."

Dimon rolled his eyes. "To anyone the trail is the path. Those words mean the same thing."

"I mean that to walk the trail is the end, the objective. The Gatto guide isn't trying to get somewhere. It's not important to him that in this place the trail is in the southlands, and then at this other place it's in the north-lands. His focus is on walking, not the points along the way."

"Does he walk with that annoyingly even pace over mountains and through rivers, then?"

"Possibly," Tagan ignored the sarcasm, "if the trail is clear and the water shallow. But my point is that the line between south and north is nothing."

"This conversation is nothing," Dimon quipped. "What about food? Do the Gatto eat? Maybe their attention is only on the trail."

Tagan didn't answer. For at that moment, four figures in Gatto gis stepped out from the shadows, one with gray hair, and three young men. The Gatto offered no greetings, but none were needed. Tagan and Dimon knew what this was, a sensei training his students. Even the hierarchy was clear. The sensei stood in charge at the rear, and a dark-haired trainee stood a pace forward of the other two young men, taking charge of things.

"Who are you?" he demanded.

"Good evening," Tagan started. "We ..."

"Bind the spy pretending to be Gatto," said the gray-haired sensei. "Kill his companion."

Tagan's eyes met Dimon's for just a split second. No verbal exchange was needed. The next step was clear enough. Four on two, where one is a Gatto sensei and one is a senior trainee, were odds neither liked. The two younger trainees hesitated, working out the situation. But the dark-haired trainee rushed forward and executed a tight set of offensive strikes. As Tagan blocked, Dimon was already running. Tagan landed a strike that knocked the dark-haired trainee back, and then he, too, bolted.

They heard a moment's commotion behind them, but as the surprise of the situation wore off, the trainees brought order to their pursuit. Evidently the Gatto trainees knew the same tricks as Tallach trainees about moving swiftly and quietly through the woods.

"Come on!" Tagan hissed, urging Dimon to speed up. They ran as fast as they could, weaving through the trees and leaping over a stream. They dodged left and right looking for the best cover.

"Those rocks." Tagan raced up an incline and dropped behind a boulder. "Now we play dead," he whispered, holding his breath to slow his heart.

The Gatto were quiet, but not silent. Tagan and Dimon heard their footsteps as they approached, and then heard a low voice.

"Find them. Take the spy and kill the other. Show me what you've learned. This is your task for today."

Tagan closed his eyes and sighed. They were pinned down. He ran through the options in his mind, trying to come up with a clever tactic to win the moment. Maybe they could trick the trainees. The dark-haired trainee was quick on the uptake, and had attacked without hesitation. He would be the hardest to elude. The others were junior, and would be less trouble. But with their sensei there, it wasn't just a pursuit; it was a test. All three trainees would be motivated to succeed. Their full attention would be on finding their prey.

Outrun them? Unlikely. They would spread out and take away the advantage the woods presented in a one-on-one situation where cutting back and circling could be used to confuse a pursuer. Fight? Another bad idea. The trainees would give it their all, with the sensei there to observe. And there wasn't time to develop a more complex strategy. Tagan could think of only one way. He patted Dimon on the shoulder. In hand gestures, he laid out the plan. Dimon's jaw dropped, and his eyes protested, but he understood their predicament.

Take this, Tagan mouthed, pulling the pendant from around his neck. *Go back. Get over the border.*

Dimon shook his head in protest, but relented and accepted the pendant. He had heard the order, just as Tagan had: The trainees were to kill him, and take Tagan alive. Dimon's peril was greater than Tagan's. By running, Tagan could give him a chance to get back over the border. Dimon grasped wrists with his friend, and with a mournful nod, ducked low and waited. Tagan peeked out, and when he saw an opening, he ran, making enough noise for two.

He tore through the woods, heading back toward their camp, figuring he could snatch the pack and maybe get away clean. But the trainees could run, too. The fastest young Gatto gained on him, and took Tagan down within sight of the campfire. He was pinned to the ground by the dark-haired young man. The trainee said nothing, but quickly bound his wrists and pulled him to his feet. Another trainee, the blond boy, stripped him of his blades. The third stood with his hands on his hips, his bald head lowered, out of breath. He left it to his companions to take care of things.

Tagan had a better look at them, now. The younger trainees were his age, or possibly a year or two younger. Maybe seventeen, he guessed. The older one might be twenty-five. And the sensei appeared to be in his fifties.

"Where is the other?" the gray-haired sensei demanded as he approached. "Hyoso? Sado? I see one. There were two."

The trainees flashed looks of guilt and dropped their eyes, realizing their mistake, all of them running at the sound; no one suspecting that their targets might have split up.

"He's on his way to the White Cliffs, I'd guess," Tagan lied. "Are you going to chase him up there?"

"The White Cliffs are Lord Torin's domain," the Gatto man said. "If your friend is running to that place, there's no need for us to pursue."

"Why don't you let me go, and I'll join him. What interest do you have in the matter, after all?"

The gray-haired man laughed. "A Tallach in a Gatto gi asks what interest we have?" He smiled at his pupils, who smiled back in solidarity, relieved that the focus wasn't fully on them for losing the second target.

"And why take me alive, but order my friend killed? That seems unfair," Tagan complained, not entirely sure why he was being so forward with the man.

"All the same in the end," the sensei said. "It's merely a question of which blade is bloodied. The master will decide your time."

"Speaking of blades, sensei, look at this one!" the excited blond boy said, holding out Tagan's Gatto blade.

The man took the blade and studied it for a long time. His students crowded him, until at a wave of his hand they stepped back. The old man turned his eyes to Tagan. "Where did you get this?"

"It's mine. And it's dear to me. Handle that with care, if you please."

"How does a Tallach boy have a Gatto blade of The Hidden? There's a dark story behind this, I'll warrant."

Tagan pressed his eyes closed. "There's no dark story. At least not in my lifetime. I didn't take it from the corpse of a Gatto, if that's what you're thinking."

"Shilla, Sado. Bring him." The old man scowled. "Hyoso, run ahead."

Shilla, the blond boy, tied a lead around his neck and wrapped the other end twice around his palm. "Walk," he said. He tugged on the rope, deliberately forcing Tagan to stumble.

"You're lucky, Tallach spy," the big boy Sado said. "The master is away. You'll have two weeks at least before you're bled."

"Does that make the young Tallach lucky?" the gray-haired Gatto mused.

"I mean, one might say …" the trainee stuttered.

Tagan smiled. The old Gatto wasn't making a philosophical point about the value of holding onto a few final days of life before execution. He was quizzing the boy on war tactics. "To be alive is to have a chance," Tagan said. "The northern hunters say, *live on, and join in the hunt tomorrow*. You can't join in the hunt if you're dead."

"The spy is correct," the Gatto said with a sour smile.

"The not-yet-dead spy you mean," Tagan corrected, and received a thump in the chest from the blond boy for his insolence. "And I'm not a spy." He dodged another blow. "I have ties to the Gatto. My mother once trained in the north."

"Your mother is Gatto?" The gray-haired man said, sarcastically. "I suppose this is her blade, then."

"She trained up here when she was young. Yes, it's hers."

"Isn't that an interesting account. Perhaps one day we'll show her the first kata." His students laughed.

Tagan had a fiery rejoinder—*Perhaps one day she'll run her blade into your gut*—but he kept it to himself. The adrenaline of the chase was wearing off, and he was starting to consider the merits of baiting his captors, or of giving them too much information.

Dimon got himself turned around. He shook his head in disbelief as he realized the error. Was it because he and Tagan had stopped to make camp, and it wasn't dark yet? Maybe that was it. Surely had it been dark, he'd have seen the stars and wouldn't have gone north instead of south, he told himself. But that was idiotic. He couldn't see where the sun was? He needed stars to guide him?

It was nerves. His friend had risked his own freedom to allow him to escape. And racked with guilt at allowing him to do it, Dimon had run north instead of south, his mind telling him that it was the right way.

It wasn't just a minor detour. He'd run for a full hour, all in exactly the wrong direction. There was no way that he could make it to the border now. He would have to find a place to spend the night, and make a plan for tomorrow. He patted his pocket. His share of the gold was there. He had no supplies, but maybe he would come to an inn, or find a merchant on the road. He walked for a long time, but there were no inns, and no merchants. Determined not to be taken by surprise again, he climbed a tree, found a high perch, and tied himself onto the branch. At least it wouldn't cost him anything, he reasoned, as he fell into an uncomfortable sleep.

He woke to a voice calling from below. "You up there. Come down. Show yourself."

"Oh, no," Dimon muttered. Could he close his eyes and make this go away? Being up in a tree was a fine way to stay safe overnight, but in the light of the early morning it was a bad place to be. It limited one's options.

"I'll come down. I'm no threat. I'll come down peaceably." He untied himself and climbed down, and dropped to the ground. Arms out in surrender, he looked at the two men who had found him, and sighed. He only knew a little about the north, but he knew what they were. "Sentries," he muttered. "Sentries of the north."

The older one stepped close, wielding twin short blades. "And you?"

"A traveler."

"Hiding in a tree? Would you like to try again?" The man's voice was firm, already growing impatient. He nodded to his companion.

"I've done no harm to anyone." Dimon stopped talking as the younger man sheathed his blades, stepped up and roughly searched him. "I wasn't hiding. I was just sleeping."

The sentry drew Dimon's short blades and dropped them to the side, then unclipped his belt and pulled it off, dropping it as well. The man looked down at the sound of the coins jingling. Then his fingers came to the pendant, and he lifted it out of Dimon's tunic.

"I'm here on business," Dimon insisted. "I have free passage. You must allow me to go my way."

The sentry unclipped the chain and held the pendant up to the other sentry. "Have a look at this. The Tallach boy has a safe passage pendant."

"Let me see." The other took it. "I've heard they sell these copies down around Steerageway. That where you come from? Are you a smuggler, then?"

His companion picked up the coin sack and dumped the gold into his hand, and gave a low whistle. "Or a highwayman. Here's a boy in common Tallach garb, carrying nothing but blades and gold."

"And a free passage pendant," Dimon argued.

"Bind him," the first sentry said. "I'll keep this." He pocketed the pendant.

"But wait. I didn't steal the gold," Dimon complained. "I got it from …" and then he closed his eyes and rued the fact that his friend Tagan wasn't there to interject with the perfect lie. "I got it from a sale. I sold a blade." Too late. A bad answer, and he'd paused for too long.

The sentries didn't even bother to ask how that could be, since he still had both of his blades. "Let's go."

"Go where? Where are you taking me?"

"I suppose we could escort you to the border and give you safe passage," the older man gave a low laugh. "But I think we'll stop at the Tenth Station."

"Hiding in a tree with a pair of Tallach short blades." The captain of the station leaned back, his boots up on his desk. He pulled out his own blade and picked his fingernails with it.

Dimon sat, wrists bound, a pair of sentries standing behind him. A day in a cell hadn't brought him any new ideas. His only play was to stick with the story. "The gold and the blades are mine," he insisted. "And the safe passage token."

"What gold?"

"No idea what he's talking about. But he did have this on him."

The captain's eyebrows went up as the sentry produced the pendant on the chain. "A safe passage token?" He turned it over in his hand. "Do you Tallachs down south suppose we still hand out silver safe passage tokens in this day and age? You might have considered purchasing a forgery of a warrant. It would have been more convincing."

"Who says it's a forgery? It's just old."

The captain opened a drawer and dropped the pendant in. He put his feet down, and leaned his elbows on the desk. "I'm told you were seen with a Gatto porter. Care to tell me about that?"

"He led me across the border. Isn't that what's expected?"

"Ah. So you arranged passage with the Gatto, but also felt the need to carry a safe passage token. I don't think so. Perhaps you tricked a Gatto into bringing you across the border, and the pendant was your backup plan?"

"I didn't ..."

"We soldiers of the north are not so gullible. Not in the Tenth, anyway." The men behind him straightened in solidarity. "Put him in his cell. Half rations. I told you this arrangement with the Gatto would come to this. They're nothing but mercenaries. They'll bring anyone across the border for a fee."

Dimon was hauled away. They marched him down a flight of stone steps and closed the iron door of a cell behind him. The cell was small, with a stone floor and walls, a small air shaft in one wall allowing only a thin line of sunshine in.

Was it night already? Dimon woke to a darkened room. The air shaft was a slot of gray. He rose as he heard someone coming down the passage.

"Hungry in there?" came the jailor's voice. A port at the base of the door slid open, and a tray slid in. "Don't break the dishes or ruin the tray. Have to tell you that. Nothing peeves the cook more than broken dishes or a damaged tray. He'll put glass in your food, or send you a bowl of maggots. No joke, prisoner. If you want to try to tunnel out, find another tool. The cook's not to be toyed with."

Dimon stepped over. The meal on the tray didn't look bad. There was a large chunk of bread, a bowl of beans, and a whole apple. "Thank you," he said, realizing he was starving. He dug in.

"The cap'n said half rations, but he didn't say half of what. So I figure, this here is a double, ain't it? There's two walls big enough for a man to stretch out along, so it's got to be. And half of that is a meal. So there it is."

"Thank you," Dimon repeated, smiling and then taking a big bite of the bread. "You're a prince."

"Oh, I'm a king," the man objected. "King of the dungeons." He laughed. "Listen, now. We don't get no Tallachs in here. Never since I been here, anyway. You the skittish type?"

"Skittish?"

"If I was to open this door so's I ain't talking to a slab of iron, are you gonna try to leap past me, and get your head bashed in by the guard up at the next door, or do some damn fool thing like trying to take me hostage? Just to be clear, they'd shoot through you and me both, and call it a good job."

"I won't run." Was he being played? Dimon wished Tagan were with him. His friend would understand the game, and know what to do. "I promise."

"And you'll stay put? I sit out here. You stay in there. That's the only way it works, if you want some company."

"I'll sit and eat."

The door creaked open, and Dimon looked over at an older man, maybe in his fifties. He had envisioned a skinny man with bad teeth and blotchy skin. Yet here was a solid looking man with graying hair neatly trimmed and combed back, smooth skin, and only a hint of crow's feet around the eyes. He was dressed nicely in gray pants, a white shirt, and a black vest, not the military outfit Dimon had expected.

"I'm Darach," the man said. "Jailor of the Tenth. Although it's only a part-time job. They don't bring me in for the day-to-day matters. Drunk soldiers, fights, and such. The duty lieutenant sees to them, and that's about all there is on a typical day. Not much going on here since the Gatto took over at the border. So I'm glad to see you. I need the money." He gave an exaggerated wink.

"Dimon. From the Western Shores."

"That true? The Western Shores? What in hell are you doing up here? I heard that's a splendid place. Merchant ships, and fire pit pavilions, and girls in them short pants that shows their legs. And that woman fighter up in Deadrise Bay."

"Talla Undine. Yes, I know the Talla."

The man grinned. "Sure you do. What port are you from?"

"Deadrise Bay. That's where I live."

"Oh, come. This is a friendly conversation. I'm a civilian, you know. I ain't enlisted. And it's true that I have to report about the prisoners to the cap'n, but he don't give a shit what I have to say. Don't even listen, really. So you can talk to me. Where are you from, really?"

"Deadrise Bay. Truly."

"Fine, then. We'll play it that way. And I'm from the White Cliffs. Lord Torin's my brother, an' I have supper with him every day."

"I'm not making a joke. I live at Deadrise Bay. Listen, Darach, it was foolish of me to sneak over the border. I understand. And I apologize to the captain, or to the northlands, or whatever it is I need to do. I came looking for my kin. My father is from the north."

"Thought you said you was from Deadrise Bay." The man rolled his eyes. "Now you're from the north? You look to me like you're from overseas. Maybe you come in on a Tallach ship."

Dimon put a hand to his head and massaged his temples. "My mother was from Ben Atallach. She died years ago, when I was small. She said my father is a soldier from a place called Lesser Mire."

"That crazy compound up over the mountains? Shit, you're telling me your daddy's a compound soldier? And he hooked up with some lady from overseas? Well, that's a good one. Ain't heard this one before. All right, I'll play along. You want to find your kin. And what's the game?

86

You figure on getting arrested at each of the border stations and see if he's there?" Darach laughed.

"I didn't plan to be arrested. I wanted to find a guide to take me to the Lesser Mire compound. I brought money."

"I'm told you brung Tallach blades, and nothing else 'cept for some little thing from a bazaar that you're trying to pass off as a passage token. That might've been a mistake, bringing that. Piss off the cap'n. He don't like pretenders."

"I know," Dimon sulked. "He's not subtle about it. Will he give it back? It's not mine. My friend lent it to me in hopes it might help me get back safely over the border when the Gatto set on us."

"Ho, this story gets better. Gatto came at you? And who might this friend be?"

Dimon almost blurted out Tagan's name, but caught himself. "Just a friend. And he pretends it doesn't mean anything to him, but if I lose it, he'll never forgive me." He stopped, and held up a palm. "I'm sorry. I don't mean to be rude. I realize it's a reproduction. But it has sentimental value."

"Hm. Tell me about this Gatto attack." The jailor scowled.

"My friend and I came north. I to seek my father, and he to pursue his own ends. He dressed as a Gatto to get us across the border."

"Why not use the token? Ain't that supposed to get you across?" The jailor feigned serious interest, scratching his chin and tipping his head.

"I'm not making this up," Dimon insisted. "My friend enjoys that kind of thing. Pretending to be a Gatto fighter, for instance. He said it would work. And it did. We crossed. The Gatto caught us later. It was just bad luck. They came upon us at our camp, and I suppose heard us talking. So we ran, and we split up. My friend gave me the token in hopes I could use it to return south. But I mixed up my directions and ended up here."

"Bad luck, indeed. Hell of a good story, though." The jailor rose. "I'd not tell it to the cap'n. Put you on quarter rations, or something, and then I don't think I could work out the math to where you'd get a good meal." He winked. "Been a pleasure. I'll be back for the tray and the dishes. And remember, the cook don't have no sense of humor at all."

The door slammed shut, and Dimon closed his eyes and shook his head miserably.

"Do you know a fighter named Aideen?" Tagan clutched the bars of the small window in his cell and called to a young Gatto trainee sitting on a stool in the corridor. "Let me speak with her. I can clear this up."

The young man looked over lazily. "We regularly give border jumpers pretending to be Gatto an audience with the master. Let me hurry and fetch her right now." He sat.

"At least tell her I'm here."

"Tell her who's here? You haven't told us your name."

Tagan blew out a breath. "Please, just arrange an audience. I promise she'll want to speak with me."

The boy rolled his eyes. "I don't even want to speak with you. Why would Master Aideen?"

"Listen to me. You must know something about the Tallach trade on the Shores. You'll receive a ransom, if that's what's needed."

"Oh yes. We often find rich Tallachs from the Western Shores sneaking into the northlands dressed as Gatto. I'm sure there will be a great ransom."

"Damn it," Tagan quietly cursed. He turned to the trainee again. "If you won't listen to me, could I at least walk outside? Or am I to be kept in this dungeon all day and all night?"

"That's what dungeons are built for." The trainee smiled thinly.

"Fine. Might I make a small request? Or is it your charge to respond to whatever I say with a clever quip?"

"It helps pass the time. What's your request? A land grant? Or dinner with Master Stetlin from the far reaches?"

"I'd like to have someone else guard me." Tagan snapped, and flashed back the same thin smile. The barb found its target. The young trainee scowled and turned away.

The guards changed twice between the morning meal and the evening meal, and twice during the night, all of them boys no older than he, and some several years younger. Tagan silently mused that this must be a perk of running a group of Gatto trainees: there was a ready supply of warm bodies to perform unwanted tasks.

He slept a little, paced around the cell, and sat to think, but couldn't come up with any options. By the time the fourth trainee had taken his place on the stool, Tagan began to wish he hadn't been so unpleasant to the first. At least the first boy talked to him. The others sat silently and didn't acknowledge him.

But it seemed that while talking was discouraged, listening and report-ing was not. Midway through the second day, the door opened, and the trainee jumped from his stool, stood and bowed. The gray-haired Gatto whom Tagan had encountered in the woods stepped in.

"I'm Taijo," he said. "Sensei at Three Rivers Pavilion. You request access to the outdoors."

"I requested that, yes."

"Not unreasonable. You can't be faulted for the delay in seeing to your situation, as surely you didn't plan to be captured while the master is away. You'll be allowed to spend time outside until she returns."

"She?" Tagan perked up. "Do you mean Master Aideen, then?"

The Gatto's eyes narrowed. "What trail did you think you were on? This is not the Pavilion of the Hidden, young Tallach. Master Caterione is steward of the lands at the Three Rivers."

"Master Caterione? Wait! I know about her! She trained under Master Aideen, right? Or in the stories she did, at least."

"Storytelling will gain you nothing, spy. If you wish to walk outside, swear that you'll be on your best behavior."

"I swear."

The master turned to the trainee. "Leg irons."

"Fresh air!" Tagan stepped outside and stretched in the sunlight, in a place he had never expected to see, the inside of a Gatto compound.

The compound was new, some structures still being built. He had heard about a compound in the southlands that was a mile across and closed in by a high stone structure in a perfect square. This one was nothing like that. In place of stone walls were wooden buildings with stockade fence in between. It seemed wood was more plentiful than stone, in the valleys. From the outside, Tagan figured, it must look more like a border station than a Gatto compound.

Inside was a village of plain huts in neat rows, and open spaces filled with gardens and walkways. Everything was lush and green, the gardens and trees fed by wooden irrigation trenches. Tagan had read about the Three Rivers, the fertile valleys in the foothills below the northern passes. It certainly seemed to be a fine location for an encampment. Maybe his mother hadn't made up the story about Caterione, after all. She would have to be important to be offered land like this.

He walked the path—or shuffled, rather, burdened by the leg irons—and took in the scene. At first it seemed no one had been assigned to monitor him, but then he picked out two young boys keeping their distance, but watching, ready to call an alarm if needed. The trainers and trainees walked along the paths, not staring, but noting his presence as well.

In the center of the compound Tagan came to the pavilion, a high post-and-beam structure with canvas walls and roof. Men in Gatto gis guarded entrances on either end. From inside he could hear the trainees at their exercises. He felt the urge to run in and spar with them. Wouldn't that be entertaining! But it was clear from the stance of the guards that he was not to be allowed entry.

Attempts to strike up a conversation were answered with blank stares, and after a while he gave up. He made his way to a stone bench by one of the irrigation trenches, and sat and watched the water flow. The stockade fence blocked his view upstream, but he assumed he would see a continuation of the trench up to the river, where most likely a gate had been built to control the flow of water.

Tagan hung his head. It was fine to be outdoors rather than in the dungeons, but it didn't solve his problem. When the master returned, he'd be back in his cell facing an undesirable end. He reached down to rub the skin of his ankle where the leg irons chafed.

"Bind your ankles with cloth. You'll lose your skin if you don't."

Tagan looked up to see a dark-skinned young girl in a brown gi, hands on her hips, staring at him from the path. She flipped a braid of long, black hair over her shoulder and stepped closer. "You're the prisoner."

"You think so?" he said, and then regretted his sarcasm as the girl's eyes narrowed and she turned to leave. "Wait. I'm sorry."

She turned back. She had a tight-lipped, unsmiling expression that didn't seem right for a girl who couldn't be more than twelve or thirteen. "You're rude in error?" she said.

"I suppose by nature. And yet I'm sorry," Tagan said. "Will you sit?"

"Sit with a prisoner?"

"I'll stand, if you're not allowed to sit."

The girl tossed her head. "I can do as I please." She stepped over and sat on the far end of the bench. "Bind your ankles with cloth," she repeated. "Those iron cuffs will rub you raw."

"Thank you. Except I don't have anything to bind them with. Can you tell me about this place?"

"I can. But I won't. Not for free," she taunted.

"I have nothing to pay you with. No money, no treats. They took everything."

The girl aimed her wide, dark eyes at him accusingly. "Where's your companion?"

"You don't know? Does that mean they didn't catch him?" Tagan smiled. "Good. This isn't his fault."

"*What* isn't his fault? If you want information, then give information. They won't tell me anything."

"Maybe the pendant worked. Wouldn't that be a fine joke to tell my mother," Tagan mused out loud.

"What joke?" the girl said.

"Ha. My friend uses that old reproduction of a passage token, and actually gains passage. She'd find that amusing."

"What are you talking about?"

Tagan turned to the girl. "Just thinking. Here, why don't we start with introductions." He held out his hand. "I'm the prisoner."

The girl shifted away and looked at his hand as if it were a snake. "And I'll break your arm if you try to touch me."

He withdrew his hand. "I'm afraid most of what I know of the Gatto is from my mother's stories. And she never said a handshake was an offense."

"Your mother. Who's your mother?"

"Oh, never mind. It doesn't matter," Tagan sulked. "And probably everything she told me was made up, anyway. Like the story of that passage token. The whole thing about Master Aideen, and her spat with the other girl, Caterione."

The girl rose and glared at him. "What about Caterione? Your mother claims to have known Master Caterione? You're telling stories. And you don't sound like a road bandit. Who are you?"

Tagan halted. He needed to be more careful! Prisoner or not, he wouldn't be safe from the gray-gis if someone were to figure out who he was. "Because I'm not a road bandit," he said. "I'm a traveler."

But a shadow crossed them and the old sensei stepped up, arms folded. "Miss Isotta," he said, brusquely, and the girl stepped away from the bench.

"Sensei Taijo," she said, and bowed.

The man waved his head, and she grimaced and hurried down the path. The sensei stood looming over Tagan. "You'll not accost the novice."

"I didn't accost her. She sat to talk. Is that forbidden?"

"The novice is not a channel to the master. That route could lead you on a worse road than you find yourself on now."

"I don't follow." Tagan stood, annoyed at being looked down upon. "The girl sat on the bench. I'm not attempting a route to anywhere, except maybe to find out what's going on around here, if anyone would care to talk to me."

"Miss Isotta is off limits."

Tagan rolled his eyes. "What is she, thirteen? I wasn't making an advance."

"She's the master's daughter. You'll not accost her."

"Which master?"

"Master Caterione, of course." The Gatto turned and stalked off.

"Ho. Well, now, that's interesting," Tagan muttered. "And dangerous. The daughter of Master Caterione? And here I am, blathering away. I should have kept my mouth shut."

He wondered if anything his mother had told him about Caterione was true. In his mother's version of the events of her childhood, she had called herself Una, and had trained at the hidden village of Gatto exiles in the woods up north. She told him of a deadly serious older girl named Caterione. Undine had always been a troublemaker, and each time she got in trouble, the master would punish all the girls, and not just Una; and Caterione would then administer justice on behalf of the other novices.

"When I got in trouble, we were all in trouble," his mother told him.

"That's how it works with the Gatto. You step out of line and you and your companions all suffer for it. Caterione handled the situation by beating me. Not that I didn't deserve it."

Tagan's mother told him of a later encounter, shortly after Undine had earned her fourth ring in Tallach fighting. Freshly minted as a fourth-level Talla, Undine had come across Caterione at that same village. Her old rival had been promoted to Gatto master, and they had sparred.

"And I got the best of her, too," his mother bragged. "I'd have defeated her, were we not interrupted."

This girl he'd just met certainly looked the part of the daughter of the person his mother had described. She was dark and brooding, and quick of temper.

He wandered around the compound, stopping to watch workers building a new structure, and took his noon meal on the same bench by the irrigation trench. Then he was led back to his cell.

He was pleased to see the talkative Gatto trainee on watch. "You again," Tagan said. "Back for more?"

When the door was closed behind them, the trainee nodded slowly. "I'm sentenced to an extra shift for having spoken to you." The trainee sat on the stool in the corridor.

"I didn't tell," Tagan shrugged. "I swear to you. No one will even talk to me. How could I have?"

"No, I did. I confessed. And my master reprimanded me—not in fact for speaking, but for choosing to be clever. I apologize, prisoner. It's not a trainee's place to be clever with those under his control." He bowed his head.

"You apologize? Oh, come. So you teased a bit. It's not as if you made me cry."

Then the door farther down the hall was pushed open, and the trainee jumped from his stool. "Miss Isotta!"

"Out, Geun," the girl said, pointing.

"But ..."

"Out!" she demanded, "and not a word that I was here."

The trainee nodded and slipped outside.

Isotta shut the outer door. She stepped up to the bars in the iron door and folded her arms, staring and silently demanding. "Tell me your mother's stories about Caterione," she said, unsmiling.

"My mother tells lots of stories."

"Let's hear them."

"All right. But not for free," he said, echoing the girls' own words. "If I tell you a story, you tell me one. Deal?"

The girl shrugged. "Fair enough."

Tagan glanced upward to gather his thoughts, and to consider how to play it. Normally something close to the truth was best: Stick mostly to a true story. It made it easier to avoid making a mistake.

It only took him a moment to come up with an idea. "You know of Deadrise Bay?"

"The port. Yes. I was just there."

"You've been there? My mother and I live there."

"And your father?"

Tagan shrugged. "It's just my mother and me—oh, and my little sister Rebecca." He smiled. Why not work Becca into the tale? It would make it more interesting, and if he ever got out of this, Becca would give him a big kiss for casting her as his sister.

"You have a sister?" Isotta perked up.

"Younger than you. She's ten. What are you, three years older?"

Isotta pursed her lips and didn't answer.

"Anyway, my mother works for the master of Deadrise Bay." This, Tagan reflected, was sort of true. His mother wasn't exactly employed by Saor Tieg, but as his daughter, she certainly did plenty of things for him.

"Your mother works for him, you say? And your sister?"

"Rebecca runs errands, and works in the kitchen." He couldn't help smiling. The most work Becca did in the kitchens was to plan how to get her hands on the baked goods without getting caught. "My mother mostly attends the Talla."

Isotta's eyes narrowed. "The deal is for a *true* story, if you want me to tell one," she said.

"It's true. Ask me anything about Deadrise Bay. Go ahead. I'll prove I'm telling the truth. I've lived there all my life. I've trained since I was little in the House Kamine pavilion that Talla Undine built."

"House Kamine." Isotta's eyes widened again. "You train there? Prove it." She rose from the stool and pressed her face to the bars.

"Open the door and we can spar. How would that be?"

The Gatto girl pulled back. "Spy! You want to trick me! I'll not talk to you anymore." She stormed down the corridor and slammed the outer door.

From his cell, Tagan could hear a storm come in. The dull roar of pouring rain and peals of thunder seemed to make the stones vibrate. He had no outside window, but imagined spectacular flashes of lightning. It continued through the night and into the morning.

When the shift changed, a damp trainee mopped an arm across his face and sat. It was the talkative one.

"Quite the storm, eh, Geun?" Tagan said, and received no response. "When will I be allowed to go outside?"

"It's raining," Geun said. "And I'm not supposed to talk to you. And how do you know my name?"

"Isotta called you Geun."

"Oh."

"And I don't mind the rain. Tell your master I'd still like my time out of doors. And I thought you were only not supposed to taunt. Now they've forbidden you speaking to me at all? That's not very friendly."

"I'm sorry." The boy turned away.

Hours of dull silence passed, and when the outer door opened again, Tagan expected to have a fresh trainee to ignore him. Instead a familiar young voice drew his attention. "Quiet," the young voice demanded.

"Yes, miss. Shall I wait outside?"

"Stay." Isotta's face appeared on the other side of the bars. "I have an idea," she said. She stared at Tagan. "You told me that you trained at House Kamine. So show me. You'll fight him. Get to the back of the cell. I'm armed. If you try to get out, I'll run you through."

Tagan raised his palms and backed up. "Now, wait a minute, Isotta."

"Don't call me by my name!" the girl demanded. "Do you think I'm your friend?"

"What shall I call you, then? I've no wish to fight, girl who doesn't want to be called Isotta. I meant a kata, or sparring on the mats, not to fight a trainee."

The lock turned, and Isotta shoved the boy in and slammed the door after him. Her face reappeared behind the bars. "Fight him, and maybe I'll allow you another chance to tell your story. Refuse, and I'll tell the master you accosted me."

Geun stood staring, his mouth open. He flashed Tagan an imploring look, as if hoping the prisoner could get him out of the jam.

Tagan looked from the frightened boy to the smug girl, and rolled his eyes. "Don't I know that look," he muttered. He sat on the floor and folded his hands. "I'll not be bullied, Isotta. If you want …"

"I said don't call me by my name!" the girl barked.

"Now you remind me of my little sister, stomping her foot and demanding to get her way. Are you ten, then, and not thirteen? Are you still just a little girl? Go, then. Tell the master I accosted you, and see what it brings. You'll get no stories that way." He gave her the universal unimpressed-older-person look, and watched her face turn from angry to annoyed, and finally to irritated.

"Fine," she stomped her foot. "I won't say anything."

The trainee's look of staggered surprise almost made Tagan laugh. Evidently this girl wasn't used to anyone telling her *no*. Even Becca would have played it out longer than that before giving up.

"But you have to show me," she insisted. "Spar instead of fighting. But I'll not believe a word you say until you prove what you've told me already."

"Fair enough. But not here, and not with an unwilling partner. Tell the master I want my time outside, and ask if I might pass time in the pavilion when it's not being used, given the storm. I'll do a kata or two. You can hide somewhere and watch. Good enough?"

The lock turned, and Geun hurried out and quickly shoved the door shut again.

"Tell the master," Isotta ordered, confirming the plan. Then Tagan heard a loud sigh. "Not right now, dummy. Do you want to get me in trouble? Get back here, and tell him after your shift is up."

Later the old master appeared in the corridor. "You may sit in the pavilion," he said. "The trainees are at exercises outside the walls today."

"Sparring in the rain?" Tagan said. "They must love that."

"Do you think, young prisoner, that fighting waits for clear weather?"

Tagan smiled and followed him out. "Oh, I know from personal experience that it doesn't."

Outside, Sensei Taijo raised a cloth umbrella and led him along the path to the pavilion. "Remain inside. We'll spare the leg irons, but I have no wish to be out in the rain hunting for you, and I've no trainees to send in my place."

The Gatto pavilion was large and well built. In the south, the canvas of a fighting pavilion would be a gigantic, painted mural, showing scenes of historic encounters and symbols of the fighting house. But the Gatto walls were plain oiled canvas. There were low tables at one end where trainees would sit for the tea ritual or for meals, and there were grass mats on the ground for exercises, but not much else inside. Tagan spotted a pot of water and a dipper near the entry, and a stack of crates in a corner. Aside from that, the room was empty.

He walked all the way around the perimeter, looking for a place the girl might be hiding. Having been trapped in the cell made him want to get on the mats and get some exercise, but he also needed to play the game. He had only two slim allies in this place, the trainee named Geun, who some-times spoke to him, and the girl, who in spite of her outwardly hostile stance and jumpiness, seemed fascinated by him. But the crates were empty, and there was nowhere else a thirteen-year-old would fit.

"She's not coming," he said out loud, as he stepped onto the mats. "Your loss, Isotta. I mean to practice anyway."

He started with a slow warm-up, bending and stretching to move his muscles. Then without stopping to consider, he began working through his usual opening, a long training kata that all House Kamine students performed at the start and end of a session. It wasn't until he had completed it and stood with his arms out in the final stance that it occurred to him that the Gatto might not appreciate a Tallach fighter performing in their pavilion.

"I suppose they might kill me for it," he mused, and smiled at the dark irony. He walked the perimeter again, to confirm that he was alone. Tagan bowed to no one, and made the opening moves of an especially tricky sparring kata that his master had been teaching him. Halfway through he stopped and whipped his arms out at the sound of a voice.

"You weren't lying. You're better than the trainees."

Tagan looked around, searching. "Isotta? Where are you?"

And then he discovered something he hadn't known about the construction of a Gatto pavilion. The walls weren't a single layer of canvas. There was an inner layer. What he had taken for seams were hemmed edges of wide canvas sections forming the inner wall.

Isotta slipped out from her hiding place between the layers and flashed a look of triumph. "I watch the trainees from there, sometimes. I can see through the stitching. They never catch me."

"You were spying on me? I thought I was supposed to be the spy." Tagan folded his arms and frowned in mock indignation.

"I wasn't spying," Isotta sternly insisted. "This was the plan. You were to prove that you were telling me the truth about your training."

"Ah, right," Tagan said, as if just recalling. "Or you would tell the master that I assaulted you, or some such thing."

She closed her eyes and sighed. "I didn't mean that." Then her eyes went wide, and she darted back behind the canvas.

Tagan heard the rustle of someone coming through the door behind him, and he carried on, talking out loud. "And what would you say, sister, if I told you I'd been in a Gatto pavilion?" He shifted his voice up, mimicking the girl's "I'd say you're a poor liar, brother." He dropped his voice again. "But then you'd ..." Tagan turned and halted at the master standing inside the door.

"Someone is here with you?"

"Here?" Tagan looked around. "Oh. Ha. Just thinking out loud. I have a little sister. She'd never believe me if I told her I'd seen the inside of a Gatto fighting pavilion. Thank you for allowing me to see it."

"You may stay and have your meal." He stepped aside, and some women carried in dishes and a covered tray.

"Thank you, master. I'm honored."

"It's a tent, prisoner, not a temple. Eat. I'll return to take you to your cell later."

Tagan sat at the low table, then rose and walked around to sit against the wall. He pulled his meal over. There was a large chunk of warm bread and a bowl of dark, rich stew, and two apples. When the master had gone and the entry was safely closed, he took one of the apples and reached behind, and tucked his hand under the canvas. A hand met his and took it.

"I like to talk to myself as I eat," Tagan said, smiling, "almost as if I were telling someone a story. You know, as if someone might be listening." The girl behind the canvas didn't respond, but she was still there. "I and my mother, and little Rebecca, we live at Deadrise Bay. Mother works closely with the Talla. *Very* closely." Again he grinned. "I'm speaking of Talla Undine. I'm sure everyone here has heard of her. I'm sure of that because everyone *everywhere* has heard of her. I could travel beyond the northernmost outposts and I'd still be in her shadow. But never mind. I'll tell a story my mother told me. Am I speaking to myself loudly enough?" The rain had picked up and was noisy on the roof.

"Tell your story," Isotta said.

"There was a girl called Una, about your age. Twelve, I think she said. Una trained with a Gatto master of The Hidden named Aideen."

"You promised a *true* story!" Isotta hissed.

"Every word is true. At least, this is the story my mother told me. If it's not true, then she's the liar, not I."

"All right. Tell it."

"There were four other girls training with Master Aideen. One was younger and pale. Una thought she looked like a ghost. Two were twins, Una's age, and one was older. The older girl was called Caterione." Tagan heard a rustling behind the canvas, but Isotta didn't say anything. "Caterione must have been around sixteen, I think," he continued, "and was stronger and more capable than the other girls. Una perhaps should have shown this older girl more respect."

Tagan smiled. The quiet "humph" from behind the canvas told him his nod to the girl's mother had worked: Butter her up, and keep her interested.

"Caterione was a fine young fighter, more fierce and more determined than Una. But Una was clever, and liked to play tricks. Sometimes she tricked people on the road, and sometimes she tricked her fellow trainees and got them in trouble. When she got them in trouble one too many times, Caterione beat her."

"She beat Una," Isotta hissed. "So she won?"

"I don't mean in a sparring match. The other girls held Una down, and Caterione beat her with a weighted sock."

"But that's not fair."

"Oh, you'd have heard no argument from little Una on that point. But the other girls were all in on it. They held her, and Caterione punished her mercilessly for getting them in trouble. And so Una ran away. Later she found her father, and started using her real name, Undine."

"Humph," Isotta again grunted, this time in disdain. "This sounds like a made-up story. Why would she call herself Una if her name was Undine? And why would the Talla be in Gatto lands as a girl?"

"I believe the deal was a story for a story. Those are two more, so you'd better think up some good ones if you want to hear those."

Tagan grinned at yet another *humph* from behind him. "There's one thing I remember that I'll tell you, though. My mother told me this part only one time, I think because she'd had more wine than usual, and let it slip. Do you want to hear a secret? She told me what Caterione whispered in Una's ear that night, the night Una ran away." He stopped and waited.

"Well?" The girl behind the canvas had dropped down to get as close as possible. "What did she say?"

"You have to promise not to tell. It's a secret between Master Undine and Master Caterione. My mother shared it with me, but wouldn't like it if she were to find out I told you." Tagan took a bite of an apple and waited.

"Fine," the girl growled. "I promise. Now tell me!"

He leaned back and put his face up close to the canvas and with a dramatic flair, he whispered, *We're not going down for you!*

There was a rustle, then utter silence from behind the canvas.

"So? What do you think? Don't you think that's a pretty good story? Master Undine might be Gatto today instead of Tallach, if your mother hadn't driven her off. But come, your turn. You said you've been to Deadrise Bay. Let's hear your story." But there was no answer. Tagan lifted the canvas to look. Isotta was gone.

10. Opposing Forces

"Annoyingly sullen, but the defiance is gone." Allton nodded grudging approval.

"The pilgrimage forces reflection," Arran said. "Miss Abigail considers her place."

"Does she? Well then, Hester," Allton said with a wave of the hand, "perhaps this walk in the woods did her some good." He turned his eyes to Arran. "And what now, tutor?"

Arran bowed. "Should it please you, I propose a regimen of physical activity and new studies. Keep her mind and body focused on the here and now, and disallow the opportunity to return to dark thoughts."

"Physical activity. My daughter is not a Gatto trainee." Allton scowled and drummed a finger on the table. "She needs to learn her place."

"I believe we see the same end. Activities create focus. Not in the pavilion, of course. As you say, she has no need for Gatto training. I propose a study of the minutia of the natural world. Let each day focus upon an element of the pilgrimage, albeit close to home. Let the lessons learned in solitude be sealed in solitude."

"Hm." Allton nodded his head slowly. "You want to keep her apart from the others."

"I do."

"But within the compound."

"The pilgrimage is finished, master. The young miss has no need to wander. What's needed is focus. There are a great many things for her to study. Wind, and water, and flora ... plenty to keep a young mind focused on her place."

"All right. Go teach her about the wind and water, then. And I don't need to hear about Abigail's every concern, but I wish to be updated on her overall progress. Your pilgrimage seems to have produced results. Show me more results."

"Yes, master."

"And my patience isn't endless, young Gatto. Impress upon her the required outcome. Abigail will learn her place one way or another."

"Yes, master."

"You talked to him?" Abigail didn't look up as Arran stepped inside.

"I did, young miss. Your father is pleased with the outcome."

"Which means you didn't tell him. I suppose that's obvious, since you wouldn't be here if you had."

"The master doesn't wish to hear about every small concern."

Abigail missed his thin smile. "Every small concern?" she growled.

"Any concern of mine is small to him." She turned and stalked to the window. "What now? I'm expected to return to the life of dull drudgery that a Turning woman is supposed to aspire to? I suppose he expects me to smile and appear content."

"You might benefit by learning to do that," Arran said. "But I proposed a different sort of training. I thought you might prefer to spend less time in the company of the Turning—at least in the short term."

Abigail spun to face him. "I prefer to spend no time with the Turning, now and into the infinite future. What difference does that make? It's not my *place* to decide that kind of thing," she huffed, "or I wouldn't be here at all."

"Then perhaps you'll find comfort in the coming weeks. I've arranged to teach you out of doors, away from the others."

"Teach me what?"

"Put on those traveling clothes and come outside."

"He said I can wear a man's clothes?" Her eyebrows went up.

"The master doesn't wish to hear of every small concern," Arran repeated. "That's his directive, and I his faithful servant." He bowed and stepped outside.

Once again Abigail felt liberated to be in a boy's pants, shirt, and vest instead of the shapeless dress of a Turning woman. If anything, if felt better this time. When last she'd put on this outfit it was to run from the Turning camp and go to Tagan's funeral. That weight had been lifted. He was alive! And Talla Undine herself had reassured her that her son would not forget the girl he'd met at Deadrise Bay. Even the smallest chance that Tagan would come for her was enough to keep her spirits up. And to pass the time doing something other than the daily drudgery of being the daughter of the Turning chieftain was welcome. Whatever Arran had in mind, it had to be better than the alternative.

"Come," he said, meeting her on the path. Arran had a pack slung over his shoulder.

"The pilgrimage wants food this time?" she smiled sourly.

"You'll see. Come."

Arran's pace was rapid, and the trail was not empty. Scouts stepped into the road. But it seemed the word had been given. There were silent nods and more than a few sideways glances at the chieftain's daughter in pants and a vest, but they were allowed to pass. Arran led her farther and farther, until they passed outside of the inner boundary and into the vast, wild acreage of Turning land.

Several times he stopped and held up a hand, and they stood silently for long minutes.

"We're not pursued," he said at length. "The master is allowing it, it seems."

"Another pilgrimage, then?" Abigail said, with a note of sarcasm.

Arran stopped and turned. "The pilgrimage is a fabrication, young miss," he said, looking straight into her eyes. "The Gatto don't use the technique. It's not a Gatto custom."

With a shrug, Abigail looked back at him. "But he believed it."

"Your pilgrimage in particular, now that was a fabrication upon a fabrication, wasn't it?" Arran continued. "A pretend custom, embarked upon to cloak a hidden purpose."

Abigail looked around warily.

"Be at ease. No one is here but the tutor and his pupil. I went along with your plan, Abigail—and engaged in trickery against the master— because I recognize grief and the value of ceremony."

"I needed to go, Arran," Abigail said. "I needed to be there for his funeral. It's good that you understand, because I can't explain beyond that."

"Let's not conflate distinct matters. You felt compelled to go, and now after the fact, you can't explain. Or you won't."

This prompted a furrowing of Abigail's brow. She folded her arms. "What do you mean?"

"Oh, come. My hope was that you would attend the funeral, vent your sorrow, and return devastated and drained, but with a sense of an end to things, a closing of a difficult time. I hoped to see you move past thin-lipped defiance to sullen disregard. Then you might face a painful, long rise from grief to acceptance, and eventually find it within yourself to move on to new things."

"And you're disappointed?" Abigail winced and looked away.

"Disappointed? I'm your tutor. I can't fault you for being cautious. Rather, I suppose I would have to scold you were you incautious, as it would reflect badly upon me. No, not disappointed. Perhaps injured, although that would be self-indulgent."

"What are you talking about?"

"You practically skipped home, young miss. There's no funeral that can bring about that kind of magic. That boy is not dead, is he?"

Abigail turned and stared. She realized her mouth was hanging open, and snapped it shut.

"I see. So come. We've more walking to do."

"What are you planning?" Abigail demanded, hurrying to catch up as Arran walked off at a rapid pace. "You can't tell. He'll send another kill team! Arran, you can't tell!"

"Haven't we covered that already, young miss? Would you care to rethink your demand?"

"Arran!" She grabbed his arm. "You can't tell my father! I'll run. I swear I will."

Arran stopped. "It seems we need a repeat of our lessons in logic. Let's work through the scenario. You play Master Allton, and I'll play myself." He cleared his throat. "Master, I must report to you that instead of taking your daughter on a pilgrimage to the mountain, I led her to Deadrise Bay, the one place she was absolutely forbidden to go." He stopped and flashed a thin smile. "Now it's your turn, young miss. You're Allton. What comes next?"

Abigail smirked, looked away, and stormed down the road. "Fine. You're right," she growled. "I'm sorry."

Arran stopped. "Abigail," Arran said, causing her to stop short and spin.

"Abigail? You've never called me Abigail," she said.

"Abigail," he repeated, "to agree to accompany you to Deadrise Bay was to declare my allegiance to you and not to your father. Do you understand? The Turning master pays my wages, but you're my charge."

A slow smile spread across Abigail's face, and her shoulders loosened. "He's alive, Arran," she beamed. "He faked his death. The gray-gis didn't get him!"

"And I'll go out on a limb and propose that perhaps he hasn't forgotten the Turning girl he met. Was he there?"

Abigail blushed and continued down the road at a fast walk. "No. He had to run."

"Ah. And have you thought about your own end of things?"

"My end?"

"Logic. Logic, young miss, and practical planning. Do you suppose your role is to sit back and wait for the young Tallach to sweep in, overcome the Turning by himself, and retrieve you? If so, I'd suggest we spend more time with lessons on basic thinking."

"My end." Abigail stopped.

"Master Tagan is clearly a bright fellow. To escape the gray-gis is no minor feat." Arran chuckled. "I've heard of men running from them and enjoying a year or so, until one day the shadow falls across their door. But I've never heard of the gray-gis mistakenly reporting a contract to be complete when the mark still lived. Never. That, young miss, is something."

With a ringing laugh, Abigail turned her eyes to him. "He's a trickster. His mother as well."

"I've not met the Talla, but I've heard tell."

"Do you know, she arranged for Tagan and me to meet, during that trade mission? Not just once, but many times. My father's soldiers discovered us on the cliff walk—or so it seems, as they made it impossible for us to see each other again. Or so they thought!"

"Come. We have work to do."

"What work?"

"I wish it could be to tune your fighting skills. Unfortunately, your father wouldn't allow me to teach you Gatto fighting."

"No," Abigail grunted. "But I don't see why I couldn't learn it if I wanted to. Didn't you just say that your allegiance is to me, and not to him?"

"I have taken that position, yes."

"You could teach me." Abigail folded her arms again.

"I could. But not in time."

"In time for what?"

"In time for whatever comes next, young miss. I told your father I'd keep your mind focused. And I may have misled him slightly on the subject of that focus," he smirked, "but one thing I said was true. There's no time for your mind to wander."

"And what is it that comes next?"

"If we knew that, the task would be considerably simpler. But we can draw from what we know, and narrow the field. We know, for example, that your young man will not likely be thinking in terms of decades. His plan is not to come find you in your old age."

"I certainly hope not," Abigail huffed.

"So, we should be thinking in terms of weeks or months. Agreed? Further, we know that the Turning way doesn't involve many different paths for the daughter of the master."

"Tell me about it." The laugh was replaced by a scowl.

"And so, we have opposing forces. And when opposing forces converge, conditions become unstable. I'm going to teach you to survive it."

"You're to be moved." Dimon's jailer seemed disappointed. "I'm sorry. Guess our little jail of the tenth is no place for a civilian. At least that's how the captain sees it."

"Moved?" Dimon said, rising. "Moved where?"

"Can't say. Not my job, you know. The captain don't see fit to fill me in on the details. Good news is, it might be a fair sight better'n this stone cage you're in now. Bad news is, might be worse."

"Thanks," Dimon scowled. "And I don't suppose I have a say. Is there a jail at the Lesser Mire compound? That would be convenient."

The jailor laughed. "You might live to think different. If I was you, I'd be hoping for a cell up at High Pines. Nice little town, and the jailor's top notch. He's my cousin. Kind of a family business, us and jailin'. Oh, here they come now." He turned the lock and pulled the cell door open, and Dimon stepped out to find a pair of soldiers marching up.

"Here for the prisoner," one announced.

"Good thing you ain't here for nothin' else," the jailor said. "All's I've got is the prisoner. And now it seems I got nothing, so why don't I follow you out and I'll be heading home."

"This way." The soldiers flanked Dimon and marched him out.

"Will they return the token?" he implored. "They can't just keep it, can they?"

"Take it up with the captain," a soldier said.

In the captain's office Dimon stood and waited while the man finished his meal.

He took his time, but finally rose. "I'm sending you to a civilian jail," he said.

"I'd like my property returned."

The captain sauntered over and stepped up close. "Do you suppose we're thieves, in the tenth?"

"No, sir."

The man stared at him, then returned to his desk and fished the token out of a drawer. "Take your *property*," he said disdainfully, and tossed it to Dimon.

"What about the gold?"

"What gold?"

Dimon was marched back outside and loaded into a wagon, and at the call of the wagoner, the horses pulled and they rode out of the Tenth Station.

It seemed this Isotta had a sense of obligation, Tagan mused. Something had spooked her, and she had run from the pavilion. But she dutifully returned to his cell the next day, ordered the trainee to wait outside, and stepped up to the bars.

"I'll tell my story now."

"And I'll gladly listen." Tagan stepped closer, but kept a few paces back. He wasn't expecting a fine tale from a young girl, but anything was better than the tedium of hours alone in the cell. And while this Isotta was nothing like his ward, she somehow reminded him of Rebecca. Maybe it was the tone of defiance. Rebecca had spirit, and so did this girl.

"I didn't go all the way to Deadrise Bay. Not to the shore. I had to wait in the village. My brother—he's older than you—he tutors for a living."

"Tutors?"

"Arran knows everything," Isotta said casually. "He tutors an important woman. And this woman wanted to go to a funeral at Deadrise Bay. If you're really from there, you must know of him. The Talla's son. The gray-gis killed him. Did you know that?"

Tagan froze, but recovered quickly. "I had, uh, heard about that on the road, yes. And I'm sure my mother knows. I told you she works for the Talla. I suppose the place is in an uproar."

"Everyone was going to the funeral. You should have seen it, all the wagons. Arran brought her to Deadrise Bay so she could attend. She knew him. Closely, I think. She was very upset."

"This woman knew the Talla's son? Who is she, then?"

"Let me tell the story." Isotta flashed him a scowl. "I had to get everything to the meeting place with nobody knowing about it. I mean, not my mother or the sensei, and not Hyoso or the other know-it-all trainees who think they're better than everyone else."

"But this woman ..."

Isotta glared. "Do you want to hear my story or not? Arran told me, *Isotta, you have set camp for the three of us. You, me, and my charge. And see to it that no one discovers us, or you'll be on your way back to Three Rivers instead of on an adventure to Deadrise Bay.* And with mother away, there was no one to forbid it. So, I got Geun and one of his friends to help. They won't say anything. They know I'll kill them if they do. Anyway, I met up with Arran and Abigail, and we..."

"Wait, Abigail?" Tagan interrupted. "The woman's name is Abigail?" Tagan stepped up close without thinking. He pressed his face to the bars. "What does she look like? Is she Turning?"

Isotta backed up, and she clamped a hand to her mouth. Her eyes widened. "I wasn't supposed to tell her name! I have to go!" she said, and rushed out.

"But, wait!"

The gray-haired Gatto caught Isotta slipping around the corner and hurrying away from the dungeons. "Isotta!" he called out, and she froze. "Come here."

Isotta padded over sheepishly and bowed. "I wasn't doing anything. I was just ..."

He put up a hand. "I'm sending you to the Crossroads. Prepare your things."

"The Crossroads? But I want to stay here," the girl whined.

"And that very fact is reason enough to send you there. Only the greatest temptation would cause you to object to a trip to the Seven Crossroads. The commander arrives soon. Prepare your bag."

"Commander Stiles? But he's so stuffy."

"Not Stiles, child. Commander Riley travels to the Crossroads. He plans to stop here on the way."

"Commander Riley?" Isotta grinned. "Oh. All right. I like him."

"Assuming he agrees, you'll ride with his caravan. You'll mind yourself. You'll stay in the wagon, and you're not to pester the commander. Am I clear on this point? He's a high commander of the north. A very powerful man. It's only out of kindness to your mother that he would have his men bring you along."

Commander Riley was imposing without being especially large. He was no taller than the soldiers and no broader, but his eyes were sharp, and the graying around his temples was testament to his age and experience. Above all of that, he wore the token of the north on his collar, a silver band with three ruby cabochons set into it, and he carried himself in a manner that convinced anyone who saw him that he had earned it.

The commander flashed a smile at the girl as she hopped and waved to get his attention. He nodded at a pair of soldiers and turned back to what he was doing. The soldiers strode over to fetch the girl, brought her to the rear of the caravan, and bundled her into a wagon.

"Can't I ride up front?" she complained.

The soldiers were already closing the canvas cover. "You're to ride here, miss," one of them said.

"But ..."

Soon she was bumping down the road. She was annoyed at being sent away from the compound just when she was starting to hear interesting stories from the prisoner, and worried about having blurted out the name of her brother's ward. He had made her promise not to tell anyone that he had brought Abigail of the Turning to Deadrise Bay. But she was as excited as ever to be heading for the Crossroads, and soon put the prisoner out of her mind.

The Seven Crossroads was the seat of power of the north. In one wing of the old castle, the Tynan lord made his plans in the great war room. It was a dark-paneled room filled with map tables and lit by bronze sconces, the ceiling stained dark by the smoke of generations. In another wing, fancy meals were served, and in yet another there were sparring rooms, baths, indoor gardens, and other luxuries. Those who had stayed in the magnificent Hawk Bill Inn in the south might demote the inn to second place, were they to enjoy a night at Castle Tynan.

To Isotta, it was like an exotic vacation. While life in the Gatto compound was spartan and rigid, days at the Seven Crossroads were like moving from one holiday to another. On top of the luxuries, there were exciting people to meet. She had once peeked into the war room, and had caught a glimpse of Lord Torin himself poring over maps. He had caught sight of her looking in, and waved her in and introduced her to his generals before the servant assigned to watch her discovered her there and hurried her out. It had been the highlight of her day.

The accommodations were remarkable as well. On her first visit, they had given little Isotta an elegant room. The daughter of Master Caterione, the servant had told her, was an honored guest. But Isotta preferred to be with the other girls her age, and so on subsequent visits she always asked to be put in a room at the other end of the castle, in the servants' quarters. She would join a pack of girls to work outside early in the day, and then spend leisure hours cavorting the dark halls and playing tag games, or sitting and playing cards in the rose room.

They all loved the rose room, an elegant marble washroom with one wall to the outside covered in roses except for an open arch looking out at the gardens.

"My grandmother Shonnie tended the roses," one of the girls once told her. "Now mother tends them. One day I will."

They weren't allowed to bathe in the copper baths of the rose room. Those were reserved for the northern lord and his generals. But sitting in the room made them feel like nobility, and Isotta didn't care where she bathed, anyway.

"We wash in the creek at the compound," she had told the others. "No need for all the fuss."

"Outside?" a girl had said, eyebrows up. The others enjoyed her visits as much as Isotta did. As creatures of the castle, they were fascinated by this wild Gatto girl of the outdoors.

Late one afternoon their tea party was interrupted by the unexpected arrival of the commander and a man with the mark of a captain.

"Oh. Apologies, girls," Commander Riley nodded. "I see you've a prior claim to the rose room."

But the girls had already sprung to their feet and were scooping up the items from the table.

From the rear entrance appeared servants lugging hot water. One glared at the girls. "Out. Scat. What are you doing in here?" they scolded.

The girls rushed for the door, but Commander Riley put out a hand. "Child," he said to Isotta. "You fare well?"

"Yes, thank you, commander." She stopped and bowed.

"The word is that your mother is soon to return to Three Rivers. You'll be home soon."

"Soon?" Isotta looked crestfallen.

"Today, I think. Don't you want to go home?" Riley said with a smile. "I was told you hadn't wanted to come in the first place."

Isotta scowled. "No, it's just the prisoner." She had tried to forget about the prisoner. What could she do about it, after all? And his death would take care of one little problem for her: A dead prisoner wouldn't reveal that she'd accidentally named the daughter of the Turning chieftain as the person her brother had brought to Deadrise Bay. But she couldn't shake the feeling. She didn't want her mother to have this prisoner put to death. She liked him.

"The prisoner?"

"I do want to go home, now that you mention it. I can talk her out of it."

"Why the turnaround? Now you want to go home?"

"I don't want her to kill him. He's important in the southlands. I'm certain of it."

A woman emptied her buckets and glared at Isotta, and nodded her head toward the door, urging her to get going.

Isotta ignored her. "When can I go home? Can someone take me now?"

"Important in the southlands? What are you talking about, child?"

"Sensei Taijo doesn't like him. But that's no big surprise. The prisoner's not Gatto. He dressed like a Gatto fighter and crossed into the north, and the sensei caught him. The prisoner is Tallach."

The commander raised a single eyebrow. "Tallach. A Tallach prisoner at Three Rivers? I see. And you've taken to this prisoner."

The condescension was not lost on the girl. "I'm not in love with him, if that's what you mean." Isotta rolled her eyes. "His mother works for the Talla down at Deadrise Bay."

Riley's other eyebrow lifted. "For Undine? The prisoner's mother works for Undine? What's his name, this prisoner?"

Isotta raised her own eyebrows at the familiarity. Not *Master* Undine or *Talla* Undine, but just *Undine*. "He wouldn't tell me. But they're from Deadrise Bay. His friend Dimon got away. The prisoner gave his friend an old passage token to help him get past the border."

"A passage token."

"My mother has one, an old silver pendant with the vine carved in it."

"This prisoner has a silver passage token? And he's from Deadrise Bay?"

"I didn't say it was real," Isotta shrugged. "Even the prisoner says it's a fake. He said his mother would think it was funny if his friend actually got past the border with it."

"I see." Commander Riley scowled. "Well, there's a curious story, Isotta. Go on, now. I'll speak with you later."

She bowed with a swelling sense of pride at telling him a story he seemed to be interested in. But instead of sending her out, the commander stalked out of the room himself, and she started to worry that she might be in trouble.

11. Baldface

The trail was easy at the base of the mountain, but gradually grew steeper. Camilla led the way, Grace right behind her, and Enzo trundling along trying to keep up. It was early, but there were others on the trail already, all heading up. Camilla kept to a brisk pace to pass those they came upon. Occasionally groups of boys raced by. Camilla and Grace would fall silent and let them pass. When they were alone, they talked.

Finally Camilla decided it was time. "He's dead," she said. "They both are." She turned reddening eyes to her foster mother, and held in the tears as a look of horror crossed Grace's face. But her expression quickly turned to resignation.

"I knew. He would have come to me." She stopped and sat on a stone, and put her face in her hands. "Oh, god. And Horace."

Enzo feigned an interest in some birds and dawdled to give them privacy.

"I'm supposed to say that it was quick and painless, but I don't know." Camilla stared at the ground. "They stormed the house. I went out through the hatch."

Grace nodded her head and wiped back the tears. "Come. We should walk." She strode ahead, too fast, determined.

"But I need to know, mom. I need to know what happened." Camilla rushed after her. "You have to tell me. How did they get on to us?"

Grace slowed, her shoulders slumped, and she took hold of Camilla's arm. They leaned in to one another, talking almost in a whisper. Enzo pretended he was hiking alone, but stayed within eyesight.

"He was trying to do the right thing, Calista. I told him to leave it to Horace, but Robbie is so stubborn." She stopped and wiped her eyes. "I told him it was too dangerous. Those men. Horace took their money, but it didn't stop them. Not all of them. Walter Turcotte set up a new company overseas."

"Walter Turcotte." Camilla's teeth clenched. "Yes, I know about him."

Horace had told her about this man. When she was a little girl, her estranged father had been hired by a company in Boston to kill a man who stood in their way, and in the aftermath, an agent tracked and killed her assassin-father. The man who had hired her father to kill for him was Walter Turcotte. And when her grandfather discovered the truth about his son, that Vergil Rand had been a hit man, he launched a financial vendetta against Turcotte's company. Horace swindled millions from them, and ran. He knew men would come after him, or at least those still standing. And so he went into hiding, and set up the home in Boston as their safe house.

"Horace took his fortune, but the man didn't give up, Calista," Grace continued, "this man, Walter Turcotte. He started up again in London, and Robbie found out about it. He wanted to stop the man, before he could build a new fortune and insulate himself. Before he regained his former wealth and power. Horace told him to let it go. He'd find a way to handle it. But Robbie felt it was his duty to take over and settle things—to let the old man sit this one out. You know we both owed our lives to him."

Camilla nodded. She didn't know the details of her foster parents' background, but she knew they had been on the run, too. Horace had set up the new pretend family for the benefit of all four of them: Camilla got parents, Horace got time with his granddaughter and peace and quiet for his remaining years, and Robbie and Grace got to stop running.

"Robbie promised to stay out of it. But he didn't. He set up a Ponzi scheme. Do you know what that is?"

"Of course I do," Camilla growled. "You take investments on a fake product, and use money from the investors to pay big, pretend returns. Then other investors see what an amazing deal it is, and they put in money too. Only there isn't actually a product. You're just shuffling the money around. Then you hook the big fish and you take the money and run. It's an old one."

Grace closed her eyes and nodded. "Yes. But it still works. It requires time and effort to set up the fake paper trails and so on. But you can still haul it off. Sometimes." She turned and took hold of Camilla's arm. "And it *was* working. Robbie pulled in a dozen big investors, and made sure Turcotte Industries—that's the name of Walter Turcotte's new company in London—he made sure they saw it. And they bit. Just a little bite, but that's how you start."

"We have to keep walking," Camilla urged, realizing they had stopped on the trail and another group was approaching.

"He talked Turcotte Industries into putting a few million into a development project south of Boston. Robbie knows the area, and he got the deed to a property there. The scam was that a federal highway project was in the works to build a new ramp off the interstate that would make the property worth a fortune. Early investors could get a hundred to one, easy."

"And let me guess. They figured out the scam."

"He's not Horace. He's good, but not that good. I told him he was going too fast." Grace stalked forward, practically running, until Camilla put an arm out to slow her down.

"We don't need to run up the mountain."

"Damn it, Calista! I told him! He should have left it to Horace. Horace knew how to do this. But he had to prove himself. So he just kept pushing and pushing, and he pushed it right over a cliff." She stopped and broke into tears.

The conversation ended, and they hiked without talking. Enzo tried a few times to make small talk, but realized neither of his companions was interested in the hike, or their surroundings, or the weather—or him, for that matter. It was a silent march, one foot in front of the other up the trail. There were no complaints at the steep parts, and no comments on the scenery when they crossed streams or heard water crashing down a valley. They just walked.

It wasn't until they had cleared the tree line that Camilla called a halt, and started to look around.

"What's wrong?" Enzo said. She wasn't communing with the beauty of nature.

"Mom, we need to set aside regrets and pay attention," Camilla said. "We need to pay attention to right now."

"You think they're coming? The men who're after you?" Enzo looked down the trail and saw no one.

"They're coming. And we can't be deer in the headlights. Time to execute a plan. Enzo, you know this trail. Tell me what's ahead."

"We're above the tree line for a while, but then the trail dips down before the next ridge. After that we'll be out in the open again. Over there it's just rocks and scrub." He pointed across a valley at a rocky rise.

"Okay. Here's what we'll do. How fast can we get to those rocks?"

Funny how the connection seemed to come at moments of tension, Camilla reflected. As she and Grace jogged the stretch of valley between the ridges, she found herself looking in on Tagan again. "Not the best timing," she muttered. But she saw that Tagan was in trouble, too. Several karate fighters seemed to be lined up, ready to take him on. Tagan was facing off with them, baiting them, it seemed.

"I guess I'm not the only one getting ready for a fight." Camilla concentrated, and spoke to him. "Good. Make them angry," she said. "Get them to show their weaknesses."

"You're in danger, muse?" came his voice.

"Don't worry about me. I've got this. You pay attention to what you're doing. Look, I have to go."

Enzo sat on the downwind side of a boulder, protected from the wind. Even in the summer, it could get cold above the tree line. He clutched his ankle and cursed, and peered down the trail. "This is crazy," he muttered. "I should get the hell off this mountain. What am I doing?" But he nursed his ankle and shin, and took a drink of water.

Several people stopped to ask if he needed help and to offer to make a phone call. But Enzo waved them off. "Nah, thanks. My buddies just want to hit the top. They're coming right back."

Then men in matching black spandex pants and running shoes caught his attention. Technically they were outfitted well enough. Each carried a black backpack and wore trendy runner's gloves. They were in good physical shape, and they moved up the trail quickly. But Enzo thought they looked more prepared for a run on a treadmill than up a mountain. And they wore the spandex well, but the top half didn't quite sync with the bottom. Instead of sporty tee shirts and sleek, lightweight shells for the cold weather at the top, they wore khaki button-up shirts and didn't seem to have jackets. And the shirts failed to conceal the Kevlar vests underneath, at least for someone looking to spot them.

"Hey. Nice day for a hike, huh?" he called out to them. "Either of you happen to have an Ace bandage or something?" Enzo rubbed his ankle.

The men reluctantly slowed, glancing at a couple of other hikers who were close enough to overhear.

Enzo could see it in their eyes, the decision metric: Ignore the man nursing his ankle and look like jerks to the hikers up ahead, possibly drawing negative attention, or lose precious moments and engage?

"Sorry, man," one of them said as they slowed to a walk. "Want me to call a warden?"

A warden? This was another giveaway. You'd call the Mountain Rescue Service, not a warden.

"Nah. The guys will be back. Just wanted to see the peak."

"Okay then, bud. Good luck." They hurried on—but not fast enough to prevent Enzo from spotting the handguns at their backs.

He watched for a minute or two, looking up and down the trail. There might be more. Then he rose and followed. "Okay then," he said to himself as he hurried after the men. "Run toward the guys with guns. Good plan, Enzo." He exhaled. "But then, I didn't get where I am by being the brightest bulb in the pack, did I?"

Don't get spotted, but keep on them, Camilla had ordered. *We need as much time as possible.*

The men were going fast. Soon Enzo realized his problem wasn't going to be getting too close, but losing them altogether. He increased his pace, and felt his heart rate rise.

The last section was a steep scramble, and a feeling of panic started to overtake him. He was losing them! But then he reached the top and scanned, and spotted the two figures not far ahead, just about to descend to the valley. Camilla had told him not to use his phone. Someone could be listening. Instead he found the highest boulder and climbed up. Camilla had a scope, and had assured him she would be watching. He did his best to relay the information in hand gestures, then repeated the whole thing.

"Okay? Am I done with this now?" he muttered, climbing off the rock. "Can I go to the restaurant and beg to keep my job?" But a few steps down the trail, he stopped. "Damn it," he cursed. He couldn't just walk away.

"Two men. Handguns and backpacks. Kevlar. I think he said, black pants and brown shirts." Camilla lowered the scope.

Grace pressed the barrel of the takedown rifle to the action and clicked it into place. She wasn't sure she would need the scope, but she took it from Camilla and slid it onto the mounts anyway, and tightened it.

"Give me that. You take the .38. We might need to draw them out."

Grace hesitated, but handed the rifle to Camilla. "Are you sure?"

"Concentrate," Camilla scolded. "They're not after me. They don't know I'm here. If one of us needs to draw them out, it has to be you."

"Right, right. Sorry," Grace said. "I do need to concentrate." She pulled out the .38 and checked it. "But we don't want to get into a close-quarters fight, Calista," she said. "Not with two of them."

"No, we don't. We have to separate. See those rocks?" She pointed. "You watch from there. If I don't get them on their first approach, you come out and draw them into the open." She pointed at an open area of low scrub, where the path ran from their current spot to the south peak. "Then book it down the trail and get behind cover. I'll take a new position and pick them off from behind."

Grace looked around, but couldn't see a better plan. "Agreed."

"Just draw them out and take cover. Don't get shot, and don't get between me and them."

"Of course not," Grace scowled. "My head's in the game, now, Callie. Relax." She looked once more, and hurried across an open space to hide behind an outcrop.

Camilla hid the rifle and flashed a fellow-hiker's nod of solidarity, as a couple walked past and started down the open stretch of trail. She scanned once more, and seeing no other hikers in sight, moved behind a low ridge of stone and stretched out, getting the rifle set. She breathed in and out, calming herself and lowering her heart rate. She concentrated on relaxing every muscle. Time to be calm, and get ready to aim.

Horace had taught her many things, but there were a few that he repeated like mantras. One of these was the importance of aiming. "The old expression, *shooting from the hip*? That's for TV. If you want to hit something, you don't whip out your six-shooter and start spraying bullets. You'll hit your own foot, or your buddy. Breathe. Aim. Then shoot."

It was the same thing with a rifle. Even with a perfectly aligned scope, the shot's only as good as the shooter's ability to aim and fire. Knowing how to pull the trigger was another essential. That's what the slow breathing was for. If you start tugging at the trigger in a panicked frenzy, the safest spot will be dead center on your target's chest: you'll never hit it.

Camilla experienced a moment's concern that she wouldn't be able to confirm the targets. Hikers in black pants and brown shirts? There might be lots of them. But when the figures emerged from the valley, it was clear as can be. They walked too fast, with the stern determination of men on a mission that didn't involve enjoying the beauty of the mountain. And when they reached the open space they immediately separated. Friends on a hike wouldn't do that.

She wished she'd had time on a shooting range with this particular rifle, or at least time to adjust the scope. "It is what it is," she muttered, and with another long breath in and out, she lined up the shot and fired.

The man on the right jerked into a pivot and dropped, and after a count of one, as the sound and the sight came together in his head, the other dove behind cover.

"Shit!" Camilla cursed. She'd seen it hit, low by several inches. She had wanted a shoulder shot: Take him down, or at least take out his shooting arm. Instead she'd seen the flutter of the khaki shirt as the bullet hit him on the Kevlar. Maybe he would have a bruise.

She pivoted and fired a shot at the second man's hiding spot, and hoped for a wildly lucky break: The bullet might ricochet and take down the first man. But no such luck. Both were under cover now, and it was one against two. Camilla fired again at a flash of black and khaki racing from one boulder to another, and thought she heard a shout. His leg?

She moved the scope to the other man. "Shit!" she cursed, louder, as she caught a glimpse of a rifle barrel. She wasn't the only one with a long-range weapon, and his probably wasn't a .22.

The second man peered out and fired his handgun, from much too far away to be effective. Camilla didn't fall for it. He wanted to draw her attention away from the man with the rifle. As the barrel once again appeared, she fired again, and saw the puff of stone dust. The rifle barrel disappeared.

But a moment later another shot rang out, not the high chirp of a .22, but the lower, louder boom of a much larger caliber. A .30-06? Camilla guessed. It didn't matter. Her opponent had a deadlier weapon, all things being equal, but either bullet could do the job in the right circumstances.

"Show me that gun barrel again," she muttered.

Behind the men, some colorful jackets appeared. No! This was bad. Accidentally killing a hiker would not be okay. Aiming carefully, she fired two more rounds, and puffs of stone dust rose fifty feet ahead of the hikers, on either side of the trail. They froze, and then Camilla breathed a sigh of relief as one grabbed the other's arm and they ran back into the woods.

But that brief interval was all the first man needed. He'd changed positions, and when Camilla turned and saw the muzzle flash, she thanked the gods that the man either couldn't, or hadn't, aimed. She ducked behind the stone, pinned down as a closer shot from the handgun ricocheted off a stone a few feet away. Three more rapid shots of the first man's rifle rang out, and Camilla was just about ready to run to a new location when a shadow flickered across her line of vision.

"Don't move! I won't miss this time!" came the second shooter's harsh command.

It was a bluff. The second shooter was moving into position, but wasn't quite there yet. He was stalling for the extra seconds he needed to get the jump on her. Camilla moved the rifle into position, but a moment too slowly. The shape of the shooter appeared, and his shadow fell across her.

Then the man grunted in pain and fired. The shot went wide—way off—and Camilla stared for just a split second as her brain caught up: Someone had thrown a rock at the man. The handgun was rising again when another shadow crossed her path, and she looked in surprise at Enzo coming at the man in a flying leap. Camilla didn't wait. She whipped the rifle around and fired three rounds at the location of the first man. Maybe he wouldn't fire and risk killing his partner, but then again, maybe he would.

Enzo fought the second man, gripping his firing arm and stopping him from getting a bead on himself or Camilla.

"His leg!" Camilla shouted.

The struggle continued for another moment—and Camilla fired more rounds to keep the other man down—and then there was a howl of pain as Enzo kicked the man in the leg where he had been shot. She heard the handgun clatter to the ground.

But the first man moved again. He rolled, aimed … and then a different gun fired, and the man with the rifle stopped moving.

It took Camilla less than a second to spot Grace closing in on her kill. She turned to size up the situation with Enzo and the second man. Enzo was holding his own, but his opponent was a trained killer. She jumped out, grabbed the loose handgun and fired. The second man's body jerked and then slumped, and Enzo rolled away and whipped his hands up.

"Don't shoot!" he begged. "It's me, Enzo!"

"I'm not gonna shoot *you*," Camilla said, and then flashed him an adrenaline-soaked grin. "Check on Grace. I've got this one."

But Grace was already coming over, holding the .38 in one hand and the first man's rifle in the other. "Come on," she said. "Let's go." She nodded at the trail, where more colorful jackets peeked out from behind trees. "Quickly. We've got an audience."

Enzo slid his backpack off. "You go," he said in a low voice. "I'll stay and keep them busy."

Camilla was about to object, but she looked at his face, then at the faces in the distance peering at the gruesome scene. "Damn it. He's right, mom."

"Pretend you don't know me," Enzo added. He raised his hands and dropped to his knees.

"Yeah?" Camilla nodded. "Listen, Enzo, I'm sorry about all this."

His strained smile relaxed. "Get going. I've got some great stories for the bar, okay? Now go on."

Camilla nodded, and she and Grace turned and ran down the trail.

"I saw the whole thing," a young woman in red lycra and a heavy jacket said, looking around as if more men with guns might show up.

"Stay away from the bodies," Enzo urged, in part because he wanted to stay away from the bodies, himself.

"You were trying to stop that guy from shooting the girl—the little one—and then her mother shot this guy."

"She's not ..." Enzo started, then stopped. It was a better storyline than the one he had in mind. "She's got to be what, fifteen?" he said. "He was gonna shoot a kid. I couldn't just stand there."

"He would have shot you, too. You saved that kid's life, and then she saved yours!"

"I'm an agent, not a mountain survivalist, honey," Grace said, as Camilla led them off the trail and into the woods.

"We can't be seen," Camilla insisted. "We can't get stopped. Not this close to the peak."

"Fine. But I don't want a re-do of *Lost on a Mountain in Maine*, Calista."

"We're in New Hampshire."

"Oh, well it's all fine, then. The mountains are friendly in New Hampshire, and no one gets lost and dies here, I suppose."

"We won't die on the mountain. Come on. I have a plan."

Camilla picked her way through the woods, parallel to the path, and Grace grumbled at first, but realized the plan wasn't to bushwhack a random path to a cold death. They kept up the slow pace, several times stopping to duck and hide as they heard voices or saw colors that weren't part of the natural backdrop. Finally Camilla felt they were far enough away from the crime scene, and she led them back to the path.

"Now we run," she said. "Only on the flat parts."

Enzo had told her about the descent. There were some long, fairly flat stretches, but much of it was nearly vertical scrambles down a narrow, rocky trail. A mountain goat might move quickly, but even the fittest hiker had to climb slowly, or risk breaking a leg or worse.

The descent was hard on their knees, but Grace and Camilla were in good physical shape. They warmed and started to sweat, but kept up the fastest possible pace. Then as they came upon groups of hikers heading up, Camilla stopped and walked, and Grace fell in behind her.

Grace heard Camilla muttering. "No, probably an old pickup truck. Too easy to spot. … SUV, for certain. Big one. … Something flashy. …" This went on for a while, until she spotted three young women, one leading a little dog up the trail. "Subaru. Bet you ten bucks," Camilla muttered.

She put a hand on Grace's arm to stop her, and waved at the group. "Hey," Camilla said, "Did you park down, you know, at that little lot off the road?" They would have had to, she reasoned, since there was no other place to park. It was a hopelessly stupid question. But hikers on the trail weren't thinking about subterfuge.

"Sure. Why, is there a problem?" One of the young women picked up on Camilla's expression.

"I think I left my car unlocked. Damn it."

"It's probably okay," another woman assured her. "Nobody's gonna do something. It's just people hiking."

"Damn, I don't know. It's my sister's car. She'll kill me. She's got her school stuff in the back seat. Did you see it? Silver Honda?"

"Didn't we park right next to a silver Honda?" another woman said.

"Yeah. Those guys in the truck took the last spot near the trail. Instead of letting me put my little Subie there, they parked that giant truck half blocking the entrance."

"So it's still there? Oh, god. Good. Hey, thanks."

"I'm sure it'll be fine."

"Listen," Camilla said, "there's a couple guys up ahead waiting for us. Like, at the sign post where that other trail starts. If they're still there," she rolled her eyes, "could you tell them to just relax? It won't take me that long. We still have time to get to the top."

Camilla hurried down the trail, and Grace followed.

"Her *little Subie*?" Grace said mockingly, when they were out of earshot.

"It's an eight-hour hike. Or will be for them, anyway. At least eight hours. If there isn't already a cop at the parking lot and we can get out of here, no one will be looking for that car for a long time."

They made it to the gravel parking area and spotted the car immediately, a blue Subaru parked next to the rental. The women had made it easy. The car was locked, but the back window on the passenger side was partly down, no doubt for the dog. The driver hadn't thought to close it. Camilla got in, and soon had the engine going.

"Horace taught you that." Grace smiled, as they drove away.

Camilla sighed, and then her face hardened. "Horace taught me to survive."

"You know, he never told me. Never. But I can see it. I wasn't certain until today."

"You can see what?" Camilla glanced at Grace, then looked back to the road as a truck screamed past.

"You're not just a girl he took under his wing because you needed help."

"Oh, I definitely needed help."

"Those of us who worked with Horace back in the day, we knew he had a son, and that his son had a child before he passed. Word was, she was gone, taken by her mother. Never thought we'd ever see his grand-daughter. His real one. But here you are, Camilla."

12. Kata and Combat

Master Caterione looked like an older version of Isotta. The girl had a long way to go in terms of poise and presence, but looking at this Gatto master, Tagan could see what Isotta might become in a decade or two. The master possessed the room when she entered, confident and powerful, an absolute force.

"I met your daughter," Tagan said, looking at the imposing woman. "She seems very much like you."

"Tell me your name, and why you're in the northlands," Caterione demanded, ignoring his comment.

"We had a nice talk," Tagan continued. "She's not exactly a chatterbox, but it was pleasing to pass a little time talking with her. I'd wager she'll make a fine fighter one day."

"Your name," the master demanded, showing no sign of interest in what the prisoner had to say about her daughter.

"My name. You know, my mother told me a fine story about a fighter staring down an invader and saying, *What name will you die by*? That's what you're asking, isn't it? You mean to execute me."

"It won't serve your interests to refuse to answer," the woman said coldly.

"It won't serve them for me to talk. You fancy I'm afraid of the Gatto? I'll admit to a healthy respect. But there are others more frightening than you."

"What others? You're a prisoner at Three Rivers, a captured spy. Spies face death. Do you fear something more than death?" The woman almost smiled.

"I was telling your trainer the old saying, that to be alive is to have a chance. But I know another one, from an old muse who told it to my mother. It's the story of an elderly statesman who was put to death for always questioning those who were in charge. They didn't like him, you see, because he was always taking them to task, bringing out what was wrong in their reasoning. You Gatto would have liked this old man. Very like the Gatto, answering questions with questions and so on, forcing them to see their own errors. He had to be extremely annoying."

Caterione sat on the edge of a table, unsmiling. "This story is leading to telling me your name, perhaps?"

Tagan waved the question away. "In the end they poisoned him with a drink laced with hemlock. And as the story's told, facing death, the wise old man *drained the cup in a single breath*. Isn't that excellent? The resolve, and the logic. You see, he understood what was about to happen. And the most respectable choice, given the circumstances, was to drink the poison and die quickly."

Caterione shifted. "An old muse, you say."

"If I must die, let me die bravely. But until then I'll hold onto to the notion that to live is to have a chance."

"Noble words for a young man. Now tell me your name. We'll learn it eventually anyway, prisoner."

Once again, the talkative trainee was stationed outside his cell door. "She looks angry," the boy whispered, as if someone other than the prisoner might hear him.

"How can you tell, Geun?" Tagan said.

"The master rarely looks angry. Stern, yes. But angry? Don't provoke her."

"If the master is so angry, why am I still here? Shouldn't I have been drawn and quartered, or skinned alive and salted, or some such thing?"

"The Gatto don't resort to torture," Geun huffed. "Don't you know anything?"

Tagan smiled. "But I'm still alive. Your master thinks I know something. Is that it? She wants information. So maybe my strategy isn't so bad after all."

"It might buy you a day or two. But then what?" The boy lowered his voice again. "Do you want to die? Why not tell her what you told me, that you're no spy? That your friend is looking for his father. She might not believe you, but isn't it better than having your blood let?"

"You know, I enjoy the time with you as my guard. The other boys sit there like fungus on a tree stump, but you have spirit. You should consider getting out of this Gatto racket. My mother says it was the best decision she ever made, to get out. You could go to Deadrise Bay and train at House Kamine. Why not learn to fight and also learn to live?"

"I'll tell them my dead friend sent me," the boy said. "It will be grand."

"See? That's funny. A bit dark, but humor is rare as hunter blades around here. You must have a streak of Tallach in you. Stop in at House Kamine sometime. I'll introduce you to the sensei."

"Humph! A streak of stupid is what I have. I shouldn't talk to you."

"Tell me about the method of execution."

The boy turned. "That's your question? How will you die? You're quite the comic yourself, aren't you? I'd be begging for my life and telling the master whatever she wanted to know, on the chance she might show mercy and put off the execution."

"Tell me the method. How, where, when—all of that. Do I die at dawn, my back to a cold wall and a dozen blades hurled at me by a line of Gatto assassins?"

"Now you're rude," the boy said, and turned away.

"Oh, come. It's my last day, or nearly. I should be allowed a bit of latitude. Tell me."

"Maybe you should choose combat," the boy said. "Never mind learning how to live. You'll only get one lesson, but you'll learn how to die."

"Again, that's funny. You're … wait, combat? That's an option? I can choose combat?" Tagan stood and stepped to the door. "Tell me!"

"No one chooses combat except for old soldiers who fancy it's somehow more honorable to die cut to ribbons than to have a meal and then sit quietly while your blood drains."

"I want to know about the combat option!" Tagan demanded, then softened. "Come, now. I've been friendly, haven't I? We've had some good chats. Be a fine fellow, and tell me about it."

"Ooh, a good lookin' one. I'll bring you twigs to clean your teeth, hon," said an older woman, leering through the bars as Dimon sat on a bench, miserable. "Teeth is the secret to good health, you know. That and not bein' in jail, but I can't help with that part." She grinned and slid a tray across the floor to the bars. "Eat. Food's pretty fine here. You got lucky, at least if you stay. You see, the jailor runs the tavern."

Dimon stared at the floor.

"Could be a lot worse, hon. They could've sent you up north. Freeze your small parts off." She laughed. "I hear they keep the prisoners in open pens in the snow in the winter, like they was animals."

His new jailor had taken his clothes and given him a rough pullover to wear, and had confiscated his one possession. "Couldn't I at least have the pendant? Did he need to take that from me?"

A voice called down the stairs. "Don't be dilly-dallying down there. We got customers."

The woman turned. "Just gettin' the new prisoner his dinner."

"Come on, then. He don't need your help to eat it."

Dimon watched her leave. He sighed loudly, and shuffled over to see what she had brought. The woman wasn't wrong. It was a good meal. And the cell was a palace compared to the stone jail of the Tenth Station. There was a tiny window high on the wall at ground level that allowed him to see sunlight in the day and sometimes the legs of passersby—although sometimes the view was the bottom half of a drunk patron pissing on the wall.

He spent long days pacing his cell, staring outside, and sometimes exercising. But his mood didn't improve.

"I suppose they'll spoil tavern food for me," he grumbled one evening, picking up a chunk of brown meat in gravy with his fingers. "I'll lose my taste for it. Doesn't that count as torture?"

In spite of his growing feelings of despair, each morning and each night he scooted close to the bars and ate his meal.

"It's hopeless," he sulked. But Dimon could hear Tagan in his head: *Until you're dead, there's a chance. Work the chance.* He did his best to find small things to appreciate.

Once convinced that his new prisoner didn't have a violent temper or a foul mouth, the jailor started bringing Dimon upstairs early in the morning. He was shackled to a heavy table in the kitchen and put to work. He chopped and peeled, and learned the workings of a tavern kitchen. It didn't lead to any fine ideas for an escape, but it was better than being in the cell.

The tavern owner seemed sad all the time. The man never spoke more than a few words to his staff, and never a word to Dimon. It wasn't until one of the locals was put in the cell next to his that Dimon discovered why.

"You ain't heard that story?" the man said, very drunk, but eager to talk. "Girl got herself killed. Ranald's daughter. Right upstairs." He pointed at the ceiling. "Fellahs was fightin' an' one o' the soldiers hucked a bottle an' missed, and pegged 'er in the head. Girl fell an' caught the edge of a table, and that was that. Gone. Dead."

"His daughter died in a bar brawl?"

"She were a young wench workin' the tables, you know. Family business. Weren't in the fight as such, just got in'na wrong place. Old Ranald's been like that ever since. And that were some lot 'o years back."

Dimon started to look forward to hearing the sound of a man being dragged to the cellar door. It meant he'd have company. Some of them told new stories, and others added on to the ones he had heard already. He learned that in the incident in which the barkeep's daughter was killed, it was an officer who hurled the bottle. A northern lieutenant was condemned to death for the killing, only to be pardoned by the northern lord's second-in-command.

"He was Lieutenant Stiles back then," a man who'd gotten in a fight explained, as he spent his night in jail. "Ain't no lieutenant now. He be Commander Stiles now."

"Commander!" Dimon said, fascinated.

"Don't 'spect he'll ever set foot in this town again, though. Not that he couldn't. A commander can do whatever in hell he pleases. But I'll guess he don't want to see nothin' of High Pines."

In his morning work in the kitchens, Dimon made an effort to talk to Ranald. But all he could ever get was a nod of the head and a grimace that said he didn't want to talk just then. Things settled into a steady monotony.

And then just as his hopes were about to fade altogether, one morning instead of the usual woman bringing his meal, a dark-skinned girl stepped down the stairs. Dimon wasn't sure what to make of her. She looked to be thirteen or fourteen, and she wore a brown Gatto gi. The girl strode over and stared at him.

"Who are you?" he said. "Where's the barmaid?"

The girl said nothing, but stepped closer and continued to stare.

"You live in the village? I've not seen you in the kitchens, or outside."

"Your name," she said, folding her arms.

"Dimon," he answered, scowling. "Yours?"

"Did you settle on that, or is it your real name?"

"My mother settled on it. Or perhaps my father. I'll ask him, should I ever lay eyes on the man."

"I mean, did you and your companion settle on that name. He won't tell me his."

Dimon tipped his head. "Who won't tell you? What are you talking about, child?"

"He said your name is Dimon. Why wouldn't he tell me his own name? He'd rather die?"

"Wait. You've seen my friend? Is he all right?" Dimon rose, and the girl rapidly backed up. He raised his palms, fearing she might race up the stairs without answering. "Please tell me. You've seen him?" Dimon sat.

Then another figure strode down the stairs, and Dimon stiffened. A northern soldier. No, a commander! The man had the mark of Tynan on his collar. Had the prisoner been wrong? Had Commander Stiles from the stories returned to town?

"Isotta, what are you doing down here?" the commander asked.

She shrugged and pointed at the prisoner. "There he is."

"Yes, I see that, child. I expected to find the prisoner in the jail cell. Go upstairs and wait for me as you were instructed."

"Yes, sir." Isotta climbed the stairs, but as slowly as possible, leaning down to try to catch the conversation.

"I said go."

"Fine," the girl huffed and disappeared upstairs.

The commander stepped to the bars. "Little Isotta tells me that you were captured crossing the border."

"I'm not a criminal," Dimon argued. "I came north to find my father. Is that a crime, to wish to find my father? Wouldn't you?"

"Tell me who you are."

"It seems everyone is interested in that all of a sudden. My name is Dimon, and I live at Deadrise Bay. I've not met my father, but I'd like to. He's at Lesser Mire. Or I think so, anyway. That's why I crossed into the north. And who are you? Are you Commander Stiles?"

The man smiled, and almost laughed. "That'll be the day, when Stiles chooses to enter this town again. I'm Riley. Now, Dimon, I'm told you crossed into the north with a companion. Who is he?"

"He's … Ask him yourself, why don't you, Commander Riley? The girl just told me she's seen him, so I assume you've got him. Why don't you release us both, and let us go our way?"

"The soldiers told me you said you went north by mistake," the commander said, raising an eyebrow. "And yet you're telling me now that you wished to visit your father at Lesser Mire."

"I do want to visit him. But the Gatto chased us, and then the northern soldiers caught me. Robbed me, too. So, as you can see, it didn't work out." Dimon sat on the bench and sulked, and the commander nodded and returned upstairs.

A few minutes later, Ranald stepped into the kitchen to find the commander arguing with the girl in the brown gi.

"Isotta, I agreed to stop here and have a word with the prisoner. We've done that."

"But don't you see? Something's going on," the girl insisted. "My mother will put the other one to death!"

"The Gatto guard the borders here, child. You know that. And your mother is in charge at Three Rivers. It's her prerogative to carry out the sentence if a foot soldier of the south is found spying. In fact, it's her duty."

"A foot soldier? But she can't! I don't want her to! At least bring this one along, couldn't you? What's the harm? We can put them in a room together and get some answers. I talked to the other one. He's hiding something. He's not just an ordinary foot soldier."

"Hiding things is what spies do. Now, come."

"I want to bring him." The girl stomped her foot.

"Shall I get his things?" Ranald said, interrupting the argument.

Commander Riley let out a long sigh. "Fine. We'll carry the prisoner to Three Rivers. But Isotta, it's the master's decision whether to speak to him or not. I suspect your mother will have him bundled into the next wagon to take him right back here."

"And this plant is called *Tears of the Widow* by the Gatto. I believe you call it *Horse Bells*." Arran cupped a spray of tiny white flowers. "The Tallachs have yet another name for it, *Bells of the Dead*—because, you see, it's quite deadly. These little flowers, and the red berries that come later, and the leaves. All of it."

"As deadly as nightshade?" Abigail put a hand to her forehead. "The Talla told me the flower I wear is deadly."

Arran smiled. "I'd say your flower would give this one a fine contest."

"So, the Talla was right? Were my ancestors assassins?"

Arran patted her on the shoulder. "Let's focus on the lesson, shall we? There are many plants you can use, and some that you'd regret tangling with. And there are some that will kill you. Watch, listen, and learn."

"But I already know which plants are good to eat. I gathered all sorts of things for the kitchen when I was little."

"Do you know which are good to heal? Do you know which will help your blood to clot, and which will take away pain?"

Abigail shrugged. "You think I need to prepare for that?"

"Would you like to return to the volume on the history of the Turning leadership? We could do that instead."

"No."

"Then listen. Do you see this vine? Not that one. That one will disturb your skin. This one, though, this is a very fine vine. Extremely useful."

Abigail nodded and watched as her tutor cut a section to demonstrate its flexibility and strength. She couldn't imagine the scenario in which knowing the perfect rope vine would be the trick to survival, but she listened. When she returned to her room at the end of the day, she was tired, and slept well. She woke the next morning still unsure of the importance of learning the minutia of the natural world, but thinking it was better than poring over tomes of the Turning while her mind wandered to worrying about Tagan.

After days of studying plants, Arran abruptly switched to a subject that seemed more practical to Abigail. "Running, young miss," he said, as they reached the safe area beyond the sight of the soldiers. "Now that you know something about the trees and the plants, and a bit about the rocks and the earth, it's time to learn how to run through them."

"I've worn the new shoes as you instructed." She hiked up her pants cuffs to show low leather shoes. "And the stockings."

"The stockings are important. Running will blister your feet if you don't protect them. Now imagine a boy growing up in Deadrise Bay. The ocean is on one side and the forest on the other. In which direction do you think his attention is focused?"

Abigail smiled. "Both. The food tents and merchants on the terraces would be a draw, but the forest would be, too."

"You make a good point. But as we don't have an ocean on hand, let's turn our attention to the forest. Let's say there's a boy named Tagan, and he's ten or eleven. He's no longer a small child. He's starting to learn about the world. Suppose he and his friends have absconded with treats from the food tents, and would like to be able to get away and enjoy them. You might imagine mischievous boys would want to make their way into the woods quickly. So, tell me, young miss, if little Abigail of the Turning were there, could she keep up?" He raised an eyebrow.

"I'm imagining ten-year-old Tagan is adorable. Abigail would run her little legs off to keep up."

Arran smiled. "All right, then. But let's perhaps temper the enthusiasm. Your father wouldn't approve if you were to return with bloody gashes or a broken leg."

The mention of her father soured her mood, and prompted her to stop talking and set out. Abigail ran into the forest.

"I choose combat," Tagan said, his usual playful smile pinched into a smirking scowl. "I understand your code allows me to choose, and I so choose."

Surprising him, the master smiled back. "The code allows it, and you may so choose," Caterione said. "But understand, boy, you're choosing death." Her stern expression returned. "You're choosing death instead of choosing to tell me who you are and why you crept over the border pretending to be Gatto. If you have something to say, say it now."

"If I win, I'm free to go?"

"Wouldn't that be fine," Master Caterione huffed. "Then the strongest, best fighters would be exempt from the law. No, boy. That's not how the Gatto operate. You Tallachs have gray-gis who operate like that."

Tagan shivered, and lost his scowl.

"But there are no gray-gis among the Gatto. If you win, you're banished from the north. We deliver you across the border. But you will not win."

"I accept," Tagan nodded. "Combat."

Caterione looked at him, then turned away and nodded to her men. They took the prisoner out of the room.

Later the sensei came to his cell. He opened the cell door and stepped inside. Over the man's shoulder, Tagan saw trainees standing in the corridor.

"Well, young Tallach," the sensei said, "you might not know this, but it's believed that the historical roots of your fighting style are common to that of our people, although less ancient. Do you know the three pillars of Gatto?"

The sensei raised a hand, and from the corridor the trainees immediately chanted, "Form! Strength! Skill!"

Tagan looked past the sensei. These were the three who had chased him in the woods. The blond boy had put a rope around his neck and repeatedly yanked it as they walked. The larger boy with a shaved head had been out of breath from the run, and the third, who was older, was the one who had tackled him near the campfire.

"Exactly so," the sensei said. "Form, strength, and skill in combat are the pillars." He flashed a contented smile at Tagan. "Were you to return to your Tallach pavilion, you might eventually come to learn that it's the basis of your own fighting style, although the third pillar is divided into two in the tradition of the Tallachs. Form, strength, endurance, and courage. Those are the trials of the Tallachs. Surely you know of those four."

"Did you read that in a book?" Tagan almost yawned. "The old poem of the four tiers, *The Tallach Fighter's Lament*. It starts with, *Show us your form, and carve in the mark*, and goes on from there. Yes, I've heard that, as has every novice who ever stepped foot into a Tallach pavilion. Little kids chant that when they're playing with sticks."

"Good, then. And so perhaps you see the lesson."

"What, that you Gatto know the old chant, too? So what?" Tagan was getting annoyed by the sanctimonious Gatto sensei.

"A convict who chooses combat faces the Gatto triad: form, strength, and tactical skill."

Tagan scowled. "I thought it was a fight to the death."

"We don't allow common road thieves or men who kill in drunken brawls to face off against a Gatto fighter. Nor do we allow young, green trainees to do so. If you want to fight for your life, you must first demonstrate that you're worthy. You'll compete in kata. That's the first trial."

"Kata? I'm to compete with one of your fighters in performing a Gatto kata?"

"With a Gatto fighter?" the sensei smiled. "We wouldn't waste their time. You'll compete with the trainees." The three in the corridor stood at attention. "It will provide them an opportunity to practice. As for the kata, show us a Tallach kata if you wish, or whatever exercise you like. You must show your form."

"Fine. I show you my form." Tagan rolled his eyes. "Then what?"

"You must show form at least the equal to that of your opponent. If you do that, you will you be allowed to proceed and show your strength."

Tagan wanted to ask, *what if my opponent's form is better than mine?* but he knew better than to give them the satisfaction of suggesting he might lose. He waved an impatient hand. "And?"

"You fight to pin your opponent. The Gatto challenge rules apply."

"Challenge rules," Tagan said sourly. "And what are those? I suppose I'll be unarmed, but my opponent will have blades."

"No blows, and no blades. It's a contest of strength. You compete to pin your opponent for a count of ten."

"All right. So, I show I can do a kata and then I wrestle someone, and then finally we get down to it?"

"Should you make it to the third round, you fight with blades. But hold for a moment. Do you see the lesson? It's not a mere curiosity that your ways stem from Gatto ways. It's a matter of cold truth. The Gatto tradition is far older than yours. You'll not win."

"The lesson is that I should plan to lose? That's not a very good lesson."

"The lesson is that you face a challenge much older and greater than you, young Tallach. It's not too late for you to choose another path. The master asks your name and your purpose for crossing the border. Why not tell her, instead of dying in the caves?"

"Ha!" Tagan huffed. "Because, old man, no matter how impressed you Gatto are with yourselves, there are more dangerous enemies than you. I'll take my chances with your three pillars."

The old man's eyebrows lifted, but he said nothing.

"And what do you mean, *in the caves*?" Tagan asked, as the man rose and walked out of the cell. "I'd guessed the competition would be up on that plateau above the river that I saw on my way here. I figured that for the spot. We fight at dawn, and my dead body is cast into the abyss. Something like that."

The master closed the cell door and stepped down the corridor.

Then Tagan witnessed something he hadn't expected. Instead of one of the boys hopping onto the stool and the others following the master out, the three trainees in the corridor immediately started to argue.

"I get the death watch," the blond-haired boy said. The door at the end of the corridor closed with a bang, and he raised his voice. "I ranked first."

"He said you won the match," said the dark-haired boy. "There was no promise about taking the death watch. I'm your superior. I claim it."

"Why should you claim it, Hyoso?" The blond boy poked the dark-haired one. "Because you're the sensei's pet?"

"You beat me because you cheated, Shilla," the dark-haired boy said, as if it were a plain fact, "As you always do, you and Sado. I'll take death watch. Neither of you deserves it."

"Cheated?" The other two said at the same time. Tagan's eyebrows rose as the big boy grabbed the dark-haired one and pinned his arms back. The blond boy punched him in the stomach. The dark-haired boy took the hit with a grunt, and stared accusingly.

"Let me hear you say that again," challenged Shilla. The blond boy punched him again without waiting for an answer.

"Unhand me!" Hyoso demanded, trying to cloak his shortness of breath. "You'll not drag me into your petty competition. Go on and take the death watch. And as you watch him, know that this Tallach boy could beat you in a fight as easily as I could."

Shilla punched him a third time, and then Sado shoved him away. Hyoso skulked down the corridor clutching his stomach, and left.

"I'll tell you what," Sado said. "You take death watch. I'll get my sleep. I want to be ready to fight him."

"You?" Tagan butted in. "Why would I fight you?"

"Are you afraid?" Sado taunted. "I suppose you could pick me for kata, and then face one of the little ones." He shoved the blond boy's shoulder and laughed. "That what you're planning? Fight a little one?"

The blond boy pushed back. "I'll fight him, Sado. I'll fight him right now! You think this Tallach trash can beat me?"

"You three are the ones I choose from?" Tagan stepped closer to the door. "Hyoso, who just left in shame, and a couple of trainees who disgraced their superior?"

"We won the competition."

"I won it, you mean," complained Shilla. "You came in third."

"Yeah, sure you won." Sado laughed, then held up a hand. "Calm down. He'll die tomorrow, anyway."

"I'll show you right now," Shilla insisted.

The door lock turned, and Tagan dropped to fighting stance as Shilla stepped inside.

"Here. You might want these," Sado said with another laugh, and tossed in a pair of wooden truncheons before pushing the door shut. He pressed his face to the bars to watch the fun.

Tagan might have objected that it wasn't a fair fight, but he could see that a fair fight wasn't the plan. The boy came at him, swinging the truncheons.

In the end it was almost a fair fight, anyway. Tagan bloodied the boy's face, and thought he might have cracked a rib. If the big boy Sado hadn't kicked open the slot at the base of the door and shoved a dinner tray in at just the right moment for Tagan to slip on it, Shilla would have been beaten in spite of being armed. Instead Shilla pegged Tagan in the back of the head as he fell, and the prisoner went down.

"Let anyone try to say I can't take him in a fight," Shilla muttered, and stepped outside to spend the rest of his shift safely on the other side of the iron door.

When he came to, the room was dark except for the glow of a lantern outside his door. The oil lamp in his cell had been spilled in the fight. Tagan groaned and tried to clear his head.

"I saw that. The little shit."

Tagan looked up, but it wasn't the boy in the corridor speaking.

"They can't do that. It's not fair."

"Camilla?" Tagan said softly. "You saw? Hyoso is the one who ran me down, and captured me. And Sado and Shilla were there, too. The sensei ordered them to kill Dimon."

"And you drew them away from your friend. Nice. That's a win," came the words in his head. "And there's no point in talking to the sensei, then. He's probably in on the cheat. And I guess you wouldn't really want to tattle on them, anyway. I wouldn't. I'd just kick their butts."

"I certainly can't speak with the sensei," Tagan muttered. "He might replace them with others that I've not met and can't prepare for."

"An even better point. The old *evil that you know* thing. Better to prepare for an opponent you know about. I'm guessing the older one, Hyoso, is the best fighter, right? And probably has the best style. So, it's between Shilla and that big galoot."

"Big galoot?" Tagan echoed.

"For the first round. I heard the sensei. You have to do a kata, then you have to wrestle, then fight. You want the weakest one for the third round. That's the one that counts, right? So, you don't want Hyoso for round three. And I'm thinking that blond weasel will be easier to beat than the big one. So maybe the big dude for kata, then Hyoso for wrestling? That one could be tough. But then it's a cake walk with the little blond shit. You can definitely take Shilla in a fair fight. You almost beat him in an unfair fight."

"Cake walk?" Tagan rubbed the lump on his head. He groaned again.

"Easy. It means easy. The expression dates back to slave plantation days. The cake walk was a dance. But, god, I sound like Horace. Never mind that. The point is, you have to decide. Make your plan. That's how I'd play it, Sado, then Hyoso, then Shilla. But even if you make your picks in advance, you want to look for tells, so you can make adjustments if you have to."

"Tells?"

"Tells. Don't you have that word? Like the one who just clocked you with the blackjack. Shilla. Did you see him looking at his big buddy for approval? That's a tell. It shows he's not sure about what he's doing. Watch for things the others do that tell you something. Find their weaknesses, and the signs that reveal what they're thinking or planning to do. Tells. You understand?"

"Yes, all right. Look for signs of weakness." His head was starting to clear. "You're right, of course, muse. I must do that. Any fighter would."

"Sometimes taunting helps. Taunt them and watch how they respond. Look for a lack of discipline. That's definitely good to know."

"Taunt them?" He sat up and looked at the light coming through the barred opening. "Is that how you were taught? You sound like my mother."

"What, you think Horace's words in your mother's head were about honor and sticking to a respectable code of conduct? I was taught to find a way to win—by the same man who taught your mother to survive."

A shape suddenly blocked the light. "You won't find any signs of weakness, Tallach trash," the gloating boy in the corridor said. "Tomorrow I'll finish up where I left off."

Tagan struggled, but rose to his feet. "Do you think so, Shilla? You'll never be Gatto. They'll expel you when they discover you can't win without cheating."

"Good," Camilla said in his head. "There you go. Insult him. That's a good start."

"And whether you defeat me or not is immaterial," Tagan said. "If you do, you'll remember tomorrow as the day you won and yet lost, because Taijo will never advance you. The best you'll be is his lap dog, the failed trainee that he forces to do his dirty work."

"I'll be ready for you," Shilla said, but his grin had faded. He returned and sat on the stool.

"Not much time for it, though, muse," Tagan sighed. "Tomorrow morning."

"You have hardly any time left at all," the blond boy laughed.

"Silence, failed Gatto!" Tagan barked, causing the boy to jump. "I've no interest in your foolish words. Sit silently at your post and leave me in peace."

"Good, good," Camilla encouraged him. "Now, listen. You have to pick your opponents, right? But did he say you have to choose quickly?"

"He said nothing."

From the corridor came Shilla's defiant voice. "Mutter to yourself, then, convict. Tomorrow you die."

Tagan moved to the far end of his cell and faced the wall. "There was no instruction as to how I must choose. Only that I must."

"Play for time. Don't you Tallach have customs? Tell him you demand to be allowed to choose in your own way."

"In our way? We don't have this kind of trial at all."

"Do they know that?"

"Ha." Tagan smiled. "I see. No, I'm certain they've never heard about our customs for a condemned man choosing his executioner. I'm sure, because I'm just about to make it up."

"Ah. You're learning!"

"Where are my blades?" Tagan complained, as he was led from the cell. They had given him his knife belt, but not the knives. "I chose combat. I demand that you give me my blades."

"Patience," the sensei scolded. "It would be wise not to wish that to come too soon."

"We've been through this already," Tagan growled. "To be alive is to have a chance. But not to have my blades returned is unfair."

"You've two trials to pass, to earn the right to have blades in those sheathes. And even if you should get that far, it will be a short, final time that you'll carry them, convict."

Tagan was put in leg irons and loaded onto a hand-drawn cart. A pair of young trainees stepped up, glared at him, and pulled.

They quietly complained as they headed the procession. "Why can't he walk?" one boy grumbled. "This is a stupid tradition."

"Why can't we sit and he pull us? Isn't he the criminal?" the other added.

But the old sensei waved an annoyed hand, ordering them forward. They pulled him along a path to the gate, where they were met by the rest of the procession. Hyoso, Shilla, and Sado took the lead. Behind them were four Gatto fighters. Then came Tagan in his cart, and then the sensei. Master Caterione took up the rear.

"He can't win, can he?" one boy whispered to his companion.

"Silence," the man said. "You draw the cart. The condemned rides. That will be all."

As he was hauled along the trail, Tagan turned the question over in his mind: Even if he demonstrated superiority, would they allow him to win? Two of the three champions had already cheated. Would there be a surprise deviation from the expected steps, something to throw him off? Or would they simply kill him anyway, even if he won?

But he had to push these thoughts away. He couldn't tell the master his name. That would lead to the gray-gis finding out, which would be to escape the pot only to land in the flames. And would it even gain him anything in the short term? By his mother's accounting, Master Caterione was a cold tool of the Gatto, with neither compassion nor any sense of justice outside of the rigid rules of their code. Telling his name could lead to a faster execution, for all he knew.

And there were other people to consider. What would happen to Dimon if the gray-gis discovered that their target had escaped and made fools of them? He would be a target for retribution. The gray-gis were ruthless, and harbored grudges. Even Abigail might become a target.

"I thought we were to face off in a cave," Tagan said, as the young boys pulled the cart onto a magnificent stone plateau above the gorge.

The Gatto sensei and his trainees had led him past this gorge on the way to the compound, after they had captured him. Eons of flowing water had carved a deep cut, and the falling water was still at work. Forced to half its regular width, the river moved over a waterfall and crashed into the cut with a singular fury. In the gorge above the rushing water everything was green and wet. Blankets of ivy covered the stone cliff faces, and stunted trees reached out for a bit of sunlight.

Tagan admired the natural beauty. Up on the plateau, the sound of the raging water was a muted roar, and he could taste the spray as he was pulled from the cart. If these were Tallach lands, this place would be a favorite spot.

"We're to fight here, after all? I'd guessed this might be the spot." He looked at the edge of the cliff, feeling déjà vu. Another jump off a cliff? He knew about waterfalls and gorges. The water would especially deep right at the base of the fall, where it would have carved a bowl. If he could figure his jump just right …

But then a black hood was pulled over his head, and he was lifted to his feet and held by the arms. Someone knelt and unshackled his legs.

"Walk," the sensei said, close to his ear. "Don't try to run or you'll be shackled again."

It was a long walk, but blessedly devoid of talking. It allowed Tagan to concentrate on his surroundings and consider his strategy. He felt the warmth of the sun overhead and hard stone underfoot. After a while he stepped onto grass, and the temperature dropped. They were in the woods. Then the grass turned to rough, loose stones, and a pair of Gatto fighters took over for the trainees. They took hold of his arms and gave instructions.

"Step to this side. Two paces, then climb. Down three steps. Down three more."

He felt the air grow cool and then cold, and the voices began to echo. They were entering a stone passage, moving underground and descending, and it was getting wetter. The trail went steadily down, the trainees several times lifting him off the ground altogether to carry him past an obstacle. Tagan imagined sharp rocks and deep crevasses.

After a long descent and a walk through more wet passages, they stopped, and the hood was pulled off. The cavern was impressive, larger than the main cavern at Deadrise Bay, and with a higher ceiling. Water dripped from the ceiling and ran down the walls in rivulets, across the floor and into a narrow, black river. The floor was smooth, wet stone, the water pooling in black puddles that reflected the yellow of oil lamps, which had been placed all around the perimeter and along the water's edge. There was an odor of sulfur, but not from matches. It was the natural odor of the place, deep underground.

The two young trainees who had pulled him in the cart were not allowed down, it seemed, as the execution party now consisted of the Gatto fighters, the trainees who would compete with him, the sensei, and the master. He expected to hear a recitation of his crimes, a declaration to the world of the charges against him. He supposed there might also be an incantation or prelude about the sanctity of the killing ground, and the tradition of the Gatto. Maybe he would be invited to beg for mercy or to offer his final words. Instead the trainees formed a line in the middle of the space, and the others formed a circle around him. The circle widened, and then without saying a word, Master Caterione pointed at the sensei, marking the start.

"Choose," the old man said, waving an arm as the trainees snapped to attention.

"We do kata first, am I right?" Tagan said, stalling. But no one moved or spoke. "I see," he grumbled. "You informed me already, and it would be inefficient to repeat things, wouldn't it?" He smiled sourly, but no one else did, so he turned to the sensei. "Might I be allowed to choose in the Tallach fashion? Our code provides that a man forced to face an opponent in lethal competition has the right of inquiry. May I inspect them, and speak to them if I choose? It's our way."

"You may," said the sensei with a dismissive nod.

Tagan moved close to the blond boy. He had already made his first pick. Camilla had been right. The big boy Sado was the logical choice for the first round. But he stared at Shilla anyway, and smiled as the boy flinched.

"Yes, Camilla, I saw that," Tagan muttered, just loudly enough for his opponents to hear. He stared for an extra moment as if sizing up the blond boy, and then shook his head. "Too jumpy," he said with a frown, and moved to stare at the next boy, the older, dark-haired Hyoso. "And this one is too quiet. He's hiding something. Possibly he's troubled at having to bear the secret of his companions' cheating."

In the north, this would rightly have been taken as an insult, and would have drawn a response. But the Gatto trainees stood quietly and allowed the spy to inspect them and utter his taunts.

When Tagan came to the big boy, he pushed his face up very close. "Did you say something, Sado?" he asked loudly, adopting the tone of a sensei scolding his student. The boy was silent, but couldn't resist an eye roll. "Ah. This one," Tagan said. "I'll show my form to this one. It'll be a cake walk."

"What's a cake walk?" Shilla whispered through his teeth at Sado.

The boy expelled a breath of annoyance, and ignored his companion. Sado wanted to be chosen for a fighting round, not kata. But he straightened, and as Tagan stepped back a few paces, Sado backed up as well. Shilla and Hyoso returned to the circle.

"Who goes first?" Tagan asked the sensei, in the tone of a man challenging the local riffraff to a competition.

"Show your kata, Tallach," the man said in an even tone.

"I start? All right, then. Good." He bowed to the trainee, turned and bowed to Master Caterione, and notably not bothering to bow to the sensei, moved into a stance and started on the kata he had shown Isotta earlier.

They all stood rigidly at first, but as Tagan worked smoothly through the moves, he saw the faces change. The fighters worked to keep their neutral expressions, but he could tell they were surprised. The trainees started to glance at the sensei and then at the master. Midway through he saw his opponent's hands tighten into fists.

"There's a tell for you," Tagan said quietly. "The fists. Are you counting, Camilla?"

"And watching," came her voice in his head. "That's an interesting exercise. Teach me one day."

When he finished, Tagan bowed to the boy and to the master, and stepped to the edge of the circle, chin up. Sado bowed to Tagan, his sensei, and the master, and offered an acceptable execution of the second Gatto kata. When he finished, Tagan acknowledged it with an over-solemn nod of his head and a fist of solidarity—which his fellow Tallach trainees at House Kamine would have understood as sarcastic, but it seemed to confuse the boy.

The sensei glanced at the master, then looked at Tagan. "The first round is yours, condemned," he said dully.

Tagan almost felt guilty. The big boy looked crushed. His shoulders drooped as he stepped back to the circle. Then the remaining two stepped into the ring again and stood at attention. Tagan thought it might be funny loudly to reject both of them and to suggest they go get one of the little boys, who might have a better chance. But the only one who might share his sense of humor was Geun, the trainee who talked to him while on watch. And Geun hadn't been invited.

He studied the two. Shilla flashed a smug grin as Tagan stepped up, and for a moment Tagan thought the boy might actually break his stance and say something. But the sensei was looking right at him, and the boy held his tongue.

"Hm," Tagan said, almost in a whisper, so that only the two facing him could hear, "this one hasn't the strength of a novice. Perhaps it wouldn't be fair." He moved on, not needing to look, to know the boy was fuming. He looked at the older boy. "What of you, though?" he muttered. He had a pretty good idea that Hyoso could fight. But he needed more information. He turned to the sensei. "I'll ask questions, if I may."

"As you wish," the sensei said, with a note of annoyance at having to repeat himself.

"We'll start with you." He pointed at Shilla—and silently kicked himself for not having planned this part more carefully. What questions should he ask? He was drawing a blank.

Then Abigail popped into his head. He remembered walking with her above the sea, and their long talks in his mother's quarters, and the stories she told him about her life at home in the Turning compound. Maybe it was the rigid order of the Gatto that brought the Turning to mind. The

Gatto were similar to the Turning in some ways, their stuffy adherence to routine, in particular. He smiled as he remembered Abigail complaining about her trainer and his relentless three morning questions.

"Yes," he said to himself. "Good idea, Abbie. Thank you for the inspiration." He stepped up close, and kept his voice very low. "What did you say you would accomplish yesterday?" he asked Shilla.

"What do you mean?" Shilla said. "Do you choose me? I'm ready. But I'd rather kill you in the third round."

"Answer my question," Tagan demanded, and then dropped his voice once again to an almost inaudible, accusatory low, as if it would be indiscreet for the question to be overheard. "What did you say you would accomplish yesterday?" he repeated, folding his arms.

"I didn't say ..."

"Do you mean you hadn't planned to accomplish anything at all?" he said in a louder voice that everyone in the circle could hear.

Shilla stared, flustered.

Dropping his voice again, he continued. "Sado gave you twin truncheons, and you set on me. That was an accomplishment, wasn't it? And clearly it was planned, or else why would your big friend bring truncheons to my cell? But you must answer for yourself. I demand it. What did you plan to accomplish yesterday? Was it to execute a strategy of cheating, and defeat a defenseless opponent?"

"I'll beat you in the ring," the boy hissed back. "There are no truncheons here. Come, let's get to it."

Tagan smiled. He was getting to the boy, and as Camilla liked to remind him, an angry opponent is a vulnerable one. He moved to Hyoso. "Your companion is understandably uncooperative, and I reserve the right to ask more questions of him," he asserted out loud—and saw those in the circle respond, several raising their eyebrows, and the master folding her arms and frowning. Even the sensei flashed a scowl at the blond boy. Shilla snapped to attention, and Tagan looked upward and grinned. "Another point to me, muse," he said.

"I saw that, too," came Camilla's response. "Good. Keep going. Get them to show their weaknesses."

"Ask your questions, convict," Hyoso said. "I'll answer."

Tagan leaned in and dropped his voice again. "What did you say you would accomplish yesterday?"

The boy stared back, but hesitated. "I made no assertion."

"I see. And were you successful? Did you accomplish nothing?" Tagan smiled, and turned to flash a grin at the sensei. "You have peculiar traditions, sensei," he said, loud enough for all to hear. "It seems your trainees start each day committed to accomplishing nothing. Is that how you train them?"

The sensei didn't respond, but Tagan thought he'd caught a reaction from the master. Her folded arms tightened.

"Wait. What's your strategy, here?" came Camilla's voice. "You don't have to fight the sensei. Why are you talking to him?"

"Don't worry about me. I've got this," Tagan smiled. He returned to his quiet interrogation. "And what did you accomplish? Come, think. Aside from being assaulted and then evicted by Sado there, who just showed us a schoolboy's version of a Gatto kata."

"I was selected," the older boy whispered back, and almost smiled. "The sensei selected me to oppose you."

"A good answer!" Once again Tagan turned to the sensei. "The advance planning isn't there, but at least this one knows that he in fact did something yesterday."

"And I'll defeat you today," Hyoso said, almost cracking a smile.

"Aha," Tagan crooned, again in a barely audible tone. "You anticipate the third question. Clever of you. Tomorrow you'll reflect on today, and you'll know that you failed. But it's a start. Hold, though. We need to revisit the second question, of what you did yesterday. You said you were selected. But what you mean is that you won, and yet your companions cheated, and so you came in third instead of first. Isn't that right?"

The boy said nothing—but Tagan sensed a tightening of his jaw.

"Better," Camilla said.

"You're the best fighter, aren't you, Hyoso? The best student in the pavilion. It seems as if many of them must recently have gone out into the world, for I can't believe you're the best Master Caterione can produce."

Hyoso glared.

"Possibly others were given the nod and have moved on, but you were kept behind. Is that it? You're older than the others. Maybe you're on track to teach one day. Is the sensei grooming you to run the little ones through their exercises? It would be honorable enough. Of course, you'd need to earn their respect." Tagan halted, and tipped his head. "Now there's something, Camilla. Did he allow Shilla and Sado to evict him from the dungeons because he's well disciplined? Or was it that he fails to garner their respect, and so they're able to treat him that way?" He leaned in close. "And you couldn't let the sensei know, could you? You couldn't make a ruckus. You'd look weak. And Shilla knows that, don't you?" He raised an eyebrow to the blond boy.

"One day they'll learn," the older boy said. "Respect, that is."

"Will they?" Tagan tipped his head. Once again, he turned and looked at the sensei. "How many times reflecting on yesterday does it take, sensei, to be prepared to accomplish what one sets out to do today? I don't think your trainees know. Not even Hyoso, here, who's clearly stronger, and certainly must be the best fighter of the three. And so I choose Shilla for this round." He pointed at the blond boy.

The blond boy visibly flinched, and Master Caterione's eyes narrowed.

"What are you doing?" Camilla challenged. "Why aren't you picking Hyoso?"

"Score another two tells for me, Camilla," Tagan muttered in response. He dropped into a fighting stance as Shilla stepped forward.

"You want the weaker one?" came Camilla's surprised response. "Why?"

Tagan raised his voice. "Because the stronger one is unsure of himself. I can beat him in the final round. He's ..."

"Stop!" cried Master Caterione. She strode into the circle.

Tagan whipped his arms out to signal an end to the match before it had even started, and he turned to face the Gatto master and bowed. "I've made my choice. I choose Shilla for this round."

She stepped up to him. "Tell me, condemned, what were your questions? I couldn't quite hear."

Tagan moved back a pace and turned to the sensei. "Is this part of the rules? I have to explain myself to the master? That's not part of our tradition. The questions are for the opponents alone."

"You deemed the older boy the stronger of the two, and the better fighter," Master Caterione said. "I could see that much. The correct strategy would be to choose the stronger opponent for the nonlethal round, and the weaker for the final trial. But you chose the weaker first. Why? What questions did you ask that led you to make the opposite choice?"

"Hyoso revealed a weakness, too," Tagan said with a shrug. "Shilla wouldn't answer me, because when I asked, *what did you plan to accomplish yesterday*, the correct answer was, *to cheat, so that the trials are a cheat*."

Master Caterione stared.

"Damn it," Camilla warned, "you're going off script. You're not supposed to piss off the master. Bad idea!"

"I said I've got this," Tagan repeated, waving a hand. He looked at Caterione. "One might argue, master, that I didn't know to a certainty. But when I asked, *and what did you accomplish*, I knew the correct answer. Ask Sado if you doubt me."

"Those were your questions?" The master's eyes narrowed.

"Hyoso tipped his hand by answering the third question before I had a chance to ask. He said he had been chosen to oppose me, and then immediately told me that today he would defeat me, before I could ask, *and what will you accomplish today?* Had he been sure of himself, he wouldn't have been so eager to boast."

"Who told you to ask those questions?" Caterione spun to the sensei.

"Taijo, you said Isotta spoke with him. Did this come from my daughter?"

"Isotta?" Tagan said, interrupting before the sensei could answer. "Do you think I learn strategy from little Gatto girls? The questions reveal the weaknesses, and what they're thinking at the moment. Hyoso is irresolute, so I can beat him. Last night Shilla could barely take me down even armed with twin truncheons and with the help of his companion over there. But he would be dangerous in the final match, because he'd break the rules. I'd rather defeat him in the second trial, without blades."

The sensei stared at him, rage showing on her face. "What are you saying, Tallach?"

And Camilla's voice came to him. "Yeah, what the hell are you doing?"

Then he saw the master's expression. "I'm ... Oh, hell in a basket, Camilla," he muttered, turning to see all the eyes focused on him. "I've overplayed it."

Master Caterione flicked a stern hand, and Shilla and Hyoso backed up until they were fully out of the circle. They turned away and knelt on the ground. She pointed at Sado, and he dropped to his knees at Shilla's side.

"Tell me who you are, condemned," the Gatto master said. "For clearly you know more about the Gatto than you're letting on, and more about fighting than I'd expect of an ordinary southern spy. Tell me who you are, and I'll show mercy. Or we'll move to the third round right now, and you can draw blades against me."

"No, no!" came the voice in his head. "Damn it. This is what happens when you go off script! I hope you've got a new plan."

"That wasn't the deal," Tagan said, backing up.

"Your companion, the boy you snuck over the border with. You realize we have him. It seems he went the wrong way, when you parted. Ran north, right into the arms of soldiers of the Tenth."

Tagan stiffened.

"That's right. The northern guard intercepted him. He's in a cell at the Tenth Station. Perhaps you'd like to consider where he might be sent from there. The northern soldiers won't hold him for long. He may already be in another place. And he could be sent to yet another."

"What other place?" Tagan demanded, but her threat was plain enough.

The master stood unmoving, staring at him and waiting for an answer. "Tell me," she repeated, "or choose your blades, and leave your friend's fate in other hands."

Tagan backed up past the edge of the circle, and the fighters turned to look at him. He reached the water's edge and held up a hand as if thinking. Everyone fell silent. Behind him he heard the water. The rumble was louder to the left. The waterfall must be in that direction.

"Blades, you say." He put a hand to his chin and drew in a deep breath.

"I brought a fine one with me. Did you bring it, Taijo?"

"I did, condemned, as I thought you might choose to die with it."

Tagan glanced at the sensei, but then looked down. He tipped his head down and rolled it to one side and then the other, slowly, as if working to loosen his neck. "As it's rightly mine, I should like it returned. As for dying, well ..." And then he turned and dove without finishing his sentence.

Everyone stared in mute astonishment as the prisoner plunged into the black water and vanished.

The sensei began barking orders. "Hyoso, after him! Shilla, you as well. The rest of you, out! Half of you go up, half down to the river. Quickly! You know the outlet, Sado. Guard it. Run!"

The Gatto fighters raced across the cavern to the exit, followed by Sado, and Hyoso pulled off his gi jacket and dove.

Shilla froze. "After him? In there?" he said, horrified. "But master ..."

"Then follow the others," he barked, irritated. "We'll discuss this later." The sensei turned to find the master standing stock-still, jaw clenched, staring at the water. "Master," he said, and bowed.

"Your trainees set upon the prisoner with truncheons? And what's this about a blade?" Caterione said, not turning to look at him.

Taijo bowed again. "The condemned wore one Gatto blade, master, and a southern blade," he said, dodging her first question.

"A Gatto blade?" She spun.

Taijo hurried to the side and drew a leather satchel from a pack. "Here it is. He claimed his mother gave it to him." He pulled out the blade and handed it to her.

Caterione took it and studied it, and her eyes widened. "This blade? The boy had *this blade* on him?" She looked up and stared, incredulous. "And you say he told you it was his mother's?"

"Master, yes. What of it?"

She locked eyes with him. "Why didn't you tell me this earlier? Do you know what this is?"

"Master, we ..."

"I have a pair just like it. Master Aideen presented them to me when I was her trainee. Do you see this letter scratched on the hilt? Fire and daggers, Taijo, find that boy! This is Talla Undine's blade!"

13. The Fire Floor

Abigail stood bent over, hands on her hips, winded.

"You run well," Arran said, also breathing hard. "So, let's add to the exercise. Put on the pack."

"What?" Abigail gasped between breaths. "But I can't run with that on. You made me fill it with books."

"Provisions. It's filled with food, clothes, and blankets for protection from the cold."

"No, it isn't," she scowled, but she stepped over and picked it up.

"Running to escape your enemy only to starve or freeze isn't a win. You'll need to carry things."

"Fine." She pulled it on, still breathing hard. "What about you? You think you could run with this on?"

Arran sighed. "Get on my back."

"On your back?"

He turned and squatted. "Get on." With a huff, she wrapped her arms around his neck, and he looped his arms under her legs and lifted her, and started down the trail.

"Not so fast," she complained as he picked up speed. "We'll fall and die!" But when he stopped running and let her down, there were no more surly challenges.

"I'll give you a head start and then pursue. See how long you can remain in the lead."

In following days, Abigail found that her instruction would become even more interesting. One morning Arran brought her farther into the woods than usual, and showed her a pool cut into the stone where a stream dropped over a ledge.

"It's cold," he said. "You'll learn to tolerate that, as you'll be in this pool at the start and end of each day."

Abigail knelt and put a hand in, and pulled it back out. "It's freezing."

"Young miss, if one day you should be running from an enemy and come across a heated pond, send word to me and I'll offer an apology." He pulled a bundle of brown clothes from his pack. "This is your new outfit. You're to put your clothes in your pack, then get in the water for a count of ten. Then get out and put these clothes on. See that boulder? I'll be on the other side of it, counting your time. We'll see what you score."

"You want me to get in the water," Abigail said, scowling.

"The morning routine is easier, young miss. This evening you'll have charcoal on your face, and the count in the water will seem all too short to get it off. Now, get out of your clothes, into the water, and into these clothes as quickly as possible. We start counting when I turn my back."

The whole thing sounded more like a punishment than an exercise, but Abigail knew what the charcoal would be for. Her tutor was going to teach her to hide. This seemed useful indeed. She had to clamp her mouth shut to avoid screaming when she hopped into the water. It felt like someone had cut off her air. But she counted a fast ten and leaped out, and struggled to pull on the brown outfit over wet skin.

The lesson wasn't just about how to hide. Arran meant to teach her how to go undetected, whether moving or stationary. She learned about wind direction and speed, and how to hide her tracks, and how to blend in.

"You won't learn in a week to be a ghost. A Gatto tracker or gray-gis won't be fooled for long. But you'll improve."

"It won't help me against gray-gis?" Abigail asked, disappointed and suddenly a bit afraid.

"That's not what I said, young miss. It might help a great deal. Sometimes all that's needed is an extra moment to reach a safe place."

"Again?" came the voice in Tagan's head, the moment before he hit the water.

He plunged into the black river, and Camilla went silent. But he couldn't help think the same thing. What was it about underground waterways? He seemed to be attracted to them. From the swiftness of the current, he had gambled that this one would lead outside to the gorge, and hoped the mouth wasn't a hundred feet over a bed of rocks. Was it a short way, or a long way? Did it end in open air at all? Maybe the passage narrowed ahead, and split into many thin channels, none large enough for a man to swim.

As he felt the primal demand to draw air into his lungs, he reached up and felt stone overhead—not air—and kicked harder. Would he drown in darkness? The river had seemed a better choice than facing a Gatto master. But as the seconds slowly passed, panic started to set in. With visions of his bones one day washing up on the rocks in the gorge, he scrambled along the stone ceiling, feeling for air pockets or a way up.

An odd thought came to him, as he felt his air expended. The ceiling of the river passage was too smooth. It didn't tear at his hands like the jagged rocks at Deadrise Bay. There was something wrong about it.

No air ... no air ... no air! He panicked and scrambled forward and checked, reaching all around him, and turned to fight the current. He had to go back. But the river was much too strong, and there was nothing but water in every direction. He was forced downstream, desperate hands searching.

Then he felt something different. An opening? He pushed upward and thrust his head into blessed air. The current pulled at him, and threatened to drag him back under. He scraped his hands on the smooth stone, trying to get a handhold in the blackness. Then his feet caught a ledge, and he held on. He pushed himself up until his head was fully out of the water, and he breathed in and out, clinging to the stone and not daring to move.

As the panic subsided, he tried to get a sense of the space. Would the air last? Would he be pulled back under if he tried to reach for a higher handhold? The air was cleaner, lacking the odor of sulfur. The stone surface was indeed smooth. That part, at least, hadn't been a sensation brought on by panic and the onset of unconsciousness.

"Another cavern?" he said out loud, and heard his voice echo. It wasn't a tiny pocket of air. It sounded like a gigantic space. He set aside his fear and felt the stone around him, seeking a way out of the water.

"It's a damned big cavern, from the sound of it." Camilla had returned to him.

"The stone tapers in above me on this side," he said. He worked his way around the opening, and his feet found a flat surface. "A floor! No, wait. It feels like a step."

"Can you stand? You need to get moving. They're after you, right?"

Tagan rose, carefully feeling above him to avoid hitting his head. He nodded, then thinking it might be foolish to nod to his muse when standing in a pitch-black space, he answered. "I can stand. But I can't see anything. No, hold. I do see something." There was a tiny spot of light, far away overhead. "There's a light up there." He dropped his voice to a whisper. "Is it them? The Gatto?"

"Oh, shit. Gotta go," said his muse, and Camilla's voice left him.

Standing utterly alone in a dark space, peering at a dot of light, Tagan drew in a breath. He moved slowly, feeling for obstacles. In the caves below the cliffs at Deadrise Bay there were ledges, giant limestone stalactites and stalagmites, deep fissures, and sharp edges. But instead of that, he felt the smooth surface of a tread and a riser, and another step above it. He seemed to be on a stone stairway leading up toward the tiny light. He turned to stare into the blackness behind him. Up or down? Up to whatever that light was, possibly the Gatto waiting for him, or back into the river?

He chose up. First he crawled, and then he rose and walked hunched over, sweeping a foot carefully on each step before standing on it, to confirm that it was safe to take the next step. The stairs rose up and up. At fifty steps he stopped counting. The light was now a vertical line, bright enough to illuminate the edges of things. It couldn't be a lantern, and it wasn't moving. Was it a fissure to the outside? That could explain the freshness of the air here, compared to the air in the cavern. He could see the shape of the stairs now, and hurried up.

At the top he stopped to look and listen. The cavern was enormous.

The space stretched for at least a hundred yards, the floor uneven, but more or less flat. Taking a tentative step off the stairs, he could hear water dripping from his wet gi, and the squish of the wet fabric as he moved, but nothing else.

He stopped and silently slipped off the knife belt and gi, discarding them on the stairs, and moved forward in his whites. Better. There was less drip-drip. He could move almost silently now.

It took a long time to make his way across the cavern, fearful of Gatto hiding in every shadow. The edge of a door, perhaps? He approached slowly, but gradually his concerns about someone waiting for him abated. There were no sounds and no smells except for the sound and smell of an old cavern; no disturbance in what he sensed. It seemed, rather, that no one had been here in a very long time.

When he reached the source of the light, he stared in awe. It was not light coming past the edge of a door. Rather, a geometric cut had been carved into the stone wall, about ten feet wide on the inner surface and at least twenty feet high, tapering in at smooth angles so that five feet into the stone the opening was a mere inch wide, a long vertical slot. He stepped into the cavity to look through the slot, and could see that it was cut the same way on the other side, opening outward at the same angle.

"Like an hourglass turned sideways," he muttered. Camilla didn't respond, but he spoke aloud anyway. "Who cut this, do you suppose? It looks ancient."

Daylight filtered through hanging ivy beyond the outside cut, so that he couldn't see clearly what was out there. But the roar of the waterfall and the smell of the river told him where he was, more or less. He was looking out through a slot in the stone wall of the gorge.

"What is this place?" he said, turning to scan the cavern. When he stepped to the side, he realized that the shaft of light from the slot cast a bright line across a gray stone floor—and discovered it wasn't plain gray, at least not in the area near the cut in the wall. There was a large, round, very flat section, and he could see images on the surface created in fine inlay. He moved closer, and discovered that there were figures in black and white set in against the gray of the bedrock.

"A kata floor?"

The light flickered and then steadied as a gust of wind in the gorge outside moved the ivy. Tagan knelt to look at the inlaid characters, and looked in wonder at finely crafted fighting figures, a figure in black and a figure in white, and more figures above and below them. The inlay was delicate and subtle, shades of blacks and whites representing motion. In one spot illuminated by the shaft of light he could see a figure in black blocking a strike from the one in white, while the other two seemed to be charging forward.

The narrow stripe of light illuminated only a sliver of the floor brightly. The rest was dim, but Tagan could see that soon the sun would catch another column of figures. He could just start to see another image of the figure in black near the one he'd been looking at, this one with his arms together, the lighter shades revealing that he had prepared for a two-arm block.

"Ah. The master has blocked this opponent, and now he's about to block this other, and then strike the third," he said, looking ahead to where the light would soon shine.

Stepping back, he realized that inlaid figures were spread out all across the flat, round section of floor. Several feet above and several feet below the first set were more sets of figures, and more above and below those. At first, he thought it might be a repeat of a pattern: a fight scene repeated across the floor as a decoration. Then he looked more carefully, and realized they weren't exact copies. Each set of figures in the column stood in slightly different positions. In this one, the figure in black was poised for a lower block and an up-thrust strike. In this other one, the block was higher. He walked across the floor keeping his back to the light so that his eyes would adjust.

He looked to the point where the line of the sun would start, and discovered a single set of figures: The figure in black bowed to two in white, who returned the bow. Just in from that, where the shaft of light would travel next, were two sets of figures. In one, the black fighter was in a high ready stance, and in the other, a low stance. The white fighters, likewise, were in different starting stances. The sun would then illuminate a third column, with four sets of characters, then eight, then sixteen. It didn't move to thirty-two, but instead there were many columns of sixteen, after which the numbers reduced to eight, four, two, and one. In the last set there was just the black fighter, standing in a high ready stance.

"It's a kata," he said, astonished. "A kata floor that illustrates a kata and its variations. Oh, look at this! The path of the sun shows the progression. And each of these sets is a variation." He talked out loud as he walked the floor, working it out. "You fend off this blow, and then perhaps you counter with this strike that the light will illuminate in another minute or two. Or possibly you choose a higher strike, like this one up here, forcing your opponent to take this defensive move. Or a lower strike, like this one." He counted the rows. "Spectacular. A kata floor, and the sun shows us the action!"

He found himself mimicking the black figure's stance and strike, then trying the one above and the one below. The sun had already shifted, showing the next set of moves. Forgetting that he was wet and cold and running from a Gatto master intent on putting him to death, Tagan moved into the next position of the black figure, who followed his two-arm block with a side strike.

Then he looked at the variations above and below. From the set he'd first looked at, either of these would also work as the next move, although he couldn't jump several rows higher or several rows lower.

"No, not unless I'd chosen one of these other moves earlier. I can only pick one that's close. What is this kata, though?" he said out loud. "Mother showed me many Gatto kata, but I've not seen this one, nor any kata with this many variations written down. What is it? Oh, this is magnificent!"

Then he spotted a long, low table, and his eyes widened again. "Lamps!" he said, and rushed over.

Twin bronze oil lamps sat on a stone table built to eating height for seated fighters. The lamps were dry, and if there had been wicks, they had turned to dust. But behind the table he discovered a low wooden chest. It took some effort to work the oxidized bronze clasps, but he got them undone, and with some effort he pulled the lid up. He laughed out loud. There was a ceramic jar of lamp oil, sealed with wax, and a leather box with wicks for the lamps, and sulfur matches wrapped in linen. He punched a hole in the wax seal and poured oil into a bronze lamp, and soon had it lit.

First, he examined everything in the chest. There were two more bronze lamps and two more jugs of oil, one open and empty, the other full. There was a stack of folded brown gis, and for a moment he thought he might have clean, dry clothes. But they had turned brittle, and fell apart when he tried to lift them.

Underneath the decayed gis, at the bottom of the chest, there was an elegant copper box with a patina of green. Tagan pulled it out and carried it over to the table, and sat.

"What treasure might this be?" he said, as he struggled to loosen another set of clasps. He pried up the lid, and emitted an audible "Ooh!" The interior of the box was polished ebony, and resting in carved insets, on a bed of brown silk, were twin short blades. "Here's a fine old pair of Gatto blades." The blades were clean and surprisingly sharp. They had ebony handles and spiral hand guards of something that looked like silver.

"But it can't be silver," Tagan muttered. "It would be black with tarnish. Nickel, perhaps?" He pulled the lamp close to examine one of them. "White gold! Oh, very nice." he said, admiring the inlaid scrollwork on the black handle and on the blade. "And a fine balance. It's a wonder someone abandoned these in this old cave. They're finer than my mother's, that's for certain."

He returned to the stone steps to fetch his clothes, and after wringing them out, he pulled on the wet gi pants and jacket, and laughed as he tightened the leather strap for the knife sheathes at his waist. It was fortunate and yet ironic that the Gatto had meant for him to die in a knife fight, or else he wouldn't have been given the knife belt. He slipped the blades in and strode back to the kata floor, feeling the part of a Gatto warrior.

There was something timeless and calming about the place. He felt safe in the old kata room, separated from the danger as if he'd shifted to another place altogether.

"They won't find me here," he said. "They don't know about this place. No one has been here for ages."

In the light of the lamp, the kata floor appeared as a gray stone fighting ring decorated with an array of figures in black and white, the boundary a ring of the same black inlay.

"Spectacular," Tagan said, walking with the lamp and admiring the workmanship. "And only with the lights out and the sun up can it be seen for what it is, the recording of a Gatto kata. I wonder what this one is called." And then he saw the answer, set into the black stone circle, repeating all the way around in tiny white letters: VATRA.

"Fire," Tagan said. "I've never heard of a Gatto fire kata. Mother has never shown me this one."

Then above the steady roar of the waterfall outside he heard another sound, a human voice. Instinctively he blew out the lamp and dropped to a crouch. It came from somewhere in the gorge. He heard it again, this time a different voice. The Gatto fighters and the trainees were out there searching for him. He crept to the wall and peered through the slot, but all he could see was the movement of the ivy and flickering sunlight. He could hear the voices more clearly, though: not words, but signals to coordinate their search.

He froze and listened. But after standing still for several minutes, Tagan realized that even if they were right outside the cut, they wouldn't see the lamplight, given the bright sun outside. More than likely, they were simply making a sweep of the gorge. Even so, he didn't relight the lamp. He crept back to the stone stairs and stood listening. The place seemed to have been abandoned a very long time ago. But could he be certain they didn't know about it? Maybe they were making plans right now to send blades up the stairs and search the old kata chamber.

Blades drawn, he hovered at the top of the stairs for a long time, but no one came. He heard the faint sound of the water below, and the occasional echo of voices outside, but no figures emerged from the water to come after him.

"So, I wait," he muttered, and returned to study the kata floor.

It was hours later that he found the storeroom. He'd discovered a smaller oil lamp on a stone ledge, and thought it should be safe enough to light it if he were careful to keep the light low and not to direct it toward the slot. He crept around the perimeter of the cavern, and almost stepped right past the low opening into the second room. He had to duck to pass under the arched doorway. A small cavity had been cut with hammer and chisel to make a storage room, heavy wooden shelves on either side of a narrow passage.

"Isn't this interesting," he said.

On one shelf was a large, utilitarian box sheathed in hammered copper. As with the trunk, it took some work to loosen the lid. Tagan hoped to find more relics of the Gatto who had once used the great hall, but instead he found neatly stacked splits of wood, dark from untold years. It explained the shallow cut he'd found near the table, and the black stain in the bottom: They had lit fires in the kata room.

On the other side of the small room were shelves containing rows of ceramic pots and jars. These had been food stores, he guessed.

"But nothing left for a wayward Tallach to eat," he muttered. Whatever the vessels might have contained had turned to dust. "Wait, here's one." He discovered one small jar in the back that was still sealed. He broke the wax seal on a short, squat jug and sniffed. "Honey!" he said, and dipped a finger in. It was sweet and good. "I won't go hungry just yet!" he laughed. He carried out an empty jug and the honey. A blade in one hand, he descended the stone stairs to fill the jug with water to drink.

Much as he would have liked to light a fire and warm up, he opted to leave the bundles of wood where they sat. A fire could give him away. There might be a fissure overhead that would draw the smoke outside. The Gatto might see a plume of smoke rising above the stone like a beacon. Or someone might see light through the slot to the gorge, or smoke wafting through the ivy. No, he couldn't light a fire.

Instead he searched the entire cavern looking for a way out. He walked the perimeter many times, carefully inspecting every notch and crack. But there were no other store rooms, no other stores, and no way out that he could find.

"But there are also no dusty bones. And someone did all this work. They got in and they got out. How?"

Next, he searched the ceiling. Was there a way out up there? Did they come down on ropes, or was there a ladder, or a way to climb? There was nothing. There were deep fissures in the stone ceiling, but none large enough for a man, and no evidence of a passage. There were no iron rings pounded in to the wall, no chisel marks—nothing.

"Whoever used to come here, they came by water and left by water," he said, and sighed. "It must be. There's no other way."

He carried one of the larger lanterns down to the water, and sat on the stone steps and stared. The surface of the water was a black swirl, the stairs disappearing down into it.

"These gray-gis that live here now, they don't know about this place, because they didn't panic in the passage," he mused. "No one considered that there might be stairs leading up, right in the middle. Why would anyone think of that? And no one was scraping the stone, desperately hoping to find an air pocket, so no one stumbled on it, as I did." He watched a bit of foam floating on the surface. "Perhaps they sent objects through at first, to see if they would arrive at the other end. A wooden float, and then something larger. A barrel, perhaps. And eventually a brave soul chose to swim it, and either die in the attempt, or prove his mettle by being the first."

He wished he'd counted his time under water. How long had he been under? He had once held his breath under water for almost three minutes, and he had heard stories of people who could hold their breath for up to five. He should have counted!

"I must have been under water for close to two," he mused. "Maybe more than two. So that rules out returning upstream."

If he had been under water for even just one minute, he couldn't possibly make it back to the cavern, swimming against the current. No one could do that. Downstream was the only option. But how far would it be, and where did it even go?

Whoever these Gatto were, maybe they trained for it, he considered. Maybe they trained to swim for many long minutes in the inky blackness. For all he knew, it might have been one of their trials, to be able to swim the channel. Maybe only the top fighters visited the cavern.

"Or maybe I'm ten feet from freedom." Tagan grumbled. "Maybe I just need to dive and kick my legs and I'll be out. He sighed. "Maybe the river wasn't always here. They might have walked through a dry cavern to get here. Or maybe the river doesn't lead to the outside at all, and when I try to get out it will be my last minutes alive."

Horses thundered down the road and stopped outside the wooden gates of Three Rivers Pavilion. On the watch deck, a Gatto fighter snapped to attention.

A single horseman moved closer and looked up. "Commander Riley arrives to speak with the master," he announced.

The Gatto fighter made a sign, and the gate guards pulled the gates open.

They rode in at a walk and stopped just inside. The lookout had climbed down, and offered a bow. "The master hunts the river for a convict," he said, moving his eyes from the soldier to the commander. Then he stiffened anew as the master's daughter raced up on foot from the rear of the convoy.

"Where is he?" Isotta shouted, grabbing the gate guard by the arm before the commander had had a chance to offer a greeting. "The prisoner. Is he still in his cell?"

"Miss Isotta," the gate guard stuttered. "I ... he ..."

"Isotta," Commander Riley said, "bring your things to your quarters. Your mother isn't here at present. We'll wait for her to return."

"Where is he?" Isotta demanded of the gate guard. "Am I too late?"

Riley looked over her shoulder at a pair of Gatto fighters leading Dimon from the wagon. He nodded his head in the direction of the dungeons, and they turned and pulled him along.

"Drowned, I suppose," the Gatto fighter said. "I'm told the boy dove."

"What do you mean he dove?" the girl demanded. "Tell me!"

Riley and his men dismounted, and Gatto guards came to tend to the horses.

"Isotta, child, come," Riley said, prying her hand off the fighter's arm. "Get your things and get settled. And you, Gatto."

"Yes, commander?"

"Tell the master I'll wait for her in the pavilion."

Isotta spun and stared at the soldiers leading Dimon to the dungeons, then spun to look at Riley. Then she emitted an exasperated breath and stormed off. Riley and his men headed for the pavilion.

The master and the sensei were both out, Riley was informed as he stepped inside. But the staff and the trainees knew who this man was, and swarmed in to offer him and his soldiers food and drink. Riley and his men gathered around a table and sat.

Riley nodded at a trainee, who stepped in with wine. "Come here, boy," he said. "I'd like to hear about this prisoner. I bring with me another who claims to know him."

"Commander," the boy stared at the floor, "it's not my place. The master will wish to tell it."

Then the boy's eyes closed as a figure stepped in and a familiar voice whispered in his ear. "Tell it now, Geun, or face me on the mats and then tell it."

"But Miss Isotta, your mother ..."

"My mother is master, and she's not here. Neither is Arran. So, I'm in charge. And I'm ordering you to tell us what happened."

His lips quivered as he weighed his options, and then the boy blurted it out in a single string. "The prisoner chose combat, and then in the caverns they discovered that the trainees had cheated, so the master disqualified them and said she would fight him herself. Then the prisoner dove into the water. And when the sensei showed the master the prisoner's blade, the master said it was Talla Undine's blade! And now they're searching for his body." Geun turned and ran out of the pavilion in a panic.

Isotta stood triumphant, arms crossed in a told-you-so pose. "Do you still think he's an ordinary foot soldier sent to spy on us?" Isotta said.

Riley had risen to his feet. "Bring the prisoner!" he barked, pointing at a Gatto fighter. The man jumped up, but looked confused. "The one I just delivered to your dungeons. Bring him!"

Soon Dimon stepped in and stood rigidly, his arms held by soldiers, his hands clenched into fists. "You've killed him." he hissed at Riley, "you northerners and your Gatto assassins, you've killed him."

With looks of astonishment, the men seated around the table began to stand, offended at the prisoner's rude, forward manner of addressing their commander. But Riley waved them away and motioned for the soldiers to release Dimon.

"Hold!" Riley said to his men, as Dimon strode forward and hands all around went to blade hilts.

Dimon glared at the commander. "Were your Gatto friends part of the plan, then? If the gray-gis couldn't kill him, they would?"

"Calm yourself," Riley said, holding up a palm. "Speak plainly. Who are you, and what's this all about?"

"It doesn't matter now," Dimon said, scanning the room, locking eyes with one soldier and then the next. "Drown me in the river and I'll lie next to him in death. Or kill me in the caves. I don't care. The trainees in that dungeon told me there's no body. Nothing emerged from the dark river. His body is entombed beneath those cliffs we passed. You've finished the work of the gray-gis. I'll not speak to you."

"Gray-gis?" Then Riley leaned forward. "Hold. What is that, boy?" He pointed at the pendant around Dimon's neck, which in the struggle with the soldiers had slipped out from his gi jacket.

Dimon grabbed it and held it tightly in his fist. "It's not yours! Kill me and take it from my dead hands if you want it. This has nothing to do with you."

But soldiers had already closed in from behind. Dimon was pinned, and the pendant taken from him. They handed it over, and the commander's face blanched.

"I told you he had that," Isotta said, stepping closer for a look. "I told you he had an old pendant."

Riley distractedly shooed her away, and the soldiers held Dimon firm. Dimon clenched his eyes and his mouth shut, and stood stiffly.

"Release him," Riley ordered.

Dimon's eyes opened, and for a moment he considered leaping at the commander in a final act of defiance. He would be cut down honoring his friend. Then he saw the man's expression. Panic? Northern commanders didn't get panicked.

"This token," Riley said more quietly. "Who wore it? Is it yours?"

"I'm sure you know," Dimon said, now in a measured, dull tone. "I told the girl, and she no doubt told you. It was his, a gift from his mother. But what does it matter? You've completed the kill."

"How old was your companion?" Riley stared at Dimon.

"Nineteen. Same as me. If you find his body, send that token with his body to his mother. It was her gift to her son. She told him his father gave it to her."

Riley dropped back a step and looked around, trying to fix on something. "His mother ..." He turned desperate eyes to Dimon. "Tell me, please. Your friend. He's Undine's son?"

Dimon's impassive stare answered the question.

Riley spun. "All of you," he waved at his men. "Search! You're to find him. Bring him back alive, or bring his body. No one rests until I see him!"

The soldiers rose, saluted, and ran out of the pavilion, leaving the commander, Isotta, and Dimon standing in a triangle, staring at each other.

"And why should you care so much, all of a sudden?" Dimon said, accusingly.

Riley held the pendant. "Because I gave this to Undine myself, twenty years ago."

14. Sotto Voce

"Don't kill me!" Enzo raised his hands and took a step backward, wishing he hadn't closed the door.

Then the gun went down, and the figure holding it resolved into Camilla. "Enzo. Oh, god. It's you. We thought someone followed us. How'd you get back so fast?"

"And are you sure no one followed you?" Grace added.

"Gimme just one second to let my heart start beating again, huh? Jesus." Enzo dropped into a chair. "That was fucking unbelievable. How'd you get off the mountain? They had helicopters and shit, searching all the roads." Enzo rose and locked the door, and sat again.

"We stayed off the trail for a while. And at the base we took a different car." Camilla raised a defensive palm. "We left it where it'll get found. They'll get their car back."

"Jesus."

"But what'd you do, Enzo? We figured you might not get back here until the middle of the night."

"Well, I didn't steal a car. I hiked back to the lot, and bummed a ride. I just reused the same story. I said I twisted my ankle, so I told my buddies I'd hitch a ride back, or if I couldn't, I'd wait in the parking lot."

"Not bad," Grace said.

Enzo stepped over to the kitchenette. "Want some coffee? I do." Then he turned. "Look, the police are gonna want to talk to me. People saw me up there. I'll stick to the story. But shouldn't you be getting out of here? I thought you'd be long gone."

Camilla shook her head. "Not yet. We need to have a plan first. Yeah, coffee would be great."

"And it's fine if you need to stay here a while, but ..."

"I've got money," Grace said. "We can pay you."

"Money? That's not it. There are two dead guys on the mountain, and the cops are gonna know I was involved. Isn't this the least-safe place for you two?"

"Hidden in plain sight," Camilla said. "It's the best place, for now. Unless you're telling us to go. You helped us a lot, Enzo. You tell me to go, and we'll go."

"No, come on. After all that? Just tell me what you need, okay?"

"Go to work," Grace said, "then do whatever you'd normally do, then come back here."

"Shit, really? Oh, wait, I see. Keep up appearances."

"Exactly. Don't change things up," Camilla said. "If the police want to talk to you, then talk. Stick to the story. And you can't stop and buy groceries for three, either. We'll figure something out for food."

"There's always pizza."

Camilla sat in the dark, peering through a grimy window at a parking area behind the building. In the alley storefront below her, a local wine-maker waited on tourists, offering them a sample of the summer's popular label. In the opposite window, Grace scanned the deck of the next building. Whoever lived there didn't seem to make much use of the deck. An old gas grill sat dejected in a corner, kept company by a broken lawn chair and a dead plant.

"How long do we stay here, Camilla?" Grace said. She had felt odd about letting her foster-daughter take the lead, until she discovered who she really was. There was no need to feel inadequate when handing the reins to the granddaughter of Horace Rand. The only thing that felt odd was to call her Camilla rather than Calista.

"Until we have a plan. It's safer to stay here. No one will have any reason to look for us here."

Grace sighed out loud. "I suppose you're right."

Camilla stared outside and focused in on her connection. "Tagan, are you there? Can you talk?"

"I have time at the moment, muse," came Tagan's voice. "At the moment I don't have much other than time. I do have a small pot of honey, and some fine blades."

"What is that place?" Camilla asked. He sat huddled in a stone cut, wrapped in what looked like a hooded silk kimono.

"It's a dojo," Tagan said. "That's the word you use, isn't it? Dojo? We call it a kata room. This one is built of stone."

"And what's outside?" She could see a line of late gray light. "What is that?"

"Outside is a gorge carved by the river. There are men and boys search-ing for me, but they can't see in. I'm sitting near the opening because it's cold in here, and the air outside is warmer. Look at the old master's robe I found. I thought it was packing material for the blades, but it's a silk robe."

"Blades?"

"I found a magnificent set. The finest pair of Gatto blades I've ever seen. Very old, I think, and yet no tarnish." He pulled one out and looked at it in the dark. "Ebony handles like the blades of the north, but with the spiral hand guard of a Gatto blade. Were I to see it in a market, I would assume it was nickel or colored steel. But I think it's gold. White gold for the guard, and something hard for the blade. A mixture of gold and copper, perhaps. I'm not certain."

"And you found them in a stone dojo? Where exactly are you?"

"Trapped," Tagan said. "They're out there hunting for me, and I'm trapped in an old kata room cut into the mountain. Even if I could swim the second run, I'd emerge only to be taken. Surely they're guarding the outlet."

"The second run. You need to fill me in a little."

"The passage to this place is under water. That's why they haven't come for me. I don't think they know this place is here. I found it by accident. They were about to kill me, so I dove into the underground river, and now here I am. I think at one time that channel might have been dry, but there's a river there now. To get out, I'll have to swim blind beneath the stone once more. I don't relish that thought."

"I'm trapped, too," Camilla said. "Not underground, but the same thing. Men are hunting for us, and so we're prisoners in my new friend's apartment. I can't come up with a plan. And do you know what it's like to eat leftover pizza for every meal?"

Tagan smiled. "I don't know what pizza is, but send me some if you don't want it. Honey is fine, but not entirely satisfying."

"I might take that trade," Camilla said.

"And say, aren't you my muse?" Tagan asked, feeling a rare moment of good humor. It struck him, that he had been lonely. It was good to speak to someone. "I'm sure you can tell me the way out—and then find a way out for yourself."

"I don't know a lot about caves," came Camilla's sullen reply. "Why don't you be the muse? I could use a muse about now."

"You'll come up with a plan. You suggested the fiddle game when my friend and I were on the run," Tagan countered. "That was brilliant." He stopped and sighed, thinking of Dimon. "Did he get away, though? I don't know. Some fine mess I've made."

"Horace taught me the fiddle game. And he taught me to run, and to hide. He taught me everything. I'm no muse, Tagan. I need help as much as you do."

"Oh, but you are. I don't hold a shadow to the muse Camilla. Maybe I can pull an idea out of my backside, now and then. But tell me your situation. You said you're trapped?"

"It's kind of similar to having gray-gis on your trail," Camilla grumbled, "but in a different time and place. You see, my stepfather set up this con, aimed at bankrupting the man who's been after us all these years. We've been hiding. Robbie wanted to end it."

She filled him in on the basics of the sham land deal and the supposed new ramp off the interstate that would make the land worth a fortune. Several times she had to stop to explain things that made no sense to Tagan.

"What's an interstate?" he asked. "And why would this spot be any more valuable than anywhere else along the road?"

They talked for a long time, and Tagan watched the slot of light grow dim. The sun would be down soon, and it would be dangerous to have a light on. But an idea came to him. He rose and carried one of the small lanterns to the stone stairs and descended, and then lit it and sat. It was cold near the water, but at least he wouldn't have to sit in the dark.

"All right, Tagan said, "so your surrogate father meant to help solve this problem by causing the financial ruin of an enemy of the great seer Horace. But he overplayed his hand, and these enemies killed both the seer and this man. It's a horrible, tragic story, Camilla. The great old seer is dead. My mother quite misses Horace."

"So do I." Camilla sighed.

"And now his enemies are coming for you and your surrogate mother, and you're hiding. But you're not exactly trapped, are you? You could leave."

"And do what? Run? Run where? No, I need a plan, and I don't have one. They'll probably assume I ran, after the shootings on the mountain, so frankly this place might be about the safest place for us to stay for now. No one knows us here, and no one has any reason to connect us to my new friend Enzo."

"I suppose we're alike in some small ways," Tagan said glumly. "Although I'm the more pathetic character. Look at me," he held his arms out, "Looking like a Gatto master on the outside, but beneath this cloak just a wanderer running from assassins."

"And look at me," came Camilla's voice, "the granddaughter of a master con artist hiding out ... Wait a minute. *Looking like a Gatto master on the outside?*"

"This is a fine old robe. Master Caterione would be envious. By all rights I shouldn't be allowed to wear it. And the blades. They're stunning."

"Tagan, it's getting dark, right?"

"Yes. That's why I'm down here. They won't see the light of the lamp."

"They're searching in the dark. They're searching the shadows looking for an escaped prisoner."

"I suspect downstream they have torches and are looking for a body. But yes, upstream they'll be hunting in darkness. It's what I'd do. And it's an impossible barrier. No one could get through. Master Caterione will finish the job and kill me, if I don't starve to death in here, or if this river doesn't take that pleasure away from her."

"And she's out there herself hunting for you, I bet. Or at least it's plausible that she is. So, listen to me. You be the Gatto master."

"I be the master? What, impersonate master Caterione?" Tagan suddenly rose, and stood with his mouth open. "Hold. Impersonate the master!" He fingered the hilts of the blades. "Oh, that's excellent! Muse, never sell yourself short. It's simple, and it's brilliant."

"But listen to me. You have to play it right this time. You can't get out there and decide it would be a great idea to go back to the Gatto camp, or carry on a conversation with someone. Got it?"

"Don't overplay my hand. I believe I've learned my lesson on that point in fine fashion today." He charged up the stairs.

"Get out of that cavern, and get out of Dodge. Got it?"

"Out of Dodge?" Tagan asked.

"An expression. It means get the hell away from that place as fast as you can. Don't be hanging around trying to do something clever."

"I promise," Tagan said solemnly. "And while you were telling me your story, a thought came to me, as well. It's not nearly as good as your idea. Do you want to hear it?"

"I'm all ears."

"Although maybe it is a good idea, since really it's yours, and not mine."

"Spit it out."

A little while later Camilla sat blinking, and had to draw in a few deep breaths to make the twinkling lights go away. "Tagan, you're the muse," she said out loud. "That's a fantastic idea!"

"Camilla?" said Grace, looking over. "Is there a problem?"

Camilla grinned. "Not a problem. A plan. Damn it, come on. I've got it. We have to get to Boston!"

"What's the plan?"

"You know where the office is that Robbie set up? For the sham highway land deal?"

"Well, yes, but ..."

"Then come on. I'll fill you in on the way. We're gonna run the fiddle game."

A week later, a primly dressed blonde woman with large glasses and a fine leather briefcase rode the elevator to the top floor of an office building on State Street in Boston. She stepped out, was buzzed in by an attendant at the front desk, and stepped into an elegant reception area. She scanned the room, stopping briefly to find the eyes of the receptionist, a young man whom she guessed wasn't over twenty. Then she strode forward and placed a business card on the counter.

"I'm Grace Worthington, of Baker and Worthington, LLP. Mr. Barnes is my client. Mr. Robert Barnes."

The receptionist's eyebrows rose. "Mr. Barnes is ..."

"Deceased. And yet still I'm his attorney. I represent Robert Barnes

Ventures. Here are the papers. I need access to his suite." She snapped a set of papers from her briefcase and neatly slid them across the counter, but kept her fingers on them.

"Let me check with my manager," the young man said. He picked up a phone and turned away, and spoke in a low tone.

Soon Grace had a key card, and was stepping into Robbie's office suite.

The first room was a small waiting room, with several upholstered chairs in dark leather and a table with magazines. To the side was a secretary's office, with a window to allow the secretary to see anyone entering or leaving. And at the back of the waiting room was a dark wood door that opened into the main office, a large, plush room with a gigantic mahogany desk and a high-backed executive chair, and heavy captain's chairs in front of it. A feeling of despair swept through her. She could smell Robbie.

To the side of the office, twin glass doors led to a conference room.

"You took your shot, didn't you, Robbie?" Grace said to herself. "And now it's my turn." She drew in a deep breath to center herself. The plan had several moving parts, and everything needed to work perfectly. She sat at the desk, picked up the phone, and dialed.

It took a moment, but someone with a British accent finally answered. "Good evening. Turcotte Industries. How may I help you?"

"Grace Worthington, for Robert Barnes Ventures. I'd like to speak with Mr. Walter Turcotte." She said the name slowly and softly, as if reading it from a list. "Is Mr. Turcotte available?"

There was a long pause. "Uh. Might I inquire as to the purpose of the call, Miss Worthington?"

"It's about the Boston property. Mr. Turcotte appears in the list of investors. I'm contacting the investors about the sale of the property."

"The Boston property. ..."

"Yes, the Boston property. As perhaps Mr. Turcotte is aware, Mr. Barnes has passed. I'm settling matters. May I speak with Mr. Turcotte?"

"Hold, please."

Grace breathed in and out, working to calm herself. A long time passed, and she thought the man might have hung up, but finally he clicked back on.

"Ms. Worthington, could you tell me what firm you're with?"

"Baker and Worthington," she said. "We took on the account last week. Happy to send papers if Mr. Turcotte would like. Is he available?"

"I'm sorry, not just now. Could I take a message and have him call you back?"

"Certainly. Tell Mr. Turcotte we've opened the first round of bidding for the Boston property to the original investors, but only for four days. If he's interested, we'll need to hear from him promptly."

"For the Boston property. Is this a joke? The Boston property was a scam, *Ms. Worthington.*" The man spat her name. "You think Mr. Turcotte would like to lose more of his money? Who is this?"

"You didn't receive the packet? Turcotte Industries hasn't lost a dime," she said in a low, even voice, meeting anger with professional confidence. "The initial investors have all been bought out in preparation for the sale. And the plans for the ramp are being filed today, if I'm not mistaken. Please let him know I called, and inform him I'll need to hear from him promptly if he's interested." Grace hung up the phone and exhaled a long breath.

A short, dark-haired young woman in a pants suit entered the records room and stepped up, unzipping a portfolio. "May I use that?" she said, pointing to a round table with a few chairs around it. "I have a few details to discuss before we file these." She tugged at the corner of a set of blue-prints. "It's the ramp project."

The man at the desk flashed a confused, do-I-know-you look, but nodded at the table. "Go ahead, ma'am. Coffee's hot, if you want some."

"Thank you." Camilla flashed him a smile, but not too wide. She didn't want to crack the layers of makeup covering the tattoo on her face. *The ramp project.* Just vague enough. He didn't ask, *What ramp project?* Probably there were dozens of ramp projects at any given time.

She opened the portfolio and spread a set of blueprints over the table, and for a few minutes she leaned over to study them, keeping half an eye on the entry. No one else came in, and she wandered to a cart with a coffee machine and poured a cup. Back at the table, she set it down and sat, and waited another few minutes.

Then her phone vibrated, and she pulled it from her back pocket, checked it, and looked over at the man she'd spoken with. "Okay if I leave these here for a minute? One's on his way up, but the others are in lobby. I'll go get them."

He smiled and nodded, and she slipped into the hall.

Less than a minute later, a man in a gray suit stepped in and looked around. The man at the desk looked up. "Ramp project?" He pointed at the table. "She went down to get the others."

"I see. Thank you." He stepped over to the table, looked at the prints, and pulled out his cell phone. Pretending to be sending a text, he quickly shot photos of the blueprints, each marked *approved*. There were photos of the site and detailed construction drawings for a new ramp. Plainly visible in several of the site photos was the old building. The man in gray put the phone to his ear, turned, and walked out.

Camilla hurried back in a moment later. "Hey, thanks," she said, scoop-ing up the blueprints. "Another round of changes, I guess. But thanks for the coffee."

"Not a problem," the man said, and watched her zip the portfolio and leave.

For three days, Camilla and Grace waited and fretted.

"They can do this?" Camilla asked, for the hundredth time. "You're sure? All of them?"

"Robbie had lots of friends, Camilla. And most of them were agents. If they can't haul this off, then it can't be done."

"But the records office. What if they call and find out the project doesn't exist? And the other investors. What if he calls one of them?"

"They don't need to call the records office. Their man got photos of the plans. And we've got people covering each of the other investors. We've set up paper trails for the payments, and we have people ready to intercept calls, or whatever else needs to be done. They're professionals. Robbie helped a lot of people out of jams, in his time. Helping us nail the man who killed him is the least they can do."

"But will it work?"

"We need Turcotte to think the ramp project is legit. That's all in place. The rest is a matter of timing. He's a greedy bastard, Camilla. He'll bite."

On the fourth day, the call came through. "Mr. Turcotte's office, for Ms. Worthington." It was a different voice this time.

"Speaking."

"Ms. Worthington, first I'd like to apologize for the treatment you received when last you called. It's been dealt with."

"I'm used to it, sir. I'm a lawyer."

"It wasn't an acceptable representation of the firm. At any rate, Mr. Turcotte would like to make an offer." The man gave her a number. "That's well above the market price we see for that property."

Grace paused, and counted to ten. "I'm sorry, sir, but the current bid adds a couple of zeroes onto that number."

"A couple of zeroes?" The man said, incredulous.

"Yes sir. But thank you for the courtesy of the call. Should Mr. Turcotte like to make a different offer, he has, let's see ... just over two hours."

An agonizing hour later, the phone rang again. "Hello again," Grace said, when the man identified himself. "Is Mr. Turcotte interested, then? You understand, it's a cash sale, and we've exceeded the minimum, so there won't be a public offer. We can sign electronically, but the funds would need to be wired today."

"Mr. Turcotte arrived in Boston yesterday. He's prepared to make an offer, and to sign papers in person."

"Splendid."

15. Commoners on the Terrace

Tagan wrapped the knives in the silk robe and packed them into the copper-clad box he had found them in, then stripped off his gi and packed that in, too, adding his knife belt. Would it be watertight?

"It doesn't matter," he muttered. "I can't swim with blades on. I'd lose one or both for certain. And so what if my things get wet?"

He looped his gi belt through the handles and tied it to his back. The swim itself had been his main concern: an unknown distance in complete blackness, under water. The box strapped to his back added to the problem, as it would make the swim more difficult. But neither was top of mind anymore.

"I'll either make it to the outlet or drown," he said with a resolute nod. "I need to focus on what will come next, if this channel leads me outside and not to my death."

It was the timing that worried him, and the unknowns. He had to swim the channel, find his way out, and then somehow get changed into his costume before anyone discovered him.

His own addition to Camilla's plan might make the difference, though. In his hours staring at the back side of the ivy and listening to the voices, he had gotten the sense that his narrow window to the outside was high up on the cliffs. If everything worked as planned, including the timing, he might have a chance.

"Is there enough oil?" he quietly asked out loud. "Will it work? Damn it, it has to work."

In the carving in the cliff wall he had piled the splits of wood from the old trunk, and tucked pieces of linen and the old, brittle gis underneath. Then he poured lamp oil on the wood and the cloth. Everything was tinder-dry. It should go up like a torch. He checked the gi belt again, tugging at the knot.

"All right, then. Time to get out of Dodge."

Tagan struck a match and lit his lamp, and turning, tossed the lit match to the oil-soaked fabric before sprinting for the stairs.

At the water's edge in the dark gorge, the trainees and their sensei looked up all at once.

"Look!" one cried out. "Look at the light! What can it mean, sensei?"

"The fire altar," the old man hissed. "A sign?"

They stared in awe as orange and yellow light flickered and rose behind the ivy, high on the cliff face. They knew about the ancient fire altar, but none of them had been up there. The cut in the gorge wall was a sacred mark of the past, spoken of only in whispers.

A story always circulating among the novices was that generations ago a Gatto novice had rappelled down to look at the old cliff carving, and had slipped and tumbled over the edge, shouting *Fire!* as he fell to his death, taking the knowledge of whatever he had seen with him. The master explained that it was inexperience, and not a mystical power, that had ended the life of the young novice, but declared the spot off limits, and decreed that anyone who should dare desecrate the ancient monument would be exiled from the Gatto. No one had tried since, and the ivy had grown thick over the spot.

"It grows brighter," another remarked. "Is it a sign?"

"Get up to the plateau!" the sensei ordered, snapping back to the moment. "It may be a sign that our mark is up there. Go find him!"

Tagan emerged from the inky black water and almost laughed. He had barely started to kick his legs when he saw the dim outline of the cavern. The opening at the foot of the stairs couldn't have been more than fifty feet from the mouth. He climbed out of the water as quietly as possible, thankful for the roar of the falls outside.

He stared, looking and listening. At the entrance to the cavern was a single silhouette. Flickering light from outside revealed this to be one of the younger trainees, no doubt ordered to stand at the entrance and call an alarm if he should see anything. Had a seasoned fighter been placed on watch there, Tagan might already have been detected. But it seemed the boy hadn't learned about nighttime watches. Instead of placing his torch inside the cavern to allow him to see anyone emerging from the underground river, the boy had set it in the entrance, to keep himself out of the dark.

Tagan quietly pulled open the box and got dressed. His gi was damp in spots, but the blades and the robe beneath were dry.

Soon he was creeping through the cavern to the river bank, a Gatto master prowling in the night, his hood drawn low.

Camilla had told him what to do. When the young voice challenged him, he spoke in a sharp whisper to cloak his voice, and mimicked the intonation and rhythm of the master's speech.

"You there!" said the young boy. "Stop and identify yourself."

"Out, boy!" Tagan whispered sharply. "Why do you linger? You see the firelight, do you not? Find the prisoner."

The boy's jaw dropped. "Master!" he cried, and turned and hurried out of the mouth of the cavern.

Patting the handles of the Gatto blades, Tagan stepped out and marveled at the sight. "Better than I could have wished for," he quietly mused. A hundred feet over the raging water, a vertical line of fire burned in the night, flickering behind a veil of ivy.

His own spot was quite high above the river, as well. He would have to climb down before he could make his way up the riverbank. He noted the figures rushing for the path, and when the way was clear, he descended the rocky tumble and headed upstream to the waterfall, and started to climb again.

Riley convened an inquiry on the plateau above the gorge. A ring of torches cast a harsh light on the old Gatto sensei, and on many fighters and trainees. They stood at attention, shocked to see what looked like fear on the face of their master. Even Isotta looked stunned. She stood silently at the back of the group, for once not wanting to be noticed. Caterione stood rigidly in the middle of the ring, as Commander Riley paced. A few of his soldiers had lined up, like a contingent on a field of battle awaiting an offer of surrender. The rest were out searching.

"Commander, we had no knowledge," Master Caterione stated. "He refused to identify himself."

"He stated that he was from Deadrise Bay. You have no agreement with the Tallachs at Deadrise Bay with respect to prisoners? You summarily execute them?"

"He was impersonating a Gatto border walker. There was cause."

Two more soldiers stepped up, pulling Dimon along with them.

Dimon stood with his head tipped down and his fists clenched. "Why did you bring me out here?" he complained. "I've nothing to say to any of you."

"I wish to understand today's events," Riley said, his voice softening, "and thought you might also wish to."

Dimon grimaced and nodded. "One day I'll face the Talla. She'll demand to know what happened."

"I demand it, right now," Riley said. He turned to the sensei. "You say others have swum the river passage."

The sensei stepped forward a pace, and Caterione stepped back. "Yes, commander," the sensei said.

"You have, yourself, I suppose. And you," Riley pointed at Hyoso, who stiffened and bowed. "You swam the passage tonight. Is that right?"

"Yes, commander." The trainee stepped up next to the sensei and bowed, and the sensei retreated. "I'm trained for it. We simulate the passage swim by remaining under water in the river. To attempt the passage isn't allowed until one can swim underwater for three full minutes."

"It takes three minutes to swim the passage?"

"Two and a half on average, sir. But there are contingencies to consider. One might suffer an injury, or muscle cramps."

"And you encountered no body when you emerged at the river below the falls."

"No, commander," Hyoso said, and bowed again.

"And you guarded the mouth, and you saw nothing? No body, alive or dead?"

"I saw none, sir, alive or dead. I dove directly after the prisoner. There would have been mere moments for him to get away, and I scanned the river banks to be certain. I then stood my post at the mouth until others came to spot me."

"The prisoner entered the underground river and never came out. This is your report?"

"Regrettably, yes, commander. The river holds him beneath the mountain."

"And then you saw the fire, and you went to investigate. All of you?"

Dimon's head rose. "Fire?" he said. "What fire?" The soldiers quietly ordered him to be silent.

"The light in the cliff face. Yes, sir. We had never seen such a thing. But I didn't leave until a novice arrived to take my place." Hyoso dropped his eyes.

"And this novice. He remained guarding the mouth of the underground river?"

"It's reported that he didn't remain faithfully, sir." Hyoso didn't make eye contact.

"Didn't remain," Dimon echoed, more brightly. "The exit was unguarded?" The guards hushed him again.

"And where is this boy?" Riley said. "I want to hear what he has to say."

Hyoso stepped back, and a boy of nine or ten stepped forward, wide-eyed and shaking.

"You left your post?" Riley scowled at the boy.

"But master," the young boy hissed, turning to flash a look of desperation at Caterione, "you ordered me to!"

"Boy, you'll address me. I'm asking the questions," Riley barked. "Master Caterione has already stated that she was not at the river tonight. She was here on the plateau, directing the search."

"But the master came when the fire started, and ordered me to look for the prisoner." The boy's lip quivered.

"Don't make stories," the sensei hissed.

"I was not at the mouth of the underground river, novice," Caterione stated flatly.

"You wore a Gatto robe," the boy whined. "And the blades!"

"Boy!" Riley barked. "You will address me! And Taijo and Caterione, you'll speak only when I say!"

Everyone fell silent, stunned.

"Now, boy, tell me what you saw."

"Yes, tell us," Dimon demanded, his muscles tensing against the grip of the soldiers.

"It was dark, sir. But I saw in the torchlight. The master in her Gatto robe, with her blades—those blades!" He pointed at Caterione's waist, where black-handled blades with spiral hand guards were sheathed. "And she ordered me to search for the prisoner. Was it a ghost, then?" The boy shrank back.

"A Gatto robe?" Dimon muttered, eyes wide, his attention fixed on the boy.

"Silence, prisoner," the guard hissed in his ear, "or you'll be removed."

"This altar in the side of the gorge," Riley demanded, turning to Caterione. "Is this a ritual of yours, to light a fire there?"

The boy rushed back to the group as Caterione stepped forward. "The carving in the cliff face is sacred, commander," Caterione said dully. "No one has climbed to it for generations. Ivy covers it, so that no one visiting this place even knows it's there."

"Then how do you explain the fire?" Riley raised his eyebrows. "Lightning? There was no storm. What, then? I don't want to hear about demons or ghosts. Is there another Gatto master walking these paths? I demand an explanation!"

Dimon broke into a low laugh. "The explanation is Tagan," he said, and received a disapproving jab in the ribs from one of the soldiers. "He fooled you all."

"Silence," hissed a soldier.

But Riley spun. "What are you saying, Tallach?" he spat.

"You didn't kill him. He fooled you, too. Release me," Dimon demanded. "Issue me safe passage and let me find my friend. Safe passage in writing, not that old pendant."

Riley pushed the soldiers aside and stepped up. "You say he lives? What makes you think so?"

Dimon looked around at the staring faces, and his own face hardened. "I won't speak in present company. Perhaps you're disinclined to harm him, but I don't trust these Gatto."

"Away." Riley waved a hand, and everyone retreated. He motioned for Dimon to join him, and stepped out of the throw of the torch light. "Yes, Tallach, I believe I understand the stakes. Twenty years ago ..."

"You're his father," Dimon interrupted. "Talla Undine makes up stories all the time. She laughs when I fall for it. But she didn't make up the story about that pendant, did she? That one is true. You gave her that passage pendant as a token of your time with her."

"And she gave it to our son."

"He didn't believe it was genuine, but that pendant represented his father. He only parted with it to try to save me."

"And you say he escaped? Come, tell me what you know, and how you know it!"

"I suppose you don't know him. Just as those searching the river suddenly look up at a fire in an old altar, the ghost of a Gatto master orders the boy guarding the river to leave? That has Tagan written all over it. Genius ideas come to my friend—although lately he claims they come from his muse, whom he calls Camilla."

"The silent one," Riley stared. "She speaks to my son?"

Dimon looked surprised. "You know about his muse? The silent one, yes, that's what Talla Undine called her. Camilla never said a word to her. But Tagan says, *she talks to me*. I'm not sure I believe it, but whether it's real or in his mind, my friend speaks to his muse and discovers impossible, clever ways to get out of a fix."

"It would please me greatly if this were true." Riley nodded slowly, and smiled.

"Oh, I promise you, it's true. It all fits. But it doesn't mean he's out of danger. Let me go. I need to find him."

Riley raised an arm and waved at his soldiers. A man ran over and stood at attention. "Gather the men at the main entrance. We leave directly." The soldier nodded and ran. "Your name is Dimon, is it not? Tell me, Dimon, why were you and Tagan in the north?"

Dimon hesitated, but there was no longer a reason to keep quiet. "He's the target of a gray-gi sanction, sir. Tagan fooled the gray-gis into believing they had killed him, and we ran north. We were bound for the White Cliffs. His mother is said to know the lord's right-side fighter."

"Indeed, she does." Riley stopped and breathed in, gathering himself. He stepped back into the circle and waved brusquely at Caterione. "Call off the search. Tell your Gatto to return to the pavilion."

"Call it off?" Dimon said. "You believe me, then?"

"I know something of Undine and her muse. If she passed that to her son, then as you say, it answers the strange questions that arose tonight. But tell me, why would assassins target the Talla's son?"

"It's the Turning," Dimon said quietly. "The Turning put a hit on him."

"The Turning."

"Tagan met the chieftain's daughter. And they ..."

"And let me guess. Allton took issue with the spoiling of his bloodline. Damnable Turning."

"Yes. That, exactly."

Riley waved his guard over, and Dimon raised both arms in surrender, but the soldiers ignored him and stood at attention.

"The prisoner escaped. And he's Tagan of Deadrise Bay."

The soldiers stared, their eyes wide.

"He's to be allowed safe entry to any station, and safe passage wherever he may wish to go. Send word to the stations. Six of you travel with me. The rest are to run. I want the guardians in the south notified as well. No one is to harm him. Understood? If he's sighted, I'm to be informed immediately."

"Yes, sir!" The soldiers nodded, then turned and ran.

Caterione and the rest of the Gatto now ventured closer, and Riley strode over to them. "You'll stay here, Master Caterione. You'll assign fighters to ride with me to Deadrise Bay, in place of the soldiers sent to carry messages."

"Yes, commander," Caterione said, but the commander was already storming down the trail to the compound. She clenched her teeth at the rebuke.

Even Isotta could see the look of frustration on her mother's face. Caterione wanted to lead a search party herself. But the Gatto held Three Rivers through a grant of the northern ruler, and this was his lieutenant's man. Riley outranked her, even at her own pavilion. But Isotta had her own concerns. Caterione turned to find her hopping from one foot to the other and waving to get her attention.

"What is it, child?" she snapped. "Go find a spot in the woods, if you have the need."

"Send me to my brother! I have to speak to Arran!"

While the border guards could pick out a young man in a brown gi pretending to be a Gatto guide, no one said a word to the hooded Gatto master walking silently along the trail. The ancient blades of ebony and white gold sheathed at his waist bore testament to his rank. Tagan had combed white ashes into his hair to turn it gray, and streaked and darkened his face with charcoal, adding crow's feet around his eyes and shadows beneath them. Gatto fighters stepped aside and bowed as the old man passed, and stood for a moment in the road to watch and wonder who it was.

Camilla's words came to him as he slowly walked the road. "You haven't met with the people you wanted help from," she objected. "Shouldn't you go north? Wasn't that your plan?"

The pretend Gatto master exhaled in frustration. "I barely had a plan, muse. Go talk to the lord of the north? What kind of plan is that? No, muse, I need my mother's help," Tagan found that he'd started stalking down the road, and he slowed to a Gatto master's pace. "Damn it. She'll lord it over me forever. But I need to swallow my pride and ask her to help me."

"There was a time when I didn't want anyone's help," Camilla said. "Now I wish I had the chance to ask for it."

"Why would you need someone else's help?"

Camilla laughed. "Go find your mother. I have to go."

Even a high Gatto master has to eat, and Tagan was acutely aware that he had no food. But after ducking several groups of Gatto patrols, it occurred to him that he didn't need to avoid them. The Gatto revered their old masters, and it was their custom to offer assistance to an elder, including food and shelter. The next time he spotted a group of Gatto fighters on patrol, instead of bowing his hooded head and walking past, he pretended not to have seen them, and ventured into an open field.

In the center of the field he drew his blades and stood in a ceremonial fighting stance. The sun glinted on the white gold of the blades and spiral blade guards. In his peripheral vision he saw that the men had spotted him. They moved silently to the edge of the field and stood stock-still, watching.

Tagan's hours in the kata room had netted him a new bit of knowledge. He hadn't learned all the variations—not nearly—but he'd chosen one thread, one version of the old kata, and had memorized the moves. Now he worked through them, not at speed, but slowly, showing the art of each small action. With no fighters to make the opposing moves, his performance was a ritual Gatto dance. The men watched intently and silently. And when Tagan had finished, they solemnly approached and bowed.

"What kata is that, master?" one asked.

"Vatra," Tagan said, adopting the raspy voice of an elder, "the fire kata."

"Vatra?" another said to his companion. "I know of Ara and Vela, the great altar and wind katas. I had thought Vatra was lost."

"Not lost. At least, not yet," Tagan said, with an old man's knowing smile.

"From where do you journey, master?"

This, Tagan understood, was a polite way of asking, *who are you, and what are you doing here?* "Do I journey?" he answered, with an inscrutable smile. "Do any of us journey, young Gatto? Or do we merely walk the path? Those of us whose descendants spar in the pavilions in the south don't feel that we journey, whether we find ourselves there or here. It's all the same." Tagan hoped he would have a chance to relate this encounter to Dimon. *The journey is the path*, he'd told his friend. Dimon had dismissed it as trivial wordplay, but now here he was, making good use of the old bit of Gatto wisdom.

"The south. You're from the compound deep in the tenth district?" They knew of that place, very remote and secretive. "How may we serve you, master?"

"The road is long. I'd not refuse sustenance. Something to carry with me."

"Yes, master." They quickly pulled packs off their backs, shuffled items between them, and presented a pack to the old man. "Thank you for allowing us to see the fire kata." They both offered a deep bow.

"And now may the road wing me away," Tagan said, delighted to have this old saying in his arsenal. His mother had told him it was something the Gatto said.

"Master." They bowed again and retreated, and Tagan continued down the road with a pack filled with food.

"I'll accompany her," Dimon said, nodding at Isotta. "The Turning have no quarrel with me. They don't even know me. I'll take her there, and he can guide me home, if he will. I'll pay."

"Nothing of the sort!" snorted Caterione. "Taijo, my son is to come immediately. Isotta, you may go with the sensei, but you're to return directly, with him and your brother. And you," she waved at Dimon, "may go your own way. Take supplies for your journey, and you'll get your papers. Leave Three Rivers. Taijo, see to it."

Dimon was about to object, but it seemed his only ally was the commander, and he was gone already. Then the girl grabbed his arm. "Come with me," Isotta ordered. "I'll take you to the supplies." She pulled a torch from the circle and marched toward the compound with Dimon in tow. "Wait until we're away," she whispered out of the side of her mouth. "Don't talk yet."

"Understood," Dimon whispered back, smiling. Perhaps he had two allies.

Isotta glanced back and grinned. "He's not following. I knew he wouldn't. The sensei doesn't want to miss what they're saying. He'll come soon, though, so we don't have much time. There's a map in the war room. I'll show you where she lives. Abigail, I mean."

"Abigail? You can't mean the girl who got Tagan into all this trouble?"

"My brother tutors the daughter of the Turning chieftain."

"Your brother ... Hold a moment." Dimon's eyebrows went down.

Isotta scowled. "Wait. She already knows he faked his death, doesn't she?" Isotta picked up her pace, and stormed down the trail. "Damn it. I should have figured it out. Everything was gloomy on the way there, and then on the way back suddenly she wants to talk, talk, talk. She didn't tell me he was alive. But she knew."

Dimon stopped. "Let me get this straight. You and your brother accompanied Abigail of the Turning to Deadrise Bay, for my friend's funeral?"

"And she found out he wasn't dead." Isotta grabbed his arm and pulled him along. "I'll show you where she lives. But you have to promise me something. I want to meet the Talla. Can you arrange it?"

Dimon tipped his head. "The Talla? What does she have to do with all of this?"

"Nothing. Can you do it?"

"You want to meet Talla Undine? Your mother wouldn't be too happy about that."

"I show you where Abigail lives, and you agree to introduce me to the Talla. Is it a deal?"

"Deal," Dimon grinned. "But this is all very strange. Tell me about your brother. How did he come to be Abigail's tutor?"

Isotta squeezed his arm, and Dimon fell silent. He saw the shadow of the man stepping up behind them. It seemed the sensei had already had second thoughts about lingering on the plateau.

He stepped between them. "Isotta," the old man said, "prepare your things, and then sleep. We leave before first light."

"But I said I'd show him the supplies."

"Do as you're told. I'll see that the southerner is provisioned. As for you," he tossed his head at Dimon, "the master says you're to receive safe passage. I'll draw up the papers in the war room."

Surely the sensei must have seen the girl's eye roll, Dimon thought. But the man stalked down the path with them, and there was no more opportunity to speak.

While the sensei's manner was brusque, he wasn't stingy in packing provisions. He loaded a pack with dried fruits and meat, jars of water and one of grain alcohol, a loaf of fresh bread, and a dozen fine apples. Was it guilt? Was this Gatto trying to make up for having imprisoned Tagan of Deadrise Bay? Dimon accepted the pack with a polite thank-you.

"Now for the papers. Then you may find a place to sleep, and leave whenever you wish in the morning." He led Dimon to another structure, a building about the size of the pavilion except with walls of wood and a solid roof. He held up a hand, stepped inside, and closed the door behind him.

"I'll just wait outside," Dimon muttered, and then almost cried out as a hand touched his arm.

Isotta put a hand to her lips and scowled. In her other hand she held a stone goblet, which appeared to be filled with wine.

The map, Dimon mouthed. *You said you'd show me.*

I know, she mouthed back. She tugged her ear, then stepped through the door, offering Dimon a brief glance at a row of wide tables and chart racks. He stepped close to the canvas to listen.

"I said, wait outside. Oh, Isotta. What do you want?"

"Sensei," Dimon heard her say, "you're writing his papers?"

"It seems every young man draws your attention, girl."

"Where will he go? Back to Deadrise Bay? Where is that, by the way? Show me."

"I'm busy, child. And you should be packing your things. I told you, we leave just before dawn."

"It's on this map, isn't it?" she said. "No, wait. This is where my brother lives."

"Child, don't touch that!"

"It's this place near the river, here. The Turning compound."

"Isotta, go!"

The door burst open a moment later, and Isotta stormed out and slammed it, and then turned and grinned. "Go in and look when he leaves."

The old man pushed outside holding the papers, and handed them to Dimon. "You may sleep in the pavilion, or find another spot. I have things to do. Goodnight." He strode off imperiously.

Dimon started to walk toward the pavilion, then circled around and returned to the war room. The sensei had left a lantern burning, as if he meant to return. There might not be much time. He slipped inside to find rows of maps laid out on the tables, and quickly found what he needed, a finely drawn map of the sector where the Turning held power, with a girl's fingerprint in red wine marking a spot. He leaned in. Most of the land was unfamiliar, but he had studied maps in the document room at Deadrise Bay, and he saw a few places he recognized. "I can get there," he muttered, memorizing the arrangement of roads.

He slipped back outside and sat on a bench. With a little more time in the war room, he might be able to plot his path home, he considered. But should he find Abigail, anyway? "What would Tagan do? What would he want me to do?" he muttered. "He won't go to the Turning, himself. He can't. I should go. This Arran will assist me. And even if he doesn't, I can give the chieftain's daughter the news, and surely she'll help me get home."

He made up his mind, and then sat for another few minutes to consider what he'd heard. The sensei had said he and Isotta would leave just before first light. "Never mind sleeping, then." His friend Tagan had once told him, *If you know where someone's going, the best way to follow is to be in front.*

Camilla had reinforced the idea of disguise. "You can be anyone," she had told him, "young or old, rich or poor—whatever is needed. *Be* that person, and others will believe you."

So far, it was working. With the Gatto master ruse, Tagan had food, and he had nothing to fear of the Gatto patrols. Keeping to the pace of a Gatto master meant a slower journey, but not a soul accosted him. The ruse worked so well that as he approached the border, he decided to abandon his original plan of changing to a different disguise. He had acquired a change of clothes along the way, stealing from unattended clotheslines, but he left them in his pack.

He walked across the border and continued as a Gatto master, and soon he encountered a southern patrol.

"Master Gatto," said a southern lieutenant, with a respectful nod, "you have business in the southlands?"

"I seek counsel with the freedman at the great sea," Tagan said in his feigned old-man voice, trying to strike a tone of Gatto inscrutability. He worried about overplaying his hand again, and listened for Camilla to scold him. But Camilla wasn't there. He would have to muddle through on his own.

"The freedman," the patrol said. "Oh, you mean Saor Tieg? The elder at Deadrise Bay?"

"I'm to seek counsel, and to offer information." It was working!

The lieutenant nodded a stiff bow and turned to his companions. "When's the next run to the coast, soldier?" He stepped closer and dropped his voice. "We can't just leave him on the road."

"A coach will pass soon, lieutenant," the soldier said, "within the hour, if there haven't been delays."

"Good. Arrange a seat for the old man. We'll settle with the coachman later. I'm sure Saor Tieg will cover it." He turned to Tagan. "We'll see to it that you have a comfortable journey, master Gatto."

"Many thanks, young man."

Soon Tagan found himself climbing into a horse-drawn coach that the soldier had flagged down. He pulled his hood low and sat. Riding next to him was a man in a Tallach outfit, who stiffened as an old Gatto joined him in the carriage. Across from him were a woman and two young boys. The woman looked at him and raised her eyebrows. But her attention was mostly on her sons, who were squabbling over a dinner basket, each trying to get the best sandwich for himself and arguing over who should have the larger boiled egg.

The man seated next to him held his place in a book, interrupted from his reading. "Those are fine blades, master Gatto," he said.

"Relics of the past," Tagan said with the slow laugh of an old man, "as am I." He glanced at the man and blanched. He bowed his head, and prayed that his riding companion hadn't gotten a good look at his face. It was a man in his grandfather's guard.

"And yet I'd wager the edges are as sharp as when they were forged. Yours too, perhaps," the soldier said with a light laugh.

"That isn't the way, I'm afraid," Tagan said. "Soon the blades will pass to another generation, and the memory of my days bearing them will fade."

"Not too soon, I hope," the man said politely.

The coach arrived at Deadrise Bay just after sunset. The first stop was in the village, where the woman and her sons stepped out. The coachman passed bags to her, and the woman thanked him, collected her sons, and headed down the street. Next the coach stopped at the water.

"Last stop before the stables," he announced.

The man from his grandfather's guard waited for Tagan to disembark and then he climbed out himself. "May I accompany you to your destination?" the guard said. "It grows late."

"Thank you, but I'll walk and gather my thoughts," Tagan said, and bowed. "Live on, liegeman." Odd, Tagan thought, that the man hadn't offered to walk the woman and her children home. Was it curiosity? Did this man want to see what the old Gatto was up to?

"Join in the fight tomorrow, master Gatto," the man said, and bowed before heading for the stairs.

Tagan wandered toward the water, but then circled back and took a road toward the village. When he was out of sight, he picked up his pace and ran. A short way down the road he turned onto a walking path that cut the corner for servants who worked up at the inn. At a spot where a narrow wooden walking bridge crossed a creek, he looked around to be sure he was alone, and stripped off the Gatto robe. He climbed down the bank, dunked his head in the water, and scrubbed the soot from his face and the ash from his hair. Then he quickly changed into the clothes he'd stolen. The Gatto robe and blades went into the pack, and he emerged in plain brown pants and a hooded shirt with wooden buttons.

As he approached the terrace and saw a crowd gathering, he realized he'd stumbled into a bit of good luck. A year ago, a new tradition had been started. A free meal was offered on each solstice and equinox to the workers and other commoners at Deadrise Bay. He'd get a good meal and a chance to wander near the inn and get a sense of what was happening.

It was his mother's muse, the old man Horace, who had planted the seed of the idea. He had drilled Undine on the importance of capturing hearts as well as minds. "Win the hearts. You'll be safer and happier for it. Little things count."

Tagan's grandfather had never seemed inclined to worry about winning the hearts, and his mother didn't understand how to do it. It didn't come naturally to either of them. It was the little girl Tagan had brought home, Rebecca, who had come up with the idea for the feast. Undine was scolding her for one thing or another, and told her about Horace's directive. "No one knows you, tether. You'd do well to consider the advice of my muse, and learn to win hearts." Then she sighed. "And of course, I should as well. What do you say, child? How shall we attempt to win the hearts, you and I?"

Rebecca, probably because she was hungry at the moment, immediately said, "Throw a feast. Everyone loves a free meal."

His mother offered some objections, but thought about it, and decided to give it a try. It didn't merely work. The feast was a fantastic success. Not only did the village turn out for it, but the ship captains offered the service of their men to help with the work. For weeks afterward, the Talla's feast was a topic of conversation among the commoners. And so, Undine established a new tradition at Deadrise Bay, the Feast of the Quarter. On each equinox and solstice, long tables of food were set up under the pergola, and a happy crowd formed a line. It was one day each quarter when there was no distinction across the terraces: People filled plates with food and sat wherever they liked.

"I'll get a meal and some time to think," Tagan muttered. He understood that he couldn't simply step up and announce his presence: *Mother, here I am. I need you to solve this problem of gray-gis wanting me dead.* He couldn't approach her cap-in-hand and beg. He would almost rather go back to his cell at Three Rivers than do that. He tugged his hood low to obscure his face, and joined the line.

"Don't think we've met," said a man behind him, tapping him on the arm. "Neil's the name. You new in town?"

Tagan turned, keeping his head low. "Geun," he said, adopting the name of the Gatto boy who had deigned to speak to him at Three Rivers. "Traveling to Steerageway. Lucky break. Didn't think I'd have a meal tonight."

"Oh, and a fine one, at that. The Talla puts on a good spread. And they buy all the provisions from the farms in the village, so we get a bonus both ways. A nice price on the produce and meat, and we get to have a taste of the stuff we don't get to eat at home. It ain't no basket of culls and gleanings here."

"They do this often?" Tagan asked.

"On the season. Fine way to call in the next one, don't you think? So have a good meal, Geun, and a fine journey."

Tagan nodded as the man turned to speak with a woman behind him in line.

As he reached the first table with his plate, Tagan felt a pang of anxiety. What was it? Then he saw her. At the next table he spotted a little girl in a bright yellow dress, dishing heaping helpings of sauce on each plate. Anxiety veered toward panic. Rebecca was pale, and looked smaller and thinner, as if she were wasting away. Her breathing was slow and rasping, and her hands shook. But in spite of it, she scooped out a large portion for every guest, and smiled. Tagan pressed his eyes closed, and worked to get hold of himself. Poor Becca!

Then as he stepped up to her, his eyes widened beneath his hood. The girl stopped, her face lit up, and she drew in an enormous breath. She dropped the dipper in the pot of sauce and stepped back, and he thought she might collapse, but instead she stood up straight.

"I can breathe! I can breathe!" she exclaimed. "Ha ha! I can breathe!" She turned and scanned the crowd. "Where is he?"

Tagan stepped quickly to the next station and tried to look like just another commoner getting his meal. Was she staring at him? Would she give him away? He silently willed her to hear his warning. *Don't give me up, Becca. Careful!*

And somehow it worked. The little girl giggled, and then turned and skipped to the inn, and a soldier stepped up to take over her post. Tagan moved away from the pergola with a full plate and a racing heart, and found a place away from the crowd to sit and eat. He glanced at the inn and saw a curtain pulled back in the small dining room. Two faces peered out, his mother's and Rebecca's.

"It's all right," he muttered. "They're just looking out." He sat and ate his meal, thinking about his next steps and feeling inadequate. He didn't have a next step. His plan had been to come up with a plan along the journey to Deadrise Bay, but the unexpected ride had shortened the journey considerably. Now here he was. Never mind figuring a way to evade the gray-gis. He needed to figure a way to save face. He'd never live it down if the message were, *I've failed. Help me, mother.*

"What do I have to work with? What are the pieces?" he said to himself, trying to consider what Camilla would say. But once again, Camilla wasn't there to give him the answer.

He took a silent inventory. He had a spectacular pair of ancient Gatto blades, and a silk robe to go with them. Of course, on the other side of the equation were the gray-gis, who would come for him again if they learned he was alive, and the Turning, and the Gatto, and probably the northern soldiers as well. Add to that Master Caterione of Three Rivers, formerly of The Hidden. So, the gray-gis, Three Rivers, the Hidden, the Turning, and the north ... everyone was gunning for him.

"Skin in the game," came the words in his head. "It's about having skin in the game."

"Skin?" Tagan looked around, and then his face brightened. "Camilla. You're back! I need your help, muse."

"Not much time. But look, this one is easy. If you don't want to beg for your mother's help, then you need to propose something instead. A play."

"A play would be ideal, yes," Tagan's smile turned to a scowl. "Why didn't I think of that?"

"Oh, feeling snarky, are we? You're the one running home to mamma.

Shut up and listen. I've only got a minute. If you don't want your mother to give you a glass of warm milk and tuck you into bed, you'd better have a plan. You have a plan, and you're offering to let her in on it. Understand? She's got a stake. Skin in the game. You follow? She gets something out of it other than just to save your ass."

"Like what?"

"Damn. Didn't they teach you strategy? You're gonna haul off something big, and maybe you could let her in on it. You're not begging. You're offering. I mean, she does want things, doesn't she? Everyone does."

"Of course. Something big," Tagan rolled his eyes again.

"Wow. I always hated that your mother couldn't hear me. But it meant I never got the attitude."

Tagan sighed. "Apologies. I don't have a big plan. And these past days haven't been ideal."

"You and me both, brother. But take control. Make something up, if you have to. Even if it's half-baked and she tells you you're nuts, you'll be in the door, right? And then she'll help you anyway, because you're her son. So, think. What does your mother want? Oh, damn. I have to go!"

"She, um ..." Tagan rose and looked out over the water. His head blanked. What did his mother want? Nothing came to mind. Then his attention abruptly shifted as a small figure who had changed from her yellow dress to an old peasant dress slammed into him. "What the hell!" Thin arms wrapped around him and a face crushed itself to his chest.

"You're here. You came back!"

A few heads turned, and Tagan felt a flash of concern.

"Daddy, can we walk on the grass?" Rebecca said, realizing the same thing. "I want to see the cliffs from up here. We never get to come up here."

Whoa. Nicely done, Tagan reflected. Rebecca eased up, but clamped a hand onto his and wouldn't let go. She pulled him along, and they walked up the stairs to the lawn in front of the inn.

"We're allowed to be on the terraces today," she said, for the benefit of a few others who were walking on the grass. "Come on!"

She tugged his arm and led him into the shadows around the side of the inn, and then sharply pulled him toward a door. The door opened, she pulled him in, and it closed again. Tagan pulled off his hood as the little girl hugged him again. He blinked as his mother came at him, too.

Undine's reception was less dramatic. "Back so soon?" she said with a smile, stopping at arm's length. "Tagan, child, I hadn't expected to see you before the end of the year."

"I've returned, mother," he said.

"I can see that." She gave him a hug and waved the little girl off. "Don't crush him, tether. So, what is it? Did you miss my cooking? Couldn't bear to miss the Feast of the Quarter? Couldn't sleep in a strange bed? What?"

"You cook?" he said, matching her sarcastic tone but feeling his hands tighten into fists. Camilla had pretty much pegged it: He'd been back for less than a minute and was already getting the running-home-to-mommy treatment.

"I'll cook whatever you want," Rebecca chimed in, "if you'll promise to stay. Ha! Talla, look. I can breathe!"

"Come," Undine said, "we'll sit and talk. And yes, tether, you may tag along. Tagan, dear, I suppose you've eaten, but we'll open a bottle of wine and talk. Is that pack filled with clothes like the ones you're wearing? Let's toss it in the fire. We'll fetch you some proper clothes."

If she wants in, maybe you could arrange it. Camilla was right. He had to come up with a plan where he wasn't begging his mother for help. But what was the play? Stun her with the amazing blades he'd found? She would certainly be interested, but then what?

"Come, tell me. I'm waiting. Did you find the north to be more hostile than you expected, dear?" Undine said, condescendingly. "It's all right. I won't let those northerners get to you. You're home now."

"Mother," Tagan said, working to relax, "I didn't return because I need you to protect me."

"Of course not, dear. Now come along. I'll have a bath drawn for you. You look like you need a wash before bed. You too, tether. Where did you get those rags, child?"

"Mother, shut up, damn it!"

The woman laughed. "All right, all right. I'm sorry, Tagan. I'm just having a bit of fun. I told you the world is dangerous, didn't I? But come, we'll sit, and you can tell me what you've been up to." She waved to a man at the bar and he followed them into the small dining room.

"I came here with a proposition," Tagan snapped, when the glasses were filled and the waiter had left.

"You came here because I need to breathe," Rebecca corrected, pulling her chair close to his.

Tagan gave her a squeeze. "I've been thinking about you, Becca. I was telling stories to another little girl to pass the time. She's a bit older than you, but I bet you two would get along. She's got spirit. Anyway, I told her you're my sister."

The girls' jaw dropped, and Tagan thought he saw a tear in her eye. Then she flung herself at him again, and took his breath away with a bear hug.

Undine sipped her wine. "All right, Tagan, tell me about this little proposition," she said with a patronizing smile. "And tether, sit down. He needs to breathe, too."

The backpack he'd placed at his feet tipped and thumped to the floor, and Tagan looked down at it—and the root of an idea came to him. "I have something of value. Something of great value," he improvised. "Old and rare. I'd venture to guess not many have seen the like of it."

"All right." His mother rolled her hand, urging him to get on with it. "What is this item of great value?"

"I'm not an expert in this particular field. But let me back up." He needed to play for time. Camilla was annoyingly absent. Maybe if he could stretch things out, she would return and tell him what to do. "You're wondering if I had a plan to get away from those gray-gis. I did. I got out through the caves, and I ran to the north. I'd planned to go to the White Cliffs and enlist the help of the northern lord to get the gray-gis off my back."

Undine raised a single eyebrow. "How exactly did you think that would work?"

Tagan held up a palm. "Listen. The original plan was to ask him for help. Maybe he wouldn't offer any, but it was worth a try. After all, you did a job for the north, all those years ago, didn't you?"

"Tagan, dear, it's a bit more complicated than that. You can't exactly say they owe me."

"All right. But what did I have to lose? The backup plan, if they sent me on my way with nothing, was to keep going north and help Dimon find his father. He's a soldier in one of the compounds up there. Maybe he could do something. Those old clans keep to themselves, but I've heard they have influence."

Undine sighed. "That was your plan? All right. And let me guess. It didn't work out. Did you make it all the way to Lesser Mire? That's where I'm told your friend's father is, and it's a long, long way. Did you take Dimon there?"

Tagan closed his eyes, and then opened them again as an idea popped into his head. Of course! It was obvious! Here he was, trying to engineer his own path to safety, with Dimon languishing in a prison cell in the north. His plan should be to do the right thing. As Camilla had pointed out, his mother would work to keep him safe, anyway. The plan didn't need to be about his own predicament.

"It's Dimon that I want to talk to you about."

"Dimon?" His mother's casual tone evaporated. "Tagan, did you get that sweet boy into trouble again?"

"He went the wrong way." Tagan shook his head slowly. "Damn it. How could he go the wrong way?"

"Son, what are you talking about? You say you have a proposition, and it has to do with Dimon? I like that boy, Tagan. If he needs my help, tell me."

"I got away, but he didn't. Soldiers of the north took him."

"Soldiers of the north have Dimon? Why? What's he to them?"

"Last I heard, he was at one of the border stations. The Gatto hold sway there."

"The Gatto," his mother said flatly. "Yes, it's quite the contract she's won up there. By kissing ass, no doubt."

Camilla, it's working, Tagan silently said. *She's not belittling me anymore.* But Camilla was still not there to observe.

His mother leaned forward, anxious to hear more. This was good.

"The border stations are still there, of course," Tagan said, "but I'm told most of the soldiers have been assigned to other places. The Gatto have taken control of a long stretch of the border. So yes, this is about the Gatto, too. Unless you have a bargaining position with the north directly," Tagan said.

"Tagan, spit it out. What's this plan of yours?"

"I want to make an arrangement. A trade. The Gatto will arrange for Dimon to be released, and I'll give them something they want. Or rather, you'll give it to them, as I can't very well approach them."

"You took something from the Gatto? You visited with them?"

Tagan laughed. "Oh, a fine, pleasant stay. No, damn it, mother, I didn't visit them. They intercepted me on the road and held me prisoner."

"The Gatto? Why? And they released you when they realized who you are, I assume? This story grows more incredible by the minute."

Tagan smiled. He'd thrown his mother off her game. Point to Tagan. Why couldn't Camilla be watching? She'd never believe him. His mother looked almost flustered. "They didn't release me, mother. The Gatto imprisoned me, and I got away."

"Imprisoned you. The Gatto?"

"And I escaped, and I took a little something with me. Something I found. Do you follow? That's where you come in. I could try to haul this off myself, but it will work much better if you do it. And there's something in it for you as well."

"Tagan," his mother said, folding her arms. "These are not people to be toyed with. You've stolen something from them? Is that why they imprisoned you?"

"Not stolen. You couldn't say I stole anything. And it was after they imprisoned me. But I do have something they want. Two things. Here's one of them." Tagan grinned and set the pack on the table. He opened it and pulled out the silk robe, and unrolled it. "I have these." He showed her twin ebony and white gold Gatto blades resting on an ancient silk Gatto master's robe.

His mother's eyes bugged out, and her jaw dropped. "Hell in a basket, child," she hissed, "where did you get these? Are they from the far reaches?"

She picked one up and turned it slowly, inspecting the workmanship and its age. "Oh, this is the finest I've ever seen—ever heard of! Old master Stetlin has a pair like this, but his are pocked and dented from centuries of use. Will you look at the sheen on the handle, and the symmetry of the hand guard. Fire and daggers, look at this blade!"

Smiling, Tagan sat back and watched his mother ogle the blade. "Are you going to draw me a bath and tuck me in, mother? Or would you like to take those blades to the Gatto and bargain with them?"

Undine didn't answer, but instead kept staring at the blade and turning it. When Rebecca leaned in and reached for the other, Undine swatted her hand without shifting her gaze, and the girl scowled and sat.

"I need something, mother," Tagan said. "Freeing Dimon is the main thing. I want you to help me do that. But I also need to get the gray-gis off my back. I don't have that part worked out yet, but maybe the Gatto can help with that as well. Maybe they can provide information, or make an arrangement with the gray-gis that the contract is to be lifted."

"An arrangement." His mother shook her head and shifted her attention to her son. "The Gatto aren't fond of making arrangements with others. And you and I, Tagan, we're Tallach. The Gatto have never made an arrangement with the Tallachs. Not that I've ever heard of."

"I want to make an arrangement with them," Tagan stubbornly insisted. "At a minimum, they can get my friend out of that jail. I have the blades. It seems a fair trade. Can you make that happen? We don't have to win their love, but I bet you'll put that nasty Gatto master Caterione back on her heels when she sees the blades."

Undine looked up and stared. "Caterione? She's at Three Rivers. You were taken to Three Rivers?"

"I was, and she was about to have me killed as a spy."

"My son? Caterione was going to put *my son* to death?" Undine spread her palms on the table and rose.

"I didn't tell her who I was, mother. I couldn't. For all I knew, they would tell the gray-gis. But listen. I got away, I have these, and I want to use them to get Dimon returned to us. Can you do it?"

"Caterione of the Gatto tried to kill my son?" she bellowed. "And you say she didn't know who you were. Does she know now? I'll show her these blades by driving them into her heart!" Undine pushed her chair back and started pacing.

"I didn't stop to ask her if she'd figured it out. Damn it, are you going to help me?"

"And this other thing." She halted and turned to him. "What is it? You said two things. You have something else of value to Caterione? Oh, yes, son. Yes, I'm interested."

Tagan smiled. Ten points at least, he thought, again wishing Camilla were watching. His mother was furious. "The other thing is probably of more value than those blades, especially to Master Caterione. Do you remember when I begged you to teach me some Gatto katas?"

"Teach me, too," Rebecca interjected. "I want to learn a kata."

Tagan patted her on the shoulder. "Shush, Becca. Let me speak with mother."

"I do recall that, son. And against my better judgment I showed you, and you annoyed your sensei to no end when you decided to show him. What of it? How does this relate to Caterione?"

"Do you remember how I begged you to show me the great altar kata and the great wind kata?"

"Ara and Vela. Even Caterione herself can't perform those two. Not at full speed."

"You once told me a story about another great kata that was lost."

Undine folded her arms. "There are many Gatto stories, dear. It's an ancient order. The lost kata is a favorite tale. What are you driving at?"

"It's not just a tale."

This earned him a glare. "It's a legend, son. A story told around campfires to impress the novices."

"You called it the fire kata. Isn't that right? But I know the real name. It's called Vatra. And like fire, it reaches out into variations. Sixteen, to be exact. More, if you shift up or down in the middle. As I say, I'm not sure just what to do with it, but maybe you'll have an idea."

"Do with what, child?" Undine said, leaning forward. "Exactly what did you find up there?"

"In the old legend, is there a kata room?"

"The great Vatra hall? The story goes that the ancients set down the fire kata to be preserved for infinite generations, only to have water vanquish fire. There are different versions of the legend, but if you sift through them it seems there was an earthquake and a flood, and the place was destroyed. Everyone died. The village burned and was completely wiped away. No one even knows where it was. It's rubble at the bottom of a lake somewhere."

"The great Vatra hall wasn't destroyed. Only the entrance was flooded."

"Tagan, the Vatra hall fell into legend dozens of generations ago."

"And it's about to fall back out, mother, because I found it."

16. Intertwined

Dimon traveled from early morning until late into the night, slept for a few hours, then rose to continue south. Twice he overslept, rising well after sunrise, and scolded himself for it.

Ironically, he wasn't stopped at the border. "But I have passage papers this time," he grumbled. "And now no one is here to challenge me?" He looked around, almost wishing a Gatto border guard would stop him, but saw no one. He crossed into the south and continued toward the Turning compound, long days of walking and short nights of sleeping.

When he started to recognize landmarks from the map, he slowed to a steady and purposeful walk. He was drawing close to Turning territory, and didn't want to arouse anyone's suspicion by rushing toward the compound.

"Would Tagan approve?" he wondered out loud. "Or would he scold me for my stupidity?"

The gate guards at the outermost perimeter seemed confused when Dimon strode up. "Who are you?" a guard demanded. "Are you lost? These are Turning lands."

"I've come with news and information for a Gatto named Arran, who is stationed here," Dimon said. He had practiced saying these words over and over, but still felt that his tone wasn't quite powerful enough.

"What news and information?"

Dimon offered a shallow bow. "Master Caterione orders me to report to the Gatto. She asks that you allow me to pass. I was issued papers at Three Rivers. You may inspect them, if you wish."

There was a moment's hesitation, but a guard waved him forward. "Come with me."

Dimon made a few attempts to strike up a conversation, but the guard had no interest in speaking, so they walked in silence. After almost an hour they reached another checkpoint. The guard escorted him past the checkpoint and continued to accompany him down the road.

It was a long way to the compound. After even more miles they passed a third checkpoint, and kept walking. Finally he saw an inner gate, higher than the others, and more heavily guarded.

"Wait here," the guard said, leaving him just inside the gate with a pair of guards flanking him. He disappeared down a path.

Soon the guard and another figure approached. Dimon recognized the aspect of the man accompanying the guard before he could make out his facial features. He'd seen two versions of this already, the girl and her mother. The Gatto tutor strode up, expressionless, and yet Dimon hardly felt he needed an introduction.

"I'm Arran," the Gatto said guardedly. "I'm told my mother sent you."

"I come with news and information," Dimon said. He concentrated on slowing his speech and keeping his tone slightly over-loud and constant. Confidence. He had to show confidence. "I'm sent from Three Rivers," he added, reflecting that Tagan might have laughed at this. It was technically true, although it would have been more accurate to say he'd been evicted from Three Rivers. "I'm to speak with you in private."

Arran nodded at the gate guard, who turned and left without nodding back. "Come," he said to Dimon, and led him along a path to his hut. "Come inside and tell me the news."

Dimon entered and stood just inside the door, feeling his heart beat faster. He hadn't practiced this part as many times. "Arran, please don't be alarmed. Your sister Isotta told me where to find you."

"My sister?" he scowled. "What mischief is she up to?"

"This is not about her. I understand you know about Tagan."

The Gatto moved his hands to his blades. "What is this? Who are you?"

Dimon raised his palms. "My name is Dimon. I'm Tagan's friend. Tagan of Deadrise Bay, the son of the Talla. We fled north together. May I sit? It's a long story."

Arran stared at him for a long time, considering, then nodded. "Sit."

"You don't need to be along at all, child, let alone setting the pace," the old sensei growled, as Isotta urged him to move more quickly.

"I thought old people wanted to make their time count," the girl huffed.

Sensei Taijo clicked his tongue. "You thought nothing of the sort, child, unless you've forgotten your lessons entirely. The journey is the path. Walk."

"But the mission," Isotta said under her breath, "is to tell my brother what's happening."

"It's not the Gatto way to mutter while walking the path, child. Chin up. Mouth closed. Walk."

"Fine." Isotta raised her nose and strode ahead, and almost walked off the side of the road.

It seemed endless, the slow days ambling along, but when Isotta looked ahead and saw the gate that marked the edge of Turning territory, she realized they'd arrived fairly quickly. The slow walks had been compensated for by the shorter rests between.

"There it is," she said. "You can walk like a snail, but I'm going to go find my brother." She didn't wait for the sensei's reprimand, but darted ahead. The gate guards nodded their recognition of the young tutor's sister and didn't stop her. They moved to the side and allowed her to duck under the gate and run.

It was late morning, and Isotta knew everyone would be up. Most would be at their duties, but not her brother. He would be outside practicing his kata. Isotta ran faster. If she hurried, she might arrive before he finished and went inside. It would give her a chance to tell him in private what had happened.

Instead she stopped dead in the road as two figures appeared, her brother and another young man.

"Arran," she said, as the figures in the road also halted. "And Abigail? Abigail, what are you wearing?" Isotta strode forward, then stopped and stared, not bothering to offer a formal greeting to her brother. "Why are you dressed as a man? You know he's not dead, don't you? You knew and didn't tell me. But I know it too, because I saw him."

Abigail's expression changed from friendly to alarmed. She stepped forward and grabbed Isotta by the shoulders. "You saw him? Tell me!"

"Into the woods. Now!" Arran barked, nodding his head at a narrow path and flashing a deep scowl at his sister. "We'll not talk in the road."

Twice as they walked, Isotta started to speak, and twice Arran held up a hand to silence his sister. When they were well into the woods, he stopped. "Now tell us."

"The sensei caught a pair of Tallach spies crossing the border," she said.

"But they weren't spies," Arran said.

Isotta scowled. "They ran, but the trainees caught one of them, and brought him to Three Rivers. The other one ..."

"Caught by Tynan soldiers. He ran the wrong way. Come, get on with it."

This time Abigail turned to Arran and scowled.

"Let me tell it!" Isotta scolded. "I spoke with the one the sensei brought in. He refused to tell anyone his name. Later we learned that he was Tagan, from Deadrise Bay. The Talla's son."

"Tagan!" Abigail cried out.

Isotta nodded. "But he got away."

"Swam the river route, and escaped into the night," Arran said.

Both spun to him. "How do you know all of this already, brother?" Isotta said, folding her arms in annoyance. "What are you not telling me?"

"A boy came earlier with news," Arran said.

"Oh, that figures," Isotta grumbled, her shoulders slumping. "Dimon got here first? The sensei has to walk the speed of a snail. How long has he been here? I shouldn't have told him where you are."

"What?" Abigail demanded, confused. "Someone came here?"

"He's not here, Isotta," Arran said. "The boy stopped in earlier this morning, and left. You've missed him by a couple of hours."

"Then what are you doing?" Isotta spun and looked back toward the road. "Aren't you going with him?"

"Arran, Isotta, what are you talking about?" Abigail insisted.

"The Tallach boy's journey isn't our affair, sister," Arran said to Isotta, still ignoring Abigail. "I gave him a map. He can make his own way."

"Maybe it's not *your* affair," Isotta sniffed, "but it's *hers*." She pointed a thumb at Abigail. "And you're staying, too, Abbie? Why?"

Abigail stepped physically between then. "What's going on? Tell me who visited!"

Isotta saw Abigail's expression, and turned to her brother. "Arran, you didn't tell her? You're impossible," she scolded. "Abbie, Tagan's friend Dimon—the one who went north with him—came here to ask Arran to guide him to Deadrise Bay, because he thinks that's where Tagan is going. He assumed you'd want to go, too. And instead my brother sent him away."

Abigail spun on Arran. "You said Tagan wouldn't go home!" she accused. "That it was too dangerous, and we should wait here for word. Now his friend has come, and you've not told me about it?"

"Young miss, this is not our affair." Arran held up a palm.

"Never mind him, Abbie," Isotta said. "My brother is about to be ordered back to Three Rivers, anyway, so who cares about him? You and I can go."

"What?" Arran exclaimed, backing up a step and looking around as if someone might be coming for him that very moment. "The boy didn't tell me that. Why am I to be ordered home?"

"Sensei Taijo will tell you," Isotta sniffed. "He'll get here eventually, at his masterful turtle's pace. Go find him on the road if you want. I'm supposed to go back, too. But I'm going to Deadrise Bay with Dimon. Don't try to stop me, brother. I'm going."

"Why is mother ordering me back?" Arran pleaded.

"Why do you think? She just tried to execute the heir to Deadrise Bay."

Abigail blanched. "She did *what*?"

"She didn't know who he was. But mother was going to execute him herself, I hear. With her own blades."

"Arran!" Abigail said, white-faced. "What is this?"

"How long do you think it will be, brother, before the Talla finds out?" Isotta piled on. "I'd guess mother wants us home because she plans to run. Wouldn't you?"

Arran took a step backward. "I hadn't considered ..."

"And I know something else," Isotta said. "Commander Riley is Tagan's father. Yes, that's right." She held up a finger and thumb. "Mother came this close to executing a commander's son."

Abigail stared first at Arran, who was as wide-eyed as she was herself, then at Isotta, who was smirking in gleeful defiance of her older brother.

"I have to go," Abigail hissed. "I have to find Tagan's friend!"

"Tell me something, Tagan, dear," Undine said, leaning back. "The kata room ..."

They had moved from the inn to the mansion, but had settled in a sitting room for the servants, to avoid interruptions. Once news of the return from the dead of Undine's son had spread, the frenzy of inquiries and visits would start. They wanted some time to talk privately while things were still quiet.

"It's remarkable." Tagan sat on a worn sofa staring at the embers in a little fireplace. A copper tub of water on the hearth had grown cold, and Rebecca, fresh from a bath and wrapped in a damp towel, was curled under his arm, asleep.

"You told me how you got in, the desperate dive to escape the damned Gatto, and finding the entrance under water. How did you get out? And how did you get away?"

Tagan grinned. "I've been waiting for you to ask me that. I got out by swimming the last part of the passage. It ends in a cavern on the side of the gorge."

"The gorge. I'd like to see that, one day. I'm told it's spectacular. But how did you get away? I'd have thought the Gatto would be everywhere, searching. Even if she wanted you dead, Caterione would want to *know* that you're dead. That's not the kind of loose end she'd want to leave."

"I got some help."

"One of Caterione's men helped you?"

"Ha. No. Nothing that outlandish. Although," Tagan nodded, "I suppose anyone but you and I would think it's more outlandish."

"Who helped you, then?"

"Someone you know, although you haven't spoken to her since before I was born. Someone I always thought you made up."

"You thought ..." Undine started to talk, but halted, and stared.

"Camilla speaks to me. She told me how to get away."

"The silent one." Undine spoke in a whisper. "She speaks to you? My old muse speaks to you? And Horace. Does he speak to you, also?"

Tagan shook his head. "Camilla says the old man is gone."

Undine let out a long breath, and wilted, putting her face in her hands. "Horace. You're gone? I'd always thought ... always hoped ..."

"She says his enemies killed him. She barely escaped, herself."

"And she talks to you." Undine looked up. "She talks to you."

"Yes, mother. She told me she could only speak to you through Horace. And when he died, it severed the connection. And then she connected to me. Or me to her. I don't know. Her voice came to me the night I fled from the gray-gis."

"Camilla. Is she with you now? I'd so like to speak with her!"

Tagan shook his head. "We connect now and then. She's running from danger, as am I. We speak when she can, I think."

Wiping her eye, Undine sat up, breathed deeply, and forced a smile. "My muse. And now yours!"

"It was her idea. I put on the Gatto gi, and pretended I was Master Caterione. I sent the boy guarding to cavern to go hunt for me. I whispered, and copied the master's intonation. Her sharp manner of speaking."

"That sounds like Camilla. And that sounds like Caterione. Tagan, dear. My muse speaks to you! Tell her, when you can, that Una misses her, and misses Horace. Tell her to say a word for him on my behalf. Odd, I don't know his custom around death. Do they say words for the dead?"

"I don't know, mother. But I'll tell her."

Undine rose, straightened her sleeves, and nodded sharply. "Well then. Here's what we'll do. I'll negotiate with Caterione, as you wish. You'll stay here. Talk to your grandfather in the morning, and he'll see to it that you're protected until I return. Understood?"

"Why should I stay here?"

"Stay here, son. Stay, and do as your grandfather says."

"What, so I'm to be a prisoner here instead of at Three Rivers?"

"The difference is that here you won't have a humorless Gatto master itching to cut you to ribbons, dear. And the food is better, I'd guess, than in the dungeons of the Gatto."

"He'll order me to stay inside for my own protection. You know he will, mother."

"Do as he says. I don't want to come home and discover the gray-gis have taken you."

"But for how long? I don't want to be locked away in this old mansion."

"Take the robe," Undine said. She tossed it to him. "I'm sure you'll go out anyway, even if both I and your grandfather order you not to. But do it at night, and disguise yourself, all right? Wear the old Gatto robe. And it seems you've lost one of my Gatto blades," she scowled, "so take one of these, and I'll give you my other one. They don't match, but it will work well enough as a costume."

"But you need the ancient blades to present to the master," he objected, "To bargain for Dimon's release."

"One will do. Your friend isn't a king. Do you realize what these are worth? You just hold onto the other for now. And listen to me. Never, never go out without that robe and the blades. Do you understand me? Here, give me the tether, and go get some sleep."

"All right, mother." Tagan picked up Rebecca and rose. He kissed the girl on the cheek and handed her over, and headed to his room.

As he walked the halls, a servant dropped a tray and screamed, and another stopped dead in the hall and stared without moving, frozen in place.

"I'm not a ghost," Tagan said to the man. "Would it be asking too much to get a pot of tea?"

Tagan strode down the stairs early in the morning, pleased to be in his own clothes. He hoped to sneak a quick meal in the back kitchens and enjoy a few quiet hours before anyone found him. But Rebecca was up already, and nabbed him in the hall before he'd even made it to the kitchens.

"She's gone," Rebecca announced, skipping in, dressed in black pants and a brilliant yellow shirt. "She left this note. I'll tell you what it says."

"The note was to you?" Tagan raised a single eyebrow.

"She says you have to carry the Gatto blades all the time, especially if you go outside. She says never go out without them, and especially not without the old one."

"Yes, she said that last night." Tagan smiled. "The old blade will be safe with me," he said, patting Rebecca on the shoulder.

"She also says, don't go out without taking Rebecca with you." The girl grinned.

"It doesn't say that. Give it to me." Tagan snatched the note from her. "Come. Let's get some breakfast in the kitchen."

"Breakfast in the kitchen? Don't be stupid. You're getting a feast. Your grandfather is in the dining hall waiting for you, along with a hundred other people."

"Already?" Tagan sighed. "All right. Come with me. I suppose I'll have to sit next to the old man, but you can guard my other flank."

When they entered the dining hall, a cheer went up, and continued unabated as the old man stepped over and hugged his grandson.

"My dear boy," said Saor Tieg. "My dear, dear boy!"

"Didn't I say I'd take you to see the northlands again one day, Tyra? And here we go."

The redheaded woman who sat across from Undine nodded. "Another adventure in your father's carriage."

"It's my carriage now, but this will be an adventure, that's for certain."

"Do you remember the time we stole his day carriage and went to a fire pit pavilion? That was a fine night."

"If you thought that was amusing, wait till you see this. You brought your blades?"

"Yes, Undine. I'm not a fourth-tier Talla, but I'll look respectable enough at your side." Tyra laughed. "I can't wait to see what Caterione looks like these days. I remember that was she was so severe. Do you think she's changed?"

"She's probably more severe. And more confident, and more capable, and more annoying. They've given her Three Rivers, damn it. I wonder if there's a hat large enough for her head. But she'll speak with me, Tyra. I promise you that."

The last time they had seen Caterione was twenty years ago. Undine and her friend had been quietly escorted to the north by Commander Stiles, an aloof man who executed his orders efficiently, and saw to it that she and Tyra were delivered directly and discreetly to the Pavilion of The Hidden.

This time Undine meant to make a show of her arrival. Behind the carriage and in front were dozens of solders on horseback.

"Mightn't they see us as a threat, Undine? All these soldiers."

"I'm counting on it. She'll think I know she almost put my son to death—and of course I do know it, although I won't state it directly. I mean to dangle it in front of her and make her squirm. I'll get her to do what I want."

"You'll get Caterione of the Gatto to do what you want? That will be a fine trick."

"As my old muse used to say, *you just watch me*." Undine smiled sadly, thinking of Horace.

"But to trade those magnificent old blades for one boy's freedom? It doesn't seem so hard. Who wouldn't take that deal?"

"Don't be silly. Caterione will never carry the Vatra blades, Tyra. I'll let her touch one, but they'll never be sheathed at her waist."

Tyra tipped her head. "No? But I thought that was the plan."

"That was my son's plan." Undine waved a dismissive hand. "He's so young. *Trade these blades and get my friend out of the dungeon. Please, mother*," she mocked. "He has no idea. She'd have to give me Three Rivers for them, and even then, I might not make the trade. Not with Caterione. No, I have a plan of my own. But I'll get that adorable boy out of the dungeons while we're at it. My son will have his friend back."

"You're not going to fight her, are you?"

"That would be entertaining. But no, Tyra. Another thing my old muse used to tell me is, *less rash and more clever*. That's what's wanted at times like this."

"Undine, we're stopping." Tyra leaned out the window to see what was happening. "Soldiers. Not Gatto."

Her own soldiers moved into formation around the carriage, weapons drawn. But as Undine scooted over for a look, she caught sight of a northern soldier, palms up, approaching. She drew the curtain closed and sat back, flashing Tyra a wink.

"They want to talk, not to fight. Relax."

The officer asked for an audience with the Talla, and at the knock on her carriage door, Undine listened through the closed curtain as her own officer identified the visitor and waited for her orders.

"He may enter," she said.

A northern captain stepped into the carriage and sat stiffly across from the Talla, at Tyra's side. He waited for permission to speak.

"I heard you talking to my guard. You're a captain under a northern commander by the name of Riley," Undine said. She flashed another wink at Tyra, and Tyra raised her eyebrows up and down.

"That's why I'm here, Talla."

This brought Undine's eyebrows up. "Hold. Riley sent you to me?"

Tyra leaned in, fascinated. A twist already? They hadn't even arrived yet.

"No, Talla. Apologies. I meant that the commander has issued orders. I recognized your carriage and your men, and I thought you should know. Orders have been given that your son is to be allowed safe passage."

Undine stared. "Orders have been given. By whom? Do you mean by Commander Riley?"

"That's my understanding, Talla, although I've scant details aside from the order itself. The order is that the young Tallach man Tagan, whose mother is Talla Undine," he nodded, "is to be given safe passage, and that should the boy be spotted, the commander is to be notified immediately." The captain paused. "I, uh, was actually hoping you might be able to tell me more about it. When we spotted your convoy, we thought it must be connected."

"Tell your commander that I thank him for the offer of safe passage for my son, and that if he should like to see Tagan, he's welcome to visit Deadrise Bay. Thank you. Good day, Captain." Undine nodded.

The man nodded and quickly departed, and Undine's convoy pulled into motion again.

"But Undine," Tyra half-whispered. "Commander Riley? He's involved in this? But you and he ..."

"That was a long time ago. And we've been over this, Tyra. A commander of the north couldn't have gone home with a girl from Deadrise Bay, any more than I could have introduced Riley to Saor Tieg. We had our time together, and then we said goodbye." Undine pursed her lips.

"Of course. I didn't mean ..."

"But I don't understand why Riley is involved with this. I didn't tell him I'd had his son. He may have guessed, but I told no one but you. What purpose would it serve? Of course, I wouldn't turn down the chance to see him again. I wouldn't turn that down at all."

"It's curious that he's involved, Undine. But will you tell me the plan? For the meeting with Caterione, I mean."

"Tyra, I asked you to come because it's much more fun with you along. But also I want someone to tell me afterward if I've overplayed or underplayed my hand. You remember my old muse, the silent one?"

"You never talk about Camilla and Horace anymore."

"Because they left me twenty years ago. I've been thinking of Camilla again—but that's another story. She had some fine ideas, Tyra. She never spoke to me directly, but Horace passed her thoughts on to me. I think the most important thing she taught me was how to play my hand. Play too close and careful and you'll miss the payoff. Play too rough and reckless and your opponent will beat you. And this play I'm about to make, it's not for a few copper pieces. We're looking at high stakes."

"I'm along to watch you play your hand?"

"Yes. I want to know afterward if I played it well."

"She's coming here?" Caterione looked flustered, and the gate guard who had brought the message retreated half a step. "The Talla is coming to Three Rivers? When? How do we know this?"

"Soldiers spotted her horsemen, master, and identified the carriage. They sent a runner. He's at the gate, if you wish to speak to him."

"How much time?"

"A few hours. If they ride on, they'll arrive before the midday meal."

"Tell the runner he may go. Then get me my captains. I want the pavilion readied. Fresh mats on the floor. I want silk under the tables, and linens. Wine. Bring wine." She rushed out to issue orders.

When the visitors reached the gate and hailed the gate guard, Caterione was ready, prepared either to entertain or to fight. A phalanx of Gatto fighters stood behind her as she waited outside the pavilion. But just two figures approached, the Talla with a spiral on her face, and a woman with brilliant red hair and a flax flower on her forehead.

"Stand down," Caterione said, and the fighters broke the phalanx position and formed lines, hands folded behind their backs.

Undine stepped up carrying a satchel over her shoulder, and flashed a tight smile. "Caterione," she said, and bowed.

Caterione returned the bow. "Undine," she said stiffly, unsmiling. "And Tyra, isn't it? Welcome to Three Rivers." She turned and nodded her head, and the rows of Gatto fighters dispersed, although they didn't go far. "Shall we sit in the pavilion?"

Undine nodded, and she and Tyra followed her in. The pavilion was lit brightly by lanterns hanging along the ridgepole. At either end a fire burned, and pots of steaming water hung from iron holders.

Tyra beamed as Gatto girls stepped in with trays of teacups. The Gatto tea ritual! She had always wanted to see it for herself. Hot water was poured into a ceramic teapot, stirred once, and then the girls stepped over and served. First, they placed a cup for the master, and then for her guests. Undine waited for Caterione to lift her cup, then she and Tyra raised theirs and drank. Then the girls collected the cups and retreated, and the guests were left alone in the pavilion with the master—except that they could hear ranks of Tallach soldiers and Gatto fighters outside, shifting and rustling.

"Did you anticipate us?" Undine asked, the formalities over. "Or have the Gatto become fancier in their everyday trappings? Silk on the floor. We never had silk when we trained under Master Aideen. I recall hard brick and thin mats."

"Three Rivers welcomes you, Talla Undine." Caterione bowed her head.

"You and I have things to discuss," Undine said sharply, a new note of menace in her voice.

"Your son," Caterione repeated, flatly.

"And the old Gatto on the road. And a few other things."

Caterione tipped her head. "The old Gatto on the road?"

"You know about the Gatto master seen heading south. I see it in your eyes, Caterione. This isn't news to you."

"I received a report. What of it?"

"Was it reported that he and my son crossed paths?"

"Our guards at the border reported seeing an old master in a silk robe, with fine old Gatto blades. Your son knows of the Gatto master?"

"Fine blades indeed," Undine said. "Look at the workmanship." She placed a Gatto blade on the table and watched Caterione's eyes fix on it. "Go on, touch it, my old friend. It's the finest Gatto blade I've ever seen. The polished ebony, and the burnished gold. Look at it." Undine slid the blade across the table.

Caterione lifted it reverently and pulled it close to study it, then flashed a look of suspicion. "Where did you get this?"

Undine shrugged. "From the master Gatto, of course. You don't find these in the port shops. But you must know something of this already. I'm told my son was here at Three Rivers for a time." She paused, delighted to see Caterione grow tense.

"He was. Although I wasn't informed that ..."

"And he walked in the path of an old Gatto master for a time," Undine interrupted. "My son has a talent for connecting with those around the edges of things, you see. He's drawn to them, and they to him. A child drowning in a lake. A Turning woman wishing for a different life. An old Gatto carrying fine old blades and fleeing to the south."

"Fleeing?" Caterione' eyes snapped up. "Why fleeing?"

"And bear in mind that yours isn't the only pavilion, Caterione, nor the oldest, nor the best known. Stetlin still holds power in the far reaches, for example. For generations his line has been there. And our old Master Aideen at the Pavilion of the Hidden. Her pavilion is new by comparison to Stetlin's, but yours is a mere baby."

"And so?"

"This man with the Gatto blades knows all of this as well as you and I. Everyone knows it. What is it, three years that you've been here? Four? You haven't even finished building it. But tell me, Caterione, do you know how Stetlin's father died? Have you been told that story?"

Caterione shook her head.

"He was an old Gatto master, too. I imagine in his later years he must have looked very much like what your border guards witnessed, an old man in a robe with fine old blades, making his way. He was set upon by bandits and was left to die in the road, and his blades stolen. Not a fine end for a master Gatto."

"Set upon," Caterione echoed.

"At one time he was a powerful fighter. But the time comes to pass the blades to the next generation. Stetlin's father wasn't allowed the pleasure of doing that in a civilized manner. Instead the son was forced to track down his father's killers and retrieve the blades that he now wears, himself."

"Unfortunate indeed," Caterione said.

"The wanderer your border guards met, he'd like not to do things that way. He would prefer to live the rest of his life without fear of being cut down in the road."

"He wants protection?"

Tyra's eyebrows lifted slightly. She was looking from one to the other, working hard to remember each expression and each movement.

"That's a fair way of stating it." Undine sat back.

"Protection." Caterione set the blade on the table and stared across the room. "And he came to you? Why?"

"An old man seeking protection isn't so very different from a young man running from those who would harm him, is he? At its root it's the same thing. Protection requires alliances. History teaches us these things. Those who seek security seek allies. And so here I am."

"You're here to negotiate on behalf of an old Gatto master?" Undine looked incredulous.

"For the bearer of those blades. Is it so strange? But let's be clear, Caterione, the fabric of your pavilion is fresh off the bolt. You and I might reach an agreement. Or if not, there are plenty of others who will be interested."

"Undine, what did you come here to ask of me?"

"I'm here to offer you something. Something that will set Three Rivers above the other Gatto pavilions." Undine retrieved the blade, carefully wrapped it in cloth, and tucked it back into the satchel. She noted Caterione's eyes following every move, watching the blade disappear into the bag. "But only if a suitable arrangement can be made."

"And what is this thing? That's a fine blade, but perhaps you overstate its value."

"No, I don't. But never mind the blade. Two of your border guards observed the man I speak for. They watched him do a kata in a field. Are those men here? Call them in."

Caterione scowled, but barked a command, and a fighter immediately entered and ran over to her. "Fetch the two who reported seeing the Gatto master."

Moments later, two fighters entered and bowed to their master.

"May I?" Undine said, rising and stepping onto the fighting mat.

"You're challenging my men?" Caterione said, also rising.

"Ha! No, Caterione. I want to show them something." Undine bowed, then dropped to a ready stance, and then started working through the moves her son had shown her, just as slowly as Tagan had performed them in the field. She didn't peek to see how they responded. That was Tyra's job. She just slowly, fluidly worked through each move, until she returned to the point where she had started and stood tall. She turned and bowed again.

Caterione stared.

"It's Vatra!" one of the border guards said. "The very thing the old Gatto showed us."

"Not as elegantly executed, I'm sure," Undine added, stepping back to the table and sitting. "I'm no Gatto master, and I can only do what I recall from seeing him perform it for me. But it's good, don't you think?"

Tyra offered an almost imperceptible nod, a silent assurance that Undine had played this particular card quite well.

Caterione remained standing. "Undine, speak plainly. What's this arrangement you mean to make?"

"Sit, sit, Caterione. Don't loom over me. Pour the wine. Let's talk."

There was a long silence, then Caterione waved her men away, and they bowed and ran out. She sat, forgetting about the wine.

"The man who carries these blades," Undine continued, "carries the secret of Vatra. That's what we're here to negotiate, Caterione, who will inherit Vatra."

"The secret of Vatra? Are you making a joke?"

"In return for Gatto protection of the bearer of this ancient blade and its mate," she unwrapped the blade and set it on the table again, "the stewardship of the sacred hall of Vatra will be passed to Caterione of Three Rivers."

"Stewardship ..."

"It will be for you and your descendants to hold and protect for generations to come. Bear in mind that the deal is for absolute protection, with no exceptions. If the blades are stolen from the bearer and he's then harmed, the deal is breached. If he dies at the hand of road bandits, the deal is breached. If a tree falls on him, it's breached. Nothing but dying of old age satisfies the deal."

Caterione looked first at Undine and then at Tyra, and finally at the blade. She smiled sourly. "The protection of the Gatto in return for the stewardship of the ruined hall of the fire kata? All that's left of that old hall is legend. What is this, Undine? What's the trick you mean to play on me?"

"It's a simple arrangement," Undine said, "with incentives for each of us to honor it. You see, if you should find that you've been tricked—if the great hall isn't where he says it is, or isn't what you know it should be—then this old blade and its mate are a pair of fine relics, but won't confer any measure of safety to the bearer."

"Agreed," Caterione scowled. "I'd hunt him down and relieve him of the blades myself."

"On the other hand, should the Gatto fail to protect the bearer of the blades, I or one of a designated few who are parties to this arrangement, will send dispatches to every Gatto master in the north and south alike, revealing the location of the fire hall. And then just how long do you think young master Caterione of the fledgling Pavilion at Three Rivers will hold the title of steward?"

Caterione nodded slowly, her eyes narrow, thinking. "You say the hall of Vatra wasn't destroyed."

"It wasn't."

"That although for many generations the legend says it was ruined, it stands."

"It does."

"And the Gatto master knows where it is."

"That man your fighters saw perform that kata knows where it is. Yes, Caterione, that's what I'm telling you. But if you're not interested, say so, and I'll be on my way. My soldiers will take me to visit Aideen."

"And what do you stand to gain from this arrangement?"

"My skin in the game?" Undine laughed. "That's an expression of my old muse, although I never heard her speak the words herself." She leaned in and whispered to Tyra, "In this case it works out rather literally, doesn't it? My skin in the game is my own flesh and blood."

"I don't see you brokering a deal for free." Caterione scowled.

"My fee is modest. I want two things. First, when my son traveled north, he came with a companion. I want Dimon released. I hear he's being held in a border station not far from here. You'll arrange to have him freed."

This brought a slight smile to Caterione's face, as she had already released the boy. "I'm to arrange for the boy's release. All right. And the other thing?"

"You've made an error, Caterione, threatening to cut down my son," Undine said, slowly and darkly. "You and your Gatto have overstepped."

"He entered the north on false pretenses. He ..."

"None of that!" Undine commanded, and Tyra's eyebrows lifted as the Gatto master stopped talking. "He's my son, the grandson of Saor Tieg. No one crosses Deadrise Bay. You're fortunate that I'm the one visiting you. My father would have come with legions of soldiers. And do you think the Tynans would stand behind you in that fight? Yet I'm told it was an error, and so I'm prepared to handle it in a less severe fashion."

Caterione's teeth were clenched, but she nodded. "I'm listening."

"Dimon will be released, and I'll take a hostage from your pavilion. I'll choose."

"A hostage?" Caterione spat.

"When I'm convinced you mean to uphold your end of the deal—perhaps after a few years—the hostage will be released. But until then, you're going to have some skin in the game, too, Caterione."

Caterione stared for a long time. "Not my son. You'll not take Arran. And you understand what will happen if this is a hoax. I'll see to it that the boy is never released."

"You're threatening me? I'm not a little girl sparring with you anymore, Caterione. I'm offering you a fine prize, and a way out of your mistake that doesn't see you facing the armies of the south. But leave the wine glasses empty if you don't like the deal, and my soldiers will bring me to Aideen. I won't require a hostage of her. All in all, it might be less complicated."

"The location of the Vatra hall," Caterione muttered, still staring.

"And Dimon's release, and a hostage that I'll hold until I see fit. Now tell me *no*, or pour." Undine nodded at the wine bottle, and Caterione hesitated for another long moment, then poured. Undine raised her glass. "The Gatto will provide protection for life to the bearer of this blade and its mate," she said. "The prisoner Dimon will be released, and I'll hold a hostage at Deadrise Bay. And in return, the location of the great Vatra hall will be revealed only to Master Caterione of Three Rivers. Are we agreed?"

"Agreed." Caterione's face was screwed into a deep scowl, but she raised her glass, clinked it to Undine's, and they downed the wine.

"Tyra, would you wait outside?" Undine nodded her head, and Tyra rose and left. "Tyra is my friend, but she doesn't know the location of the hall," Undine explained. "I prefer to keep it that way. And please know that aside from me, none among that chosen group knows who the others are. Is that clear? Should you happen upon the identity of one of them one day, it won't help. You won't discover them all."

"Where is this great fire hall?"

"I'll tell you where it is and how to get to it. But I won't tell you here, with ears all around. Walk with me to the plateau above the river. Tell your men to remain here."

Caterione hesitated.

"Oh, please," Undine complained. "Do you think this is an elaborate ruse to trick you into walking to the plateau alone with me? Bring your blades, then. If I should attempt to kill you, you'll get your chance to finish our little match that was interrupted twenty years ago."

The reluctant look changed to a thin smile. "Come, then," said the master Gatto. "To the plateau."

Rebecca's eyes drooped and closed, and her head landed on the table with a thump, narrowly missing a water glass.

"Stop it," Tagan hissed, poking her. He looked at the man standing across the table from him and nodded. "I thank you for the generous gift, captain, and look forward to many years of profitable trade with the mainland."

"You're the one falling asleep," Rebecca said. "I can't help it."

The man bowed and moved off, and the next in line stepped up in his place and set a case of wine on the table. "It's a miracle, son of Undine," the man said, as a servant took the case and carried it to a side table that was already piled high with gifts. "I hope the wine will suit your taste. All of us on board salute you, and drink to your health."

"I thank you for the generous gift, steward, and look forward to many years of profitable trade with the mainland," Tagan said, and then leaned in to Rebecca. "We're not even done with the sailors yet, Becca, and then there's everyone from the village. Just sit and be quiet, or go do something else. It can't be helped."

"I have to sleep," Rebecca said. She pulled her chair close to his and leaned on his shoulder as the man moved away and the next man stepped up.

"The mates of *Ocelot II* send their greetings and wishes for a long life, son of Undine," the man said, placing a sack of imported fruit on the table.

"I thank you for the generous gift, midshipman, and I look forward ..." Rebecca yawned loudly, and Tagan elbowed her. "I look forward to many years of profitable trade with the mainland."

The next man stepped forward, and Tagan tipped his head. Had he cut the line? The sailors weren't nearly done, and yet here was a northern officer. A commander! He stiffened.

"Ho!" Rebecca's head snapped up and her eyes flew open. "What's going on?"

"Hush," Tagan whispered.

The man reached in his pocket and discreetly slid something across the table. Tagan saw it and rocketed up from his chair. "What is this? Where's Dimon?"

"It's your old pendant," Rebecca said, picking it up by the chain. "He's found your pendant, Tagan."

"Apologies for the abrupt approach," the commander said. "I didn't mean to startle you. May we speak in private?"

"Look, Tagan, he's a commander!" Rebecca said, and Tagan's hand clamped over her mouth.

From the other end of the table, an old man rose and strode over.

"Saor Tieg." The commander bowed. "May I have your leave to speak with your grandson?"

"This way," Tagan said, not waiting for his grandfather to answer.

The old man glanced at the pin on the man's collar and nodded, and the commander nodded back and stepped around the end of the table. Saor Tieg waved the next one in line forward and stood in for his grandson.

"Wine!" Tagan barked at a servant stationed in the hall. Then he paused and tempered his voice. "If you please," he added. "We'll sit in my grandfather's library."

"Yes, sir," the servant said, and hurried off.

The commander strode forward to walk at his side instead of in his wake, as Tagan rushed down the hall. They climbed a flight of stairs and stepped into a room that was more of a sitting room than a library. There were bookcases between the windows and along one wall, but the focus of the room was a circle of captain's chairs around a large coffee table.

"Tell me, commander," Tagan said, "where did you get this?" He held up the pendant. "Is my friend safe? What can you tell me of my friend Dimon?"

"Shall we sit?" Commander Riley said.

"Yes, of course. I'm sorry. I'm being rude. It's just that ..."

"And the girl," the commander said, as Rebecca hopped into Tagan's lap. "She's to stay while we talk? A younger sister?"

Rebecca beamed at this, and wrapped her arms around Tagan's neck. "That's right," she said.

Tagan gently pushed her off. "You're too big to get on my lap." He turned to the commander. "Very much like a sister," he said.

Becca frowned and folded her arms. She huffed across the room, then thought better of it and huffed back, taking the chair next to Tagan's.

"But yes, she can stay," Tagan added, and the girl's scowl softened. "Please, though, I must know. Is my friend all right? I was told northern soldiers seized him."

Riley raised a comforting palm. "Dimon is all right. Your friend was intercepted by soldiers. Later I brought the boy from High Pines to the pavilion at Three Rivers."

"Three Rivers! You brought him there?"

"He's in no danger." Riley opened his mouth to continue, but they were interrupted by servants sweeping in with wine, glasses, and plates of bread and cheese. A small feast was laid out on the table, and the wine was poured. Rebecca looked hopefully at the servant with the wine bottle, and Tagan nodded. The man poured a taste of wine into a glass and gave it to the girl. She scowled at the scant quantity, but took it and sat forward, copying Tagan's method of holding it by the stem.

When the servants had left, Riley took a sip of wine and set down his glass. "Your friend is safe," Riley said. "We can talk about him later. The pendant." He caught Tagan's eyes. "That's what I'm here about, Tagan. You asked where I got it. It was from the silversmith who cast it, son. I insisted on paying for it from my own wages. And then I hung it around your mother's neck, twenty years ago."

Tagan stopped breathing, and Rebecca's eyes bugged out. She let out a wheezing gasp, and her glass fell and shattered on the floor. White-faced, Tagan reached a hand out and found the little girl's arm. He patted her wrist and then squeezed her hand, all the while maintaining his stare, his eyes locked to the commander's. A tear formed in Rebecca's eye and ran down her face, and the commander glanced at her, unsure if she was crying or in pain.

"She told me, a northern soldier," Tagan finally said, his voice wavering. "But how could this be? You're a northern commander! You? And my mother?"

Rebecca wheezed, her breath coming back to her. "Tagan, he's your father?" she gasped.

"She told you a northern soldier?" Riley offered a thin smile. "I suppose that isn't incorrect. Once a soldier always a soldier. And yes, I'm a commander. But son, the scales weren't tilted in my direction on that count. Did your mother tell you what she was doing the day I met her, at the Pavilion of the Hidden?"

Tagan stared.

"She had just put everyone including Master Aideen herself back on our heels. That's another story for later. I volunteered to bring Talla Undine home, and was thankful for the privilege to do so."

Tagan rose and stiffly approached the man, and Riley rose and stepped up. "Father," Tagan said, solemnly offering a hand. The man smiled and shook it, and then Rebecca stepped behind Tagan and shoved him. The commander opened his arms and accepted his son into them. Rebecca collapsed into a chair.

Tieg was more disgruntled than the people in line, at accepting gifts on behalf of his grandson. "Where is he?" he repeatedly demanded of a servant. "What's he doing? These people are here to see him, not me."

He was about to demand that the servant find Tagan and drag him back if necessary, when Tagan reappeared. Rebecca clutched his arm like a child afraid of being lost in a crowd, and on his other side strode the northern commander, a hand on his newfound son's shoulder.

Tagan stepped up to his grandfather and whispered in his ear, and the man's eyes widened. He stood and turned, and distractedly waved a hand to order the captain of his guard to take over at the receiving line. Murmurs broke out. Those waiting to present their gifts to the resurrected heir to Deadrise Bay might have felt slighted at the third in line stepping up to receive them, but they were too fascinated to dwell on it. Saor Tieg, his grandson, and a northern commander stood in a huddle. What was going on?

Back in the library, Tieg motioned for the commander to take the seat next to him, and waved Tagan to a chair across from them. Rebecca climbed onto his lap again, and this time Tagan let her sit.

"My daughter," Tieg began, "left out the fact of the boy's father being a northern commander. Forgive me for appearing unsettled. I'm not merely surprised, but astonished."

"Is Undine here?" the commander said. "I should like to offer my respects, and to speak with her."

"She's traveling north," Tagan said, and received a scowl from his grandfather for interrupting.

"North?" Riley's eyebrows lowered. "Not to Three Rivers!"

Undine saw the question in Caterione's expression. "You think this is a trick. I mean to trick you into swimming that channel. Send one of your fighters, then, Caterione, and let him be the first Gatto of our time to lay eyes on the great Vatra hall."

Caterione glared. "I'll swim the channel. My men will accompany you to the cavern in the gorge. You'll wait there. Tell me the distances."

"He didn't count it, as I mentioned. But he said the route out from the stairs was quite short. The entrance to the hall will be very close to the outlet at the gorge."

Caterione waved to her men. "Accompany the Talla to the cavern at the end of the underground river. Wait for me there. I mean to swim the channel, but I may be some time. No one is to come after me."

"Yes, master," the men said, bowing.

Undine was impressed at the discipline of the fighters. She sat dipping her feet in the water, then got bored and walked up and down the gorge for a while, and finally returned to the cavern and paced. The fighters stood at the mouth of the cavern like statues, waiting as ordered, only their eyes moving. Each time they looked at her, she tried to strike up a conversation, and each time they said nothing, and looked away. Finally, annoyed by her attempts, they turned away altogether, and stared out at the gorge instead.

Undine grinned. "So predictable," she muttered, and started her search. It didn't take long for her to find the old copper box, tucked behind a pile of stones deep in the cavern. Even in the dim light she could see that it was exquisite. She would come for it later. The box was not part of the deal.

It was almost two full hours before they spotted a figure surfacing in the cavern. Caterione rose from the water, ran her hands across her face, and stepped onto the rocks. The fighters turned and stood silently, and Undine raised her eyebrows and waited.

"We have a deal," Caterione said, with a dark smile.

"We didn't pack for this. Isotta. Abigail, hold. We can't pursue the Tallach boy unprepared."

Isotta clicked her tongue. "We didn't pack? That's your concern?"

"And you're calling me Abigail again. Isotta, race!" Abigail broke into a sprint.

"Young miss," Arran pleaded. His sister let out a war cry and raced after her.

A long run later, they stood bent over, hands on their hips, breathing hard. "What was that, a mile?" Abigail said.

"At least. Maybe two," Isotta said with a grin.

Arran jogged up and hovered over them. "I see you're having a fine adventure," he said. "I hope you don't plan to eat. We've two apples and two slices of bread, young miss, that I brought for our midday meal. Nothing for you, I'm afraid, Isotta. Are you hungry yet?"

"The Tallach boy has provisions," Isotta said, "And so do I."

"It will be fine," Abigail said.

"And do you mean to run to Deadrise Bay dressed as a man?"

"What's in the pack?" Isotta asked. "Abbie looks better prepared than you."

Abigail laughed. "It's books. He makes me lug them around."

"Books? What for? Arran, you make her carry a bag of books through the woods?"

"For training," Abigail said, "not for reading. But now it's time to put that training to use, so I don't need to carry these anymore, do I?" She stepped to the side of the road and dumped the books.

"Young miss!" Arran cried. "Those are valuable!"

"Then you carry them. Come on, Isotta." Once more they broke into a run, and Arran sighed and ran after them.

They realized after another long run that Dimon knew how to move. They could follow his tracks, but even with all the running, they hadn't caught sight of him.

At the first crossroads, Arran took the lead and turned right, but Isotta grabbed Abigail's wrist. "Wrong way, brother," she said,

Arran turned and scowled. "His tracks go this way."

"That's not the way to Deadrise Bay. He went that way." She pointed to the left.

"Ah, I see." Arran folded his arms. "You feel you've improved your tracking skill so that you can smell his trail, perhaps, sister, and don't need to follow the tracks?"

"That's the way to Deadrise Bay. He went that way," Isotta insisted. "Maybe he's smarter than you. Maybe he wanted anyone coming after him to think he went the other way."

Arran opened his mouth to say something, but closed it again. "Wait here." He jogged up the road and stopped a couple of hundred yards down, and studied the markings in the dirt. Slowly he worked his way to one side of the road, then the other. A moment later he was jogging back. "Perhaps you're right," Arran grudgingly admitted. "But allow me to check."

He ran down the left-hand road, and after a few minutes stopped and waved them on. Isotta grinned, tugged Abigail's sleeve, and ran after him. "Told you so," she muttered.

Midday they stopped briefly for food. Arran proposed that he and Isotta split one apple and Abigail take the other, but Isotta grunted her disapproval. "Don't be stupid," she said. "I told you, I have food. Take some of this, Abbie." She pulled a bag of dried meat and a leather wineskin from her pack. "You can have some too, brother, unless you want to test your skills at not eating."

"Fine. Walk and eat," he snapped. "We can't linger. The master's men will pursue."

This caused both Abigail and Isotta to turn.

"Soon," Arran added, to put a point on it. "The master might not think to ask until his midday meal. Then it will take some time for the reports to be given. They'll report that you arrived, sister, and the sensei."

"So?" Isotta shrugged.

"So, Isotta, when the sensei informs the master that he's here to fetch me back to Three Rivers, questions will follow. Who was the earlier visitor? What was his message? Sooner or later the master will ask after you, young miss. If her tutor is to leave directly, where is Miss Abigail, then? And soon enough, they'll pursue. Or possibly they're already coming."

"But they'll be on horseback, Arran!" Abigail said.

"I'm sure my sister has a plan for outrunning horses. Let's hear it, Isotta." Arran lowered his eyes at the girl.

Isotta glared back, and once again broke into a run.

Just down the road, Arran halted. "Stop!" he called out, and turned to run back up the road a short distance. "He's left the road. This way. He must have found this path on the map. It cuts off a good section of road."

"A shortcut?" Abigail asked.

"Somewhat difficult, but it shaves a half day off the journey. It seems our friend is in a hurry."

"Of course he is," Isotta said. "Tagan's his friend."

Arran sighed and shook his head. "Fetch some boughs. We'll redo our tracks down the road and then circle back, just as the boy did at the cross-roads. Your father's men," he nodded at Abigail, "will be following your tracks, not the boy's."

Soon Abigail and Isotta were following him along a narrow trail into the woods. "Remember what you've learned, young miss," he admonished, as he picked his way along. "Clearly this boy knows his way in the woods. Don't reveal us or him to your father by making our own trail easy to follow."

Abigail noted that he didn't say anything to Isotta, but soon she realized why. Isotta was far better than she was at hiding her trail.

Suddenly Arran halted again, and flashed his palm, silently ordering them to stop. He pointed to his eyes, then to a large tree ahead of them. He started to give them more signals, outlining his plan, when Isotta stepped forward.

"Dimon," she called out. "Come out of there."

"Isotta!" her brother scolded.

"He knows who I am, Arran," she said. "We've met already." She turned back to the tree. "Dimon, you can come out."

A figure peered at them from behind the tree, then he stepped out. "Isotta? It's you following me? Why? And your brother. And who's that with you?"

"My brother and Abigail."

Dimon approached. "Abigail. I wasn't there when you visited Deadrise Bay and met my friend."

"Do you have news of him?" she demanded, fists clenched in excitement.

"I know he escaped the Gatto. But I'm sure my young friend told you that already."

"Of course," Isotta confirmed. "We think he's going to Deadrise Bay. We'll go there with you."

"You will?" Dimon looked confused, and turned his eyes to Arran. "You said it wasn't your affair, and that Miss Abigail had made her peace and understood her place. That she had no wish to rejoin Tagan."

"You said what?" Abigail stepped up and punched him hard, and Arran stepped back and raised his palms.

"Young miss, it was too soon. Unplanned," Arran insisted. "Don't you see? And Isotta, what's your place in this?" Arran raised his eyebrows at his sister.

"Tagan is my friend, too," Isotta glared. "At least, I think so."

"Your friend. Have you forgotten every detail of what you've learned, little sister?"

Dimon pursed his lips. "Tagan is heir to Deadrise Bay. Not a bad friend to have. But perhaps you should turn back, son of Caterione. Tagan might vouch for your sister, but I don't know that Master Caterione's son will be welcome at Deadrise Bay."

"We should turn back," Arran scolded. "Come, Abigail. Come Isotta. Let's end this fool's errand and return to the compound. There's still time to fix all of this."

Abigail folded her arms and planted her feet. "Arran, I mean to go to him."

"Perhaps if you'd consider ..." Dimon started, but Isotta stepped between them.

"Just shut up, all of you," she barked. "This isn't a contest. We're going to Deadrise Bay with Dimon. Arran, you should come, too." She turned to Dimon. "My brother likes to control everything. But he's good in the woods, and good with a blade." Isotta turned and strode down the trail without waiting for agreement, and Abigail stepped around Arran and Dimon and strode after her.

"Oh, isn't this fine," Arran muttered, but he followed, as did Dimon.

Gradually Arran's mood seemed to shift from sullen disapproval to the consideration of what he could control. "All of you stop," he said. "We need to make a plan, and I have an idea. Let me show you on the map."

After a brief conference, they agreed that his plan was a good one, and they stepped off the trail and made their way in a new direction. Another mile or two through the woods brought them to a long, narrow lake. It was bounded on one side by a forested hill, and on the other by a steeper hill that was almost a cliff. A tumble of rocks swept upward at a steep angle to a rocky ridge barren of trees.

"We have work to do," Arran explained, stepping up to the edge of the water. He carried a long, thick branch he had collected from the woods. Dimon followed with two shorter sections. "Shoes off, and roll up your pants," Arran ordered. "Walk into the water. Isotta, drop a sock at the water's edge."

"Why should I lose a sock?" the girl complained. But she complied, leaving one sock half in the water.

Arran pressed the branch into the sand, perpendicular to the edge of the lake, and Dimon pressed his to the sides. They backed up, carving into the sand an emulation of a small boat being dragged in.

"Now come," Arran said. "Stay in the water and walk on stones wherever possible. Avoid stirring up the mud."

They waded in the shallow water, following the edge of the lake until they were a hundred yards away. Then where a line of rocks reached into the water, Arran climbed out and jumped from one to the next until he was on the shore. The others followed, and soon they had their shoes back on and were scrambling up the rocky hillside.

"Will it work?" Isotta said, grinning as they crested the hill.

"Let's not stay to find out," Dimon said with a wink. "Come on. Time to run."

17. Lex Camillae

"Camilla, this man has a history with your family. Let me handle the signing." Grace paced, while Camilla sat in a plush leather chair next to the wet bar.

"He killed my grandfather. I want to see him sign those papers."

"He'll sign. Leave that to me. And he's going to be signing over everything he's worth. We couldn't have asked for this to go any better."

"And if he doesn't sign?"

"He'll sign. It's all green lights. Camilla, it's working."

"But it's not done yet."

"Listen, your disguise was good enough to fool an inspector downtown, but this is different. Turcotte knows about you. He knows Horace has a granddaughter, and he knows your age, and he probably knows what you look like. They probably have a portfolio of photos of you, and variations for what you'd look like with different hair and so on."

"He probably has that on you, too."

"But I don't stand out, Camilla. I'm average all around. And my friends will be here to back me up and make the signing look legitimate. He won't suspect the blonde lawyer in the group is me. It won't occur to him. But you can't give him time to sit and look at you. It's too dangerous."

"Fine. I can at least watch, right? The secretary's office has two-way mirror. I guess so the secretary can watch meetings and come in at the right time with coffee or papers, or something. I can pin a curtain over the window so they won't see me when they come in, and I can watch from there."

Grace nodded. "All right. I don't like it, Camilla, but all right."

"You took care of the receptionist in the lobby?"

"Honestly, Camilla, stop. Everything is set. The regular man will be off to a show, and our man will be at the desk. The meeting is after hours, so no one else will be on this floor."

Walter Turcotte entered the suite dressed in a fine black suit, followed by two men in gray. The receptionist smiled and greeted them, and directed them down the hall, but Grace was already stepping up.

"Gentlemen," she said. "Come in, come in."

She led them through to the conference room. On the table were a computer and a neat stack of papers, a pitcher of water, and glasses. Four men were already waiting, but none were seated. There were just two chairs at the table.

"Introductions," Grace said. "These are my colleagues from Baker and Worthington." She introduced each man, and each stepped forward with a warm handshake.

At a light knock, Grace turned to see the man they had placed in the outer office.

"Coffee or tea? Or a cocktail, sir?" he said.

"No, thank you," Turcotte said, and Grace waved him away and closed the door.

"Well then, have a seat, Mr. Turcotte. You've reviewed the documents?" Grace let him sit first, then pulled her chair close and sat next to him.

The men in gray took up positions against the wall near the door, and the white-shoe attorneys stood behind the chairs to look over their shoulders as Grace and Horace engaged in a little chitchat and then started the signing.

Grace picked up each page in turn, briefly explained what it was, then handed two copies to Turcotte to sign or initial. Then she signed or initialed each one herself, and carefully laid them upside-down adjacent to the stack, forming two new stacks of completed documents.

When she reached the last page, she waited for him to sign, but rose before signing herself.

"And now the transfer. You're welcome to use the firm's machine. It's on a secure network. Or use your own device if you prefer." She clicked on the computer and spun it to face away from the group, and Turcotte rose and rolled his chair around the table to make the transaction.

After a few minutes, he closed the laptop and smiled. "It's complete. You should see the funds in your account now."

Grace looked to one of the attorneys studying a handheld device, and he nodded.

"Well, then," Grace said, smiling at the mirror on the wall and then sitting. "I'll sign here, and we're finished." She signed the final sheet, flipped over the signed copies and handed one set to Turcotte. "Congratulations, Mr. Turcotte, on your acquisition." She shook his hand.

Then heads turned at a rap on the door. Instead of the receptionist, a short woman in a low-cut black dress and delicate white gloves stepped in.

"Is it time?" She said. "Champagne, sir?" She carried in a bottle of champagne and a rack of glasses, and set them on the table—and without waiting for a reply, she popped the cork and poured.

Grace shifted her chair back as if to make room. "I'm sure Mr. Turcotte would love some, wouldn't you?" she said, drawing his attention. The men playing her white-shoe attorneys maintained their solid, professional demeanor.

"Ladies first," Camilla said sweetly, placing a glass in front of Grace. Then she filled one for Turcotte.

His eyes fixed at first on her low neckline, but shifted to the bursting bubbles of the fine champagne that represented his lucrative deal. This deal would save him! It would fix all the missteps, and put him on solid footing. He'd finally be fully recovered from the disastrous loss of his wealth and power.

Camilla set the bottle down, and with a dramatic flourish, she raised the glass and reached to hand it to him.

Turcotte followed the movement of the white-gloved hand and the delicate glass of sparkling champagne—and missed the movement of her other hand.

"Here you are," Camilla said. She neatly drew a Sig 226 from a pocket in her dress, brought it up next to the glass, and fired it into his forehead.

Turcotte flew backward, and blood and bits of flesh and bone sprayed across the wall behind him.

The men in gray reached for their waists, but Grace's men were on them instantly. It was swift and decisive. The men pretending to be white-shoe attorneys laid out Turcotte's men before either had a chance to draw a weapon. In moments they were unconscious on the floor, and Grace's men were binding their wrists with zip ties.

Grace stood tugging at her ringing ears. "Earplugs would have been nice," she said, but smiled. "Hard to work into the scene, though."

"*Now* it's done," Camilla said. She calmly placed the Sig into Turcotte's hand, careful not to step in the blood spatter or otherwise disturb the scene.

Grace's men finished what they were doing and backed away from the table. "Was this part of the plan?" One of the men said with a thin smile. "I don't think we were fully briefed."

"Better as a surprise," Grace winked.

"You know Occam's Razor?" Camilla said, stuffing the gloves into her pocket. "*Lex parsimoniae*. The *law of briefness*. It's a principle of logic."

"I've heard of Occam's Razor, yes," the man said.

"People think it means, *the simplest solution is usually the best one.* But that's not really right. It means, *the hypothesis that requires the fewest base assumptions is probably the best.* Horace taught me that." She stepped back and put her hands on her hips, inspecting her work.

"That sounds like Horace," one of the men said, drolly. "And that explains this, somehow?"

"What do you see? What are the assumptions?" Camilla folded her arms as the men looked at the dead man on the floor and the spatter on the wall, and the blood pooling on the floor. "Someone swindles him, and someone convinces him to come here by himself, and then for some reason they kill him after they already have the money? Or option two, he falls for a scam, and when he realizes he's ruined, he offs himself. Occam's Razor."

"But the one with fewer assumptions isn't the right answer," Grace objected, with a light laugh.

"Oh, I think we can make it work," one of the men suggested, nodding at the still shapes on the floor. "We'll make these two go away. And they'll find residue on his hand. She had the gun right there."

Camilla grinned. "I call it *lex Camillae*. The law of Camilla. Make it so your scenario involves the fewest assumptions, and people will believe it."

"Wait," one of her men said. "Camilla?"

"That's his granddaughter's name," another offered. "Hold on. Are you're Horace Rand's granddaughter? And you just shot the bastard who killed him?"

Camilla nodded, feeling herself tear up as the adrenaline of the kill waned and the memory of Horace took its place. The man started to clap slowly, and the others joined him. They clapped a solemn approval, and then passed around glasses of champagne.

Grace raised her glass. "Here's to Robbie," she said, "the finest man I'll ever know."

"And to Horace. I miss you, grandpa Rand," Camilla said.

18. Tethered

When Undine's carriage pulled up to the mansion, Tagan was waiting anxiously. He started to panic when only his mother's friend Tyra stepped out. Had something gone wrong?

But Tyra waved a confident hand. "All's well," she reassured him. "Undine is fine. Your mother stayed to take care of something, and said she'll be home in another day or two."

"She stayed behind by herself?"

"Not exactly by herself. Her soldiers weren't about to leave her to return home unguarded. Most of them are waiting on the road to accompany her back."

"But why did she stay?"

"Come, let's go inside," Tyra said. "She'll want to tell you herself. But I'll fill in a few pieces."

Saor Tieg stepped up as Tagan and Tyra were entering. "Where's my daughter? I'd like to speak with her."

"Look at me, covered in road dust," Tyra said with a laugh, "Apologies, Saor Tieg. I need to wash. Undine said to convey to you that the negotiations were successful, but there's an item she means to recover and bring back with her. I think it has to do with this." She drew the Gatto blade from her bag and handed it to Tagan. "She told me I'm to put this right in your hand, Tagan."

"But the blade was for the arrangement to release Dimon," Tagan said, frowning. He took the blade and inspected it as if there might be something wrong with it that he'd missed earlier.

"Undine says it's yours now, and you're to wear it and its mate whenever you go out. She says the blades will keep you safe."

"Safe from gray-gis?" said Tieg. "My grandson is developing fine fighting skills, Tyra, but wielding a master's blades doesn't make one a master."

Tagan scowled at his grandfather, but said nothing.

"She'll explain when she returns, sir," Tyra said. "I promised to pass along her message—that you're to wear the blades whenever you go out, Tagan—and to keep my mouth shut and not spoil the rest of the story for her." Tyra winked.

"Humph," grunted the old man. "All right, dear. I know I'm no match for my daughter's willfulness. You've had a long journey. Will you join us tonight for dinner?"

"I'd love to. Thank you. And Tagan, your mother insisted that I impress upon you that *whenever you go out* means every single time."

He smiled. "It won't be a chore to wear them. So yes, grandfather,"

Tagan rolled his eyes at the old man, "I'll obey my mother. You don't have to tell me, also."

Tagan picked out one of his better outfits, a fancy white shirt with ivory buttons, wool pants edged with purple thread, and a black satin vest that shimmered in shades of blue in the light.

With the commander in town, Tagan felt it shouldn't be necessary to sneak around. He he strapped on his knife sheaths and slid the elegant old blades into them, and looked at himself in the mirror. "Oh, damn, that looks fine," he said out loud.

"I keep telling you that," came a young voice from the doorway. He spun to find Rebecca grinning at him. She was scrubbed and combed, and dressed in yellow, this time a summer sundress with gold ribbon straps and an enormous bow in back. "Fine indeed."

"I meant the blades, Becca," Tagan smirked.

"Oh, well those are nice, too, if you like that kind of thing. Come on. Your father is at the saloon." Rebecca caught him looking at her, and she folded her arms and shook her head. "Nuh-uh. No telling me I can't go. I get to go."

Tagan stepped over and gave her a squeeze around the shoulders. "I was going to say that you look nice, too, all cleaned up."

"I hope so. I have to look nice. He's a commander."

Tagan laughed and stepped down the hall. "Let's go."

The cheers were deafening when Tieg's grandson stepped inside. Men lined up to shake his hand, and others waved. Rebecca stood behind him and grabbed hold of his shirt for fear of getting separated.

Tagan raised a hand. "All right," he said, "thank you, everyone, but it's not the first time I've been in this place." He grinned. "Not by a long shot," he muttered as an afterthought.

"First time since you was dead," one man called out, and there was more cheering.

Some of Riley's men stepped up, and the revelers shifted away and went back to their seats. Riley rose as Tagan approached, and two of his men got up and stood aside to give seats to the commander's son and the little girl.

Riley smiled. "I thought you told me your mother was to trade those blades. And yet now you have both? Very fine indeed. But is that good or bad?"

"I'm not sure yet."

"It's good," Rebecca said. "Don't be stupid. It's Talla Undine. It means she didn't give 'em to that nasty old Gatto after all, and she still got what she wanted."

Tagan started to object, then he laughed and patted Rebecca on the shoulder. "She's probably right. We are talking about my mother, after all."

"And where is she? I'm told her carriage was in town."

"She always changes plans. Tyra says she stayed behind to get something. Who knows?"

A waiter stepped up. "What can I get for you, sirs? On the house."

"No, no, come on," Tagan objected, "you're embarrassing me. I've come here countless times, and I always pay my tab."

"I'll pay it," the commander said.

Rebecca's elbow told Tagan to shut up. He started to object, but then smiled and laughed. "Thank you, then. A beer, I think."

"And you, child?"

"A beer as well," Rebecca said, offering a fine imitation of the confidence Tagan had expressed, as if it were her usual.

"Oh, fine," Tagan said. "Get her a small beer." Rebecca grinned. He held his thumb and finger apart to show exactly how small he meant.

They sat and talked. But the beer was just a prop. Neither Tagan nor his father cared about the drinks. Tagan was eager to learn more about his father, and the commander about his son. Soon Rebecca had sipped the last of the shot glass of beer the waiter had brought her, and she scooted her chair over and took up her favorite spot, leaning on Tagan's arm.

When he realized she was asleep, Tagan smiled. It was late afternoon, so she wasn't sleepy from a long day.

"She's content, the little one," Riley said. "One day I'd like to hear her story."

Tagan looked at Riley. "Shall we walk outside? I could use some fresh air, and to see the ocean."

"That's a fine idea."

"And maybe the fresh air will keep Rebecca up, and I won't have to carry her home." He patted her shoulder to wake her.

They ambled down the road, continuing their conversation. Rebecca clung to Tagan's arm, and the commander strolled next to him on his other side. Keeping their distance, several of Riley's men followed. They split into smaller groups and walked on both sides of the road. By all appearances, they were just soldiers on leave, out for a stroll, themselves. They stopped and said hello to people on the street, and looked at wares for sale. But they didn't allow their commander to get too far ahead.

When Tagan led the commander up the footpath to the ledge that overlooked the ocean, they pulled back farther, not wanting to intrude on a father-son moment.

"Isn't this the spot where the gray-gis came at you?" the commander asked. "The villagers told me about it."

"Yes, up here." Tagan led him to the rocky ledge. "You see, it's a sheer cliff all the way into the water. It's plenty deep, and safe to jump. There's nothing to hit under the water. But there's nowhere to hold on when you surface."

"I can see that. You'd be pounded against the rock face."

"And it's slippery. Every wave pushes you in, then pulls you out to throw you back at the wall. But there's a secret. Just under the water is an opening to the caverns. Don't tell my mother that I told you about it." Tagan grinned.

"Tagan, who are *they*?" Rebecca tugged his arm, and they turned to see a small figure in a brown gi rushing out from the scrub and running toward them. At a distance, three large figures in gray approached, seemingly chasing the small one.

Suddenly the small figure halted and spun, and drew blades. "You'll not take him!" cried a young voice. "He carries the blades of Vatra. No one may harm him!"

Tagan stared for a moment, and took a step forward. "Isotta?" he said. "Fire and daggers. Isotta?"

The scene was almost comic. A young Gatto girl was facing off against three gray-gis, in broad daylight. Riley had already drawn his blades, and Tagan drew his as well.

What none of them could see were two more gray-gis who had stepped into the trail farther down, to engage Riley's men, and to keep them from protecting their commander and their mark.

"Isotta, run!" Tagan urged, moving toward her. "What are you doing?"

"My duty!" Isotta said, backing away from the gray-gis, but stopping to hold firm, several paces in front of the commander and Tagan.

"To their flanks," Riley calmly ordered, and he and Tagan separated and moved to the sides as the gray-gis approached.

Rebecca froze, then dropped to a crouch and clutched her arms around her knees, terrified.

The gray-gis closed in. Two ran at Tagan, and the third at Riley. The girl in brown gave a war cry and charged the nearer of the two coming for Tagan. With a single, heavy sweep of his gigantic arm, the gray-gi caught Isotta across the chest and hurled her back, lifting her completely off the ground. She flew backward, her blades clattered to the stone, and she tumbled past Rebecca and off the cliff.

Tagan stood ready for him and the other gray-gi, and in the split second before they engaged, he glanced over and cried out in terror as Rebecca rose and ran for the edge. There was a flash of yellow, and she, too was gone.

"No!" Tagan cried, and lashed out at the gray-gis with everything he could muster. He felt the burn of blood as a blade nicked his arm, but he fought on, deflecting blows and looking for a chance at a deadly strike.

He fought the impossible battle, two-on-one against adversaries with much greater strength and fighting skills, and wondered in those first moments why they hadn't cut him down already. One fell to his knees, and then the other. Were they surrendering? Impossible! As they fell face-first to the ground, Tagan saw the answer, multiple blades in their backs.

A half dozen Gatto warriors appeared from the scrub and spread out on the ledge between Tagan and the trail, blades up, facing the trail, ready to take on any others who might come.

Tagan stared in amazement. Riley, who had dispatched his adversary, was just as astonished. His men came up the trail at a run, and the Gatto backed up to form a tighter line.

"Stand down!" Riley called to his men. "It's their blades that killed those two." He nodded at the dead gray-gis at Tagan's feet.

The soldiers sheathed their weapons, and the Gatto nodded and moved to at-ease stances and let them pass. Then they spread out again, and went back to ready. Riley's men formed an inner line and waited for orders.

"This is an alliance I've not been informed of, Gatto," Riley called out. "What does this mean, your presence here?"

"The child stated it," a Gatto said, without turning. "The boy carries the blades of Vatra. We're sworn to protect him."

"Sworn to protect him?" Riley said. "It seems your mother made an arrangement, after all, Tagan." He turned, but found that Tagan had stepped up to the edge of the drop, and was unfastening his knife belt.

"Rebecca!" he called out. "Isotta!" He spun to Riley. "I have to go after them! Hold my blades!"

Swimming was not on her list of favorite activities. Rebecca was terrified of the water. But as she plunged into the sea hoping she wouldn't land on top of the girl in the brown gi, she couldn't tell whose terror she was feeling. She'd seen the assassins charge at Tagan, and had watched one of them fling the girl over the edge like flicking away a crumb. To run after her had been an odd reflex, she thought, in the moment before the crushing cold of the water took her breath away.

But the strange clash of terrors—the water, the assassins, the girl hurled off the cliff—seemed to dull one another. Or maybe it was the dangerously cold sea water. Instead of being seized by the paralysis of a moment of terror, her mind calmed. She opened her eyes. She'd seen this young Gatto before, on the day she had walked with Abigail from the funeral to the man waiting to take her home. But she didn't see her, now. Where was she?

Rebecca surfaced, drew in a lungful of air, and dove. This time she saw the dark shape against a backdrop of stone illuminated by the afternoon sun. She pumped hard, and caught hold of the body. Soon she had Isotta's head above water. But what now? There was nowhere to climb out. It was vertical rock all around.

"The cavern," she said.

She'd been in the inner cavern any number of times, but had never swum the underwater passage to get to the smaller outer cavern that the tides alternately filled and emptied. Tagan had told her about it, but wouldn't have been so cruel as to try to make her swim to it. Now she would have to. She wasn't strong enough to carry Isotta and swim all the way around to the wharves.

She pulled the girl toward the waves lapping against the stone, found the spot, and ducked under, hauling Isotta with her. She could do it, she told herself. The passage to the first cavern, Tagan had told her, was only a couple of feet. And as promised, soon she was drawing in blessed air again.

It was dark in the cavern, but not pitch dark. A shaft of sunlight penetrated the low-tide water and made its way in. Rebecca found the edge, and dragged the limp girl up onto a stone ledge. The next part she had never done, but knew intimately, for it had been done to her. She didn't remember it, but she had repeatedly demanded a retelling of the story. She knew every detail by heart. She held the girl's nose shut and breathed for her, and then forced the air out with several sharp shoves on her chest.

"Keep going, tether," she said out loud to herself, imagining the Talla scolding her. "Again."

It took several tries, but she ordered herself to continue. When the girl started to cough and retch, Rebecca turned her onto her side to let her throw up the sea water.

"Quiet, now," she said, as the girl tried to get up. "Rest. We're safe. Tagan will come."

"Tagan," the girl wheezed, rolling onto her stomach and trying to draw her knees up so she could rise. "I failed him. The gray-gis ..."

"No, I don't think they got him. I'd feel it." Then Rebecca halted, and felt the hair on her arms stand up. "But I don't! Oh, no! Is he dead?" She broke into tears, and soon it was the girl in brown urging the one in yellow to rest easy.

Riley took the blades from Tagan, and announced in a loud voice, "I hold these on behalf of Tagan of Deadrise Bay. I declare that Tagan himself holds them, as long as they remain in my hands!"

A Gatto warrior turned and nodded. "Agreed, commander," he said. Two of the Gatto set down their blades and stepped to the edge.

"Follow me," Tagan said. He leaped off the cliff, the two Gatto right behind him.

Riley pointed at his captain. "Down to the water! Run!"

"To the water," echoed the Gatto leader, pointing at two of his companions. They ran down the path with Riley's men, while he and the other backed up closer to Riley, but kept their attention on any threats that might come from land.

"I'll remain here until we have a report," Riley said, and the Gatto nodded. He knelt and leaned over the edge.

In moments, one of the Gatto who had jumped with Tagan surfaced. He looked up, and in sharp hand signals, relayed his message and dove again.

The commander rose, and emitted a quiet laugh of relief. "They're all right. Both of them. Come. They await a trusted vessel. Let's see to it." He ran for the path, and the Gatto followed.

On the road, they passed teams of soldiers tending to wounded comrades. The bodies of two gray-gis had been unceremoniously rolled out of the way. Saor Tieg's guard had already flooded into the street and were locking down the town, ordering everyone to go inside and demanding that they stay inside until further notice.

By the time the commander reached the wharves, one of the larger working boats had been commandeered by his men. Riley got on board and they pulled hard for the cliffs. It seemed that every other small boat was already converging on the spot, so it took some time to get everything in order. The Gatto who had made the report surfaced again and hovered, treading water, as Riley's men ordered all the small boats back. Not until Riley's boat was anchored ten feet from the cliffs and the two Gatto on board nodded agreement did he dive again. Shortly after, the same man emerged towing a figure in brown; and behind them came Tagan, with a figure in yellow on his back. The second Gatto took up the rear.

The girls were lifted out of the water by many hands, and a cheer went up, seemingly from the whole town. More hands reached down and pulled Tagan and the Gatto men up, and the boat started to move back toward the wharves. Men with stretchers ordered everyone out of the way, and the Gatto re-formed their defensive line. Riley ceremoniously returned the blades, and Tagan put them on, and then stepped up to take Rebecca from the arms of a solder.

It was a minute before Tagan looked up and saw a familiar figure waiting on shore.

He hurried over, the Gatto clearing a path around him as he went. "Dimon!" Tagan was soaking wet, and held Rebecca on his hip, but he gave his friend a hug, anyway.

The Gatto recognized that there was little danger of another attack. The terraces and the streets above were crawling with soldiers, both from the commander's unit and from Saor Tieg's guard. They faded into the scenery, and allowed Tagan and his friend to walk back to the mansion.

"Go wash and change," Tagan told Rebecca, and she reluctantly let him set her down. She was escorted down the hall by a pack of servants.

"You need to do the same," Dimon said. "Let's go. A hot bath and a change of clothes."

"Dimon, tell me. Did you see my mother?" Tagan said. "You must have. The commander said you were taken to Three Rivers."

"Your mother?" Dimon looked confused.

"Didn't she arrange your release?"

"Your mother?" Dimon repeated, looking more confused. "At Three Rivers? She wasn't there, Tagan. Why would she be? Master Caterione released me. I haven't seen your mother since we left Deadrise Bay the night the gray-gis attacked. The first time."

"But, wait." Tagan stopped. "Mother didn't negotiate your release?"

"What are you talking about? Commander Riley brought me from some place called High Pines to that Gatto master's pavilion. The place was in an uproar. They thought you were dead—so did I—and everyone was running around hunting for a body. Then the commander realized who they were searching for, and I thought he might run the Gatto master through, on the spot. You should have seen him."

"My father."

Dimon smiled, and whacked him on the shoulder. "Lucky dog. You've found yours. Here I am, still hunting."

"Dimon, we'll look for him. We'll find your father."

"Oh, shut up. I'm joking. Trust me, nobody including me is thinking about my father right now. "Come on. Let's get you a bath. Me too. You got me all wet. But more than that," the smile faded, "I have to tell you something, and not outside."

Rebecca woke to find Talla Undine hovering over her. "Talla, you're here," she said.

"Yes, Rebecca. Are you all right? I understand you've had quite a day."

"Talla?" she said, rising to sit. Her face fell. "You called me Rebecca."

"It's your name."

"But, you heard, then?" She dropped her voice. "I cut my tether. I'm not joined to him anymore. All it needed was to pass on to someone else what he gave to me. At least, I think that's what it was."

Undine sat on the bed next to her, and put an arm around her shoulder. "Good for you, Rebecca. Maybe it was that. Or maybe it was facing your fears and choosing to jump into the ocean. Whatever it was, good for you."

"But the thing is ..." Rebecca seemed about to cry. "Do I have to go, now?"

"What do you mean, go? Are you all right, child? Maybe you need more sleep. You've had quite a shock."

"Do I have to go away? Since I'm not tethered."

Undine couldn't help laughing. "Go away? Child, Tagan would put me out before he sent you away. You just get some rest." She patted her on the shoulder and rose.

In the next room, Isotta was laid out on a gurney, dressed in a white gown, her head resting on a pillow. Her eyes were closed, and she breathed slowly, with a raspy sound. Undine stepped in, and the two men attending the girl turned and nodded.

"She'll recover. Miraculously, it seems nothing is broken. But whatever hit her, it certainly gave her a wallop."

"It was a gray-gi," Undine said.

The man's eyes widened. "A gray-gi hit a little girl? Why?"

"Because she challenged him. Is she awake?"

"Challenged him? This little girl challenged a gray-gi? Did she want to die?"

Undine waved a hand. "Is she awake?" she repeated.

"Apologies, Talla. She's had rather a lot of laudanum. But she'll wake soon."

"All right." Undine stepped back into the hall to find Tagan approaching. "The Gatto girl will be all right. But go check on Rebecca, son," she said.

Tagan halted. "What's wrong? They said she just needed sleep. Is she injured?"

"She's fine," Undine said, "except she's worried that now that's she's gotten past the terror that joined you, you're going to send her away."

"What? That's ridiculous! Why would I ..."

"Just go see her. She's frightened."

"I will. But mother, I need to talk to you. Dimon's told me something. I need your help. And maybe the commander's help, too."

Undine tipped her head and looked at him, and her face darkened. "I'd offer you a hot bath and warm milk, son, but that expression isn't one I've seen before. All right. Go get Rebecca before her little heart breaks, and meet me in the library. I'll send someone to find Riley."

When Riley stepped into the library, Tagan and Dimon were seated across from Undine, and Rebecca was sitting on the floor resting her head against Tagan's knee.

"Come in. Please sit," Undine said, and the commander flashed her a smile and sat next to her.

"What is it, Tagan?" Riley asked.

"Tell them, Dimon."

Dimon nodded. "After the master released me, I traveled south."

"And about that," Undine interrupted, "how in blazes did you get here so quickly? Caterione must have sent you on a team of horses for you to be back so soon."

"Horses? She saw that I had provisions and papers, and sent me away. I walked for many days."

"Many days? When did she release you?"

"I was just telling Tagan. It was the day the commander arrived, Talla."

"Wait. *Before* I met with Caterione? That sneaky wretch. She'd already released you! She didn't tell me that."

"Mother, let him tell the story," Tagan objected.

"Apologies, son. Go on, honey, tell us." Undine gave Dimon a smile.

"The sensei at Three Rivers drew up passage papers for me, and Isotta showed me on a map where Abigail of the Turning lives. I wanted to find her. Isotta said that the master's son is her tutor."

"Arran is Abigail's tutor?" Undine couldn't help interrupting again.

"Mother, please!" Tagan objected.

Dimon drew in a breath. "Isotta told me that Arran took Abigail to Deadrise Bay for the funeral. And so I knew that Arran knew the way. I wanted to ask him to lead me here, and I thought Abigail would wish to come as well. But I didn't encounter her, and Arran turned me away. He did give me a map, however, so I started for home on my own. Then later that day they caught up with me—the young girl Isotta, her brother, and the Turning girl."

"So Arran changed his mind?" Undine asked. "Odd. Unlike a Gatto tutor, and very unlike a child of Caterione."

"He wasn't happy about it. But it seemed the sensei was about to order him back home, and Abigail and the girl said they'd travel with me whether he came or not. And so Arran reluctantly came along as well. We worked to hide our tracks, as Arran and Abigail said the Turning master would pursue when he discovered that Abigail had run off."

"I'd imagine he would. But hold, Dimon," Undine said. "And Tagan, relax. I want to understand the story. Dimon, you're here, and so is Isotta. She's in a room downstairs, laid out from being thrown into the ocean by a gray-gi, but there she is. Where's Abigail, then? And her tutor?"

"That's what I need your help with, mother," Tagan said, leaning forward. "The Turning soldiers caught them on the road."

"They had no interest in Isotta or me," Dimon said. "But the Turning chief called for Arran and Abigail to be brought to the compound. Isotta and I were left to make the rest of the journey on our own. Some Gatto met us on the road and accompanied us the rest of the way. They told us about the Vatra blades."

"Mother, what will he do? Allton, I mean. To Abigail?" Tagan stared at her without blinking. "We have to help her."

"And what will he do to Arran?" Dimon added. "Perhaps that's not our affair, but he doesn't seem a bad fellow, overall."

"So, they let you and the girl go," Riley said, "but took the young lady and her tutor to stand before Allton. That doesn't sound good for her or for the Gatto. Allton's not one to be crossed."

Undine shook her head slowly. "It will be more than Abigail can deal with on her own." She turned. "All right, son. I understand the stakes. Leave us to consider this. You and Dimon, go. And you, Rebecca. Go check on the young Gatto. She should be awake by now."

Tagan rose and patted Rebecca on the shoulder. "Go on. Go see how Isotta is doing. Come on, Dimon."

"Wait," Undine said. "Get your grandfather. Tell him the commander and I would like to speak with him."

"Grandfather?" Tagan said. "Why?"

"Just get him."

Undine pushed the door closed behind them and turned to the commander. "Riley, I've been thinking about that Turning girl ever since Tagan first set his eyes on her. It's bothered me. Didn't I hear something about the Turning chieftain being descended from a Gatto line?"

"It wouldn't surprise me. The Turning are a young clan compared to the Gatto. They all came from somewhere."

"We'll ask the old man. He's always studying these old volumes."

"Why the interest in the chieftain's lineage? Probably half the southlands has a Gatto ancestor, if you go back far enough."

"I'd forgotten about it, but then I thought of something. It might be nothing. But I might have an idea."

When Saor Tieg stepped into the room, Undine had already retrieved a half dozen volumes from the shelves, and had them spread across the table.

She looked up. "I can't find it, father. Do you know?"

The old man smiled. "I know some things, and not others, Undine. Is there something particular you're interested in?"

"The Turning chieftain. Allton. His family line. I know I've heard you tell me things about them."

Tieg scowled and pushed the door shut. "Allton? Why do you want to know about that old bastard? Confounded Turning. They want to trade with us, but feel the need to perform ablutions whenever they touch us, as if they're holier than the rest of us."

"But his lineage," Undine insisted.

"You want to know the source of his foul temper, perhaps? Or his rigid posturing? His lack of empathy? I've a fine little tome on the roots of Turning philosophy that you could read. It will make your blood run cold."

"I want to know what line he comes from."

Tieg nodded. "Let's have a look. I believe I know the line, although I've not had a great interest in dwelling on the roots of that clan. There are better subjects to study."

"Still, I want to know."

"Commander, sir," Tieg said, "would you fetch me the large volume over there, on the low shelf? The one in brown leather." Riley rose and stepped over to the shelf. "Yes, yes, that one. Thank you. Bring that over." Tieg glanced at Undine. "Let's see what we can see." He pushed the other books out of the way, and set the leather-bound volume on the table. "Quite rare, this volume. *The Gatto of the Northern Passes*," he read. "Only two known copies. Do you know where the other one is?" He tapped the title. "The title tells you. It's in the library of the Tynan ruler, in the underground halls beneath the White Cliffs, up in the Northern Passes. That copy is older, mind you. This is a copy of that one, I suspect. But it's a good one. So here, let's have a look."

They leaned in, and Tieg slowly flipped pages, muttering to himself as he scanned and flipped to the next. "No, not this line. Ah! No, no, that's not it. Not this one either, although this name is similar."

Undine and Riley watched him for some time, until finally he looked up. "Here it is. You see this?" He pointed to a finely drawn flower entered as a section header.

"Nightshade, isn't it?" Riley said. "Quite a killer."

"Exactly!" Undine said, slapping the table. "I thought so."

"It's a family symbol," Tieg said, "and this is the family line. Have you seen what the young Turning lady has tattooed on her forehead?" he tapped the flower.

"I've seen it, indeed," Undine confirmed. She leaned forward to study the page.

"I'd wager there are many among the Turning who think that family mark originated within their own walls—that it sprang to birth at the advent of the Turning movement. Allton himself would probably say as much, although he knows it's not the case. It predates the Turning clan by many hundreds of years. Perhaps thousands."

"I see his name, there," Riley exclaimed. "Look, there he is, in the second paragraph."

"Exactly. Of course, this book is four hundred years old, so we're not reading about the same man. But it does indeed list Allton. And here's another Allton, and here's Hester. That's his wife's name is it not?"

"That's right," Undine confirmed. "Abbie told me her mother's name is Hester."

"And another Hester, and yet another Allton. And here's an Allerton, which was his father's name. And Abigail. There you are. One, two ... I see three Abigails just on the first two pages. Yes, this is the old bastard's line. I've another volume that verifies it, dear, if you need more," Tieg said, "a more recent account that ties his line to this one."

"So, he does come from a Gatto line, and that's where the flower comes from. I knew it," Undine said. "What, twelve or thirteen generations back? And father, you say Allton knows this?"

"It's a point of pride. He uses that symbol to elevate his own importance. All others in the clan are nameless peasants, you see. The chieftain has the blood of hundreds upon hundreds of years of fighters in his veins. The nightshade flower symbolizes his superior lineage."

Undine jumped up, startling them. "Wait here. Don't move!" She ran out of the room, and returned carrying a cloth bag with something large inside. "This is why I stayed at Three Rivers. This is what I wanted to get."

She pulled open the bag, and set on the table the copper box that had held the Gatto blades.

"Oh, dear me, what have you found, Undine?" Tieg said, running a hand over the metalwork. "Daughter, this is a fine old relic!"

"It's the box the blades were in," she explained. "The blades that Tagan wears now. I told him I went back for it, and he chided me for returning to fetch it."

"Chided you? Foolish boy," the old man muttered. "This is exquisite. Finer than any Gatto relic in my possession. And that's saying something. Undine, that was a well-spent trip."

"Now look inside," she said. "I'm sure Tagan missed it. It was dark. But I saw it in daylight. Go on. Look inside."

The old man very carefully lifted the lid, and set it aside gently. He looked in, and let out a single, sharp laugh. "Look at that. There it is. Oh, marvelous!"

"There *what* is?" Riley leaned in. "I don't see ... oh!" In the center of the bottom of the box, delicately carved and outlined in white gold, was a single nightshade flower. "If he'd seen that, he would definitely have mentioned it."

"Tell me, daughter, where did my grandson get this?" Tieg tipped the box to the light to search for any other marks.

"He found it, with the blades still inside, in the Vatra hall."

"The Vatra hall. What do you mean? I heard that the young Gatto called Tagan's blades *the Vatra blades*. Do you mean, the old legend of Vatra? I have that story here somewhere, as well."

"There's a kata room in the caverns at Three Rivers. A slot of sunlight illuminates fighting figures set into the floor."

"A slot of light ..." Tieg's eyes widened. "A slot of light?"

"You can only see one set of characters at a time, as the sun outside moves across the sky."

"Wait a moment. A slot of light in an otherwise dark chamber?" Tieg leaped up, and Riley and Undine rose, concerned that the man was experiencing a medical issue. "The sun, in darkness!" He shouted, and strode to his bookcases. He started running his hands across the spines. "I know it's here, somewhere. Where is it?"

"Father, what is it?" Undine stepped behind him.

"I have it! I never understood it. *Draw nightshade blades*, and *Follow the sun in darkness?* Poetic nonsense. Or so I thought."

"But father ..."

"Hold! Let me find it." Tieg raised a palm to silence her, as he read the titles. "Yes! Here it is."

He very carefully drew from the shelf a small parcel wedged between two volumes. A brown silk cover was tied with ribbon, the bow pressed flat. Tieg returned to the table, cleared a space, and set the item down, then gently pulled the fragile ribbon to untie it. He pulled back the cloth and inside it opened a leather envelope, and drew from it a thin, ancient item. Two paper-thin slices of polished ebony were drilled and stitched along one edge.

"I understand it now," he said, as he gently opened the black cover to reveal a single leaf of paper. "This is far older than the volume we just looked at. Far older. Here, listen." He read aloud.

Draw nightshade blades on the fire floor.
No oil, no wick, no tinderbox or match.
Follow the sun in darkness
To see nightshade's fire.

Tieg looked up and laughed out loud. "It's the Vatra hall! Do you see? *Nightshade blades on the fire floor.* The blades. Probably all the Gatto who trained there wore blades like that. And to see nightshade's fire—to see the Vatra kata of the nightshade clan—you must *follow the sun in darkness.* Extinguish the lights, and let the slot of light illuminate the kata."

"That's exactly how Tagan describes it." Undine leaned in to study the ancient page, and Riley leaned in to look, as well.

"Outstanding," Tieg said. "Outstanding, Undine. Never mind that the sour old clan leader has a connection to those old Gatto blades. I've read this poem a thousand times, and could never follow. Now it finally makes sense. And the old Vatra hall, not just a legend! Our boy found it, you say?"

"He did. And I've promised to keep its location secret, as Caterione establishes herself as its steward."

"A nice piece of negotiation," Riley smiled.

Tieg raised an eyebrow. "What do you mean, Master Caterione is steward of it?"

Undine held up a hand. "Tagan found the blades in the ancient kata room. He discovered the location of the Vatra hall."

"Yes, yes," Tieg whirled an impatient hand. "But young Master Caterione, steward of the great Vatra hall? Why? How? Tell me of this negotiation."

"I made an agreement with her. Protection of the bearer of the Vatra blades, in return for my silence as to exactly where the old Vatra hall is located. They keep Tagan safe, or she'll lose the stewardship for certain, to Aideen, or Stetlin, or another superior in her order."

"Keep Tagan safe." Tieg scratched his chin, and then smiled. "Yes, commander, I'd have to agree. A fine bit of negotiation, indeed. The stewardship of that hall is a prize any Gatto master would kill for. And our boy has the protection of the Gatto. Very nice."

"And don't discount the connection between the nightshade clan and Allton," Undine added. "That's no small thing, either."

"But how can we use it to help the Turning girl?" Riley asked. "It's an interesting connection, but where does it get us?"

"We need a distraction," Undine explained. "I'll never get close to Abigail with Allton in the compound. But with a little help from this old blade box, Caterione is going to provide a distraction."

"Caterione?" Riley asked. "I thought you and she didn't get along."

"She wants her son back. That's her skin in the game. I want Abigail. That's mine."

"Skin in the game. I'm not sure I follow ..."

"An expression of my old muse. I need you to ride to Three Rivers and bring Caterione to me, Riley. I'll explain when we meet."

Dimon bumped into the Talla as she was heading for Tagan's room. "Talla Undine," he said, "May I ask you something?"

She glanced at him distractedly and almost walked past without answering. But she stopped and turned. "I'm working on a plan, dear. I don't have all the pieces in place just yet, but it's starting to come together."

"This is about something else. The Gatto girl, Isotta. Would you mind ... would it be asking too much to, uh, give her an audience?" Dimon winced. "I promised her I'd arrange it. I didn't think she'd ever actually come to

Deadrise Bay."

"Give her an audience? The child wants to petition me on some matter?" Undine raised an eyebrow.

"I think she just wants to meet you, Talla. That sensei and the others, they're doing their best to drive the spirit out of her in that awful compound in the river valley. But they haven't quite killed it yet. I think Isotta just wants a bit of excitement."

"Excitement?" Undine smiled. "And she means to get it from me? Although I suppose compared to Caterione, I'm a whirlwind of excitement."

Dimon smiled back. "Talla, compared to anybody, you're a whirlwind of excitement. Except maybe Tagan. He's gaining on you."

"All right, honey. I'll talk to the Gatto girl. But I need you to do something for me, if I'm to do that. Go find Tagan. Tell him we're leaving in the morning. Make sure he has something to eat, get him ready to travel."

"Yes, Talla. Thank you!" Dimon spun and hurried back down the hall, and Undine turned down a different corridor.

From outside the door she could hear laughter and talking. "No, not like that. Hold your arm straight, like this. And don't let your feet point outward. Straighten them. Ha ha! See? Better. All right, go."

Undine stepped in to find Rebecca giggling as she practiced the opening move of the first Gatto kata, and Isotta sitting on the edge of the bed swinging her legs. Isotta jumped up and stood at attention.

Rebecca turned and waved. "Look, Talla! I'm a Gatto!"

"Rebecca, wait outside, please. I wish to talk to Isotta." The girl nodded, grinned at Isotta, and ran into the hall, returning to close the door after herself. Undine took one more step. "I'm told you've requested an audience," she said, sternly. "On what grounds, and on what matters? I'm very busy."

Isotta's mouth moved, but it took a moment for sound to come out. "Talla, I uh ... what grounds?"

Undine laughed. "Come, sit. I'm teasing. That's how Master Aideen used to receive us, when we interfered with her precious free time. Talk to me, child. Dimon says you requested an audience."

"Thank you, Talla," Isotta relaxed. "I was afraid I'd made a mistake— *another* mistake, I mean."

"You don't have to walk on eggshells. I meant to talk to you, anyway, to see how you're doing. Tell me, what's on your mind? I see you're out of bed. Are you feeling better?"

"My ribs are sore, but your physician says nothing is broken. I'm on medication. It doesn't hurt too much."

"Good, good."

"Your son told me stories, at Three Rivers. One was about my mother.

He said you were about my age, and mother was older. That's what I wanted to ask you about."

"Those are days I'll never forget, child."

"But did she really say it?" Isotta stared. "Did she say what he told me she said? He said she beat you, and then she said it. *We're not going down for you.*"

Undine's smile faded. "Water under the bridge, Isotta. Your mother and I didn't get along as children. But we both made out all right in the end. Caterione has Three Rivers, and here I am. No regrets."

"But the thing is ... you see ..." Isotta looked away, and her shoulders drooped. "When I lose a match, or if my score isn't perfect. Or if my attention isn't fully on the task ..."

"Spit it out, child. What's troubling you."

Isotta hung her head. "She says it to me, too."

Undine stared incredulously, and her mouth dropped. "Your *mother*? She says that to *you*? Oh, that woman's going to pay! She says that to her own child?" Undine started pacing. "It's one thing for a trainee to say it to another. We were children, forced together, and I got them in trouble. I understand that. But to her own flesh and blood?" She stopped and scowled at the frightened girl. "Who *will* she go down for, then? Fire and daggers, she's going to take that back!"

"But Talla, I didn't mean that I wanted you to do something. I just wanted to know. Please don't tell her!"

Undine sighed and raised a palm. "Yes, you're right, child. Your mother gets under my skin. I apologize. It's not my place to fight your battles. We'll arrange to send you home."

"No!" Isotta blurted out, then clamped her mouth shut and dropped her eyes.

Undine's eyebrows rose. She tipped her head and looked at Isotta. "You don't want to go home?"

"It's just that ..."

"Do you like it here, child? I know you've been here only a short time."

Isotta nodded vigorously. "The freedom. And other girls to talk to. It's like visiting Seven Crossroads. Not that I don't want to go home ..."

Undine looked at the girl, thinking. "But maybe not just yet?"

Isotta winced, and nodded her head.

"All right, then. I'm taking you hostage. On your mother's honor, you're not to leave the city limits without my permission, until and unless I grant your freedom. Now, go get Rebecca, and tell her to find you a room."

"I'm ... but, what? Hostage?"

Undine leaned in. "Not really, dear. You tell me when you want to go home, and I'll arrange it. But keep that between the two of us, all right? The only way you get to stay here is if you're my hostage. Understand?"

Isotta shook her head.

"I negotiated a deal with your mother. I demanded a hostage, and Caterione agreed. Her only stipulation was that it not be her son. And you're not her son, are you?"

"You demanded a hostage? Why?" Isotta's eyes went wide.

"Frankly, just to pile on. I had extra negotiating room, and meant to use it. I wasn't really expecting to go through with it, and force some Gatto to live here. But then again, I wasn't expecting an interesting one to come along."

"I don't understand."

"It's simple, honey. Your mother agreed that I would take a hostage, and the position is open, if you want it. Stay for as long as you want. Rebecca seems to like you—and that means my son will like you, too. He'll do anything for that child. But I really do have things I need to do. So, if you want to be a hostage and live here in Deadrise Bay for a while, go find Rebecca, and she can help you settle in." Undine strode out of the room, leaving Isotta staring at the open door in a daze.

Riley arrived with Caterione at an inn south of the border, and found Undine and Tagan waiting. They had taken over one of the small dining rooms that could be closed for privacy. Tagan rose as they entered.

"Talla," Caterione said. "And your son." She kept a neutral expression as she nodded at Tagan, offering no acknowledgement that she had recently meant to execute him.

"You left your men at a distance, Commander?" Undine said to Riley, ignoring Caterione. "Surely the Turning have spies watching us. I want them to report a small party."

"They're across the border. It's just the master and me."

Tagan, for his part, stood silently. Undine had ordered him to be sure no one saw him enter the inn with the ancient Gatto blades at his waist. He wore a long Tallach robe to obscure them.

Undine finally looked at Caterione and offered a quick nod, and they all sat. "Caterione, you understand the situation? Allton encountered your son and his daughter absconding west. We can assume your son is in a cell, or worse."

"I hear he was taking his charge to Deadrise Bay," Caterione said coldly. "So, it seems you have a part in this. It's not all on Arran."

Undine shook her head slowly. "No, that tack won't get you anywhere. To free him is your concern, not mine. My task is to get the girl out of there. Abigail lacks the means to stand up to Allton—as do you, on your own."

"Abigail is the chieftain's daughter. It's not my affair."

Undine raised a single eyebrow. "And what of Arran, then? You won't go down for him, I suppose."

Caterione pursed her lips. "What do you propose?"

"A diversion. I want Allton and his guard to leave the compound, and I want you to make that happen. Allton's line, you see, reaches back to an old Gatto line. There's a connection to your people. The symbol on Abigail's forehead is an ancient Gatto family mark."

"I'm aware of that, as is the chieftain."

"Yes," Undine said, "I hear that Allton trots out that bit of information when it suits him, to bolster his image and to set himself apart from others. And so, I'm confident that he'll be interested to hear of your stewardship of the Vatra hall."

Caterione stiffened. "Why? Why should he hear of it? We have an agreement!"

Undine raised a palm to halt the objections. "There's no need to tell him where it is. I'm not asking you to give the Turning chieftain a tour. You'll make an arrangement that will please Allton, and you'll see your son returned to you."

"That will be a neat trick," Riley said, but with good humor, watching them spar. He leaned in to Tagan. "Did she tell you the plan, or are you waiting in suspense, as well?"

"Tell me the plan? Why would she do that?" Tagan said with an ironic smile.

"Tell *me* the plan," Caterione bluntly demanded.

"Commander," Undine said, "you'll be interested in this, too. The arrangement I propose involves the Gatto, the Turning, the north, and the Tallachs. All of us have skin in this game, this time."

Tagan grinned. "*Skin in the game.* That's an expression I understand, now."

His mother flashed him a wink.

"An arrangement with Allton," Caterione said with a scowl. "What arrangement?"

"You want your son released. I want to get Abigail out of Allton's clutches. The north wants to trade with the Turning. Isn't that right, Riley?"

"Indeed," Riley said. "The north has been working for years to establish trade relations with the south. The Turning have been most resistant."

"And what is it that Allton wants, then?" Caterione huffed.

"I know exactly what he wants," Undine said. "Don't you? He's just like you, Caterione. Above all else, he wants to raise his own image. He wants to be admired, respected, and feared."

"That's my impression of the man as well," Riley added.

Caterione clenched her teeth and remained silent.

"Here's the plan. Caterione, you'll offer a new border agreement. You'll establish a no-man's land stretching north and south of the established border. It will allow Allton to trade with the north without deigning to enter northern territories. Which is to say, without appearing to consort with people outside of his clan. It will serve you both. Your Gatto will have free reign to patrol south of the border and stop enemies before they reach the crossing itself."

"An interesting idea, Undine," Riley again chimed in. "We know that the main barrier to trade with the Turning is Allton's reluctance to engage in trade outside his own territory."

"His council fears it will lead to moral corruption," Undine said. "A no-man's land at the border provides a solution. His people can meet in neutral territory, instead of on land controlled by the north."

"Trade is why Abigail came to Deadrise Bay," Tagan added. "They were on a trade mission. We wouldn't have met otherwise."

"And it's why Abigail and your son, Caterione, are in a tricky spot, now," Undine said.

"If this border agreement is such a win, then why hasn't the north offered the arrangement already?" Caterione folded her arms.

"Because we didn't think of it," Riley said, grinning at Undine.

"And how does it change matters with my son?"

"It changes matters with your son," Undine said, "because you'll make the offer with the condition that Allton release your son and agree not to interfere with the Gatto."

"He's Turning. That agreement would last until the first time his men encounter mine," Caterione objected.

Undine put her palms on the table. "Tell me, Caterione, do you mean to honor the agreement you and I made?"

Caterione scowled deeply, and glanced at Riley and Tagan, whom she regarded as outsiders as far as her agreement with Undine was concerned. "I stand by it. Each of us stands to lose something if we fail to honor it."

"Ah. We both have skin in the game, eh?"

"Allton might see this border deal as a profitable arrangement," Caterione huffed, "but he'll pick away at it around the edges. There will be incidents, and then skirmishes, and soon we'll be spending all of our effort at the border in disputes with the Turning about the terms of the border agreement."

"Frankly, I don't care about the border agreement, Caterione. I want you to get Allton out of the compound so I can fetch Abigail and bring her to safety. But I've anticipated your objection, and I have one more card to play. You'll offer him an extra incentive, that will keep him in check, and that he won't turn down."

"And what's that?"

"Bear in mind who he is. There are things he wants more than trade, or money, or goods. You're going to feed his ambition, to offer him a symbol of his powerful lineage."

"What symbol? What do you mean?"

"And it won't be his to keep unconditionally. It will be like the hostage I demanded of you, except rather than a person, you'll offer a Gatto relic that represents Allton's power. He'll be allowed to hold it, to admire it, and to display it to his council as a symbol of his invincibility—so long as he honors the agreement."

Riley was now leaning forward, grinning, and waving at Tagan not to interrupt. They had both guessed Undine's final play.

"I have no ancient relics," Caterione said. "My pavilion is new. We hold no sacred objects."

"Tagan, bring the bag." Undine nodded, and Tagan stepped to a side table and returned with a cloth bag and set it on the table.

"You have one, Caterione. Or rather, I have it. But I'll give it to you, provided you agree to do your part. And then we all win. You get your son back, and you and the north get a new trade agreement with the Turning. But only if you get *that old bastard*, as my father calls Allton, out of his compound for at least three days, so I can get Abigail out of there."

She slid the box out, and Caterione jumped to her feet. "Where did you get this?" she shouted. "It's stolen! You or your son. I know the blades this box held. There's only one possible set!"

"Show her," Undine calmly nodded at Tagan. "Now's the time."

Tagan pulled off the Tallach robe to reveal the Gatto blades sheathed at his waist. For a moment, he thought the Gatto master might strike out at him, or faint dead away. Caterione went rigid, and her eyes seemed to lose focus.

Then she caught hold of herself and breathed in. "The Gatto master ..." she hissed. "What did you do?"

"I never said there was a Gatto master, Caterione. The agreement was that the Gatto would protect the bearer of the Vatra blades. Tagan found them, and he wears them. They're his. And so, too, is this box that they came in."

"Trickery!" Caterione shouted. "You've made a deal in bad faith!"

"Nothing of the sort," Undine countered, rising to her feet. "But if you don't like the terms, we can end it right now. I'm prepared to speak with Aideen and the other Gatto masters any time you wish."

"You sneaky Tallach wretch!"

"You don't know the half of it, you sour old Gatto."

"Enough." Riley stood and put his arms out to separate them. "Sit down, you both."

They glared at one another, but sat, Caterione pulling her chair back to put more distance between herself and her adversary.

Riley stared them down. "Caterione," he said, in a low, measured tone, "do you want your son back, or not? And to be steward of the Vatra hall. That's a position every Gatto master, north or south, will covet. In return, you provide protection for a single man, and you feel the deal is unfair? Who wouldn't agree to that?"

"But I agreed that ..."

Riley snapped his hand up, and Caterione fell silent. "The border agreement will be a win for Three Rivers and for the north. I approve. And Caterione, in light of recent events," Riley nodded at Tagan, "right now might be a fine time for the master of Three Rivers to achieve a win."

The threat beneath his words was clear: Caterione, knowingly or not, had threatened to execute his son. It was time to start demonstrating her value to the north, or she might be removed from Three Rivers.

"You'll make the offer," Riley continued, "and travel with Allton to Three Rivers to seal the arrangement. You'll allow him to possess the blade box that bears the mark of his line, as part of the arrangement. And when I return to the north, I'll report on the fine work Master Caterione is doing at Three Rivers. Agreed?"

"I want three days," Undine insisted. "Keep Allton away from the compound for *three days*. I need time for surveillance, and then to get Abigail out of there."

Caterione sat rigidly, but she looked at Riley, and nodded. "I understand what's required of me," she said. She rose, bowed, and stalked out of the room.

"Nicely done, Undine," Riley said, after closing the door behind Caterione. "Nicely played."

Undine grinned.

"Yes, mother," Tagan said, releasing a breath, "*that* was certainly interesting."

"You think so, dear? Wait till she discovers I've taken her daughter hostage," Undine laughed.

"Isotta?" Tagan said, tipping his head and turning serious. "You can't take Isotta hostage, mother. She's a child. And Master Caterione ..."

Riley raised his eyebrows and waited.

Undine smiled, and then laughed again. "Tagan, pay attention. The girl ran all the way to Deadrise Bay and tried to save your life. And did you see her with Rebecca? That child of the Gentry is finally sticking to some-one other than you." She turned and looked at Riley. "Isotta can leave whenever she pleases, commander. But we don't need to tell her mother that. And she won't discover it from Isotta, I can promise you."

Tagan grinned. "Isotta wants to stay at Deadrise Bay?"

"And she knows her mother. Caterione might fume and spit, but she won't threaten her new little empire for her daughter's sake, any more than she's agreeing to this new arrangement to save her son. Did you see her eyes light up when she realized the deal would allow her Gatto to run patrols south of the border? Caterione is pursuing her own ambitions, Riley, just as Allton is." Undine rose. "And now it's time for us to see to ours. Commander, will you stay here with Tagan? When we receive the report that Allton has left the compound, I'll go get Abbie."

That night, as Tagan lay sleeplessly in bed, his muse came to him. "Hey," Camilla said. "Are you awake? Tagan, I did it! Your idea worked. Like a charm."

"The fiddle game? That was your idea, muse. I just parroted it back. But it worked? You freed yourself of the danger?"

"Ha. I did. And I added my own little touch to the plan, to make sure we would stay safe."

"Of course you did. You're the great muse Camilla." Tagan smiled. "You should have seen my mother's face when I told her Camilla speaks to me. I think she actually cried with joy. I almost feel as if it's a cheat, though." Tagan grew somber and reflective. "I'm the grandson of Saor Tieg, and heir to Deadrise Bay. How can I fill my grandfather's shoes, or even begin to fill my mother's? I rely on you, muse. I pray you won't leave me."

"Listen to me. When Horace was killed, I thought I was lost," Camilla said. "I was running, and I was scared, and I didn't know what to do. But Horace had already told me what to do. He told me it's my time, now."

"Your time?" Tagan echoed.

"Once it was his father telling him what to do. Then one day his father was gone, and Horace took over. Do you think he felt ready? And now it's time for me to make the plans."

"I understand. The mantle passes to the next generation."

"And we're never ready, are we? But you have to do it, anyway. Your grandfather is still with you, and your mother is still powerful. But you know what I think? I think it's time for Tagan of Deadrise Bay to call the shots. Look at what needs to be done, and make your own plans. Do it yourself."

Tagan sat up. "Do it myself. Yes, muse. You're right. It's time for that, isn't it? Time for me to make the plans."

"Mother," Tagan said, as Riley and Undine met him early for a morning meal, "I'm changing the plan."

"Tagan, dear, what do you mean? It's all set. We've just gotten word that the chieftain and his guard are traveling north. You and the commander will wait here, and I'll be back soon. I'll get her out, I promise you."

"No. You'll wait here with the commander. I'll get Abbie."

"But son, it's all planned," Riley objected with a frown.

Tagan rose. "I bear the blades of Vatra. I found them, and I wear them. I'm the heir to Deadrise Bay. It's for me to go in and bring her home with me. It's not your task, mother."

"Tagan, honey ..." Undine started.

"How do you think that would play? I profess my love to the Turning woman, and my mother fetches her for me?"

"But Tagan, that's not how it will be."

"Hold, Undine," Riley interrupted. "Our son is right. It's his task, not yours."

"But he's not ready! He doesn't have the skills to penetrate the Turning compound. He'll be caught."

"Were you ready, mother, when you were sent overseas? Were you ready when you received the fourth turn of the spiral, and became a fourth-tier Talla?"

Undine winced.

"Is anyone ever ready? I'm going to do this," Tagan insisted.

"But Tagan, it's dangerous."

"Camilla told me something last night. She said, *Look at what needs to be done, and make your own plans. Do it yourself.* She's my muse now, and I mean to follow her advice."

Tagan didn't feel that he was going in completely blind. Dimon had told him everything he'd seen on his brief visit to the Turning compound. There were very few particulars, but Tagan understood the general terrain, the distances, and the location of the gates and structures inside. He also understood that the compound was enormous, and the land surrounding it even more enormous. Getting in wouldn't be so hard. The hard part would be finding Abigail and getting her out.

Three days, he reflected, as he ran silently through the woods. It wasn't much time. It would have been better to do this at night, he thought, as he made his way into Turning territory, but he couldn't afford to wait. Tagan had enough experience with the Gatto master that he didn't trust her to keep the arrangement. He planned to be in and out in two days, or two and a half at most. He moved past the first perimeter, and ran.

He traveled through the woods, but frequently ventured close to the road to check the movements. There were very few Turning soldiers on the road or at the gates. Allton's own guards were gone, of course. Allton wouldn't go anywhere outside the compound without his trusted men to protect him. Tagan wasn't certain how many fighters were left, but he suspected that they were concentrated in the compound. With the master away, they had pulled back most of the men to guard the inner perimeter. It also meant that while the approach would be easy, getting to Abigail would be hard.

In the end, he decided to try a particularly risky maneuver. It was something Camilla had once mentioned. "Sometimes you have to just to walk right in like you're supposed to be there," she'd said. "I've gotten into buildings like that. Just go right through the main entrance like you own the place."

Tagan didn't plan to walk through the main gate. But a variation of the idea might work. He turned his robe inside-out to expose the plain gray lining, which was pretty close to the color of a Turning outfit, and waited for that perfect moment between the time the last rays of the sun vanish and the time darkness completely sets in. It's a short window, when the eyes can't fully adjust. Not that the men walking the compound couldn't see him, but what one sees at that time of day is less distinct, and the mind fills in the gaps with what's familiar. A gray-cloaked man becomes a fellow Turning soldier making his rounds.

"All right, Camilla," he muttered, crouching behind a boulder, "here I go."

Tagan rose and walked directly in. There were Turning soldiers at a distance, but he nodded and kept walking without changing direction or pace. And it worked! He made it to the cluster of buildings without a challenge. *Here's to you, Camilla,* he silently cheered.

Now came the hard part. Where was Abigail being held? He slipped among the buildings, peeking inside. Each time he detected a soldier nearby, he walked briskly along, just another soldier on duty. It was a slow and dangerous search, in which he was repeatedly forced to move away from a building without finishing his search, and return later.

His break came late at night. He had checked a dozen buildings, only to find them either empty or filled with sleeping men or Turning families—but no sign of Abigail. He was starting to wonder if the chieftain had foiled his plan by taking his daughter with him, when he peered into a window and halted at the sight of an older version of the girl he loved.

Hester sat at a table, a single lamp burning. She held a book, and seemed to be reading intently. There was a closed door behind her, and another closed door in front of her. Tagan slipped around the building to check the room in front, and quickly ducked away as he saw a pair of armed Turning soldiers sitting at a table, guarding the outer door. He went to the rear, but the windows were covered from the inside.

Could he rely on Abigail's mother? He breathed in, and decided he had to make a play. He tapped once on the window, quietly, with a single fingernail, and ducked out of sight the moment the woman's eyes rose. A moment later he reached up and tapped once more. He froze, and waited. Then he heard the soldier's voice.

"What are you doing in there?" The voice was harsh, accusing.

"Opening the window. It's stuffy in here. Would you like to come do it for me?" Hester's voice was firm, annoyed. "Or go stand outside, if you fear I might choose to slip out for a nighttime stroll." She pulled the window up a few inches.

The soldier grunted something unintelligible.

Next Tagan slipped the chain holding the free passage pendant over his head. He silently set it on the sill and pushed it inside, and a hand took it from him. Everything was silent for a long time. Then he heard singing. He risked a glance inside, and found Hester back at the table. She started low, then let her voice rise. He'd never heard the tune before, but he knew the genre. It was a slow, plodding war ballad. A warrior was polishing his armor, preparing for his final battle. By the end of the tune, the warrior would surely be dead.

Hester caught sight of him, and with rapid hand signals, told him what he needed to know. *Back room. Go now. You have ten minutes.* He understood. Some of these old war ballads went on for much longer than that. The men outside would keep quiet and not dare interrupt the chieftain's wife singing the old dirge. Her voice grew louder, and Tagan nodded and slipped around to the back.

Abigail was ready, dressed in a man's clothes, including a pullover with a hood. She slipped out of the window, and Tagan took her hand and squeezed, then stepped away.

"Walk," he whispered. "Two paces from me, like the others." He'd seen how the soldiers moved, and surely Abigail knew. They never walked abreast. If there were pairs, they walked two paces apart, in single file. Abigail dropped into the pace of a Turning soldier, and they walked.

When they reached open woods, Tagan took her hand, and they ran. He had worried about this part. His sensei had taught him to move quickly and quietly through the woods. Would he be able to do so, with Abigail along? But she surprised him with her skill. She wasn't silent, but she wasn't noisy, either. It was good enough. They hurried, working their way toward the outer perimeter.

Both understood the stakes, and the timing. At the late meal, the soldiers would bring in food for the matriarch and the daughter, and they would discover that the girl was gone. Then everything would change.

Every man in the compound would be sent to find them. They needed to be well outside the outer boundary: no time for a tearful reunion or even an embrace.

Had they remained by Hester's window, they would have heard her song abruptly stop at the shout of a soldier outside, calling the alarm. Abigail had closed the window, but it wasn't locked. As the soldier on his rounds pushed on each window in turn, one of them moved. He pulled a wooden matraca from his pocket and spun it, the rapid clacking sound loud in the night. In moments, soldiers were streaming out of the building, and converging from other parts of the camp.

"The chieftain's daughter is not to be harmed," the man on duty shouted, as he gave orders. "Whoever is with her dies. Go!"

Tagan and Abigail heard the alarm as well. They had made good progress, but the night was quiet, and the sound stood out.

"We're discovered!" Abigail exlaimed. "What now?" Her voice was unsteady, frightened. She looked around in the darkness, as if expecting to find a contingent of Tallach soldiers waiting to take them safely away.

"Follow me." Tagan gripped her shoulder, then turned and ran.

These were not gray-gis, but the tactics of the Turning soldiers seemed similar. The gray-gis had come for him out in the open, and chased him along the road and up to the drop. There was no effort at stealth. Likewise, the Turning didn't try to sneak up on them. Sounds rose as men called out to one another, coordinating their hunt. Soon Tagan and Abigail saw the flickering of torchlight. The Turning men meant to catch their prey by means of a direct confrontation.

At first Tagan feared he and Abigail wouldn't make it. On his own, it would be a fair competition. He would have a chance to outrun them and outthink them. But with Abigail along? Then he realized he wasn't slowing to accommodate her pace. He didn't have to. She could run, too, and she was navigating the terrain skillfully.

"Arran taught you?" he ventured, as they paused to choose a route over or around a high stone outcrop.

She nodded, winded, and followed as once more he ran.

At their next short rest, Tagan whispered his plan to her, and Abigail nodded. Her eyes widened, but she didn't argue. Arran had warned her that others had greater skills in the woods than she. He had noted that sometimes the right solution was to hide rather than run or fight. *Sometimes all that's needed is an extra moment to reach a safe place*, he had told her. Had she been on her own, she might have looked for a place to hide the moment she'd heard the matraca.

Tagan's strategy was more refined. "We need to hide, Abbie, but I need to find the right place."

He studied the formation ahead of them, a rocky area, mostly open, but with clusters of low scrub. The moonlight revealed the contours, and finally he saw something he liked.

"Follow," he whispered, and then he sprinted among the patches of low growth, careful to keep his footfalls on the rocks. Halfway across the open space he reached the spot. There was a slight rise, where bedrock pushed up and denied any vegetation a place to take hold. Behind it, the grass was thick and tall, fed by the water runoff from the stone outcrop. Tagan motioned, and they dropped and lay facedown, and wriggled their way into the grass.

It was a risk. If the Tallach soldiers were to study the scene as Tagan had, he and Abigail would be caught. But Tagan gambled that they wouldn't. They heard the footfalls and voices, and soon saw the torchlight. Abigail held her breath, and Tagan clutched her arm as the sounds and the light drew closer. But there were no excited shouts from the soldiers, no swarming toward the hidden spot. Tagan patted Abigail's arm, as they heard the soldiers doing exactly what he'd hoped they would do: They were taking the most direct path through the meadow, anxious to get past the open space and get back into the woods, where surely their targets must be.

"It worked!" Abigail whispered.

Tagan held her arm for another long moment, and then as the torchlight dimmed, they silently rose and backtracked, now behind their pursuers.

They crossed the field, and were well into the woods again, almost ready to breathe easily, when Tagan's head whipped around. He started to raise a hand to call for silence, but Abigail was already frozen at his side. There was no time for a signal, anyway, as a hurled blade sank into Tagan's leg.

Instead of stumbling forward, he lurched to the side, taking Abigail with him behind a tree.

"Some of us have done this before," came the smug voice of a senior Turning officer. "Come out of there, Miss Abigail. It's time for you and your friend to return, you to your quarters, and your companion to another place."

Abigail said nothing. She reached for the blade, but Tagan caught her arm and shook his head. She clenched her eyes shut, and fought to calm herself. Of course! She knew better. Rushing to draw a blade from a wound without being prepared could be a fatal mistake. Arran had taught her that. Now here she was, ready to act in a panic.

The soldier stepped closer, another blade at the ready, but for a long interval there was no movement on the other side of the tree. "Come out of there," he repeated. "I know you're still there. You'll not bluff your way out of this." Again, no sound. "Let's not be stubborn. You're discovered, Miss Abigail. Let's be done with this."

Behind the tree, Tagan clenched a fist, struggling with the pain. Then he patted Abigail's arm, and started to make signs. Her jaw dropped, but she nodded.

"I'll come out," she called to the soldier. "My friend is down. I'll come out alone." She didn't wait for him to respond, but instead stepped out, then briskly moved away from the tree. "Don't hurt me!" She cried, pulling back as if the soldier were about to strike her. "I'm unarmed!"

But her companion was not. In the split second her display of fear drew the soldier's attention from the tree, a blade flew at him, and sank into his throwing arm. The soldier shouted in pain and surprise, and his own blade fell from his hand. Abigail defensively dropped to the ground, a safe but unnecessary move. Before she'd fully flattened herself to the grass, another blade sank into the soldier's chest.

Tagan stepped out and limped over, catching the man's look of surprise as he sank to the ground. "I know. Tallachs don't throw blades. Am I right?" he said to the dying man. "My mother insists that's true." Then Tagan himself dropped to the ground, and uttered a moan. "Damn it, Abigail, I hope your Gatto taught you about stab wounds."

Abigail almost smiled. "He did."

It took a long time to get to the safe place. First Abigail had to retrieve Tagan's blades. Then she struggled to drag the soldier's body out of the open. That alone could make all the difference in keeping the others off their trail. Then came the first stages of seeing to Tagan's wound: a tourniquet of supple vine, removal of the blade, and then binding of the wound with long strips of cloth torn from the soldier's shirt. She propped Tagan up on his wounded side, got him to his feet, and they hobbled through the woods.

Several times they had to stop, and several times Abigail found panic returning, but she fought it back. They would make it! They had to. Finally came a difficult descent through thick scrub trees that scratched and pulled at them. But the panic had subsided. They were almost to safety.

"I can get all that I need here," Abigail quietly told him, as she helped him into a reasonably comfortable position in a shallow, hidden cave. "Arran showed me this place. I trained here. There's water, and I know where to find the plants I need. But first, a fire."

He would have objected, but Tagan could see that the spot was perfect for it, hidden in a low area carved over time by running water, but now fairly dry. It wasn't especially comfortable, but the spot was sheltered from view, tight growth all around them. And the night would mask the smoke.

"All right," he said. "I'm all right, Abbie."

She kissed him on the cheek and disappeared, returning with kindling and wood culled from the forest floor. "You'll be warm soon," she said. "And then we'll take a look at your wound. Talk to me, Tagan."

"How will you light it?" Tagan asked, struggling to speak. He didn't need to ask, but he understood what she wanted of him. She wanted him to reassure her that he was conscious and aware.

"I trained here, but didn't see the need to lug everything here and back every day. I left a few things, and Arran didn't notice."

"I suppose he didn't join you in wriggling into this little spot."

"Ha, no. *It's for you to learn, and me to teach, young miss.*"

"And I might make sport of your Gatto's style, *young miss*," Tagan tried to smile, "but it seems under the circumstances that gratitude would be more appropriate. Remind me to tell Arran thank you."

Abigail pulled a small pack from a nook, and drew out a tinder box, and soon had a small fire burning. "Drink," she said, passing him a wineskin. "This is one of the things I tucked away to make it more enjoyable to pass the time, here."

"Aren't you resourceful."

"Drink," she repeated. "The hard part comes next. We need to get you cleaned and stitched."

"It's a win, Abbie. You're away from them, and back with me. That alone is enough to get me through the pain. But this will help." He raised the wineskin and drank.

19. Getaway

Camilla climbed onto a brand new, jet black Ducati, and pulled her helmet on. Out of habit she patted her hips, but her blades were in her backpack. She hadn't forgotten them, and it was okay that she wasn't wearing them. For the first time in a long time, she didn't feel the need.

Time to have a little fun, she thought, as she sped out of the driveway. The sun was up, and it was warm. She slowed at the corner, and took it easy as she headed through town. No need to rush. No one would be following her, this time. And when she got to the highway, there would be no need to watch for someone waiting to shoot her. This time she wouldn't be flying over a concrete barrier or hiding under a bridge.

It felt strange. She couldn't remember ever experiencing this: just going somewhere because she wanted to, and not as a tactical step. There was no need to plan how to evade her enemy; no need to cover the spiral on her face with makeup; or to dress to look older or younger. For the first time in her life, she didn't have to do any of that. She turned onto the ramp and headed north.

At the New Hampshire border, she exited the highway and took the back roads. It would take longer, but what was the point of a motorcycle ride if all you did was drive up the highway? By midday she had reached Portsmouth, and opted to drive downtown.

"I can have lunch. Any place I want," she said out loud.

Camilla took her time picking a restaurant, and the strategy was new to her. She didn't need to find a place with the ideal location for a quick getaway. It wasn't necessary to circle around and inspect each exit route before going inside. For the first time, she could choose whatever she wanted. She found a seafood place that looked good, walked right in, and sat at the far end of the bar. Then she laughed as she realized she had subconsciously picked the perfect spot to see every part of the room. A long mirror behind the bar showed everything behind her, and she could see the entrance and the door to the kitchen.

"What can I get you?" The bartender said, flashing a smile.

"Beer. Something local. You pick. And a menu."

"You got it."

A group of three young men and one old one came in right after her, and took the seats to her side.

The old one sat on the stool next to her, tipped his baseball hat, and smiled. "That your bike down the street? Black Ducati?"

"Yup."

"Hah! Told you, guys!" He shoved the shoulder of the man next to him. "Nice ride. Can I borrow it?"

Her immediate thought was that this could turn into a problem. What was his game? But then he turned to his friends, and they all ordered beers. Just friendly banter at a bar.

She took her time with her lunch, first a Rueben sandwich, then an order of fries, and then a dish of ice cream. The men asked about the motorcycle, and they chatted about riding and seeing the world. It was a strange, ordinary conversation.

Later, as she continued up the back roads heading north, it hit her again: She'd had a meal in public, and didn't have to be thinking about her next move. Her next move was to do whatever the hell she wanted. She dawdled her way north, stopping when she felt like it, and exploring side roads that looked like fun. It was late evening when she reached the downtown strip in North Conway.

Enzo's apartment was the same as when she had left, except that there was a gas grill parked in his otherwise empty, single parking space. Still plenty of room for her bike.

The door lock didn't offer any resistance. Not for Camilla. "He won't mind if I drop my stuff in here and clean up, will he?" She looked around for evidence that someone besides Enzo might be staying there. They hadn't made any commitments, after all, and it would be awkward for another woman to walk in and find her there. But the pizza boxes and empty beer bottles seemed to say, one guy.

Even midweek, the restaurant was packed. Camilla pushed her way in and spotted Enzo behind the bar, helping two other bartenders handle a small mob of patrons. All the tables were filled, and every bar stool. People hovered behind the people on the stools, leaning in to call their orders and waiting for an opportunity to snag a seat. At the far end of the bar she thought she saw someone about to leave, and she worked her way over. The moment the man slid off the bar stool, she slid on. It earned her a scowl from a man who had been coveting the seat, but he had moved away a step or two to talk to someone, and had thus given up his claim.

A woman bartender stepped up. "What can I get you?" she said.

"Can you get me Enzo?" Camilla smiled.

The waitress glanced over at the big Mexican at the other end of the bar. "You a friend?"

"I think so. Hope so, anyway."

"Sure, hon. I'll send him over."

Camilla craned her neck to see. The waitress worked her way over and tapped Enzo on the shoulder, and said something. He nodded, but didn't look over. Camilla guessed she'd said something like, *spot me for a minute*, as the waitress then ducked under the counter and disappeared. Enzo poured drinks, took orders, and eventually made his way closer.

"What'll you have?" he asked, distractedly flashing no more than a glance in her direction. He'd noticed a new body on the last stool, someone without a glass or a bottle, but hadn't actually turned to see who it was.

"Anything but pizza," Camilla said. "How about you? Can I have you?"

Enzo turned, confused for a moment, and then his eyes lit up, and he laughed out loud. He tossed down his bar towel, ducked under the bar, and swept her up in his arms. "Oh, man it's good to see you! You're okay? Is it over? What happened? What're you doing here?"

"That's a lot of questions," she said, hugging him back.

"Okay. Let's start with the last one. What are you doing here?"

"Nothing, yet. But I have an idea or two, if you're game."

He set her down and flashed a mock look of consternation. "Does it involve someone shooting at us?"

"Can't really say. I don't think so. Wanna come?" Camilla grinned.

He leaned down and kissed her. "You bet I do. Let's go!"

20. Nightshade and Fire

Making their way through the woods took a long time. They moved quickly through the open areas where the trees were thin, and moonlight showed the way. But in parts the canopy blocked the moon, and they picked their way through in utter darkness, all the while mindful of Tagan's injury. He leaned on Abigail, aware that to tear the wound open again would stop them.

Finally, they made it past the outer border to a small road that circled around the perimeter and joined the main road from the compound.

The edges of things were starting to appear more vividly. Tagan slowed. "Abbie, let's stop for a minute. It's almost dawn. Let me rest."

The wind had picked up, and the dark silence of the woods transformed to a steady rustling of leaves.

"Will we make it?" Abigail asked, clutching her arms across her front.

"We'll make it," Tagan said, taking her hand in his, "And if we don't, I'll return again and again until we do."

Abigail pushed her shoulder under his arm. "Let's go."

Around the next turn, Tagan slowed. "The crossroads is just ahead," he whispered. "I recognize the look of it. The main road runs right and left, and is wide and open. To the left is the inn, a few miles down. To the right is the compound, and straight ahead, this road leads to the passage north."

"The road to the inn is the only road I want to take," Abigail said. "Let's go."

But as they stepped into the crossroads, Tagan gripped her arm and stopped. Something was wrong. It was early morning, with just enough light to show shapes, but not enough to paint color on the scene. Straight ahead the road was a narrow gray line, and to the left a wide, brighter gray line. But to the right, the road was dark.

The moment they stopped, they knew why—not by the look, but by the sound, the steady, low rumble of horses.

"But you said three days," Abigail hissed. "It's only been two!"

"Damn it," Tagan whispered. "That's what you get when you make an agreement with the Gatto from Three Rivers."

"She broke her promise?"

"She thought my mother would be bringing you out."

"Your mother ..."

"Ask me later."

It was too late to run. Allton's guard had already spotted them.

"Stand right there," boomed the chieftain, "the two of you! Don't annoy me further by running."

The Turning chieftain himself approached on his gray stallion with a phalanx of men on horseback stretching out behind. He halted just short of the crossroad and raised his arm. His horsemen slowed and formed lines behind him. Allton made a single motion, dropping his arm and pointing at Tagan and Abigail, and twenty men dismounted and approached.

Tagan drew his blades and made an effort at a fighting stance—and Abigail cried out in alarm and ducked behind him. Then she looked to one side and then the other, as more figures appeared from north and south, converging on them.

"Tagan!" she cried.

He had seen them, too, and recognized the shapes. "Here?" he cried out. "How is that possible? Friends, Abbie! Friends with unexpectedly excellent timing."

Tagan maintained his strained fighting stance as a dozen, and then two dozen Gatto fighters flowed like water into the road between him and the approaching Turning men. The Gatto drew blades and formed neat rows. More and more figures appeared, and Tagan grabbed Abigail's wrist and backed her up as Gatto filled the space in front of them. More Gatto surrounded them and began to fill in behind. Abigail stepped up and pushed her shoulder under Tagan's arm again.

The Turning soldiers stopped ten feet from the front line of Gatto, dropped to fighting stances and froze, awaiting orders as one more Gatto fighter stepped to the front. This one stood tall.

"Ah, I understand. The master," Tagan whispered, astonished. "We've spoiled her game. We've surprised her."

"Master Caterione?" Abigail whispered.

"Here to watch Allton intercept the Talla who tasks her so. But she came upon a different scene than she'd expected. That's why they're here so quickly. They were following your father, so she could watch."

Allton calmly slid off his horse and strode up to stand face-to-face with the master. "What is this?" he barked, standing tall himself, and looking down his nose. "We agreed that I'd retrieve my daughter, and there she is with the Tallach wretch. Move aside. I'll run that boy through, and take my property home."

The Gatto shifted one step, all at once, turning the focus of their attention and their blades to Allton.

"I agreed that I'd not stand between you and the Talla," Caterione said, coldly, "We agreed that I'd not interfere in that fight, should you choose to take the Talla into custody for attempting to abscond with your daughter."

"Then stand aside. Here I am to do it."

"This is not the Talla. You may not approach the bearer of the Vatra blades."

"The bearer of the Vatra blades? I know a bit about those blades now, Gatto, as you well know. I hold the box the blades came in. My ancestors carved it, and forged the blades. And now I'll have the blades, too."

"The Gatto protect the bearer of the Vatra blades. The young master may go his way."

"Young master? You keep saying that. I see nothing but a Tallach boy, daring to touch my daughter. He'll learn his mistake."

Then his soldiers looked up at the sound of more horses. From a rise on the road from the inn, a cloud of dust rose, and the sound grew louder. A hundred northern soldiers rode up. Gatto fighters shifted around Tagan and Abigail, until they fully surrounded them several rows deep, all facing outward.

"Make way, Gatto," called a powerful voice. "I'm Riley, Commander of the north. I'll speak with the chieftain."

Caterione waved a hand and her men parted to let a single horseman through. They shifted Tagan and Abigail to the side. Commander Riley walked the horse, taking his time. He dismounted and stepped up, one pace forward of Caterione.

"Lower your arms, Allton. Order your men to do so," he said, "and you'll be allowed to return safely to your lands. This business is done."

"And what business is this of yours, commander?" Allton spat. "I'm here for my daughter! I mean to put an end to the Tallach scourge that plagues my kin. That boy has violated the sanctity of our soil, and threatens the sanctity of my bloodline." He pointed at Tagan who straightened his back to stand tall in spite of the pain, and squeezed Abigail's hand in solidarity.

"That boy?" Riley flashed a threatening smile. "Do you mean the heir to Deadrise Bay? The young man wearing blades forged centuries ago by the Gatto line symbolized by the nightshade blossom? I believe I see that same mark on your daughter's forehead."

"The Tallach boy has nothing to do with my line!" bellowed Allton.

Riley took a step closer. "*That boy*, Allton, has something to do with *my* line, and that of Talla Undine. Tagan is my son."

This sent a low murmur through the ranks of Turning men.

"And he wears the Vatra blades of the Gatto. Do you follow? *That boy* has the power of the north, Deadrise Bay, and the Gatto behind him. So, try, then." Riley waved a hand. "Try to put an end to him, Allton. You'll be cut down along with all your men."

Allton stared, then brusquely waved an arm to his side, and his men sheathed their blades and stepped back a pace. "You outnumber me, commander. But this isn't finished."

"It's finished, father," came a surprisingly strong voice. "I don't reject my family line, but I do reject the place you've assigned me in it."

"Silence, Abigail! You'll do as I say!" Allton bellowed, stepping to one side to move around Riley.

"I'll do as I say," countered the girl. "Go home, father. My affairs are my own, now."

Allton moved forward, and Riley deftly shifted, coming nose-to-nose with the chieftain.

"See what will happen, Allton," Riley said in low, cold voice. "Choose your time and place, or do it now. Wherever and whenever, you'll face what you see now. Or perhaps you might consider taking another look at *that boy*, and give up this arrogant insistence that somehow your line is purer than his."

Allton stared, fuming, then took a step backward and turned. He waved to his men, and they all mounted. Rows of horsemen turned and retreated.

The Gatto kept their positions, blades drawn. They kept their focus on Allton and his men, but deftly parted to allow Riley to lead his horse back through their lines. He stopped when he reached Tagan and Abigail.

"Abigail," he said, offering a bow. "Pleased to meet you. The north recognizes that your affairs are your own."

"Pleased to meet you, commander," Abigail replied with a smile and a bow, "and thank you." She understood the commander's words. He was declaring no allegiance with her father. The north wouldn't stand in her way.

"And Tagan," he said, handing him the reins, "you ride today."

With the help of some Gatto fighters, Tagan mounted. Abigail climbed on behind him, and the fighters shifted to the sides of the road to make way.

Tagan rode at a walk through the ranks of northern soldiers. "Are you ready?" he said, turning to flash a smile at Abigail. "You didn't bring a bag."

"Shall we go back?" Abigail raised an eyebrow.

Tagan glanced behind them. "Why don't we get you new things."

Abigail leaned forward and hugged him. "I'll need a new hat."

"That could be dangerous. I know what you can do with a hat."

Tagan snapped the reins, and they headed down the road, ranks of northern soldiers and Gatto forming behind them.

Acknowledgments

Thanks once again to my editors, Sarah Dole and Lisa Wesel, for finding things to fix, and thanks to Braden Todd Curtis for another fine cover.

Also by Todd Woofenden:

Gunners of the White Cliffs
Trail of the Gunners
Gunner's Blade
Undine of Deadrise Bay

Sign up for email notifications of publishing dates and author news:
https://www.gunners-book.com/subscribe

The Gunners Trilogy, and other books by Todd Woofenden:
https://gunners-book.com

About the Author:
https://www.gunners-book.com/about

Signal Light Books:
https://www.signallightbooks.com